Ang Tak

Helen Yeomans

GUARDS PUBLISHING

Published by Guards Publishing

helenyeomans.com

Library and Archives Canada Cataloguing in Publication

Yeomans, Helen, 1949-
Ang Tak / Helen Yeomans.

Includes bibliographical references.
Also issued in electronic format.
ISBN 978-0-9693219-3-4

I. Title.

PS8647.E65A55 2012 C813'.6 C2011-907752-3

The lines on page 319 are from the poem "Seaside Golf" by John Betjeman (John Murray Publishers Ltd.).

Cover design: ivanzanchetta.com
Printed in the United States of America

For my father,

a player and a sportsman;

and in memory of my mother,

who loved the Masters.

ACKNOWLEDGMENTS

I'm grateful for the help of many people, starting with Lhundup Sherpa and professional caddie Bob Whitbread. Their knowledge, patience and unstinting help gave me the backbone of my story. My thanks too to journalists Cam Cole (Vancouver Sun) and John Boyette (Augusta Chronicle).

On the Nepal side, Lori Goldman, Shirley Blair, Jhabindra K. Subedi and Mitra Pariyar provided extensive assistance. Thanks also to Dallas Biddescombe, Gene deVries, Marlene Dance, Penny Smith, Stephen Lu, Susan Milner and Yaz Jiwa. For reading the first draft, I'm most grateful to Debby Hallinan, Evelyn Dewar, the late Lynda Ursaki and Pat Moret, with a special thank you to Linda Brotherston for that and much other help besides. Ruth Binney, old friend and colleague from my London days, read the penultimate draft and alerted me to a missing piece of the puzzle.

Background research: David Owen's *The Making of the Masters*; three books by John Feinstein: *A Good Walk Spoiled*, *The Majors* and *Caddy for Life: The Bruce Edwards Story*; Alan Shipnuck's *Bud, Sweat, and Tees*; and Dawson Taylor's *The Masters: Golf's Most Prestigious Tradition*. Online resources included the websites of the Augusta *Chronicle*, *Sports Illustrated* and *Golf* magazine, and masters.org, the official website of the Masters.

On Nepal and the Sherpa people: *Massacre at the Palace* by Jonathan Gregson; *Sherpas: Reflections on Change in Himala-*

yan Nepal by James F. Fisher; *High Religion* by Sherry B. Ortner; *High Adventure* by Sir Edmund Hillary; and *Living in the Middle* by Donna M. Sherpa. My favorite videos were Ian Carter's entertaining *Pilot Guide to Nepal,* and *Caravan* (renamed *Himalaya*), a short film by Eric Valli. Online resources included sherpakyidug.org, nepalresearch.org, the backgrounds and stories of the children of SMD school at himalayanchildren.org and the websites of *Nepal News, Nepali Times* and *The Himalayan.*

This is a work of fiction with a factual setting. Everyone has heard of Arnold Palmer, Jack Nicklaus and Tiger Woods, and many people have heard of Bobby Jones, considered the greatest amateur player of modern times. For the benefit of non-golfing readers, the following golfers mentioned in the story are also real: Ben Crenshaw, Ben Hogan, Bob Rosberg, Byron Nelson, Fred Couples, Fuzzy Zoeller, Gary Player, Greg Norman, Ian Woosnam, Ken Venturi, Lee Trevino, Nick Faldo, Roberto de Vincenzo, Sam Snead, Seve Ballesteros, Tom Watson and Tom Weiskopf. Their exploits at Augusta National over the decades add immeasurably to the allure of that storied course.

To the best of my knowledge, TaylorMade does not at present include a tonal component in its golf clubs, such as my protagonist uses. And finally, research and help notwithstanding, any technical errors are solely the responsibility of the author.

Ang Tak

o o o o

Funeral of Chhiri Sherpa

KATHMANDU: Hundreds of mourners witnessed the funeral of Chhiri Sherpa, killed last Friday along with nine members of the Royal Family at Narayanhiti Palace. Chhiri was Nepal's most famous Sherpa since Tenzing Norgay. He is survived by his wife Mollie, son Lhakpa Gyeltsen, 7 and brother Pemba.

--*The Everest Times,* June 5, 2001

WEDNESDAY-THURSDAY

O O O O

Amen Corner

People say it really began years ago, what happened last April at the Masters. Not for me. It began for me the night before the tournament, when I stood on the Hogan Bridge at Amen Corner and said a prayer for Josh.

Maybe I should give you a few details about myself. My name is Katrina Archer but I mostly go by Kat. I'm thirty-four, from Vancouver. I went to school there (Lord Byng) and university. I've always loved sports, golf especially. I used to play the public courses, Fraserview and McCleery. Then my dad got a membership to Vancouver Club through work, and we used to play there Fridays and weekends. You might say I grew up playing hills.

I wasn't really happy at UBC, except for meeting Josh, so I took off for Florida to try to break into the LPGA. Long story short, that didn't work. I was sort of en route home when I stopped off in Hilton Head to watch the PGA event and I happened to be hanging round the parking lot the Thursday morning Charlie Jorgensen fired his caddie. The guy had been coming to work late and hung over ever since Charlie won the Masters two years before, so now he was history and Charlie started for the pro shop to see if they had any caddies available and I practically fell all over him. He looked me over—I'm pretty well set up, five foot nine and strong—and I wonder how many decisions in this world get made just because someone wants a quiet life? Charlie said he'd give me a try and that was eleven years ago. We hit it off and we had a relationship that was a mixture of professional and friendship. Charlie had a solid marriage and two kids, and Josh and I were tight. But we spent more time together than with either of our families. We both love sports and we're both what you might call opinionated.

Caddies make good money if their players do well. Charlie got as high as eighth in the world a few years ago. Now he lies around forty-fifth, but in the years I've worked for him he never made less than a million in winnings any year except for the last three, and generally much higher. Caddies take home anywhere from five to ten percent of their player's winnings, and Charlie's deal with me was a flat ten percent, so I was always able to afford plane fare. Josh was a landscape architect, so we had pretty much the same busy season. We got married the year after I hooked up with Charlie. And that's why I was at Amen Corner that Wednesday night. Josh used to come to the Masters, and he'd spend most of his time down here, at the low end of the property. It was like a kind of shrine to him. I'd always give him a backward tip of the cap as we crossed the Hogan Bridge, and sometimes I'd try to spot him when I was on the other side looking back at the stands. Not often, because my mind was on the game. But Josh died in January of liver cancer, and so on the Wednesday night before the competition I went down there to say goodbye.

I hadn't expected to be at the Masters this year, because Charlie's back had been acting up and he phoned in early March to say he was canceling. It suited me. But he hadn't finished.

"I want you to caddie for the kid who won the British Amateur."

"No thanks." I knew the kid he meant. English-Asian hothead. Made the news last year when he socked a spectator he claimed was making racist remarks.

"Yes, Kat. It'll be good for you, and he needs your experience."

We went back and forth on this for a while but in the end I didn't care enough either way, which is how I came to be at Augusta in April as usual.

I stood on the Hogan Bridge that night looking down at the stars in Rae's Creek. I thought about Josh and I said goodbye in my mind. Thought about pine-scented air freshener and how it's not the same as the real thing. Then I looked up past the black pines at the night sky. Midnight blue is an amazing color.

I could hear the softest echo of my footsteps as I walked off the bridge. Never noticed that before.

Kathmandu

At midday, the narrow side street off Asan Tole market was busy but less noisy than the main bazaar. Two tourists hovered round a tea-seller's stand. One ate *momos*, dumplings filled with water buffalo. The other watched as the tea-seller scooped a ladle of frothy milk from the rolling boil in the saucepan into a plastic glass of tea. The glass and five rupees changed hands.

From a portable radio next to the saucepan, a program was audible in the quieter side street. "You're listening to DuChat, 96.3 on your FM dial and today the Coca-Cola Hour is devoted to golf, golf, golf. Tonight begins the Masters and our guest is the secretary of the Royal Nepal Golf Club—"

Two dogs fought over garbage, the loser barking noisily; sellers advertised massages, watches, cauliflowers, transportation. "Rickshaw to Durbar Square only fifty rupees. Fifty rupees! . . . Okay, sir, for you only forty rupees."

"It is the first time a Nepali has been invited to this most exclusive tournament and we should be very proud—"

Honking horns answered an annoyed moo. Overhead, amid a maze of wires and shop signs, washing hung from balcony rails, and women leaned on the rails and chatted across the narrow street. The whirring of sewing machines issued from open windows in the narrow buildings, and the air smelled of spices and dung and sewer odors.

"Right!" The radio host was enthusiastic. "Let's take another call, this time from Dharan."

Next to the tea-seller, a thin woman in a faded crimson sari squatted against the wall with Raju, a street musician. Today he was selling handmade flutes, a hundred rupees each, along with a meager assortment of leather belts. He glanced at his watch and then at his companion. "Time to eat, *didi*." Older sister. He was in his mid-thirties; so was she but she looked much older. She was a street sweeper.

The high-pitched voice of a female radio caller carried over the street sounds. "It is very good that Lhakpa has done so well. But we should not forget his father. I myself could never believe that the Crown Prince killed Chhiri. He liked him! And I think—"

"Oh, that is a bit off-topic, caller—"

Raju grunted. "She has a point, that person."

The radio host continued: "Let's talk about Lhakpa's style of play. Do you think it is suited to the Augusta golf course?"

"I never believed it was the Crown Prince, myself," said the tea-seller. "The Maoists had the most to gain from the king's death. But where have they got us? *Bandhas*." Strikes. "Nothing but bandhas."

A small boy dashed along the cobbled street, yelling, waving a cut down three-iron and wearing a baseball cap, green with white lettering: *Lhakpa*. Two more kids followed, one dragging the other on a piece of stiff corrugated plastic, both laughing their heads off.

"We have someone else on the line. Good morning, caller! Do you have a question for our guest?"

"I want to say that the last person was right. Surely we should recognize by now that King Birendra was killed by his brother. It was to his advantage to kill him."

"We are here talking about golf—"

The caller ploughed ahead. "The Crown Prince may have pulled the trigger but his uncle was behind the whole thing."

Raju snorted again. "If they had ever listened to me, they would know who pulled the trigger!" He got to his feet. "I am so sick of this. Who was driving the jeep that night? Who?"

The street sweeper put her hands over her ears.

The tea-seller stared at him. "What jeep, Raju?"

"The jeep! The jeep! The jeep that drove out of the south gate at 9:05 that night! Right after the shooting! Who was driving that jeep, I want to know?"

"Did you see the jeep, Raju?"

"Yes yes yes I saw the jeep! But I was on the other side of the road. It was getting dark. I could not see who drove. One man. It was one man."

"You told the authorities, of course."

"Of course I told the authorities! But they paid no attention. What does an ignorant street musician know?" He turned away in disgust. "Pah!" Then in a calmer tone, "Time to eat, *didi*."

Leaving the tourists to eat in the street, the two entered a small restaurant, and as they did so, the street sweeper spoke. "I know who can help you, *bhai*." Brother.

"Who is that?"

"Mingma."

O O O

"Have you got anything for me?" Rab Manga was the principal talent at Dharmedia, hired at great expense from an Indian TV station. His salary was more than the combined pay of all the other employees, including the group manager.

"We're evaluating these leads on the massacre," answered the group manager. The two men had crossed paths in the lobby.

"That's stale."

"It's all we've got at the moment." He added, "The public doesn't seem to think it's stale."

State-owned Nepal TV had a stranglehold on Masters coverage, and Joy TV, the television arm of Dharmedia, was scrambling to find anything to run against it. The response on DuChat 96.3 had taken everyone by surprise, and three reporters were following up on all calls.

"Can't you get the kid?"

"He's tied up," said the group manager, an expatriate New Yorker, drily. "We're trying to get his caddie."

"His caddie? Who cares about his caddie?"

The group manager shrugged. "We can't compete with NTV. They've got the resources of the country behind them."

"That's not saying much, is it?" Rab Manga scowled and his eye fell on the sign in the lobby. "And get rid of that bloody e," he said and strode off.

The owner of Dharmedia was a Buddhist. While caste had been officially outlawed in Nepal more than fifty years earlier, it remained alive and well among the Hindu majority and even among some Buddhists. When he bought the media group the owner had caused a sign to be placed in the lobby in both Nepali and English: *Caste is Past*. The janitor had added a final *e*. "It is silent," he explained to the group manager, "but it adds a pleasing symmetry to the phrase, do you not think?"

"Very pleasing," the group manager had agreed, appreciating the sign's inadvertent accuracy. Regretfully, he had explained the difference between "past" and "paste," and the final *e* had been taken down. Unfortunately, the letters were adhesive, a Chinese knockoff of an American product, and the final *e* took with it the surface of the underlying veneer, also of Chinese origin, leaving a faint outline that no amount of scrubbing would remove. Now, as Rab Manga disappeared down the hall, the group manager gazed at the sign for the umpteenth time. He was seventy-three, informal editor/production chief for all of Dharmedia, training the editors, reporters and production staff under him.

A load-shedding moment washing over him. "What to do," he murmured—*ke ho ke ho*, almost a national refrain—and turned away.

As he approached the conference room for a progress report, the door opened and one of the reporters, Vineeta Bhool, passed him, cellphone to her ear and headed for the lobby. She disconnected as she came out on to the front steps of the Dharmedia building. Two Nepalis had just arrived, one holding a cellphone. He gave the customary greeting, putting his hands together and inclining his head.

"*Namaste*, Vineeta." He was nineteen, small but strong. A Sherpa.

"*Namaste*, Mingma, how are you?" She had met him last year while writing an article on his school, part of a series on education in Kathmandu.

Mingma lost no time. "I must return to the school, but here is Raju, who listened to your radio show and knows something about the killing of King Birendra. I have told him you will hear his story." He raised a hand to them both, turned and jogged off down the street.

Raju looked skeptically at the reporter and waited.

"Hello Raju," said Vineeta. She motioned him to follow her into the building. Raju waited in the lobby until she returned for him and took him to the empty conference room, where they sat down across from each other at the table.

Raju thought he might as well get this over with. "I am a Dalit," he said. It was an uncharacteristic remark but Raju was in a mood. He was actually one of Nepal's six thousand *gandharbas* or street musicians; one of the many untouchable classes lumped together under the catch-all term "Dalit."

"So am I," said Vineeta.

He stared. "That is impossible! Dalits are street sweepers and musicians."

"And reporters." She returned his gaze and waited. Vineeta had broad features, a stolid expression and a quick mind.

Raju said nothing for fully twenty seconds. Then finally, "Ha!" His mood lightened and he regarded the woman with respect.

"What can you tell me?" she asked.

"I was at the palace the night of the massacre. I was walking past the south gate. At 9:05 a jeep came out. I was across the street. I saw the jeep with one person in it. It turned west and I was going east. I thought no more about it until the next day."

Vineeta noted the details. "What were you doing there at that time of night?"

"I was going to play at the Yak and Yeti. A group of Japanese tourists wanted sarangi music." The sarangi is a traditional Nepali stringed instrument, not to everyone's taste: it sounds like a seagull in a certain amount of pain.

She questioned him further but there was little he could add. He had not heard the gunshots. The jeep had had no particular markings; it was just an ordinary army jeep. He was sure about the time because he'd just glanced at his watch, worried about being late for his gig.

She promised to look into the information and he left, walking on air because someone had at last listened to his story. She ran the details past the group manager.

"Interesting," he said. Unlike the reporter, who was too young to remember the details, he recalled that night very well, and the days that followed. He did not recall ever hearing this particular bit of information.

"I will interview the servants."

"And the surviving royals and their ADCs. Palace security. But check online first. You should be able to find the official report." He glanced at his watch. "Is your laptop charged?"

She reminded him that the city's power would be staying on at night during the golf tournament, and left to find her computer.

Brain's not what it was, muttered the group manager sourly to himself. In his youth, he had been assistant managing editor of a New York daily. He had left to write the great American novel and had found himself, after many diversions, in Kathmandu, and here he had stayed. The novel was in a suitcase in his room, not quite finished. It had been not quite finished twenty-five years ago, but he had become attached to this little country, whose population ebbed and flowed with tourists, Tibetan refugees and

Indian gangsters. Sandwiched between two superpowers, it had been struggling for a decade to define its republican self and move forward.

He checked his watch. Five-thirty Thursday afternoon meant 7:45 Thursday morning in Augusta, Georgia. Nearly time. He could hear the television as he neared the lunchroom.

o o o

Two men, one a colonel in the combat dress of the Nepal Army, sat at a table in the restaurant of the Yak and Yeti casino. The room was filling up; the television screens placed strategically around the walls showed talking heads, volume low, against a background of Augusta National Golf Course. They could hear the roulette wheels upstairs.

The Chinese diplomat, a heavy-set man of fleshy features, raised his drink, glanced at the screen nearest him and decided to change the subject. "Do you follow the golf, Colonel?" He took a sip.

The Colonel refused to be deflected. "So you can tell me nothing about these men?"

The diplomat shook his head impatiently. "Do you really think China is invading your northern border? Of course not." He was conscious of the Colonel's scrutiny. Sounds of excitement from upstairs penetrated his thoughts. "Shall we have a wager, Colonel? I wager that if we fly up there, you and I, we will find not a trace of this horde of Chinese invaders."

"No horde. Just a team of engineers, by the sound of it. I'm still investigating." He nodded and stood up. "And I have no doubt they've hiked out by now."

"Oh come, Colonel. Perhaps it was a party of tourists. Or perhaps your villager was daydreaming—or drunk. Here, let us have a bet on our two players. Lin Jinhai against your Lhakpa Pinasa." He savored the sweet blended liqueurs of his drink, gazing at the opening ceremony now displayed on the screen.

The Colonel studied him. "Lhakpa Pinasa is an amateur. What are you trying to prove?"

The Chinese threw up his hands. "Very well. Lin against the field, if you prefer."

"Good evening." The soldier turned and strode out of the restaurant.

THURSDAY

O O O O

It is nevertheless a game of considerable passion, either of the explosive type, or that which burns inwardly and sears the soul. –Bobby Jones

Kat's Story

"Fore please. Lhakpa Gyeltsen Pinasa now driving."

Patrons milling round behind the tee box, volunteers with arms and signs held high for silence. The picture froze as Tony went through his pre-shot routine. Just under six feet, good shoulders and a well-setup body, wearing a creased off-white shirt and chinos, color-coordinated shoes. He wore a visor and his hair stuck up on the crown of his head. The best thing about him color wise was his skin: bronze with a tinge of pink. I checked that online and that's his exact color.

He addressed the ball and produced a smooth swing, clean contact and a slight draw. Nice. The ball dropped about two hundred and eighty-five yards out, just before the crest. Mild applause (it was only eight-fifteen and we were the first group). First-tee jitters are the same for golfers everywhere, but they're magnified at a major and it was good to get away.

Stillson started off as I took the driver, inspected, wiped, replaced, covered it, picked up the bag (only thirty-five pounds, five less than Charlie's) and took off after Tony. That's what he prefers to be called; suits me.

Augusta National is full of traditions. The honorary starter is a good example, where old champions, the great ones, get to hit first to start off the tournament. For years Sam Snead and Byron Nelson did the honors together. Arnold Palmer took over for a few years. Sometimes it can take a while for the starter to get going. Maybe you know: old bones and early mornings don't mix. We'd waited inside the ropes, Tony and I, then Stillson and his caddie, Monk, joined us. I braced myself.

"I'm sorry for your loss, Kat," said Stillson. He managed to grasp my hand in both of his. "I've been praying for you and for Josh's soul."

I muttered something and shot Monk a grateful look when he changed the subject.

"When's Charlie back? Miss his smiling face."

"June probably." I managed to extract my hand and looked for something more to say. "Me too."

Then the starting ceremony began and now we were off and running, only a few minutes late.

The fairway drops down about thirty feet in front of the tee box and I paid attention to my footing. Caddies wear tennis shoes at Augusta National, not spikes. It means less wear and tear on the course, but in the rain or early morning, when there's moisture on the ground, you don't want to make a fool of yourself going up and down slopes. So I hustled with care down the slope. The two players, the width of the tee box apart, were well out on the fairway as I caught up with Monk. His real name's Mike, but he's bald under his cap except for a fringe round the bottom. That plus his player gave him his nickname.

"Heard from Bullet last night," he said. Normal Thursday-Friday play is in threesomes. We're only a twosome because Bullet's player fell down the stairs last weekend and tore a ligament.

"How was he?"

We were walking fast to catch up with the two players. Monk gave me a sideways glance and I got his drift. "Oh man." Everyone wants to come to Augusta, caddies as well as players.

"He's out for six to eight weeks," said Monk.

We matched stride for stride, marching down the fairway in our white jumpsuits and green caps. "Poor Bullet," I said. Monk grunted as he veered off toward the left trees. Stillson's ball was in the pine straw under the trees, clearly visible against the rust red. I reached Tony and planted the bag. He was pacing around, not exactly impatient but with energy to burn. I glanced at him, not saying anything. It was enough. Sometimes rookies have to be reminded to breathe, and we'd discussed yesterday how I would remind him if he seemed to be getting quick. Now he closed his eyes, looked down at the ground and became very still. I assume this is some kind of meditation thing but I'm not asking. We're not on those terms.

The members go to great lengths to make amateurs feel comfortable at the Masters. They get a dinner and pep talk on Tuesday night, and that aside, everyone goes out of their way to help them and put them at their ease. The draw is set up to be supportive of the amateurs. Our threesome had included a marquee player and Greg Stillson, both of whom had played Augusta National many times.

The job of a caddie is to adapt—to do and be whatever his player wants. I'd played three practice rounds with Tony earlier in the week. We'd discussed some ground rules and I'd formed some impressions. He was something of a loner, I found, maybe because of his reputation as a hothead or maybe from inclination. He liked to keep his own council. He also soaked up information wherever he found it. For our practice rounds he'd had me suggest the club and the shot, and on the greens the line and the break. For the tournament we had agreed that he would describe what he planned on each shot and I would put in my two cents whenever I felt it necessary.

For someone with a completely undistinguished amateur career—his only win of any significance was the British Amateur, which he'd won last year after coming second three times—he had plenty of confidence. The good kind. He didn't brag or anything; he just seemed comfortable in himself.

Stillson finished conferring with Monk and took a club. He hit eventually, going up over the trees and coming down long and left of the green.

We had one-fifty-five on an upslope to a slightly elevated green. The first hole can be quite brutal but it was playing short today with no wind. Common practice is to shoot for the middle of the green and try for your two-putt. But the pin placement was front right and Tony had wanted to try something different. I waited to see if he would stay with his game plan.

"I'm going to draw it in to the front." It's a nice shot but testing, and if he'd been Charlie we'd have discussed it. Control your distance and the ball will land just off the green so that it comes in and runs toward the hole, with the slope behind the hole as a backstop.

"Nine," I said, pulling it out.

"You think?"

I put it back. "Better a hard nine and come up short. You don't want to be down at the back there behind the green."

He agreed and I pulled out the club and handed it to him. Stayed put while he got the picture. Swing. "This'll work fine." Swing. "I had this shot at the under-sixteens in Bremen," swing, "fifth hole." I picked up the bag. Swing. "Oh momma." I moved away. He went through his routine and took the shot. A beautiful draw, higher than most.

The ball landed just where it was supposed to and ran into the slope. We were lying about fifteen feet from the hole. "Nice." We exchanged a smile.

"Great shot, Tony," Stillson said and as they headed down the fairway I heard him ask, "Is this your first time at Augusta National?" I didn't hear the answer but Tony had said earlier in the week he'd been here twice since winning the Amateur: last October for two weeks, and then again in March for another two. He'd played thirty-six holes most days so he'd got plenty of rounds under his belt. But not under tournament conditions. The shot he'd just hit had been good by any standard.

Patrons were scattered round the green with one or two in the stands and a threesome in the left trees just ahead: a man and two women. I'd met Tony's mother, Mollie, and his uncle, Gordon Menzies, yesterday. Hadn't met the girlfriend, Tashi. She flew in last night.

I'd spoken on the phone a couple of times with Gordon. I asked him once if he'd considered getting one of the course caddies for Tony. He said they didn't have the tournament knowledge or experience any more. At one time players had to use Augusta National caddies. In fact, they set the standard for what a caddie should be. But there was a ruckus one year when none of them turned up on time, so after that players were allowed to bring their own. Some went on using Augusta caddies just for the Masters—Fuzzy Zoeller was one, and Ben Crenshaw. But the original caddies got older and eventually retired, and nowadays most players bring their own. So while Augusta National's caddies have plenty of course experience they haven't worked the tournaments, where the course plays very differently.

Stillson took a gazillion practice swings. Tony was standing quite close to his family but didn't talk to them, nor they to him. Stillson chipped to within about five feet—not bad by Masters standards: getting the ball to stop near the hole is always a challenge, even on Thursday. On the plus side, this morning the greens are pristine: not a mark on them; a far cry from what they'll be like tomorrow afternoon when we come this way again.

Tony surveyed his putt from both sides, and so did I. "Left edge," he said and I agreed. He uses a center-shaft blade putter. He made a good, smooth stroke, a tad too hard I thought—it looked as though it might roll by the hole—

but it caught the left edge and dropped. He straightened and grinned at me, and I walked over and replaced the flag and gave him a high five. Birdie. On the first hole, first day.

"Nice," I said as he handed me the ball. He walked off in a springy way toward the second and I heard Stillson's "Great birdie, Tony" as I followed. There had been a smattering of applause in the early morning light, and now I saw Gordon give him a thumbs up as we passed. Mollie looked thrilled and then her expression changed and I didn't figure out what it was until much later. Tashi was looking at me as I went past, and I nodded.

The bunkers at Augusta National are filled with white feldspar. Standing at the front of the tee box, Tony had the fairway bunker on number two as a backdrop. Seen like that, his outfit looked even more dingy. It's not respectful wearing clothes like that, and that's all I have to say on the subject.

He would be first to play and I wanted to allow time for the adrenaline to dissipate so I was slow putting the bag down by the right tee marker, and slow to clean the ball.

You probably know this hole: it's a par five, five hundred and seventy-five down the hill. Long hitters will try for a drive of three-twenty to three-forty taking the fairway bunker out of play and permitting a long-iron second shot. For Tony, the ideal shot is a drive that kicks off the bank near the bunker and continues down the hill. No wind to speak of, and the pin today is behind the left-hand greenside bunker. The easiest approach is from the middle right.

Tony was gazing at the fairway with his hands shoved in his pockets. I decided to put something out there. You don't want to agonize over these things. He'd been in the bunker once but that was bad luck. "Draw your drive off the bank?"

"Yes, of course," he said. "I was just looking at the dogwoods." He came back to the bag, pulled out the driver and gave me the cover. I hefted the bag and moved off the tee. I've been finding there's a lot to like with his game, and the more I watch him the better I like it. He's neither quick nor slow with each shot. He's deliberate, as a conscious choice. Like many aspects of his game this is based on his idol, Nicklaus. But I would call Jack on the slow side, though I never saw him play in his prime. Tony is deliberate but with flow. You can count the steps or stages through each stroke, but he doesn't linger over any one of them. This is especially true of his putting.

So now, he took his two practice swings, studied the line from behind the ball, glanced at the trees, took his stance—distance from the ball, grip, right foot, then left (closed for a draw)—gathered himself mentally, glanced at the target, one waggle then take away. It was a pretty shot: hugging the right then curving back into the fairway and dropping behind the bunker, with a kick off the slope toward the middle.

Stillson is a long hitter, and this time he found the fairway. We moved off, the two players in front. They'd got to religion by now. I met Monk's sideways glance as we walked behind, but his expression didn't change. I have to say, Stillson isn't one of my favorite players. He's a Southern Baptist and when the going gets rough his game slows to a crawl. I don't know for a fact that he recites the entire Lord's Prayer before every shot, but it sometimes seems like it.

"So I guess you'd be what—a Hindu?" *None of your goddamn business*, I glared at him but Tony was okay with the question.

"I'm not really anything in a formal way, but if I were I'd be a Buddhist. Or maybe a militant Anglican." *You tell him, kid.*

I reminded myself that it was Thursday, and this was pretty typical Thursday conversation. Even at the majors, Thursdays tend to be relatively easy going. You can't push yourself up to a Sunday pitch on Thursdays and hope to maintain that kind of intensity all four days. In any case, on Thursday all the mistakes, the misclubs, the disasters, lie ahead. It was a beautiful morning—a really exquisite morning if you want to know, with a temperature of about seventy and no clouds. Augusta National is outrageously beautiful: the greenest greens, rust-red pine straw, those white bunkers, and the flowers. Dogwoods all down number two and somewhere in the woods on the left I heard the call and rat-tat-tat of a flicker getting its breakfast.

At any course, early rounds are wonderful: the quiet, the dew on the grass. Setting out lifts the spirit: the round is still a mystery filled with promise, waiting to unfold, the surroundings are beautiful and unless you're really unlucky the company is fine. At a major, Thursday and to some extent Friday are for small talk: sports, family, appearance fees, or in the case of types like Stillson, religion.

"I heard Charlie had to twist your arm to get you to come," said Monk.

"Yeah."

"Sorry?"

We exchanged a glance. He could see the answer to that one.

"Who do you like for tomorrow? Atlanta?" I asked. I knew he was a Braves fan and tomorrow was their first game. We talked baseball—no use trying to interest Monk in the NHL playoffs—until we reached our ball, then he split off to join Stillson.

"Nice lie," I said to Tony. It was sitting up perfectly with a slight downhill stance. It's about a seventy foot drop to the landing area Tony wanted, seventy-five feet from the pin, and he faded a shot in there nicely. Twenty yards further down the fairway, Stillson striped his second into the neck of the green between the two bunkers. It hopped forward and ran onto the green, trickling down to the back. He'd be putting for eagle.

Before we go any further we should deal with two things. Just skip over this stuff if you know it already. A draw (or a hook) is a right-to-left curved shot; a fade (or a cut or slice) is a left-to-right curve. At Augusta, both shots come into play. "Working the ball" means a golfer is able to shape his shots to suit any situation—to get round a tree, say, or avoid a bunker. You do this by changing the position of your feet or the ball, or the line of your swing. Some players have only one ball flight but Tony isn't one of them. He works the ball.

He told me he was a runt until he was sixteen, so he learned a lot of different shots to compensate. I also discovered, however, that he prizes control over length off the tee. He's very good with his irons, three and up. His short game generally is good, and his putting is outstanding. His big weakness is sand. He's spent a lot of time on that. He plays Mizuno irons and he told me one of the happiest weeks of his life occurred when he was seventeen and the Mizuno rep came to town. "Mr. Dowling invited him to stay the week and since it was November, he did."

Tom Dowling is his teaching pro, working out of Widemouth Golf Course on the north coast of Cornwall. His lies and lofts are precise to within a tenth of a degree; apparently the Mizuno rep had a van full of equipment, tools and machines for working your will on any golf club, and had showed Tony how everything worked. "I used to go out and hit a hundred balls, then adjust the lie on this club or the loft on that one, then hit another hundred. And so on. It was wonderful. By the time I'd finished I could absolutely nail my yardages on every club." He doesn't own a gap wedge. "I found that my lofts were coming out about a degree higher each club, and it almost eliminated the gap, so why bother?" His sand wedge is fifty-three degrees, not fifty-four.

The ball, when we reached it, was actually seventy-six yards from the flagstick by my reckoning. My yardage book is pretty marked up and I had a note on the distance based on one of the right-hand trees. It's good to see some short shots early on, just to settle the nerves. We were looking at an elevation of maybe ten feet. Tony's wedge shot landed twenty feet from the back left pin and ran forward, but less than he'd expected, leaving him about five feet to the hole. I heard him muttering under his breath, swishing the club against the grass. I just waited, and eventually he handed it to me without a comment, and took the putter. Stillson missed his eagle putt but both made their birdies so now we're looking at two under for my player after two holes on the first day of the Masters.

The players eat all they want at the Grill Room in the club house, and Mollie had also given me a box of Tony's favorite energy bars, but coming off the green he decided to inspect the cooler behind the third tee and returned with a banana. He and Greg seemed relaxed and were still talking religion between shots. Patrons began to show up in greater numbers in the trees along the fairways and in the stands, and the sun warmed up the pines. There was a scent of pine and jasmine in the air.

Holes three, four and five form another corner on the course, just as tough as the better known Amen Corner, but both players followed up par at the third with another at the fourth. The fact is, they had the good fortune to be on a roll. Stillson knew how unusual that was, but Tony probably did not. In any case neither Monk nor I wanted to rock the boat, so we did our jobs quietly, unobtrusively and quickly. We were the first group out, we had no delays and few distractions, the weather was perfect and the players relaxed. Or so I thought.

I brought out a fresh ball on the fifth tee. Unless your player really crushes it or the cover is scuffed, you don't have to change balls. I just got into the habit with Charlie, about halfway through each nine. I checked that it was marked correctly: a star cradled in the tail of the Titleist capital T. Tony hovered at my elbow and I gave him the ball. Stillson and Monk were over the other side.

"Anything wrong?" He wasn't as composed as I'd thought earlier. Nothing much I could see, just a tiny bit anxious.

"I don't want to talk right now."

"Okay."

"I meant, to Greg."

"Okay." I offered him an energy bar but he declined. "Did you tell him?"

"I said I want to focus on my game."

"Perfect."

"It's not rude?" He must have discerned something in my expression because he went on, "He was telling me about his church."

"Makes no difference." I gestured over toward the right rough, about one-fifty out. "Look at that magnolia." He couldn't see it because they don't come into bloom for another month, but it got him turned well away from the others. "Listen," I said. "He may be older and a pro, it doesn't matter. You have every right to be here."

"I know that." He looked offended. Better than anxious.

"And to talk or not talk. Your call." We turned back to the bag and began to discuss the hole and the tee shot.

The fifth is four hundred fifty-five yards, a dogleg left that rises about thirty-five feet to the landing area. The bunkers on the left are eight feet deep. Unless you plan to drive them, which requires a tee shot of at least three-fifteen, you want to land as close to the right of them as you can. The landing area is narrow and the ideal shot is a draw. I studied the tree tops: still no wind. We both had our yardage books out.

"I'm going to land about there," Tony indicated a point midway along the length of the nearest bunker. That's a shot of about two-seventy. I pulled out the three-wood.

"Give me the driver."

I put the three-wood back. "You don't need the driver. Hit a hard three. Better than an easy driver." I thought he had some adrenaline in there, maybe from Stillson. In any case, a three is easier to work than the driver and he'd want to draw the ball. I met his stare calmly, waiting. I wasn't going to pull out a club until he made a decision. He looked out at the fairway. We could see the corner of the first bunker.

"Okay," he agreed at last.

I handed him the three and he took some practice swings, staring down the fairway and commenting between each one. Sounded like he was getting the picture, and he finally walked to the tee and went through his routine. He produced a sweet draw, landing about as close to the bunker as you'd want to be.

We waited for Stillson. It was nine-thirty and getting nicely warm. The group behind us had just reached the third green as we started off. Our twosome was drawing further and further ahead even with Stillson's deliberate play.

We discussed shot options as we walked up the fairway. Tony enjoyed this. I'd learned that when he first played here he asked his caddie to do what I did: namely, give him all the options for each shot. That was last fall. He went back home with his yardage book and a notebook full of thoughts, and he seemed to have spent the winter visualizing his way round the course. He returned in February and did the same thing all over again with a different caddie, then went home and put all his notes together.

Now, on number five, he ran down all the possible options for the second shot, depending on the lie and the precise distance, and whether it would be better to land long right or middle left.

The fifth green is a huge, undulating monster. At the front is a five-foot-deep flat apron. This rises sharply through a swale running across the width of the green, to a plateau. Hit too long and your ball runs off the plateau into a trough or bowl which itself rises to a smaller flat area near the back. We'd had some fun here on Monday, when Tony had been seemingly incapable of dropping a putt.

We reached the ball. Stillson had used his driver and was thirty yards ahead. The flag was left center, on the plateau. "I'm going to aim for left middle. If I miss it'll end up in the rough; if I make it should stop on top."

That told me he planned on a fade. There are two magnolias on the left beyond the bunkers, and we were opposite the second. That put us at one-sixty-five to seven, call it one-sixty-six. Eight-iron. Open stance, tremendous force on the downswing and the ball was launched. Would it cut? Christ it was high, heading for the left trees. It turned finally, but not enough, and landed in the rough all right, deeper than he wanted. I heard some muttering as I came back with the divot and he tamped it down with the club. We stood and waited while Stillson did his thing.

"He seems awfully big on religion," said Tony.

"Did he want you to visit his church?" I've heard him say that before.

"I think he was working up to it."

"So . . . you're a Buddhist?"

"I'm a Sherpa. We're originally from Tibet. That means I'm a Buddhist." He paused then added, "Except when I lose my temper."

He looked rueful and I had to laugh. I'd read somewhere that Buddhists are nonviolent. In fact, I did quite a lot of research on this kid last week. I'd had several questions and now seemed like a good time to ask one. "So—Sherpas are—well, like caddies for mountain climbers, right?" Now it was his turn to be amused.

"Sort of. That's quite funny, actually."

"So why do you call yourself a caddie? You're a player."

"Sherpa's an ethnic group as well as a job description. My dad was a Sherpa sherpa. I'm just a Sherpa."

"I get it, he was like what's his name. The one who climbed Everest with Edmund Hillary." I know most sports but mountain climbing is a bit out of my field.

"Tenzing Norgay. Yes, he was."

We started walking toward the green. "So, your dad's last name was Sherpa." I'd been wondering why his wasn't.

"Nepal's an interesting country. There are over fifty different ethnic groups. Sherpas and Newars and Nubris and Tamangs—that's what Tashi is."

"And Gurkhas, right?" I'd heard of them.

"Well—not quite. Gurkhas actually come from four different ethnic groups." He went on, "Anyway, many people take their ethnic group as their last name. But women often take a clan name. Pinasa's my dad's clan, so my mum took that name when they got married. I traveled on her passport because we left right after my dad died."

We'd reached the green and come round to the left rough. I lowered the bag and Tony finished absently, as he crouched down behind the ball, "I could add Sherpa to my name. But it's long enough as it is. . . ."

Got that right. I crouched down with him. The ball was sitting up in the longer rough, the second cut, as they call it here. In other words, it was sitting on grass an inch and three-eights long, so you have to be careful. Your club head can go right underneath and grab almost all air and no ball, which will cause it to pop up and drop down, leaving you another chip from pretty much the same place. Tony had ten feet of rough, two feet of fringe and thirty-five feet of green to the pin. If he failed to hold the line, the ball would roll off the plateau. It was like trying to roll a ball along a length of two by four over a ravine.

He didn't miss his line, he just misjudged the distance, using a seven-iron and landing it in the fringe. The ball ran out of steam about twenty-five feet from the pin. He gave that putt his best shot but it slid by about eighteen inches, and he just stood there glaring at it, then looked off to the trees and made some choice remarks under his breath. He was perfectly calm when he sank the bogey putt and I thought he was handling himself well.

We went to the sixth one under for the day.

Television doesn't show the elevation changes too well at Augusta National. Standing on the sixth tee, we had the fifth green to our left, about ten feet higher. On the right is the sixteenth green, about ninety feet below.

Stillson had the honor, so I left the bag and went to the washroom, thinking about Tony's background. He lost his dad in 2001, when the Crown Prince of Nepal went postal and gunned down his entire family during a Friday night get-together. He had several guns at home because he served in the Nepal Army. So he put on his army fatigues and took a semi-automatic and he killed his father, mother, brother and sister, plus a lot of cousins, aunts and uncles. The king's brother wasn't there and many people found that suspicious, and wondered if he was behind the murders. So although he became king he didn't last long because no one liked or trusted him. They booted him out and in 2008 Nepal became a republic.

It seems this massacre stuff won't go away, though. Some new theory's always cropping up about who did what and who was behind it. It's like the Kennedy assassination, I guess.

I couldn't see why Tony's dad would have been at the palace until I read that the Crown Prince used to do a lot of trekking and Chhiri was the one who arranged it, so he was in a study somewhere in the Prince's house with one of the royal cousins, working out the details of their next trek, when Dipendra—that was the Crown Prince—went on his rampage.

Earlier in the week Tony had discovered Augusta National's pimiento cheese sandwich, and when I came out of the washroom I picked up a couple from the concession stand and headed back up toward the tee. A big man, army by the look of his boots, was leaning against a pine staring at the bank of azaleas behind the booth. My head was still back in Nepal at the palace and for a crazy moment I thought I was seeing Dipendra—big man, army gear—mourning his terrible deed: this guy had tears streaming down his face and he turned away when he saw me and at the same time I looked away and hurried by, and came back to the present. Because Dipendra, on seeing what he had done, did not weep: he put a pistol to his head and shot himself, rather badly I guess, because he took two days to die.

Augusta National takes people in different ways. It's a very emotional experience for some. I think that's partly the beauty, partly the peace and the civility of the members and patrons, and partly the ambiance. I can't tell you how Josh loved it here.

The sixth is a hundred and eighty yards from an elevated tee, so Tony took the eight-iron. There wasn't a breath of wind. Coming off a bogey he had his tee shot completely under control. I picked up the bag and started off down to the green. He called after me and I realized I hadn't taken the club.

"Sorry," I took it and wiped it while I walked. When we reached the green he took his putter and I carried the bag over to the left, up through the pine straw to the seventh tee. I wondered if Charlie was watching. Both players made par.

Its effect on patrons and visitors aside, Augusta National tests the complete golfer, not only physically, but mentally as well. Number seven is a good example. Just when a player has got used to the wide open fairways, he's confronted by this hole: tree-lined, narrow and intimidating. Tony seemed unfazed by it, and faded his tee shot up the right for a better angle to the left pin. We walked off the tee and he said, "You should meet my cousin Kenchi. She's a sirdar. She leads treks and expeditions for my dad's company." He said the company had been run since his dad's death by an American woman who used to do all the office and secretarial. She'd become the majority owner after they left.

"Are there a lot of women sherpas? I mean, who work as sherpas?"

"Oh sure. They carry more than the men, some of them. And most of them aren't as tall as you." We reached the ball and he added, "This doesn't impress me. We needed to be further up than this." By my reckoning we had one seventy-eight to the small green bounded on all sides by bunkers.

It's not so bad landing in the front bunkers but the back ones are no good at all.

The yardage was awkward, but in the end Tony decided on a seven-iron, and hit a high, soft fade to the left-hand pin. I was going to say "nice shot" but at Augusta you always wait to see where it ends up and sure enough, the ball landed front-left then ran sideways across the green, finishing about thirty feet from the hole. His first putt stopped left of the hole, leaving a slippery four-footer with six inches of break in it. He spent quite a lot of time over that putt and so did I. In the end he managed to par the hole. He walked off the green, Stillson joined him and they went to the eighth together.

"Nice round, isn't it?" Monk was with me.

"Yeah, very." I glanced at him, assessing. Monk's been around, and he's been with Stillson a while. "I want to keep it that way, too."

"Can the God stuff, huh?"

"You guessed it."

"Greg's usually pretty good about that; doesn't overstay his welcome, if you know what I mean. The kid was asking him questions."

"He was being polite."

Monk absorbed this then shook his head. "Those crazy mixed up Brits." He grinned, then added, "Maybe Greg felt he might get decked if he didn't answer."

That had not occurred to me and I stared at Monk in consternation. "Shit. Tony doesn't make a habit of throwing punches, tell him."

He laughed. "I'll see what I can do," he said.

You have to know I asked the kid about this fight business pretty early in our relationship. From what he told me, and I saw no reason to doubt him, it didn't seem to justify the media coverage. He'd socked a racist spectator who had swung first. It was late in the match, when he and his Pakistani partner had put up with the guy's mouth for sixteen holes. They were playing a German pair, and Tony said his partner finally got so upset his hands were shaking when he tried to putt. "It was in the Midlands," Tony said, "and a misty day. That's what made his stuff so effective. It seemed to be coming at us from all around." He'd finally gone over and talked to this creep and that's when the punches got thrown.

From the way he described it, I couldn't see why anyone had raised a fuss, but apparently when some official questioned them afterward, one of the two Germans changed from saying it was okay to saying he wasn't sure it was okay. So then word got around, an article got written, then another one, and so on. My vote was on the kid.

Who now seemed agitated. He was staring out at the seventeenth green directly behind us, hands shoved in his pockets, frowning.

"Anything wrong?"

"I'm trying to think." He was curt, so I left him alone.

I wondered what the hell Stillson had said. I found out a long time after: nothing much. All he'd done was talk when Tony didn't want to talk. That was all. The putt on seven had been difficult; he just wanted to clear his mind and get focused on the next hole.

Number eight is a par five, a potential birdie opportunity, but long and uphill, with a slight dogleg left. The fairway isn't as wide as you think because of the bunker on the right, but bailing out to the left gives you no shot at the green. Today's pin was back right, difficult to get at.

Tony had said during practice that he would be playing all the par fives in three, taking three shots to reach the green instead of two. He proceeded to make a dog's dinner of this one. I deliberately stayed low-key because it was beginning to dawn on me that we had a problem.

I'm thirty-four, Stillson and Monk both early forties. For at least a decade, the amateur events have been dominated by kids. It's not like the old days where men in their twenties and thirties used to play top-line amateur golf. I'm sure such people still exist, but they don't get into the top amateur events because the competition from the ankle biters is so stiff. These kids are coming out of fancy golf clinics and schools, and roaring through the amateur events trying to get themselves a look-in at the PGA. Tony, who was in his early twenties, was coming from an environment where he'd be a senior player into one where he's quite junior. It shouldn't bother him, but I suspected he was having trouble asserting his authority. Someone who's had trouble doing that in one area might go out of his way to do it in another. He'd had trouble with Stillson. I didn't want him overriding me with a dumb decision.

"Give me the driver."

I handed it over, no comment.

"I know we talked about laying up, but I feel like going for it."

"Why not? You're playing well. What are you thinking for the second?"

"Fade a three from two sixty."

I didn't say a word. To fade into this green you've got to

hit it high and very long. If you get hung up on the mounds round the green—well, let's just say there are wonderful opportunities for big trouble, right under the eyes of the gallery.

I hefted the bag off the tee box and waited. Tony went through his routine and hit a screamer straight right up the fairway. It caromed off the slope in front of the bunker and I prayed, *go over, please go over.* It didn't go over. It took a small hop off a peninsula of grass and snuggled down in the bunker under the left edge.

"Hm. Interesting," I said lightly, taking the driver.

"Yeah, well, not quite what I had in mind."

The lie, when we got there, was challenging: about a foot inside the left edge on the downslope. The bunker's not that deep so theoretically he could use a three, but why bother? A lay-up was the sensible choice, some would say the only choice. I said nothing.

"It's sitting clean."

Talk about grasping at straws. I debated telling him to go for it as a sort of reverse psychology thing, but I couldn't bring myself to say something so stupid.

"Let's go for it." He pulled out the three.

"Let's think about laying up for a moment."

"Nah. I'm okay with this."

Give him credit, he caught it clean and hit a beautiful fade up over the trees on the left, but further left than he had planned. We couldn't see it land but it was likely on top of one of the mounds at the left.

The stand was almost full so we had an audience for the rest of the hole. As I'd feared, the ball was on the top of the left mound. The green runs away from you there, and even on Thursday it's slick. A wedge to the fringe is what you need but that requires the utmost precision and a pinch of luck and even then the ball would be difficult to stop. By the time we were done there was a six on the card, a six on a hole that many players would birdie.

That's an amateur for you.

Stillson was up first on nine, and we watched as he and Monk conferred. I opened my mouth to discuss the hole, but Tony spoke first.

"I think it's best if I do my own thing from now on."

I looked at him in consternation, and he must have seen it but he went on, "I prefer it that way. I can focus better on my own."

I couldn't agree to this. It wasn't what I was hired for, and I'd be falling down on the job if I let it go. "Look. I should have said more back on the last tee. I'm sorry now I didn't."

He gave me a gimletty stare. That's not racist, it's just what it was, a piercing look from skinny eyes. "Are you saying it's your fault I got a six?"

Oh shit. Which way was he blowing on this? Charlie was always straight up about his golf. Some guys look to blame their caddies, but he never did: "I'm the one who hit the shot," he'd say.

"Well, I'm the one with the experience—"

"I don't care. I'm the player. It's my responsibility." We watched as Stillson, having decided his strategy, walked to the tee. "Do you know what that stupid old bugger said to me?"

O. K. "What?"

"He said not to worry, I'm an amateur and this is great experience." I tried to look—I don't know, shocked?

Disgusted? What was so terrible—but he was going on in a fierce undertone, "Does he think I'm here for the experience? Do you? *I'm here to win, just like him.*"

Luckily we had to shut up then, while Stillson hit his drive. It was a good one, long and middle-right. A driver is of great benefit on this hole because the longer the shot, the more the green opens up for you from the fairway. There's a gully (a deep one, believe me: you can't see the bottom of the flagstick from there) in front of the green, and longer drives can end up in the bottom, with a flat lie, rather than being on the downslope. It makes the second shot much easier. I took a deep breath.

"Let's talk about your strategy. Just think of it as spelling it out for yourself. But do it out loud."

"I want the driver, partly because I hit such a bad one on the last hole and I'm going to need it on the next. And I'm just going to try and do what that ass did."

Oh boy. The next twenty-eight holes would be interesting. We were stuck with Stillson until the close of play tomorrow. I handed Tony the driver. He turned a quarter away from me, toward the back of the tee, gazed at the ground and became totally still. I watched curiously. His eyes were closed, and he seemed almost limp; even his hands relaxed to the point that the shaft of the club was barely caught in the slight curl of his fingers.

A draw works best on this right-to-left hole. On Monday we had discussed drawing the ball off the oak tree visible up the right-hand side of the fairway. Tony began his practice swings, commenting under his breath between each swing. I resolved to do whatever I could to keep the communications open, partly because it was my job and also because there was plenty to like about this kid's game even if he was a pill.

He hit a good drive, good enough to erase memories of number eight, a draw that was out there. I reckoned we'd have a good second and I said so after taking the club, cleaning it and hurrying after Tony. I had to hurry because he wasn't lingering. I caught up.

"Mind if I say something?" He turned and slowed slightly, and I sorted out my thoughts. Began with the positive. Told him he had good imagination. You need that on this course. Tony was able to see all the ways a shot could be played, not just all the ways he could play it. And he wasn't intimidated by the course, another plus. "Okay," I finished. "My job is to do what you say. You don't have to talk to me, or ask my advice. If you want to play it that way—well, you're the boss." Resisted words like *stupid* and *dumbass.* "But I have to say, you don't have the experience here. You've got the game but not the experience, especially on the greens. I think you know that."

We reached the crest before the gully, and for the first time today we found that Stillson wasn't the longest off the tee. Tony's ball was down in the bottom on the flat, facing the full length of the green. With a middle-left pin placement the trick is to use enough club to get past the false front. Otherwise your ball just rolls back off the green and down to your feet. Not nice.

Stillson had about one-sixty to the pin off a downhill lie. He bailed out to the right and we walked down to the bottom. About one-forty-five, plus one and a half clubs for the height. Call it one-sixty into a bit of breeze. Eight-iron.

"I'm thinking a seven to the back with spin."

That's young nerves for you. The percentage shot is one that comes in low, bouncing forward from the front portion of the green. Start playing with spin on this green and you risk overcooking it so that the ball motors back past the pin and off the green. But Tony was comfortable with the shot so I handed over the seven-iron and he took his practice swings. He was going for the very back of the green, and while there are no stands on the ninth, plenty of patrons had set up folding chairs, and we heard a smattering of applause after the ball landed. It didn't come beetling back down the hill, so I breathed out.

"You got away with one there."

It turned out to be six feet right of the pin, a straightforward birdie putt that he holed, earning more polite applause. We ended the front nine at one under. I glanced at the leaderboard. Here's another Masters tradition. The Thursday leaderboards always show last year's winner in the top spot followed by the winners of the U.S. Amateur, U.S. and British Opens and the PGA. In sixth spot they list the British Amateur winner. I could see Tony enjoying the sight: Pinasa, with a red one after nine holes.

We split an energy bar as we walked over to number ten. "Lot of golf courses in Nepal, are there?"

"The place is littered with them," he replied. "You must have seen the calendar." Thank God he had a sense of humor.

"I've seen the course on top of the Matterhorn. I didn't know there was one on Everest as well." I wanted to ask if he'd ever been up there, or his dad. I guess he must have. But Tony was staring down the fairway, considering his shot.

The tenth hole is downhill, a slight dogleg left. The safest tee shot is a draw, landing on the left-hand slope. Go right and you're looking at a truly scary second shot, downhill and sidehill, longer than it would have been if you had caught the slope on the left. You'll need a long iron to reach the green and it'll be tough to hold, especially on the weekend, because it runs away from you. Best to draw the ball on this hole.

Do that and it's not so bad. It used to be the hardest hole on the course but that was years ago. These days it's middling hard. There's a seventy-eight-foot drop from tee to green and a good tee shot will cut sixty feet out of that, landing you on the ridge at the left where the ball can bound forward and down the bank to end up behind the fairway bunker.

It was after ten-thirty, and up behind us, crowds were teeming around the practice green. The Eisenhower cabin's along the left on this fairway, along with the Butler and Jones cabins. Don't know who Butler was, but that cabin is used by CBS during the tournament. Everyone knows who Mr. Jones was.

I studied my yardage book after putting the bag down, then walked slowly over to Tony. There's really only one option here, but I wanted time for the adrenaline from his birdie to dissipate. Eventually, he took the driver and hit a beautiful draw. There are some really ugly lies in this fairway: it slopes right to left as well as up and down, with deep undulations running across it at the dogleg. These can feed your ball down to the left, but the unlucky player may find his ball hung up on the downside of one of these undulations, with a difficult lie and stance. That was Stillson's misfortune, and he ended up bailing into the right-hand bunker down by the green. Could be worse.

Tony had a good lie, fairway bunker ahead. He took the eight-iron. The tops of the trees were swaying. "Half a club of wind," I warned. He hit quite a good, easy eight that caught the wind, landed front-middle and ran across the green to the back. He overcooked the putt a little and it stopped about fifteen feet beyond the hole. He kept to his unvarying routine—look from both sides, consult, look again if necessary, then address the ball and make the stroke—and sank the putt for par.

Stillson bogeyed, and they walked off the green together. The atmosphere was no longer relaxed: more people and a stronger breeze combined to notch up the tension a little. But Tony seemed to be handling it well, and I thought we might be able to build some kind of rapport on the back nine. Funny how life works. The unexpected lurks round every corner.

It sounded as though they were back on religion. "I've often wondered," I heard Stillson say, "whether there's a link between Buddhism and socialism. That seems to be the way of life in Buddhist countries, doesn't it?" Oh brother. I yearned for Charlie and the wonderful world of sports as I followed the others through the trees. The championship tee on eleven is so far back it's about level with the fairway bunker on ten. Tony was holding his end up, conversation-wise, though I couldn't hear what he was saying. But when we got to the tee box the players separated and he seemed to be fully focused on the fairway.

From the tee, the fairway looks like a long chute before opening out. Tony hit a draw, which is the right shot, but it started down the center, landed in the first cut on the left and hopped into the trees, about two-eighty out. He took a bad-tempered swipe with his club before tossing it back, and swore succinctly. I heard the tail-end of his party-of-one conversation as we waited for Stillson. "How do you expect to play on Sunday if you can't focus on Thursday? This is so weak. So weak."

Monk gave me a let-me-know-if-you-need-help signal as we set off. I dropped the bag at about the two-eighty mark. We were looking at trees in pine straw and the ball was visible, not nestled against a trunk but clear and sitting up cleanly. You want to watch out for tree roots when you walk on this stuff and I warned Tony. You can tread on a root and its movement will run out subterraneously and shift something five feet away.

He walked in carefully to stand a couple of yards behind the ball, looking through the trees ahead of it, out to the fairway, planning a line. From my angle it looked as though he might get off quite lightly. There was no need to chip out. A low punch shot to the front right should work fine. Many players bail on this hole because of the pond on the left and water at the back, and because the green runs down to the left. Ben Hogan used to say if you saw him on in two it was a mistake, and that was before the hole was lengthened.

"Give me the four. I'll punch it through down to the mound."

I handed him the club, staying back and behind. He took a few practice swings, watching his line, then took his stance. Peripherally I saw his head move as he studied the line, but I was watching the ball. It moved.

"Oh Christ!" It came out involuntarily.

"What?" He looked down. He looked at me.

I looked away. Why not just shut up? "The ball moved. Step away, for God's sake—"

I stopped because there was no mistaking that glare. He was angry, big time. I shut up and watched in silence, my stomach knotted, waiting. He was utterly immobile for an age. Then his gaze moved to the ball, out ahead to the gap, back to the ball. There is no way you can hit like that, without moving anything but your arms . . . the club came back in a half swing, connected clean and solid, and the ball was out, through and down the fairway, stopping about twenty yards from the right of the green.

He came back out. I took the club. "Thank God it's only a stroke—"

"I didn't see it." I could see the anger in his eyes again.

"I did!"

He was furious, and he was holding it in. "We'll talk about it after the round." He turned away.

"It's a stroke penalty. It's over. Take it and—"

"I didn't see it," he said through his teeth, and set off down the fairway.

"You think I'm lying?"

"We'll talk about it later. I've got to focus."

I calmed down, hoisted the bag and followed more slowly. I didn't see how he could focus and I was right. He managed to push it down while he finished the hole, producing a "nice par, Tony" from Stillson, who was in the dark. Then the fun began.

He took a bogey on twelve after pulling the shot so far left the ball dropped on the hillside above the path from Hogan's Bridge to the green. It didn't stop there. It took a giant bounce in the direction of the green and dropped, lo and behold, in the fringe. Compared to what might have been, his chip was a non-event. He should have made the putt too, but he refused to believe me when I said it was straight in (one of the few that is on that green), missing to the left.

On thirteen he took a nine. There. I won't dwell on it. Another colossal pull into the creek that runs down the left-hand side of the fairway. Found the ball, dropped and we're hitting three. This time, it went into the creek in front of the green. Found the ball, dropped, hitting five. This one went into the middle of the three back bunkers. The pitch-out is not necessarily that difficult, unless you're lying five and your hands feel like cement slabs. In that case, all you can think of is the creek on the far side of the green. The creek you've already visited twice. Three times. Found the ball, dropped, hitting eight. He made the putt.

The group behind had caught up. I saw Gordon and Tashi looking upset as we walked off the green; Mollie wasn't there.

I took the kid aside on the fourteenth tee box while Stillson made ready to tee off. I spoke matter of factly because he had a fixed, slightly stunned look. "You've done your research. You know what Augusta can do to a player. Any player. Your nine isn't the worst score that was ever posted on this course or even on this hole. Do you hear me?" I got in his face. "Do you?"

He nodded, and I made him eat a piece of energy bar. "Let's forget that hole and think about this one." I could see an official hovering. I guessed he would wait until Tony had teed off and then tell us we were on the clock. I was right.

Normally, being timed wouldn't be a problem for two players ahead of threesomes, but the kid didn't need more pressure right now. The person it really harmed, however, was Stillson, and I felt bad for him. Being on the clock meant taking no more than forty seconds after reaching your ball before taking the next shot. He normally took far longer.

But Stillson's a pro, so he found a way to cope, and by the time we'd cleared fifteen we were off the clock. The kid bogeyed fourteen, but managed to par his way in after that, quite an impressive feat after the melt-down. He had become quite calm after the tee shot on fourteen, and I wondered if his meditation techniques were responsible. We spoke very little beyond a stilted attempt to discuss baseball. He was slighting about it, as Brits sometimes are who don't know any better. He even annoyed Monk, who put in his two bits' worth when I got bogged down explaining triple plays. We came in in silence.

Par at Augusta is seventy-two, and he'd shot seventy-eight, including the penalty, after a fine front nine of one under thirty-five. Of course, it remained to be seen if he would declare the extra stroke on eleven.

"I like the way you hung in there, Tony," said Stillson as they shook hands. "You've got plenty of game, and tomorrow can put you right back in it." Tony muttered something to him and to Monk as they shook hands. He came over to me as I was putting ball and glove in the bag. I didn't want to shake hands so I was slow about it. Maybe he knew why because he just nodded to me.

"I'll deal with that shot now," he said, and followed Stillson into the scorer's cabin. I hefted the bag and climbed through the lines of patrons toward the bag storage area. Gordon stopped me en route, with Mollie and Tashi hovering.

"Hello, Kat. Did you two have an argument? What happened on eleven?"

"Yeah, I guess you could say we had an argument. I saw the ball move. He didn't. He said he'd talk to the officials about it." I decided not to say anything else.

"What does that mean—," said Tashi, then turned to Gordon, "what does she mean?" She looked at me. Attractive Asian girl, with high cheekbones and tousled hair. "You saw it move, but Lhakpa didn't?" I nodded. "How interesting!" She was obviously not slow on the uptake. "What if—is it Kat? Shall I call you Kat as well?"

"Unless you want to get formal." I smiled but I was feeling tired and short-tempered.

"What if no one had seen it move?" She looked at me, then at Gordon, and then made as if to reach for her purse, realized she didn't have it and said—not for the first time, I'm guessing—"honestly, I don't know how you manage without a phone here!" Cellphones are prohibited for spectators. "Do they write the rules down? May we see a copy?"

"Slow down, Tash." Gordon had been reading between the lines and he was about to ask a question, then changed his mind and said, with a rueful look at Mollie, "At least he didn't throw his club."

Stillson had emerged from the scorer's cabin and I happened to meet his eye. "Kat!" He strode over. "Did you know about this? What were you thinking—." He saw my expression and fast forwarded right away. He knew perfectly well it's not up to the caddie to declare a score. "I'm disgusted with him, Kat, I will tell you frankly." He glanced at the others unseeingly, and went on: "He said he doesn't know how many wrong cards he's signed." He paced round in a tight circle, then added, "He said *I—I*, Kat—I don't know how many wrong scorecards I've signed!"

Monk appeared at his elbow. "Hey Greg, let's go." But Stillson was just getting started. I exchanged a look with Gordon then glanced over toward the cabin. No sign of the kid. Tashi was listening in fascination. Stillson's eye fell on her. That was when I began to appreciate just how angry he was.

"These Asians. They're not like us. They don't have our values. This—this is cheating, plain and simple."

"Now just a minute," Gordon and I spoke together. Tashi stepped in front of Stillson.

"Lhakpa is the most honest person I know," she said politely, looking him straight in the eye. She wasn't aggressive, but she wasn't backing down either. I decided to intervene.

"How is it cheating? He's acknowledged it, hasn't he? So he's taken the penalty—"

"He should have said something at the time! Not waited until the round's over. Hell—," Monk looked startled because Stillson doesn't swear, "suppose this had happened tomorrow instead of today? He could wait to see if he was going to make the cut before declaring it!"

Couldn't say anything to that.

"Ahgh," he waved his hand in disgust, and turned away. "They're not like us, Kat!" he shot back over his shoulder. Danny Chu, the reporter, was all over him, sensing a story but Stillson brushed him aside and ignored Tony, who had just emerged from the cabin. He headed straight over to the oak tree and I began to feel really, really tired. Any time a player wants to speak his mind, he can just stand under the oak tree and reporters will gather like flies to honey. I foresaw a long session for Stillson under the tree.

I glanced at Gordon. "He's got a point. Sorry." I hefted the bag and headed off as Tashi turned and went to meet Tony.

"My poor love," she said as they embraced. His head dropped on her shoulder and he groaned. "Whatever happened?"

I dropped off the bag beyond the pro shop and as I came back round the club house I saw the club manager looking out from the verandah. I raised a hand but he didn't respond, and I forgot it a minute later when Tony appeared in front of me. I must have looked weary, or maybe just disgusted, because he said,

"I really put you through it today." He turned to stare out at the oak tree, and the reporters gathered round Stillson. "I so screwed up. I dumped my game plan. Weeks of work and I just forgot it. Out the window." He turned back. "Perhaps this'll sound strange, but today was a red-letter day for me. I didn't throw my clubs or dig up the course or anything like that." He ran a hand over the hair sticking up on his crown. "All I did was piss off my caddie. . . ." He stopped and I was about to head for the caddie building. But he hadn't finished. "Look. I know it would have been better if I had talked to you. But I have to control my temper. It's top priority. So it seemed safer to shut up till we were finished. Kat, I learned so much from you today. Can you forgive me? Because we have a lot to do before tomorrow. . . ."

I must have looked surprised because he'd said earlier in the week he didn't want my help on the range. I guess he'd changed his mind. "Maybe there's hope for you yet," I said.

We arranged to meet in a couple of hours, and I continued along to the caddie building.

"Kat! What the hell—I thought Charlie was out of it?" Jake Witterich was just going out as I came in.

"Hi Jake." He's about my age, six foot five, skinny. Most of his weight is in his nose. "I'm on one of the amateurs' bags. Just finished."

"How'd you do?"

"Right now we're DFL."

"Oh boy." He looked sympathetic. No one wants to be last.

"I'm thinking trunk-slammer." That's a player who fails to make the Friday cut. I pulled a face as soon as I'd said it. You can think anything you want about your player but you shouldn't say it, not to others. I was more tired than I'd realized. Jake looked surprised, and then fell all over himself.

"Oh shit, Kat. I mean—I'm sorry about—for your loss."

Nothing to do with Josh, I thought but thanked him. "You just heading out?" He was in the afternoon draw, which meant he'd be finished late today and starting early tomorrow. There are pros and cons to both draws. Sometimes the weather can be the deciding factor for players in one draw over the other, but that didn't seem likely this week.

I wished Jake luck, went through to the locker room, stripped off my jumpsuit and shoved it inside my locker. They take a piece of ID when you're issued a jumpsuit, so you don't leave it lying around. I'd have to put it on later, but for now I wanted a bit of freedom. I twirled the knob on the combination lock, and strolled into the lunchroom to get a sandwich. Some of the guys were watching the action on the wall screen and I was about to wander over and join them when someone called over. "Hey Kat! Security wants you."

I glanced over. Most of the doorway was filled by a guard. My heart sank. I walked over.

"Hi there." I smiled at him.

"Boss wants to see you, Ms. Archer." He wasn't smiling.

"Oh? Okay, maybe later. I'm just—," I was feeling like one of those fugitives that seek sanctuary inside a church. But this wasn't a church. He took my arm.

"Now."

Security is based near the main gate, so we turned right onto the main path that lies between the first fairway and the practice range.

"Excuse me, Kat?"

I stopped and turned, and the guard pretty much had to do the same. Hustling along the path about as fast as anyone could go without actually running, came Danny Chu. I was never more glad to see him than at that moment.

"You promised me an interview, do you remember?" Danny spoke quite precise English. I think he was educated in Singapore. He was representing media in several Asian countries.

"Yeah."

"How about—," he glanced at his watch, then back in the direction of the first tee, "fifteen minutes? I would like to hear from you on this Greg Stillson matter." His glance widened to include the guard. "Is everything okay?"

"Everything's fine," said the guard. "Ms. Archer's tied up right now." He took hold of my elbow and Danny's antennae shot up, but we'd turned away and I didn't dare do a thing except go along. My stomach was knotted and my ears were back on the path behind us, but I couldn't hear Danny's footsteps.

We veered off the path just before the main gate with all its turnstiles, and came to a low green-sided building. The guard leaned forward and opened the door and I could sense his hand in the small of my back as I went in. The entrance area had a high counter with another guard wearing a headset and seated on a tall stool behind it. The light was dim, and I could see multiple TV screens reflected on his buttons.

"Sit down. Wait."

My guard indicated a row of chairs against one wall, and disappeared through an unmarked door in the rear. I didn't even bother trying to make conversation with the guy at the desk. He looked severe and all business and his eyes never stopped, running from one side to the other, looking at all his screens. Only now he added a stop just for me, like a comma at the end of each sweep.

It was like the dentist's office. Why do they do that? Make you suffer? I could have used a bathroom. This was a side of Augusta National that I'd never seen. I knew a lot of the guards. Until this minute I'd have said I knew most of them. But I didn't know the guy who had come to get me, and I didn't know this guy.

I heard the guard's voice, though not what he said. I stood up to check and just because I wanted to. His stool was on casters and was built for comfort, with a padded back and armrests. He was relaxed back into it, speaking into a small mike on his headset. A pause, and he glanced over at me. I sat down again.

The inner door opened and my guard came out, motioning to me to follow him. In the back was a long corridor with doors leading off it. Lunch, Conference, Men, Women. We went right down to the end. H.D. McWatters. He opened the door and I was sort of helped inside. Then the door shut behind me.

It was awfully quiet. Couldn't hear a thing. The room was empty. It held one large desk with a large, comfortable-looking chair. There was another chair in front of the desk. Small. I sat in it. Not because I wanted to, but because I thought it would please H.D. McWatters. Right then, that seemed important. The door opened behind me and I resisted turning around. It closed and a large individual came round to the desk. He wore the same uniform as the other guards, but with some sort of flashing that indicated rank.

He sat down across from me. He had black hair and heavy black eyebrows and a thick, fleshy face. I hoped his mind wasn't the same.

"What were you doing here last night at 10 pm?"

I really did not want to talk to this man. "I didn't cause any damage."

"Not the point." He stared at me. "You recently lost your husband?"

I nodded.

"That's too bad, but we can't have people using Augusta National as a cemetery."

"What?"

"Weren't you scattering his ashes in Rae's Creek?"

Jesus wept. I stood up. "No, I was not."

He was unmoved. "Sit down."

I sat. "I was just . . . I was just saying . . ." I stared at him, filled with loathing. "My husband has been here many times. He sits—used to sit—at Amen Corner. He was a landscape architect and he loved the twelfth." I drew a breath. "I was just saying goodbye to him."

He put his hands on the corners of a desk blotter and aligned its edge with the desk edge. Then he looked back at me. "You persuaded one of my guards to let you on the course after hours. You cost him his job."

Oh God. "Don't do that, please—he was only being kind. You can't fire someone for that."

"Normally, you'd be barred from ever entering the grounds again." He paused and frowned at his two hands, spread at the corners of the blotter. "I don't think you realize what a responsibility we have here. We cannot permit people on the grounds without permission at all hours. Did you ever stop to think what would happen if the course were damaged? Does it even occur to you how easy that would be to do?"

I wasn't taking it in properly. My mind had got hold of the word "normally" and stuck there.

"However, you work here. There's an extra step involved before I can make it permanent. So you will be escorted off the grounds and barred from the course unless and until I say otherwise. Is that clear?"

I nodded. "Mr. McWatters—"

"You can go."

The door behind me opened. Great timing somehow. The guard was next to me, waiting to take me out.

o o o

I rent a car while I'm in Augusta. After they'd escorted me off the course, I drove out of the lot and home without seeing much of anything. Over and over in my head I kept thinking I shouldn't have done it—but I still wasn't sorry I had. Josh deserved that quiet moment. I'd just never thought there would be such a ruckus. And firing Chad—the guard who had let me in through gate five—that shocked me.

Tried watching TV but nothing penetrated. Would they let me back in? The question whirled round in my head like a hamster on a wheel, so I went for a workout at a gym I always use here, then headed out to the Riverwalk and wandered along in a daze. Bought something to eat and sat on a bench waiting for McWatters to call. I know they work long hours during Masters week, so his "extra step" might happen any minute or not until midnight. I had my phone and I just waited. The Riverwalk runs along the Savannah River. It's a popular spot for joggers and families, and I was glad to have something to watch.

On the far bank were some modern homes, good-sized houses each with a little jetty and some with boats tied up. A couple of joggers called the standard greeting, "Ha-ay," as they went by. A tour boat came into view, headed downstream, an ungainly craft looking like a shoebox with outboards attached. Kids in the bow stared across the river at me and waved. I raised a limp arm and let it fall again. How long before I heard something? A boat tour might pass the time. The shoebox went on its leisurely way. Where did it tie up? Did it just go on till it reach Savannah? Savannah . . . where Bullet Barnes lived. I sat forward, thinking.

"Hello, Kat, may I join you?"

I glanced up to find Mollie Pinasa hovering. I mustered a smile as she sat down. Bullet, whose player was our missing third this morning because of a torn ligament. Bullet, the dean of caddies, who'd taught me more than ten years ago. Bullet knew everything and everyone at Augusta National.

"I'm so sorry about today," Mollie said. "I left on thirteen, I'm afraid. I can't bear to watch that sort of thing."

Told her I understood. "Don't worry about this afternoon. It'll all blow over, you'll see." Asked how she liked the course and she brightened and talked about the rhododendrons while I thought about Bullet. He might speak up for me. He might even come up if I asked him. Savannah lay south of Augusta, three hours away by car.

"They bloom earlier in Nepal, but then it's much further south."

"Right," I replied vaguely and got to my feet. "Would you excuse me for a moment? I have to call someone."

I walked over to the railing and looked through my cellphone directory. Charlie had sent me down to Savannah years ago to meet Bullet and I'd had his number back then. And still did. I dialed it and a woman answered. I'd met his wife, too, and luckily she remembered me. We got through the introductions and condolences and then she told me Bullet had left for his favorite bar. I asked if he had a cellphone and she said no, then added,

"Well, he does, but he never turns it on, Kat." She gave me the number for the bar and took my number for Bullet. He hadn't been seen at the bar, so I returned to the bench and apologized to Mollie, who waved it away. Something she said earlier came back to me.

"You said Nepal is further south than Augusta?" I'd always assumed it was around the same latitude as Vancouver, but it seems Kathmandu is about level with Miami. Amazing the things you learn. I'd wanted to be alone but as Mollie talked I found it comforting to sit there in the sun learning about flowers and shrubs in Nepal and round Augusta National. Mind you, the course used to be a nursery so the fact that it has some exotic plants is not exactly worth a news flash. But that didn't matter.

I like Mollie. I met her yesterday and again briefly this morning. She has a face that doesn't hide anything, and you can see laughter there and temper as well, and what you might call an echo of grief. She has light brown hair and I reckoned she was in her late forties. She's actually two years younger than her brother, but she looks older.

I thought of a question I'd had earlier in the day, and when she'd pretty much wrapped up the shrubs, I asked it.

"Did Tony's dad ever climb Mount Everest?"

"Seven times," she smiled. I'd guess she's answered that one before.

Thought about it as two more joggers went by ("Ha-ay").

"Must be quite an experience."

"For tourists, Kat. For Sherpas, it's just a job." A livelihood, she said. "Someone—I can't think who it was—wrote that Sherpas are strongly individualistic but with a capacity to work for the greater good. It's why they're so valued on expeditions."

"No kidding?"

She went on telling me about how Chhiri lost a friend on his last Everest climb and after that he decided to call it a day and stick to trekking. It seems they call it an expedition when you're mountain climbing, and a trek when you're hiking.

"But they're both dangerous, Kat," she said, although she admitted she felt relieved when Chhiri began to build more business from trekking. I learned he had proposed to her in a rhododendron forest on one of his favorite treks, called the Annapurna Circuit. I also heard a bit about his brother, who was a trader.

"That would be Kenchi's dad?"

She smiled. "That's right. They used to try to outdrink each other when they got together. His wife and I used to go in the other room and leave them to get on with it."

"Competitive, huh?" She laughed and agreed. I'd thought of another question. "Say, Mollie, was that king a good guy? Birendra?"

She looked out over the river and for a moment I regretted asking. But she was only collecting her thoughts.

"That's why it was such a tragedy, Kat. He was kind hearted and well-educated, and he was doing his best to bring the country along. You know how poor Nepal is?"

I nodded. Nepal's in the cellar in the wealth league. She went on: "He was trying to bring it into the twenty-first century and that's not easy when your population is diverse and largely uneducated. Some people say he should have set the army on the Maoists back when they were just a local insurgence, in the early nineties. But that's hindsight."

I remembered reading about the Maoists. "What's up with them? They always seem to be going out on strike."

Mollie said nothing for a moment. "I despise them, to be honest. They killed Lhakpa's uncle. He had a difficult time when he was younger, my boy did, and I've always felt that

that's what set him off on the wrong path. It was just the last straw for him."

It seemed like a good idea to change the subject. "Tashi seems to be pretty quick on the uptake," I said, and Mollie agreed.

"She was full of questions all day long. Gordon's a very good golfer, so he and Tashi had a lovely time."

Tony and Tashi were serious, Mollie said, planning on marrying but they hadn't yet set a date.

"He's staying in the Crow's Nest, isn't he?" All amateurs had the option of sleeping in the small dormitory at the club house.

"I know." Mollie answered my unspoken question. "Tashi says she doesn't mind." She looked out at the river again.

"I wouldn't worry. He'll probably move out tomorrow." The Crow's Nest is filled with history, but I don't know that it's that comfortable.

"Personally, I think it's a long way to come when you don't play golf yourself. But she says they have lots to talk about."

"Kat?"

I looked round to see another woman, late-forties, whose face seemed familiar.

"Ann Jameson, Kat. Eric's mother?"

"Of course, hi Ann." I knew Eric Jameson quite well. I'd met his mother briefly a few months ago. She asked about Charlie and I explained I was on Tony Pinasa's bag. "We had the opening tee time, with Greg Stillson." I introduced her. "Mollie Pinasa, Tony's mother."

They shook hands. "I thought Stillson was paired with an Asian," said Ann.

Mollie was used to this, I guess. "Anglo-Asian," she said with a smile. "His father was a Sherpa."

Ann looked interested. "From Nepal?" It seemed she and her husband had spent three weeks there a few years ago. So, after expressing her condolences to me, she sat down the other side of Mollie. They started in on tigers and temples and stuff while I wondered whether to try Bullet again. They were similar in age, two mothers whose sons were competing. I thought it would be good for Mollie to have another mother for company.

Another jogger went by. I surreptitiously checked my phone, but McWatters hadn't struck me as the texting type, and I had no messages. By this time the two mothers were talking about their respective homes. Ann was from Missouri, I knew. Mollie lived in Marstow, on the north coast of Cornwall. Turns out she and Tony went back to Nepal last year for the first time since 2001. Ann wanted to know more about her life in Kathmandu, so Mollie told her about Chhiri's business and Ruth Cameron, his partner, and her husband, Pete, an ex-Peace Corps volunteer who became a general contractor in Kathmandu. "He built our house," Mollie said. "We had the sweetest little house off the Paknajol Road. Two bedrooms and a mango tree in the front garden and a *karesa bari* in the back. Gordon always gives me such stick when I call it that. He says it's being pretentious." She smiled. "It means kitchen garden, but I like the Nepali word better."

I could relate to that. "Like saying fade instead of slice."

"Oh yes?" Mollie went on to talk about her garden and all the vegetables she grew there, and they were back on exotic plants and seemed to be getting on fine, so I left them to it.

Along the Eleventh Fairway

Gordon Menzies sat on a green collapsible chair at roughly the three-hundred-yard point of the fairway. It was warm and sunny and quiet. He was alone except for one other chair and occupant about thirty feet away. He ate his barbecue sandwich and shoved the green translucent wrapper in his pocket. He drank the beer in his green paper cup. Beer and sandwich had set him back fully four dollars and fifty cents. *God, I love this place,* he thought.

A ball smacked into the ground, hopped, rolled and stopped in the fairway opposite him. He could hear the applause down at the twelfth, but crowds didn't appeal to him right now. He lit a cigar and made himself relax. Watching Tony on thirteen had been hard. Looked at square on, without sentiment, it seemed likely he'd played himself out of the tournament on that one hole. After he'd come back from trying to make things right with his caddie, they'd bought a couple of beers and sat under one of the green-striped umbrellas near the oak tree, looking down over the course. Tashi and Mollie had gone to buy a rule book.

"What was all that business about incorrect score-cards?" Gordon asked.

"I was just trying to make him see that it's a pretty funny rule when you stop and think about it. I mean, if Kat hadn't seen it move then I wouldn't have taken the penalty, so then I'd have signed an incorrect card, and then I might have been eliminated like Roberto de Vincenzo. I just began to wonder how many times I've signed an incorrect card. Or any golfer has." He swallowed some beer. "Greg didn't seem to get it."

"Did Kat?"

"We weren't on chatting terms by that point." He leaned forward. "It was a way of focusing, after thirteen, you know?" His uncle nodded. "I just pictured the ball, sort of nestled down in the pine straw. No one around. And then I pictured how it might move."

"Why weren't you talking to Kat?"

After a pause, Tony replied. "I think I swore at her. I'm not sure."

"For telling you the ball moved?"

"No! I don't know. For existing." He looked at his uncle. "You know what it's like. I just explained it to her. I have to control the anger before anything else."

Gordon liked the way Kat had handled herself, especially after the round when she'd tried to defend Tony to Greg Stillson. He knew how difficult the boy could be, and yet she hadn't made a single disparaging comment. He reminded himself that the boy had, in the past two years, become a man, at least most of the time. That saddened Gordon: it meant he'd be seeing less and less of him. He wondered if it was technically possible to love a son more than he loved his nephew. He reminded himself that he owed Kat a check. That reminded him of finances, which he didn't want to think about now. But one thing was certain: if they ever came here again, he'd do what others did, and rent a house. Much cheaper. And eat at the course. He grinned.

A caddie arrived at the ball opposite, followed by his

player. They consulted their yardage books, while farther out in the fairway two other players and their caddies waited. Gordon could hear them: "Look at the trees." The tops of the trees behind the green across Rae's Creek were swaying. "Yeah, but that's down there. What about up here?" Along with the two men, Gordon raised his head to look at the trees above him. "One-eighty in front. One seventy downhill. Cross wind." "Draw it in there."

The player hit and they moved off, stopping and waiting for the other two players to hit. Gordon's counterpart thirty feet away appeared to have dozed off, his chin resting on his chest. Gordon became aware that he had an audience. He looked around and saw two children standing on the utility road, one ebony, the other, smaller one, Nordic white. The black child had tight hold of the smaller one's hand. They were perhaps eight and six respectively, and they smiled angelically at Gordon. He wasn't deceived.

"Hello, kids," he said.

"Hello," said the black child. He tugged the blond child's hand.

"'Lo." Gordon had the impression he'd somehow disappointed the child. Then he was distracted by the next group walking up the utility road behind the children. He turned round the other way to watch as they made their way to the tee. Surely that tall, serious figure was Lin Jinhai, the young Chinese phenomenon? He'd never won a Masters and he was tipped as one of the favorites after Alex Figueres. Gordon had money on Alex but he liked the look of the Chinese player and now he waited with interest for the tee shot.

On his right he heard a faint "Boo!" followed by a thump

and a snicker. *Those bloody kids,* he thought as he turned, and sure enough, there was the other patron, picking himself up off the grass as the two children looked on.

"Oy!" said Gordon, and, startled in their turn, they shot off down the road toward the twelfth, legs pumping, the black child still holding the hand of the white one. A green-jacketed member stepped into their path and slowed them down. Gordon grinned. *Bet he gives 'em hell for running.* A security guard joined the group and after a pause they all moved sedately down the path.

"You all right?" He called over and the other patron raised a hand as he righted his collapsible chair and sat down again. Gordon decided he could use a small amount of company, say one person, so he picked up his chair in one hand, beer in the other, cigar clamped between his teeth, and walked over to join the other man.

"I saw those kids earlier. Should have shooed them off," he said. "Mind if I join you?"

"I'm not much good company right now," said the other man.

Gordon had seen the army boots. "Just back from overseas, are you?"

After a pause, the soldier responded. "Yeah. Flew into New York late yesterday. From Bamberg. Germany."

"I'm ex-RAF. Served in the Gulf War, first one. Gordon Menzies." He held out a hand.

"Oh yeah?" The soldier—he appeared to Gordon to be in his late-twenties—took his hand and they shook. "Mike Ostriewski. Were you a flyer?"

"Logistics officer. Not exciting. I'm with Swan Air now."

A ball landed abreast of them and stayed just in the

fairway. Gordon pulled out his program. "I think LinJin's in this group."

"I heard he's pretty good. But I'm kinda committed to Alex."

Gordon grinned. "Me too. But this kid could give him a run for his money."

"You been here often?" asked the solder.

"Never," replied Gordon. "You?"

The soldier shook his head. "I got the pass from my boss. My new boss. Joining his insurance company. I'm from Dayton, Ohio. He had to go into hospital. Said why didn't I enjoy the Masters before coming home and settling down."

"Marrying the girl next door?" Gordon smiled.

"Yeah, something like that. If I can get my head straight."

The players had reached their balls. Lin's was the far side of the fairway. Near them was a young player who fashioned an exquisite shot to the green that landed just in the fringe and rolled forward toward the pin.

"Jeez," said Mike reverently. He and Gordon both applauded the shot, and the player turned, grinned and tipped his cap. He had blond hair and a fresh complexion.

Gordon studied his program. "It's RJ Gardner," he said, and Mike nearly fell off his chair for a second time.

"Oh my God, that's RJ?"

They exchanged a look. "That explains the shot," said Gordon. The young Kentuckian was tipped as the next Tiger Woods.

Lin decided discretion was the better part of valor and bailed out to the right. After the third member of the group had hit, they all moved off toward the green.

Gordon cocked an eye at his companion. "You've seen some action. Were you wounded?"

"No, my sergeant was. Lost an arm and a leg." He scrubbed his face with both hands. "Suicide bomb. A woman lying by the road. I told Will to check her out. Carefully. He knew better than I did to be careful. She was crying and I thought she was in pain, but Will and I were discussing this the other day and he said she was warning him off and he should have backed away." He paused and his head lowered as though he was warding off a blow. "See, that's the kind of guy he is. He says things like that to make me feel better." After a moment he went on, "He put his arm under her shoulders to help her sit up and she screamed at him. She was lying on a landmine."

"Christ."

"It's the nightmares. I can't shake them. They land all round me. An arm. A leg. A head. And then they start to move."

"That's cheerful." Gordon pulled on his cigar and gazed thoughtfully at his companion.

"Cheerful? You want cheerful? Goddamn Will's already been fitted with his prosthetics and he's practicing walking like mad and he's so fuckin' cheerful I hate him."

"Have a cigar."

The soldier stared out at the fairway, leaning forward, forearms on his thighs, then sighed and turned toward Gordon, and took the proffered cigar.

"The doctor said the nightmares'll stop eventually."

"They will."

"I don't think Will's ever going to stop being cheerful." He leaned forward to the match Gordon was holding out.

"I wouldn't hold your breath," Gordon agreed.

They sat there companionably among the pines off the

fairway. After another group had come and gone, Mike said, "Is it my imagination or does this course seem unusually green to you? It's something that struck me this morning and I can't shake it."

"The fairways are bermuda oversewn with rye. That's why."

"I thought they were bent grass."

Gordon blew a smoke ring. "That's the greens. The greens are bent grass, the fairways are bermuda."

After another long silence, Mike said, "Y'know, I remember when Tiger Woods won by twelve strokes. I was just a kid.

"Mm. I was a kid when Seve Ballesteros won by—by several strokes anyway."

After a silence, Mike said, "A lot of people think they ruined this course when they Tiger-proofed it. I have to say, it doesn't seem ruined to me."

Another silence, then Gordon said, "Funny. It was after Seve's win that they changed the greens to bent. I suppose they overhaul the course whenever it looks like being too easy."

"When did Seve win?"

"About 1980."

"Every twenty years? Guess we're okay for a while yet."

They sat on through the afternoon in the lengthening shadows, as group followed group and the golfers came, lingered briefly and moved on.

Kat's Story

I always stay at Miss Grace Feeny's for the tournament. Shady suburban street lined with laurel oaks, older homes with big verandahs. Same sort of house you see in East

Vancouver, only a bit bigger and nicer. Miss Grace has three rooms to rent for the Masters and she's fussy and that's how I like it. She cooks like a dream, breakfasts are included in the price and dinners are available if you let her know in advance. Josh always liked it here.

The other two caddies were in the bottom half of the draw so I wouldn't be seeing them until tomorrow night. By now the kid would be on the range, wondering where I was. Maybe he'd already figured out why he was pull-hooking his tee shots. I wondered if they would have kicked up such a fuss if I'd been on Charlie's bag instead of some unknown amateur. I decided not to tell Charlie. I was glad he wasn't here. I work hard at being a good caddie and if that's not enough to get me inside the gates then to hell with them. . . . I knew it wasn't enough. They have would-be caddies lined up from here to the coast. I wondered if anyone would speak up for me during McWatters's "extra step" process, whatever that was. Tried Bullet again, without success. I know a lot of people—guards, volunteers, patrons, not to mention caddies and players—but when the chips are down, none of them really count for much. I don't count for much. The tournament is what counts. They were probably introducing the kid to one of the local caddies right this minute. Come to think of it, having a younger, male caddie would probably do him good. Maybe I should just be glad it was over, and go home. But oh God, what would I say to Charlie? Maybe by next year it would all have died down. Maybe they'd forget it and let me come back. Then I remembered McWatters. No way would he forget.

"Dinner in fifteen minutes, Kat."

I realized I'd been staring unseeing at the TV. Miss Grace

had come and gone by the time I turned to answer. The later groups were coming in now, with maybe another hour's golf to play.

Who did I know who might put in a good word for me? I remembered the club manager earlier today. Normally he'd be good for a wave or a chat if he had time. Today he'd been expressionless though I was sure he'd seen me. Probably he'd be the one holding the axe. I went on worrying right through dinner. Declined Miss Grace's peach cobbler and it knocked her back, I could see. Then she recovered and said, in her soft southern voice, "I perfectly understand, honey. Don't you worry about one little thing." I knew she was thinking about Josh: she'd served her Vidalia onion and cucumber salad, one of his favorites. I didn't say anything. I didn't have to: you could hear the front door bell clear through to the back patio. After she'd gone to answer it, I checked my phone. No messages except a text from Charlie asking for a call when I had time. Then Miss Grace was back and Gordon Menzies was with her.

The backyard is big. I asked Miss Grace once if she'd never wanted to move to a smaller place but she has a kid come in and do the gardening, she told me, and she likes her privacy. There's a tall hedge all round—holly along the back and a privet hedge on both sides. If you watch college football, you've probably seen the privet hedge at Sanford Stadium, where the Georgia Bulldogs play. Miss Grace's is like that but about twice as high. She's got a camellia in one back corner and an oak in another. There's a swing seat and some all-weather easy chairs and a picnic table, where I was sitting. Gordon joined me at the table after Miss Grace offered him some peach cobbler and I told him he'd be nuts to refuse it.

Gordon has dark blond hair, hazel eyes and a pleasant expression, and just then he seemed very light-hearted. "I've had a wonderful afternoon, Kat. I saw Alex play eleven. He was as close to us as that chair. And Miguel. They were both puffing away on cigars and having a fine old time." Miguel was Alex Figueres's caddie and a character.

He recollected something and brought out his wallet. Took out a check and handed it over. "As agreed."

This had all been negotiated with Charlie; I would not have had the nerve to ask so much. Since Tony was an amateur he couldn't receive any prize money, so they had agreed on a flat fee. Any golfer who made the cut was guaranteed a weekend minimum of around twenty thousand. Charlie had taken ten percent of that and added a thousand for expenses.

I was embarrassed taking the check. For a moment I was tempted to tell Gordon to hang on to it. But this security thing was a private matter, so I decided if I was barred from the course I'd just hand it back. Miss Grace returned at that point with a tray holding a large helping of peach cobbler and ice cream, along with two mugs of coffee plus fixings. In between bites, Gordon told me more about his afternoon.

"It was sublime, Kat. Except for the crowds following Alex we were alone out there." He'd watched Lin Jinhai and RJ Gardner. "What do you think of him?"

"Some people think he'll take over where Woods left off."

"You don't?"

The front door bell rang as I replied. “The press are always looking for a new messiah. But RJ shows a lot of promise.” A moment later Tony came out onto the patio. He looked at his uncle without really seeing him, then at me. He saw me.

“Where were you? Did you change your mind?” He seemed unsure whether to be concerned or annoyed. I glanced at my watch: ten past seven. I was going to have to tell him. I looked at Gordon.

“Excuse us for a moment.” He offered to leave. I told him to stay put. I was enjoying his company.

I walked out with Tony to the front porch. We sat in a couple of wicker armchairs and looked out at the street. A white Escalade was parked behind my rental car.

“Did anyone approach you about using one of the club caddies?” I asked him.

“When?” He looked totally mystified. “Today?” I nodded and he added, “No. Why would they?”

I took a breath. “Look. There’s a chance I may not be able to carry your bag tomorrow. I did a thing the other night and now they may not let me back on the course.” He began to interrupt and I went on, soothingly. “Look. It could work in your favor. If that’s what they decide—and I should find out any time—then they’ll have to give you a local caddie. You’ll likely get one of the young guys and they’re good, believe me—”

“ARE YOU MAD?” He was on his feet, his face reddening under the bronze, hair stuck up on top and I suddenly felt sorry for Custer. “I don’t want any—,” he pushed my hands away, “STOP MANAGING ME.”

I saw a curtain move across the street and Miss Grace

came to the door. "We're fine," I said to her, "let Gordon know. Please."

Tony was sitting again. "What the *hell* have you done?" Before I could answer he went on, "I can't believe it's because of me. They can't bar you. It's completely and absolutely unacceptable. I'll go to the Chairman. I'll go to the British Consulate. The Canadian Consulate. The Nepalese Consulate, if there is one. This is outrageous. I'll say it's discrimination—"

"Shut up." I tried to marshal my thoughts.

"You're pulling my leg, aren't you? You're paying me back for the way I behaved today."

The phone rang. My phone, in my pocket. I stood up, pulled it out.

"Ms. Archer?" It was McWatters.

"Yes."

"You're cleared to return to the course tomorrow." My legs felt weak and I leaned against the porch rail as McWatters continued. "I want you to understand that if you ever do anything like that again I'll make it my personal mission to bar you from this course for the remainder of your natural life."

Jeez. Like a prison sentence. "You don't have to worry. It won't happen again. And—thank you—." But he'd already hung up. Not my favorite person but I expect it was mutual. I hit the End button and closed the phone. I punched the air. "Yes!" I did a little dance. "Yes. Yes. Yes. Yes!"

I turned. Tony had the gimlet look. "Can we get down to business?"

Yes sir! I sat down.

"What time are you checking the pin placements?"

"What time do you want me on the range?"

He ran a hand over his hair. "I haven't been able to see what I'm doing wrong. Eight o'clock?"

"Say ten, then."

"Do you mind if Tashi comes with you?" He stood up and started down the steps. "She's getting all gung-ho. I think it was the ball moving and no one seeing it that got her attention." He reached the car. I rested on the porch railing, watching as he went round to the driver's side. "Very Zen." He opened the door and stepped up, facing me across the roof. "We went to the driving range this afternoon. I showed her how to hit the ball." He suddenly lifted his head and laughed and in the evening light, he looked young and very appealing. I suddenly thought of something and beckoned.

"Come here."

He frowned, then stepped down and came round the Escalade, hands shoved in his pockets. He stopped halfway along the path.

"What are you wearing tomorrow?"

I got a semi-gimlet this time. "You're as bad as mum," he said. "I won the Amateur in that shirt, you know."

I had a mental picture of Mollie's expression this morning, off the first green. Chagrin, that's what it was. I looked it up, just to be sure. "A feeling of vexation marked by disappointment." She might not know anything about golf, but she knew what was proper and what was not. I looked at her son.

He turned and went back to the car. "I won't wear it tomorrow."

I stood up. "Tell Tashi to meet me at the caddie building at ten sharp."

He opened the door and again stood on the step looking across the roof at me.

I got tired of waiting. "What?"

He lifted a hand in a wave, got in and drove off.

My phone rang again. "Bullet! Gee, it's good to hear your voice."

"How ya doin', Kat? What's up? The hell happened on thirteen?"

"Oh Jeez. . . ." I gave him a short version of the meltdown on thirteen. It seemed to lead nicely to a wrap up: "In fact that's why I called, Bullet. I was thinking maybe the kid would be more relaxed with another guy and I couldn't think of a better one than you."

"Uh huh," he said, sounding completely unconvinced. No surprise there. What caddie would voluntarily pull out of the Masters?

I went on: "But he was just here and we seem to be getting on much better, so I dunno, I think everything's okay. But I really appreciate you calling."

I stopped off in the kitchen to tell Miss Grace I could manage some peach cobbler, and she told me she'd bring it out. Gordon was stretched out in the swing seat when I returned. He raised an eyebrow.

"Did my nephew put that spring in your step?"

"No, but listen, I don't feel right about this check. Can we discuss a new deal? It's too much." I didn't like to add, "especially if it's only for two days," but I had a nasty feeling he knew what I was thinking.

"There's nothing to negotiate, Kat. You're going to do well tomorrow and on the weekend, and Tony will learn enough about playing Augusta National to last a lifetime."

For such a pleasant man, his expression wasn't encouraging, so I decided to change the subject. "Would you tell me about Tom Dowling?"

He sat up and took out a cigar. Miss Grace appeared with the cobbler plus fresh coffee. I ate while Gordon lit his cigar and told me about Tom.

"He's a Yorkshireman. Retired furniture manufacturer and successful at it, too. He and his wife had planned to retire to our neck of the woods, but she died. So when he sold out he decided to move there anyway. The thing about Tom is he's a scratch golfer and he spent a lifetime watching and talking to other golfers. He'd formed some very definite ideas about the golf swing."

He blew a smoke ring and I savored my cobbler and listened.

"You know, it's funny," he continued. "I didn't get a bill for weeks, once he started teaching Lhakpa. Tony. Weeks—hell, it was months—"

"Wait a minute," I said. "Is he a pro? How did you find him? Where was he teaching?"

"Oh—at our club. Widemouth." He pronounced it *widmuth*. "I suppose he'd taken the necessary courses or whatever you do to get accredited as a golf pro. I really don't know. All I know is, our pro, who was leaving, interviewed Tom over several days then told the Board they'd be in good hands with him. We took him on and never looked back. What do you think of Tony's swing?"

I considered. "It inspires confidence. It's solid. Not a lot of moving parts."

Gordon seemed satisfied. "Tom says everyone has a swing inside them, waiting to get out. I told you I didn't get a bill for ages. You'll have to ask my nephew, but all he did at first was teach him how to hold the club. When did they start?" He gazed out at the holly hedge. "Oh of course, what am I thinking—late March. I suppose I may have had a bill in May, but I don't think it amounted to much. And it wasn't because he doesn't charge. He said once that people don't listen unless they have to pay, so he charges all right." He stretched his legs and blew another smoke ring. "I took it up with him at the end of April. He said he hadn't done that much. He was waiting until Tony got the bile out of him."

"The bile?"

"The anger. He had a lot of it back then."

He had plenty now, I thought.

Gordon was going on. "I'd been quite worried because they got off to such a rocky start, you see. Tom kitted him out with a set of odd clubs, took him out to the range, showed him how to hold the club and left him to get on with it. He'd given him two buckets of balls. At six, he came out to take in a sale sign and found Tony swiping at the daffodils in the bed next to the pro shop with a seven-iron. He'd taken off almost all the heads. The boy had enough sense to see how angry Tom was although all he said in his slow way was 'Eh lad, a golf club is for hitting a ball and t'grass under it. Nothing else.' Tony said he was sorry but Tom told him to apologize to the plants. And to make amends."

"To the plants?" I was just kidding but Gordon nodded.

"That's exactly what he meant. He took Tony's clubs and his sale sign, and went back inside and locked the door. That was one of the worst days of my nephew's life. He thought he mightn't get another chance with Tom." He stood up. "And now I really think I should leave you to get your beauty sleep."

"But it's early! And this is the high spot of my day, believe me." He laughed and I added, by way of explanation, "Nothing to do with Tony. I did something I shouldn't have, yesterday . . . I don't want to say any more."

He sat down again. "You never do say much, do you?"

"That depends—"

"It's all right. I approve." He eyed me. "Why did you ask about Tom?"

"Because we may have a swing problem, and I thought it might help. Has Tony had any other teachers?"

"Not one. He thinks the sun rises and sets on Tom Dowling." He settled back in his chair. "In fact, if you were to ask him, I think his three heroes would be Jack Nicklaus, Tom and Lama Sangwa Dorje." He held up a hand. "Ask Lhakpa."

"He told me to call him Tony." It wasn't exactly a question because I didn't want to pry. Gordon didn't seem to mind explaining.

"I go back and forth. I suppose we both do, though Mollie usually calls him Lhakpa. The 'Tony' started when he was—oh, nine or so."

The stress continued to drain out of me as I sat back in the chair and listened. I was feeling wonderful.

Gordon used to drive down to Cornwall every Friday after work, he said. Sometimes he was able to take one of the four-seater planes reserved for top executives at Swan, but in the early days he mostly drove down. He lived in Staines near Heathrow during the week, and worked there too. He'd arrive in Marstow around eight, and Mollie would have a drink and some dinner waiting for him and they'd chat about the week's doings.

It was on one of these Friday evenings, while Gordon was finishing his dinner, that Mollie went to answer a knock at the door and found a policeman there in his electric yellow vest, Panda car behind him on the roadside beyond the garden. He asked if Tony Pinasa lived there, and Mollie said no, she lived there with her son Lhakpa. Then she happened to glimpse a little face in the car, and the policeman turned and signaled, and her son climbed out of the back seat and came up the path. Mollie learned that he'd been caught along with a gang of other kids wrecking the playground equipment at a kindergarten in town.

"They left once they saw that we weren't going to just ignore the incident," said Gordon. "I don't know how long it was before we got around to the 'Tony' part. We were—I suppose we were like lots of families, caught completely off guard by this behavior. Mollie thought he was tucked up in bed, for God's sake. He'd been climbing out of his window and going off for hijinks with the gang for weeks. Anyway, when we'd covered crime and punishment to the full, we turned to the name business. Why Tony, we asked? It seemed that one of his friends had an older brother called Tony who had killed a bloke."

"Oh boy," I said.

"How do you know he killed a bloke, I asked him. 'Well, it wasn't a bloke,' said Lhakpa, 'it was a kid.' Oh, sez I. Just a misdemeanor."

I laughed as he went on. "It seems that older brother Tony had been seen fighting another boy and the next day the boy had disappeared. So naturally, Tony must have murdered him." Gordon had extracted the boy's name from his nephew and called the police. "It turns out that this boy

Lhakpa's friend's brother had supposedly killed was in fact alive and well and living with his parents in Sutton Bassett."

He eyed me and shook his head ruefully. "You may well laugh. I'm afraid the news did nothing to dampen the appeal of the name Tony. He'd become attached to it, and nothing we could say would change his mind. Mollie was worried because she didn't want him forgetting his cultural heritage. This subject used to come up a lot between them. I never got involved. Lhakpa means Wednesday, and as he said to his mother, how cultural is that? We finally negotiated a compromise: he could be Tony everywhere but at home. There he'd continue to be Lhakpa." Gordon shook his head. "I sent him off to bed after that. Mollie looked absolutely used up and we both felt as though we'd been through the wringer. And we thought that was the end of it. . . ." He looked over at me. "You don't have kids?"

"No."

"Nor me. I'd just been through a divorce when Mollie came back to England. We'd had no kids because my wife wasn't interested. So in a way, Lhakpa was the best thing that could have happened to me. I wasn't due to join Swan until September, so I spent the whole summer in Cornwall. I loved that little boy from the moment he first climbed into my lap and told me a story. But we had some rocky moments, I can tell you. The Tony business was just the beginning."

THURSDAY-FRIDAY

O O O O

Kathmandu

Mingma Sherpa sat in classroom three of the School for Hill Children replying to a letter from his younger sister. In less than an hour he would be leading the Friday afternoon ethics class. He took this honor seriously and had lain awake for much of last night planning. Mrs. Chandra Lama, the teacher who normally held the class, had taken him aside a week ago.

"Your meditation skills are so good, Mingma. Some of our other students would benefit from your help, I'm sure." The ethics class, which because it was on Friday tended to be a "bit of" class—a bit of this and a bit of that—always ended with five minutes' meditation practice. Mingma knew Mrs. Chandra Lama was trying to encourage him to set his sights higher than janitor. He didn't mind. Mingma had no ambition for himself: it was all focused on his sister and younger brother. But if she wanted him to take the Friday class, he would do his best.

He bent over his letter, and continued writing: "Nyima understands what you are saying. He asks me to say he is being more critical in history and social studies." He stopped and referred again to Chonyi's letter. Yes, that was the part. "Please tell our younger brother," she had written, "that it is not enough to copy words out of the text books. He must learn to think critically! This is what I have discovered. It is hard to do, elder brother. It even sometimes hurt my head. But it is worth the effort!" On re-reading the passage, Mingma was not so sure that thinking critically and being critical were the same thing. He decided to have Nyima email Chonyi directly.

His sixteen-year-old sister was in Norway. She had gone there last August on a scholarship. Mingma was so proud of her that he sometimes wanted to tell everyone he passed in the street. He referred to her letter again. "I am learning so much about the world that it amazes me. My teachers are so helpful and encouraging. But I miss both my brothers very much and I think of you every night. I am glad the spring is coming. The winter here is very harsh. It remind me of when we were small. . . ."

Classroom three, where Mingma sat, held desks, blackboards front and back, and windows along one side wall overlooking a courtyard. On the opposite wall was a plaque displaying Buddhism's Eightfold Path, the precepts governing right thought, speech and action that Buddhists follow to gain wisdom and learn compassion for others.

Mingma glanced at his watch. Less than half an hour. He

was sitting at Mrs. Chandra Lama's desk and now he stared at the blackboard at the back of the room, where he had written several ethical questions, and some other, more general questions, as prompts to get the class going. He bent over his letter once more, writing carefully and neatly, telling his sister about the honor Mrs. Chandra Lama had bestowed on him. "I think our brother will be the most difficult student," he wrote. "You know how he hates to be still." Nyima was twelve and a computer whiz. He had taught himself to type long before he was old enough to join the computer class, and he had taken a computer to pieces and put it back together when he was only eight. He had also informed his older brother that one day he would find a way to wire the whole of the Himalayas so that all villages could have light and online access. "Then they could learn from home, brother! They wouldn't have to wait to get into the school!"

Mingma thought that sounded very fine. He also thought his young brother had probably forgotten what the village was like, or he wouldn't make such a remark.

Mingma was ten when his father slipped on the icy path and slid off down the mountain and over the side into a crevasse. He had made no sound. Following the two yaks, Mingma watched in horror. His bowels turned to water and he fell to his knees and for a while he fainted. He could not have been unconscious long, because the two yaks had scarcely moved. He crawled down the path and stood up next to the rear yak. With legs that trembled, he urged the animals on. Yaks never move quickly regardless of the altitude; they just keep the same steady pace all day long. Now Mingma and his two animals continued their way from thirteen thousand feet back down the mountain. When he reached a point where it was possible to look over the edge into the crevasse, Mingma called and called, but his father did not answer. The walls were sheer and he could not see the bottom. He stayed there for an hour, calling and waiting, calling and waiting. Once he rested his head on his elbow and cried.

His mother had died two years earlier, a year after Nyima was born. No one seemed to know why she had died, or at least, no one told Mingma. She just died. Before that, the whole family had lived in the high mountains with their yaks, a nomadic existence, hard and cold. Mingma remembered huddling under the big tarpaulin with the animals—they had had four yaks then—and his parents and Chonyi and the baby Nyima. Life consisted of herding the animals to a fresh grazing area, and finding firewood, except at the higher elevations, where they used yak dung for fuel.

After his mother died, they came down to the small village at ten-thousand feet. His father made arrangements for Chonyi and the baby to stay with a family while he and Mingma took the animals to pasture, often staying away for weeks at a time. When they returned Mingma would comfort Chonyi, who missed them terribly. She was not strictly speaking being mistreated, but the family gave her and the baby no affection, and when she was put in charge of watching their herd of goats she had been beaten once or twice with nettles when one of the goats strayed.

Mingma returned late that evening, after taking a party of villagers back to the crevasse in a vain search for his father. He found his sister asleep with Nyima in her arms. The wife made him some of the thick soupy Sherpa tea that is a staple in the Himalayas. While he drank it he broached the subject on his mind: he wanted to sell his yaks, and take his brother and sister down to the plains where they would try to make a better life for themselves. The family felt sorry for him, and tried to argue him out of this plan. But they were poor themselves, and so they did not argue as hard as they might have. It would have made no difference if they had: Mingma's mind was made up, because of the tourists.

Last year in the spring, just before the monsoons, a party of tourists had come into the area. He had seen these tall, well-dressed people with their Sherpa porters and guides and had wondered about them. "They are tourists from Kathmandu," his father had said, but could not tell him more. Mingma had never forgotten them, and now he had decided he would take his family to Kathmandu and find out how to work for a tourist.

The following day they set out, having swapped their two yaks for five goats. Mingma was not sure he had got the best of this deal, but the goats would keep them warm at night and give them milk to drink. And Chonyi would help keep them from straying. Chonyi in fact was thrilled with this change in their fortunes. Her father had been a distant figure, but she loved and trusted Mingma, and now they would stay together. While Mingma carried Nyima piggyback she went on ahead, herding the goats. And so, in the weeks that followed, they made their way out of the mountains into the foothills and thence to the great Terai plain, arriving eventually in the outskirts of Kathmandu.

The city would have overwhelmed Mingma except that he was befriended almost immediately by a tourist. At least, he thought the man was a tourist: he was white and tall and dressed in a suit. And he was being swarmed by street kids begging for a handout. Instead of paying attention to them, he noticed the boy across the road carrying a smaller boy piggyback, a younger girl by his side with a goat. He crossed the street, curious at their stillness amid the noise and frenetic life of the street. If their yak-hair footwear hadn't given them away, their speech did. They knew only Sherpa. He knew a little Nepali: "*Namaste,*" he said.

"*Tashi Delek,*" replied the boy, and the little one, who had been resting his head against the boy's shoulder, sat up and surveyed the stranger with bright eyes.

Everyone deserves one big break in life, and most of us get one, sooner or later. This was Mingma's. The tourist was an American who worked at the Coca-Cola factory. He had not been in Nepal long enough to have hardened his heart to the extreme poverty. The boy Mingma seemed to him to convey self-reliance coupled with an urban helplessness that the American thought he could alleviate. So he arranged for the children to stay with their goat in a corner of a field owned by a family from whom he bought his vegetables. And later that day, when he arrived home, he wrote to his sister in Nebraska.

Six months later, the School for Hill Children notified the American that they had room for two of his three Sherpa children. He got word to the farm owners, saying he would call for the children the next day, and Mingma didn't stop to argue. He left Chonyi and Nyima with instructions to wait for the American's arrival and go with him. He promised he would see them soon. And he disappeared into the street life of Kathmandu. He could not see any other way of handling the matter. It was easy for him: he could cope on his own; the others could not.

He was quick to learn and a hard worker, ready to undertake anything for the price of a meal. He was filling up on *dal bhat* one day at a restaurant near Asan Tole, when he felt someone watching him. Glancing over he saw a thin woman along the table with an empty dish. Buddhists are taught to share, and when the owner asked if he wanted more, Mingma nodded and after the bowls of rice and curried lentils had been replenished he invited his neighbor to join him by sliding himself and his dishes along the bench.

"Eat, *aama*." Mother. "I don't like to eat alone."

The street sweeper had lost two children, daughters, one to the coughing sickness, and the other to an infection from playing in the river after grazing her leg. The older would have been Mingma's age if she had lived. The woman slept in a public rest house next to a small temple, and after that first meeting, Mingma stayed there with her, glad to get off the street.

Two years later, when he was nearly thirteen, he joined his brother and sister at the school. He soaked up knowledge, aware that he would never catch up with his siblings. He didn't mind. He had his eye on a job as assistant janitor at the school. Failing that he would drive a taxi: he knew a man who always needed drivers, and Mingma could speak English, Sherpa, Hindi and Nepali.

Now, in classroom three on Friday afternoon he considered the blackboard at the back and its list of questions. Friday afternoon class was meant to be fun as well as fruitful. The students at the School for Hill Children worked six days a week. Saturday was their day off. Friday afternoon always ended with a meditation session, for practice. Before that it was for unwinding, for progress reports on class projects, and for considering ethical questions or proposing new projects.

"Is it all right to steal?" That was Mingma's first question, only because he knew the answer. "Take only what is freely given," the Buddha had said. But if you had starving children to feed you did whatever was necessary to feed them and begged forgiveness later or tried somehow to make amends.

"How can we help the street kids?" That was his second question, and he thought it might be developed into a project, because there were too many of them, lying naked in the streets, or sniffing glue, or if they were little girls and pretty, being taken away to be sent to the Middle East.

He had several other questions and suggestions listed, more as aids to himself than anything else, because like a lot of fledgling teachers, Mingma had not yet learned the knack of letting the students do the work. He had spent a restless night dreaming up ideas.

Students were coming into the classroom now, each wearing the dark blue v-necked sweater and grey trousers or skirt that formed the SHC uniform. Classroom three had desks for twenty, but it was becoming apparent that demand would far outstrip supply. Mingma was puzzled: many students preferred to play football on Friday afternoons. He had expected ten or fifteen, but it looked as though he had closer to forty or more. There were even some little ones, holding on to the hands of older children and looking round with interest.

"Some of you, come up here, please," he called, and they came up and sat on the floor to his left, while the remainder, once the desks were filled, stood around the walls.

Each student on entering the classroom had bowed to the teacher. Even Nyima, who stood at the back with several other boys. Mingma surveyed the gathering, welcomed them and asked what they would like to talk about. He was ready with one of his suggestions, but it wasn't necessary.

"Mingma, sir?" The speaker was one of the older boys, Pasang, seated down on the floor at the front of the class. Mingma nodded at him to continue. "May we talk about Lhakpa?"

Lhakpa? Mingma had a moment's panic, and then he remembered. Of course. "Lhakpa Gyeltsen?" The former student who was playing golf in America.

The students nodded enthusiastically. Mingma was not sure where this was leading. He'd heard vaguely that Lhakpa Gyeltsen had not done well; he had no idea what that meant and he had been too busy preparing for this class to find out.

"Of course we can." He ran his eye around the room. Not every student was known to him, but there was Dolma, a nice girl in his English class. "Dolma, what would you like to say? Please stand, so everyone can hear you."

Dolma stood up, a self-possessed twelve-year-old. She turned to face as much of the class as she could. "It's wrong to say Lhakpa cheated," she said decisively, and focused on the group of boys in Nyima's vicinity. "He said what had happened at the end of the round. So he did not try to evade his responsibility or make a false score." Mingma was grieved to see Nyima stick his tongue out at her, but Dolma wasn't deterred. Her voice became severe. "You boys should be more careful when you say bad things—"

"Thank you, Dolma." Mingma thought it prudent to intervene. "Please tell me—Dolma, you may sit down now—who will explain what Lhakpa did?" Every hand went up and he chose a studious boy, Ang Tsering, who stood up and enlightened him.

"Why would that be called cheating?"

Several hands went up. "Because it happened on the eleventh hole," continued Ang Tsering, "but he didn't say anything until the eighteenth hole."

There was a general buzz of conversation, and Mingma let it continue while he tried to formulate a question. Ang Tsering remained standing, watching him attentively.

"Is golf played outside?" he asked finally.

"Ah! Yes, Mingma sir." The student explained the layout of a golf course and its component holes.

"Where would one find such a place?"

"The Royal Nepal Golf Club is near the airport," said Ang Tsering. The club had several Sherpa members, he added, and they were paying for lessons for him and Arjun, another of the older boys.

Voices intruded. "He has a girl porter," said one student. "He needs a Sherpa boy for his porter—"

"Caddie!" said several students at once, and Mingma asked what they meant. After they had explained the caddie's function, he asked what they thought Lhakpa should have done and whether he had cheated. This led to a vigorous discussion. At the end of it, the consensus seemed to be that he had not cheated, since he had owned up to the stroke at the end.

"We know it is a serious matter, to blacken a character with such an accusation," said Mingma. He didn't want to know who the culprit was—but his own brother chirruped up right away.

"They said it online, Mingma, sir. We didn't make it up."

Mingma was relieved, but nevertheless thought it would be useful to discuss Right Speech for a moment, so they talked about why it is important to avoid lying and careless talk that might hurt another and try always to be positive. Then Ang Tsering had his hand up, so Mingma nodded and he stood.

"But I think also that Lhakpa's mind must have been in turmoil. He would have been so much happier if he had spoken at once about his extra stroke. He wouldn't have bogeyed number twelve or shot a nine on number thirteen."

"He would have shot an eagle instead!" Nyima didn't wait for permission. His wiry little body sprang forward into the aisle between two rows of desks and he took a mighty swing with an imaginary club at an imaginary ball.

Mingma would have spoken seriously to his brother about waiting your turn, except that he was distracted to hear that golf involved killing. "Shot an eagle?" So that led to an explanation of bogeys, birdies and eagles, and within a few minutes, Mingma found he had a fairly good grasp of the game of golf.

"So what can we conclude of this game? Is it better to speak up immediately when you make a mistake, or to wait?"

The overwhelming consensus was "speak up." The students then explained that the next round (there were four altogether) would start in a few hours, but that Lhakpa wouldn't be playing until the middle of the night. The Administrator, who was English and thus had a double interest in the tournament, would be taping the broadcast for all to watch tomorrow morning.

"So!" said Mingma. "I for one will be most interested. Now—is there anything else we would like to discuss?"

There was a general shifting in seats as students looked at each other, then Dolma put up her hand.

"But Mingma, sir. What about the weekend?"

Mingma discovered there were still things to learn about the game of golf as the students began to educate him on the cut.

"Let me understand this," he said at last. "Lhakpa needs to play very well tonight to be chosen to play on the weekend?"

"Or everyone else must play badly."

"We should not wish for that," said Mingma automatically, and several heads nodded in agreement.

"But we thought we could help him, Mingma, sir," said Arjun, the other boy who was taking golf lessons. Everyone nodded, pleased: now they were getting down to business. Arjun explained that they wanted to meditate for ten minutes, if Mingma would help the weaker ones.

"*Ten* minutes?" Five minutes was hard enough unless you were a monk. But they were so clearly determined to do this that Mingma said he would be glad to assist. "Although we know that this is not really rational, is it? To think that our meditation will help Lhakpa."

"But it may be that our knowledge is imperfect, Mingma, sir. We cannot be sure it will not help, can we?"

Mingma was forced to concede the truth of this. "We'll need more room than we have here," he said, and suggested they move out into the hall. When they opened the door they found another fifteen students sitting waiting. Everyone filed out and joined them, sitting cross-legged with hands resting on their knees, palms upward.

"How did you learn to be so good at meditation, Mingma, sir?"

"Ah. When we came down from the hills I carried my younger brother, didn't I?" He bent and put a hand gently on Nyima's head. "And when I was weary I used to listen to my breathing and it made the time go by. I found I could carry him a long way without resting if I did that." His eyes roamed over all the assembled students up and down the hall. He smiled. "If you were to tie a sack of tsampa round your neck every morning, you would soon learn to meditate. . . ." The students laughed and his eye rested momentarily on Nyima, who once he had his brother's attention put his hands together and bowed from his lotus position. *Imp*, thought Mingma and then realized Nyima was in earnest.

"So. Close your eyes and listen to your breathing. . . ." and he paced quietly up and down the hallway among the students, speaking in the same even tone, while for ten minutes they each tried to meditate about Lhakpa Gyeltsen and his round of golf.

The following day Mrs. Chandra Lama, recovered from her dental appointment, thanked him for his help. "You do such a good job with them, Mingma, will you help again?"

"Next year, Mrs. Lama," said Mingma. He had asked Nyima to check the date. "April sixth next year."

o o o

While Mingma led the students in meditation, elsewhere in Kathmandu the investigation into the 2001 palace massacre continued. The group manager sat at the computer in the Dharmedia conference room and scrolled through the online transcript of the official investigation, listening as Vineeta Bhool, the reporter, gave him a progress report.

"I interviewed two of the Prince's servants. Neither of them said anything that isn't already in there." She paused then as he continued to read she added, "They were very upset, those investigators. You can tell. I think it is not a reliable document."

The manager grunted in agreement. "I haven't looked at this in years." He leaned back in his chair, removed his glasses and rubbed his eyes. "What we need is the transcripts of the original interviews. That would be the quickest way of pinpointing where to look first. Compare the testimonies, see if you can find contradictions."

She was ahead of him. "The army did not keep the files. They say the Secretariat had them. But the Secretariat was part of the palace government and so it is not there any more."

"That's right." He pondered. "I'm betting the Home Ministry has all that stuff. They never get rid of anything." He thought a moment longer, then leaned forward, took her pen and wrote a name on her pad. "This is the fellow to ask. He's an undersecretary. Remember that sting we reported on last year or the year before?"

"Where the officials were taking bribes for expediting land sales?"

"That's the one. This fellow was involved in a minor way. He helped us get the top dogs in return for anonymity." He glanced at her. "Want me to call him?"

"I would like to do it, please." Vineeta had already taken out her cellphone and found the phone number. She punched it in while the group manager sat back in his chair, hooked another chair round and put his feet on it, and closed his eyes. "Please connect me with Mr. Shakmaya. I am Vineeta Bhool with the *Everest Times.*" After a few moments, she disconnected.

"He is on holiday. I will try his home." Some searching, and soon she was dialing again. She spent some minutes speaking to a servant at the home of the undersecretary. Finally, "It directly affects his job at the ministry. It is critical that I speak to him." After a pause, she wrote down a number and disconnected again.

The group manager cocked an eye at her, amused.

"I am going by what you told me," she said, responding to his look. "I must presume it affects his job." She looked at her pad and punched the number. "He is trekking in Solu-Khumbu with his family. I have his cell number."

This time the wait was lengthy. Eventually the call was answered and after the preliminaries were concluded Vineeta explained what she wanted. "I believe that the findings and all the original investigation transcripts are stored at the Home Ministry. With your permission, I would like to review these documents." A pause. "No, it cannot wait until next week." Another pause. "New information has come to our attention, Mr. Shakmaya. It is most important that we follow it up. Could one of your assistants find the boxes for us?"

She turned the earpiece in the direction of the group manager and he could hear a man's voice, high-pitched and agitated.

Vineeta broke in. "Mr. Shakmaya, you were so helpful to us last year in the matter of the land titles scandal—" Another spate and she covered the mouthpiece and spoke to the manager. "You promised him we would never refer to that again," she said reproachfully.

"Sorry, it slipped my mind."

She spoke into the phone: "Oh thank you! And will you call him immediately?" A brief pause, then, "If you would give me his name and number, I will leave at once." She made notes, then disconnected after offering profuse thanks.

"Don't go overboard thanking people, Vineeta. They'll think they were had. He was just doing his duty and he had to be prodded to do it. A simple thank you is sufficient." He got to his feet. "The corruption in this country makes me sick. And they're so shameless about it."

"He wasn't shameless."

"Yeah, well, he's one of the exceptions."

"So perhaps it was right to thank him with excessiveness?"

He turned and looked at her. "Get outta here, Vineeta, before I fire you."

That meant she was right. She liked to know these things. She gathered up her belongings, and headed out for Singha Durbar, the government offices.

o o o

Friday night in Kathmandu. The Chinese diplomat, Mr. Hu, finished his dinner, pushed aside the table and moved to a settee, the only other furniture in the small room, whose walls were draped with heavy silk hangings. It was his favorite restaurant, where the private rooms allowed patrons to enjoy both food and other pleasures of the flesh.

Mr. Hu relaxed against the cushions, savoring his brandy and the day's satisfactions, chiefly two. First and foremost, the engineering team was back on Chinese soil, and he hoped the team leader would receive a sharp reprimand for his foolishness.

China was building hydroelectric plants throughout Tibet, generating terawatts of power for its manufacturing heartland from dams along the length and breadth of the Tibetan plateau. This particular team had been working up near the headwaters of the Karnali River, which runs south through western Nepal. Two dams were already in place on the upper Karnali, and the team had been evaluating the area for other possibilities. They had followed a promising river three days' hike into Nepal as it gathered strength and eventually plunged precipitously through a narrow gorge. They had been surveying the gorge and its surrounds when they were discovered by some villagers.

The engineers and villagers had exchanged stares. The Chinese were the first to move, turning away to gather their belongings. One engineer thought he had seen a cellphone, but none of the others could confirm it. The incident had occurred on Monday. The Ambassador had instructed Mr. Hu to stay on top of it, but no photograph had since turned up, and it seemed to him now that none would. He gazed absently at the heavy silk wall drapes and wondered if his country would approach Nepal with a proposal to build. Quite likely. China could always use more power.

He glanced at his watch. Lin Jinhai had played a careful first round at the Masters and would begin his second in a couple of hours. The antics of the hapless Nepali golfer had come as no surprise. To perform on the world stage required focus and dedication, qualities China had in abundance. Neither quality was much in evidence in this foolish, feckless country. Mr. Hu had been tempted to phone the colonel and offered his condolences on the performance of Lhakpa Pinasa, but thought better of it.

The hum of other voices was momentarily louder as the silk hangings were pulled aside and a girl entered, quite a young girl, thought Mr. Hu, perhaps fourteen. She wore a thin shift and sandals and had a smile on her face. They were trained to smile. Mr. Hu had been firm about that. "I want to know that I am giving pleasure," he had said to the proprietress.

He gazed at the girl, sipped his brandy and gestured her to approach him. She had large eyes and the awkwardness of adolescence. He frowned slightly: was she even fourteen?, would she have to be taught? and glanced at her feet. *Aieee.* Big feet. Big hands. Why did they always send him farm girls? He tried to repress his irritation and leaned back against the cushions.

The girl did not have to be taught, but oh—those hands! Mr. Hu hastily closed his eyes and made himself relax and let his thoughts drift to an ideal world, a world of delicate maidens with dainty hands and feet, oh yes. . . .

FRIDAY

O O O O

The harder you work, the luckier you get. –Gary Player

Kat's Story

Gordon phoned soon after seven, wanting to know if I'd seen the article. I was eating breakfast and hadn't seen anything. So he read it out, a piece titled "Allegations of Cheating?" I gave most of my attention to Miss Grace's scrambled eggs and biscuits.

"What was that bit about the trees?"

"'Rumor and innuendo swirled through the Georgia pines in the late-afternoon sun.'"

Amazing the things they find to say. "I guess you had to be there."

He laughed shortly. "I was, and I didn't hear anything like that. It's going to hurt him, though. Isn't it." He spoke flatly.

A good round would erase the rumors, I said, and rang off. But I drove out to the course thinking that Tony seemed to have a knack for attracting bad press.

I found him hard at work and frustrated, unable to get rid of the hook. Many players have swing coaches trailing along after them for exactly this sort of problem. Weird stuff can creep into any swing and cause a whole lot of trouble before it's weeded out. I lay awake for a while last night visualizing Tony's swing and trying to see what might have gone wrong, without success. Tom Dowling, responding to his email, had only seen brief glimpses of him, and only on the thirteenth. He expressed frustration with the TV coverage, and offered a couple of suggestions, neither of which did the trick.

Tony had experimented with ball placement, moving the ball forward or back in his stance, closer in or farther away from his body. He'd rejected these options almost the second he tried them: they didn't feel right or look right. He'd then gone back to basics on his grip, and showed me: nothing wrong there. We checked his alignment, broke his swing into its components and reassembled it—still nothing wrong. Yet every other drive was a severe pull.

So often it's something trivial. I'd gone to pick up some more balls and as I came back I noticed his posture. Instead of being aligned with the pines that split the range into left and right fairways two hundred yards out, his silhouette cut across them.

"Whoa! Stand up straight."

He broke off in mid-swing, glanced at me, and straightened up. Addressed the ball.

"What do you normally do?"

"Wiggle my toes." He did that. Rocked forward infinitesimally. Pulled the trigger. A beautiful draw.

Augusta National is a hilly course. A player spends all day compensating for uphill, downhill and sidehill lies that when he gets back on the flat he forgets how it feels. Especially if his mind is clogged with other stuff.

He hit another drive. Then another and a fourth. All perfectly shaped draws. "That's it!" His voice sounded triumphant. He went on hitting.

"Yeah," I said at last.

"Fade." A fade. "Draw." A draw. "I've got it. Big draw." Big draw. "High fade." That too.

Once we were confident the hook was history, Tony was anxious to get to his sand practice. He took a break to visit with his family and we agreed I'd find him after checking pin positions. I parked the bag next to the ball building, opposite the short-game practice area.

Back in the locker room once again, I climbed out of the jumpsuit and into my civvies. Took my yardage book, locked up, grabbed a cup of coffee and the daily pin sheet, said hi to several other caddies and snagged a chair on the porch. It's always pleasant to watch others working and I sat there in the morning sun and relaxed. We'd accomplished a lot and the day had hardly begun.

I sipped my coffee and studied the pin sheet. People used to refer to "typical" pin positions for a given day. These days the positions are as likely to be based on the weather forecast and the preceding day's scores as they are on tradition. That's just my hunch. Today's positions, I found, were a mixture of easier, harder and diabolical.

"Good morning, Kat." Tashi came up the steps to the porch. For someone who'd had a front-row seat on yesterday's controversy, she seemed calm and cheerful. "We went to the driving range," she said. "I hit my seven-iron one-twenty."

"Well, all right!" I liked the way she didn't add "yards."

She pulled out a rule book from the rear pocket of her shorts. "And I find these rules to be quite bizarre in places." She paused, looking out over the practice range, then added, "I don't know why we couldn't have come here."

I laughed. The practice facility at Augusta National is, like everything else, top line. One thing it isn't is open to women. It offends some people that the club is male only. For me it's an argument that got old a long time ago. If I wanted to form an all-women club I'd be majorly pissed off if someone told me I couldn't. Same applies to the men here at Augusta National. I think they're dumb to exclude women, mind you, but it's their call.

From the porch we had a great view of the whole practice area. Between us and the entrance lay thirty or so tee spots, all in use right now. Behind them, on our left, was a low privet hedge and behind that the stands, where patrons can sit and watch their favorite players. Opposite us, on the far side, just inside the entrance, is the ball building, and in front of it the short-game area, where players can practice wedge and short-iron shots to one of the two greens. We could see Tony working in one of the bunkers over there.

I finished my coffee and we set off to tour the greens. It was another wonderful day, temperature in the low seventies, sunny with little puffy clouds. There was some chance of rain but not much. Yesterday I'd feared I would never see the place again. Today it seemed as fresh and new as though I were looking at it for the first time. The patrons were doing their usual thing, some purposeful, others aimless, and the patio tables with their green umbrellas were already full.

We headed down through the valley that runs between eight and eighteen, to check out the locations on two and seven. As we went, I learned some more about Tony's background.

Charlie and I never used to mingle much outside office hours. We would meet for the round, sometimes on the range, and otherwise go our separate ways. I had a number of tasks this morning to help Tony dig out of yesterday's hole, but the more I knew of him the better I could help him. So I wasn't averse to spending time with his family. Besides, they were newcomers and kind of like babes in the wood.

Tony and Tashi went to the same school when he was little, she told me, then they met again when she went to the UK on a high-school scholarship. "I used to drive down with Gordon for the weekend." She'd watched Tony practice at home and walked round the course with him once or twice, but she'd never been interested in the game until now. "I used to think he had become rather peculiar and besotted," she said, then added, "Of course, most of the time he was playing in the pouring rain, that may have had something to do with it."

They had fallen in love last year, when Tony went out to Nepal. "Lhakpa says he first fell in love with me years ago, at dinner one weekend, when I said he and Kalden were lucky because they both knew what they wanted to do. But I think he exaggerates."

"Who's Kalden?"

"His cousin. He trained at Guy's Hospital in London and now he's practicing at a clinic in Nepal."

Tashi had a science degree, and earned a little money from tutoring. She had tried teaching but found herself to be too impatient. "Gordon wants me to interview at Swan Air, but I am more interested in hydroelectricity." Nepal had six thousand rivers, I learned, and a shortage of power. "Do you know, we could easily be net exporters of hydro power if we just put our minds to it?"

"Oh yeah?" We passed a security guard in the trees off the tenth fairway and I gave him a glassy stare, while Tashi waved cheerfully.

"People are awfully polite here, aren't they?"

"Polite?"

"Not just here, but in Augusta, too. Oh, I'm sure there's prejudice, too, we hill people are used to that at home. But they're much more polite here than in England, I find."

I asked if she had anything specific in mind.

"I was looking at a display window in the hotel lobby, and I nearly bumped into a man behind me. He tipped his hat and said 'My apologies, ma'am.' No-one would say anything like that in England, I can tell you." She thought for a moment as we walked. "And the way they behave towards Mollie. We're brought up to be respectful to our elders. They seem to share that view here. I find it quite like home in that way."

There was no one around the tenth green. The first group would be here shortly and I debated waiting, just to see how the shots held, but we had a lot to do.

"It looks so inviting, doesn't it," said Tashi. "Can we walk on it?"

"What do you think," I said drily and she laughed.

"What are we looking for, Kat?" She glanced at my pin sheet. "Interesting . . . these are contour lines?" The pin sheet showed the green with all its undulations.

I gave her a quick lesson in strategy. How the pin position determines the best place to land the ball, on or off the green. How that landing spot dictates the best position for your approach shot. How that determines the tee shot. She seemed to soak it all up.

I checked out fourteen as we headed toward Amen Corner, and saw Monk and another caddie down the fairway, crossing in front of the tee box. As we approached the refreshment stand behind number twelve we bumped into three Sherpas. I left Tashi talking up a storm with them while I checked the pins on eleven and twelve. When I came back they all looked at me in an interested sort of way and Tashi introduced us. They all bowed slightly, so I did too. I didn't really catch the names: something like Furball, Kinko and Jude. They were all shorter than me by a couple of inches, and not as bronze-looking as Tony.

"We'll be following you round," said Furball. He spoke English with what sounded like a Bronx accent. "Would you tell Tony we're all behind him one hundred percent?"

"One hundred and ten," said Kinko.

I promised to pass on their good wishes and we moved on, walking down through the trees, saying hi to the bored crossing guard at fourteen.

Tashi shook her head. "Those Sherpas are crazy."

"Are they friends of Tony's?" Tickets are not easy to come by is why I asked. They closed the waiting list in 1972 and I don't think the ticket price has ever been adjusted for inflation. It was two-twenty-five then and I believe it still is. That's a series badge for the four days. You can get tickets online sometimes for about three thousand dollars.

"Not at all. They work in the New Jersey area. They were called by the Nepalese Embassy asking if they'd like to come because they all play golf and I guess their names were on a list somewhere. Do you know what? I think when Lhakpa declined his extra tickets, they gave them to the Embassy to use. Is that likely, do you think?"

I doubted it, but I have no idea what the Admissions Committee does when it receives unwanted tickets. Falls over in a dead faint, probably. "Does Tony have any friends here?" Every player has the option to get ten invitations at a hundred dollars apiece, and so far I'd only met three.

"He didn't want the distraction. Tom Dowling and one friend were the only other people he really wanted to come, and the friend fell ill, and Mr. Dowling said the excitement would be too much for him."

I checked thirteen and on fifteen we saw a couple of turtles sunning themselves next to the pond. Then we made our way through the trees to number five. We could see crowds now, milling around in the trees, seated in the stands.

Tashi was still thinking about the Sherpas. "Do you know what they're planning? They're saving up to move back to Kathmandu and they're going to build mansions with their American dollars."

I could relate. "I had an uncle who made a fortune in Silicon Valley then came home and built this place on southwest Marine you wouldn't believe. About five thousand square feet. Like your guys."

Tashi was not sure she approved. We talked about it as we came through the trees to the crowd around the fifth. The stands on the far side were full. Just beyond them is gate five, the secondary entrance to the course, so there's always plenty of activity around here. I decided we'd stay on this side, so Tashi and I made our way behind the patrons.

We found an opening near the front, beyond the bunker. I studied the green. The flag was directly behind the false front, the flat apron that extended about three strides from the edge to a steep swale. They'd done some work on this green a few years ago, expanding and flattening the top middle section. It gave the players options: a high, soft shot could work, or you could punch a low running shot in there. Today's position was a relatively new one, front and left.

Two balls were on the middle front of the green, and the third was in the second cut on the right back. The player was preparing to chip, and Tashi suddenly got interested in the rules of golf after he chipped on, because the ball ran to the hole and dropped in. At least, it would have dropped but for the wind, which pushed the flagstick against the side of the hole, trapping the ball against it. Player and caddie walked up to the hole to moderate applause.

"Oh I see," Tashi said softly, and pulled out her rule book. "Wait, wait—"

"I'm not going anywhere." I wanted to see the next group's approach shots.

Tashi watched as the caddie straightened the flagstick. The ball disappeared into the hole.

I glanced at her. "Rule sixteen?"

She nodded, leafing through the pages. "Definitions. I'm afraid I really thought some of this was quite foolish. I mean, is it really necessary to define a ball in the hole? But now I see. . . ." She had found the right page and was reading the definitions. Rule sixteen is all about the putting green and what you do on it. Sounds straightforward enough. But as Tashi was discovering, the rules have to cover all the possibilities.

"What if the caddie had pulled out the flagstick and the ball with it?"

"If the ball was below the lip it would be deemed holed. Otherwise, he'd have one angry player on his hands." She wanted more. "He'd have to putt. It would mean at least one extra stroke. And one dumbass out-of-work caddie." I remembered the stuff about politeness. "Sorry."

She had other questions, but I motioned her to wait while the two remaining players putted out. And then we waited for the approach shots. It was nearly eleven o'clock now. I took a quick glance at her program and looked up the fairway at the players.

"Watch this guy. He's a great player but he has a low, flat trajectory. Perfect for the British Open."

"Why?"

"Much more wind. A low ball flight is generally an advantage in the Open."

In view of the pin placement, he opted to drop the ball ten yards short and it ran on to the green and halfway up the swale, where it stopped. Tricky putt. Probably easier if it had rolled back down to the flat but it stubbornly refused to move.

"Tom Watson won the Open and he won here as well," said Tashi. She saw my glance and added, "Gordon thinks well of him."

I nodded. "Winning more than one major—that separates the great players from the good ones."

She thought about that then asked, "What kind of trajectory does Lhakpa have?"

"Fairly high, and he's been good at hitting the high ones."

The next player hit exactly that kind of shot, and it landed middle front, just beyond the swale, then kicked to the left and rolled toward the pin.

"Very nice," I said.

The third fairway shot also landed and held, although it was too long. I thought of waiting for the putt, but we had some greens yet to visit, and time was marching on. Tashi had a different question as we moved back into the trees.

"What do the numbers mean? The numbers you wear on your overalls."

"Jumpsuits," I said mechanically. "Nothing, except for number one, which is always given to the returning champion. But all the others just show how early the player checked in. I did hear once that the number eighty-six was reserved for Nicklaus after his win in 1986. But that's the only case I know of." Tony had been given number five, so that's the number I wore.

"Rule 13-3," said Tashi as I noted the sixth pin location and glanced down and over to the sixteenth. I didn't answer until I'd studied it.

"Building a stance? What about it?"

"Why would you?"

"Mostly you wouldn't want to. Suppose it was a muddy area, you might simply be trying to get a solid footing. The thing about the rules, though, is the interpretation."

"Oh?"

We started up toward the fourth. "There was a famous case of a player whose ball was under a bush. He had a shot, but only if he knelt down. So to keep his pants clean, he knelt on a towel."

"You're not going to tell me that's building a stance?"

"One TV viewer thought it was. He phoned in, and the officials reviewed the film and agreed."

Tashi consulted her rule book. "So he had to take a two-stroke penalty?"

We were coming up to the fourth green. "See—he should have taken a two-stroke penalty, Tashi. But by the time it all came out, he'd already signed his card."

Tashi stopped and looked at me. "This is going to end badly. I can see it coming."

I nodded. "He was disqualified for signing an incorrect card."

She stared at me, and her expression, which was normally lively, went completely blank.

"The Buddha said life is suffering. . . ." she said at last.

"Did he golf?"

"No, but . . . why would you want to play a game like this?" She stared at me, puzzled. "Do westerners play golf because they think they ought to suffer?"

Jeepers. "Wait until you hit a good shot, Tashi. It's like your whole self is riding that ball. It's wonderful. . . ." We walked a little way in silence. "That shot you hit yesterday with your seven-iron. It pleased you?"

She smiled and nodded. "Yes, it did."

"Wait until you really get into it." I had trouble putting it into words. "Some people say golf is like life, just as great or just as horrible." I thought some more. "It's the most frustrating game in the world, Tashi. But the feel of a well-struck shot, when the club meets the ball just so and the ball goes where you meant it to. . . ." She was watching me attentively, and I shook my head. "You'll see. I love all sports, pretty much. But there's nothing like golf."

We finished the way we started, walking back up through the valley between eight and eighteen. Patrick Geoghan, the color commentator, was over near the putting green. I wanted a word with him, so Tashi and I split and she went to find the others.

"Kat Woman!"

"Hi Patrick. Knock it off." He knew I disliked that name.

He watched as Tashi walked away.

"She's Tony's girlfriend, and she wants to build hydroelectric plants, so watch your step."

He gave me a mock scowl. "You women. You're so encroaching."

"Yeah." Patrick's a likeable guy and an okay commentator, probably because he used to be a pretty good player. "Did you interview Tony, by any chance?"

"I did. He was forthright. It sounded to me like he made a mistake and wouldn't listen to you. I hear he's got game." He looked a question.

"Yeah, that's not his problem." Danny Chu joined us and after the greetings I asked, "What about Stillson?"

Patrick grunted. "Cross as a bag of weasels. I told him to put a sock in it. All that 'they're not like us' religious rubbish—"

"His mother thinks it was racist, not religious." Gordon had mentioned it last night.

Both men shook their heads. Patrick said, "You know Greg. He's a bit ponderous about religion and belief systems and so forth." I nodded. That was a good description of Stillson's manner. "I told him if he went on like that much longer he wouldn't do himself any good at all." He glanced at his watch. "I'd better find some color to comment on." He nodded to both of us and turned on his lapel mike as he walked away.

"I spoke to Greg this morning," said Danny. We walked along to the caddie building. "Tell his mother that when Greg says they're not like us, he means those Buddhists or Hindus or Muslims. He doesn't mean those Chinese, or Indians or Saudis."

"Maybe you'd pass that on to Mollie if you see her."

"I will." I turned to go inside. "Where were you yesterday, Kat?"

I remembered he'd seen me with the guard. I didn't want him pursuing that, so I made some excuse and promised to sit down with him either later today or tomorrow. He wanted to interview me about what caddies do. "Show up, keep up, shut up" is how it used to be described. Could be a short interview.

o o o

I sipped my coffee and watched Tony work the ball with his seven-iron, hitting draws then fades. We were back on the practice range. His driving was fine now, and he'd been working through his irons, hitting easily. Something had been niggling at the back of my brain since yesterday, and now it came to the front.

"The caliber of play at the British Amateur must be a whole lot higher than I thought, if it took you four years to win it."

He flashed a grin without stopping. "Yer, well, I was down a club or two, wasn't I?"

"What do you mean?"

He flipped a ball onto the club face and tapped it into the air in the golfer's dribble. "I was minus my sand wedge and four the first year. Wouldn't want to do that again, I can tell you. The second year I was minus my six; pitching and four the third year—I really should have won that year but I had astonishingly bad luck all day. Last year I didn't have my pitching wedge or my seven."

"You mean, you won without having a pitching wedge or seven-iron in your bag?" This from a guy who didn't even possess a gap wedge.

"That's right." He exchanged the seven for an eight and began hitting fades. I watched for a while.

"All right, I'll bite. Why didn't you have those clubs?"

He told me, in between shots. Years ago, Gordon told him if he threw a club, or took a divot with a practice swing after a bad shot, or was too loud with the bad language, he would forfeit that club for two weeks. He always got a bit strung out in the weeks leading up to the Amateur, so that's when he was most susceptible to breaking these rules, which was why he always ended up one or two clubs short. "I didn't really mind. I mean, of course I did, I was furious with Gordon for enforcing that bloody rule, but—." He stopped hitting and began dribbling again. "The thing is, I grew five inches when I was seventeen. And my game went to pieces, and Mr. Dowling said why not just play with one or two clubs per round, and get inventive. Well, I did and it was interesting but I wouldn't want to play a serious match without my sand wedge. But you can compensate for a lot if you have to. Like Seve Ballesteros, remember?" Seve had learned to play with a single club, a three-iron.

I strolled thoughtfully back to stand behind him. "How about a couple of knockdown shots before we quit?"

O O O

"That's one crazy flag." We were looking at the flag of Nepal.

"It's the best flag up there."

"How come it's got two flappy bits?"

"Everyone should have two flappy bits. It's the wave of the future." He paused then added, "They're called pennons."

"Oh."

The flags of all the players' countries are flown above the main scoreboard off the first fairway. Today, twenty-nine flags flapped gently in the breeze as we gazed up at them. Unlike the others, which were all rectangles, Nepal's flag consisted of two right-angled triangles, one on top of the other, crimson with a blue border. The top one had a white crescent moon cradling a sun.

"Is the bottom one a rhodo?" Mollie had mentioned that the rhododendron was the national flower.

"It's another sun. The red means that all Nepalis have the same color blood."

"Oh."

He should have quit while he was ahead. "They used to have faces on them. Sun and moon."

"You gotta be kidding! Like smiley faces?"

"You're awfully rude, you know."

"Yeah. So—are you British or Nepali?" I knew he had dual citizenship but I was curious to know how he saw himself.

I waited awhile. He shoved his hands in his pockets. "I'm British," he said at last, then added, "but my heart's often in Nepal."

"You mean, because of Tashi."

"No. When I remember my childhood I still get a—it's like a little heartache. Do you know what I mean? Not only because of my dad. Because I remember it as so happy."

We headed toward the clubhouse. A quick peripheral movement made me glance back to see two players looking after us, exchanging a comment. I chose to ignore it. You couldn't do anything about it, and anyway I was feeling better about the whole "cheating" thing after talking with Patrick and Danny. Earlier, I'd seen another player veer off into the trees when he saw us coming. I don't know if Tony saw; he didn't say anything. However, not everyone wanted to avoid him.

"Mr. Pinasa!"

We were passing the patio tables. Zachary Anderson was just getting to his feet, the eighteenth hole announcer in his crimson jacket. He would be going out to the green at any moment, and he had what looked like a beer cooler next to his table. It was open and we could see it was filled with A to Z file folders.

"Is it 'Lhakpa Gyeltsen Pinasa'? Have I pronounced your name correctly, sir?" His "I's" were "Ahs" and "sirs" "suhs".

"Thank you, yes," said Tony, smiling. "You can call me Tony if you want. I'm happy either way."

"Thank you. I don't have anythin' to say about you, Mr. Pinasa." He gazed benignly at Tony, "I really do not." He waited expectantly.

A sizable number of patrons bring their chairs to the course each day and just go directly to the eighteenth green. They settle down around it and stay there all day long. What Mr. Anderson does is tell them a bit about the players currently in the fairway, so that when they reach the green the patrons feel they know them. Sort of short biography stuff. I could well believe that his bio for Tony was brief.

"I'm sorry, Mr. Anderson. I haven't done much, as yet. But I will."

"That's fine! But now come come, sir. You must have won other tournaments?"

"Yes, but they aren't much."

He cited a couple of regional events and I nudged him. He stopped and looked at me and I made a suggestion in an undertone. He wasn't impressed, but I gave him another nudge toward Mr. Anderson.

"Okay, I came second three times in the British Amateur, before I won." Mr. Anderson jotted this down on a three-by-five card. Tony looked at me doubtfully and I gave a sharp nod. "And I won last year without my pitching wedge or my seven-iron."

"Is that so? And why was that?"

"They were confiscated." As Mr. Anderson looked up, he went on. "I'm not allowed to play with a club for two weeks if I throw it during a round. It's a sort of family rule. And I'd thrown both of those. If you really want to know, I've never played the Amateur with a full set of clubs. If I had done, I'd have been here before now."

Mr. Anderson made a note or two then looked at Tony with a twinkle.

"I can think of one or two other players who would benefit greatly from that discipline, Mr. Pinasa." He held out his hand and shook Tony's. "I thank you for these facts, and I wish you good fortune today."

Sitting at Amen Corner

Mollie cupped her hands gratefully around the green paper cup. Hot chocolate provided a welcome warmth when you'd been sitting for an hour in a weak early morning sun. The dew on the tee box had now disappeared and the sunlight streaming from behind the eleventh green spread its warming rays over the twelfth hole and Rae's Creek. And over the stands.

She was sitting with her two new friends, Bill and Ben the flowerpot men. That was how she privately thought of them; their names were actually Bill Harder and Ben Trask and they had been coming to the Masters, as far as Mollie could determine, since the world was young. They both had the papery skin of the very elderly. Bill had a round face, Ben's was long and thin. They had met here as boys or young men; they had brought their wives each year; they had shared a rented house for the week of the tournament; they had found solace in each other's company after their wives died; and today Mollie had been witness to a momentous decision by the two ancients: they were going to buy a house together. She had learned more of their medical histories than she really cared to know. Bill had two artificial hips and a pacemaker; Ben had one artificial knee, a hernia and a hearing aid. "But we figure we can manage well together, Mollie. We found out enough during one week over the years to come to a good decision about the other fifty-one."

Bill, she learned, had been an auto parts manufacturer in the Detroit area ("That would be back when cars had character, Mollie.") and Ben a lawyer. She guessed they were in their eighties or nineties but if they had said they were a hundred and three she would have had no trouble believing them. They both wore jackets and cloth caps, with gloves shoved in their pockets and they both sat on cushions. "We watch the world go by," said Ben. "All day long."

A small part of the Masters world had already gone by this morning, and except for a couple of wild tee shots up into the slope beyond the bridge, the players had provided little drama. But a breeze had begun to manifest itself an hour ago in gently stirring flags, and it was becoming noticeably stronger. Mollie had heard all about the wind at Amen Corner, and now Bill and Ben were wrangling gently about a study commissioned (Bill said) in the '90s by *Sports Illustrated* to determine wind patterns by using a scale model of Amen Corner; yes (said Ben) but it was the University of Waterloo, not *Sports Illustrated,* that commissioned the study. Mollie half-listened to them while trying to name all the flowers, shrubs and trees on the bank behind the green. Bill won that point eventually, but Ben won the date wrangle: "Not the '90s, Bill, because Melissa was still a child. It was just after she'd had our second great-grandchild, so it must have been two thousand and… two. There."

Mollie joined in the applause for the group walking over from the eleventh. "What is *Sports Illustrated?*" she asked, looking from one to the other. "Is it a television show?"

They stared at her, then explained that it was the best sports magazine in the world, and even though that didn't mean much any more, what with so few magazines being left, it was still well worth a tree or two. She could see them reassessing her as a person of comprehensive, and hitherto unimaginable, ignorance where sports were concerned.

"Does it really make such a difference, the wind?" she asked, in an effort to get off the subject, then answered her own question. "I suppose it must, if they went to the trouble of building a model."

"There you go," said Bill.

They saw the threesome hit off, two balls landing on the green, the third in the front bunker.

"I think he caught a gust there," said Ben and Bill agreed.

"What's the worst we might expect?" she asked. "Let's see, it's a par three. Six, perhaps? Or seven?"

The two old men exchanged a look.

"There was Tom Weiskopf," said Ben at last.

"He shot a thirteen, Mollie," said Bill. "One, three."

Coming off Lhakpa's nine yesterday, which she had been unable to watch through to the bitter end, this was a staggering number, especially on such a short hole. Mollie's heart sank and she wished she hadn't asked.

"We've never understood what his caddie was thinking."

"You go over to the drop zone if you have to hit another ball." Bill pointed, and she turned to look at the circle to the right of Hogan's Bridge as he continued, "He should have moved Tom back so he could get a different lie, but he did nothing."

"Although it might have been Tom. He could be very irascible, Mollie, and his caddie may have been afraid to interrupt him."

"He just kept putting them in the water. They'd hit the bank and roll back down."

"Remember Greta?" Bill looked at Ben, then said to Mollie, "Ben's wife. She couldn't stop crying. It was, you know, painful to watch. Ben finally had to take her to the washroom. It was one of those portable things back then. Poor Greta, she never got over it."

"Of course she got over it," said Ben testily. He added, after a pause, "It took a while, though."

Mollie wondered if her son was aware of this Tom whatever-his-name-was, then mentally chided herself. Lhakpa knew everything, but everything, there was to know about the Masters. *Well,* she thought, *fun and games.*

When she first joined Bill and Ben earlier this morning she had explained that this was her first time at the Masters, and told them her son was a player. They had asked her to mark his name on their program ("Memory isn't what it was, Mollie," Bill had said). She had waited for some reference to the "cheating" article, but none came, although they both remembered him coming through, the amateur whose tee shot landed up in the bank and ricocheted down toward the green.

Mollie decided to stretch her legs. The two old men were fine, they said, and would keep her place. So she wandered back to the washroom then looked at the hexagon stand of phones, where one could call anyone in the United States free of charge. Mollie couldn't think of anyone she might call except for an old school chum. That would require hours of explanation just to establish who she was, and she smiled at the thought and changed her mind, strolling over to the thirteenth fairway, then realized where she was and turned hastily away. It would be a long time, if ever, before she could look at that hole again.

A loud cheer went up from a crowd along the eleventh, and she hurried back to her seat in case someone among this mass of people tried to take her spot.

"Did I miss anything?"

"This is Alex's group, Mollie."

Mollie joined in the applause for Alex Figueres and his two companions, aware that he was the favorite to win the tournament this year. He was a tall, slender man with an olive complexion. His caddie, Miguel, was short and heavyset, with a cigar clamped between his teeth. They stood side by side studying the flag. The breeze had stiffened and the flag was blowing to the left, toward the eleventh green.

"Look at eleven," said Bill. Mollie turned to look: the flag on the eleventh was pointing toward them.

"How can that be?" She watched as Miguel took a drag on his cigar and let out the smoke. It drifted upward . . . then to the right. The flag flapped desultorily to the left, then dropped, flapping in front. . . .

"Gosh," said Mollie, "I see what you mean. Isn't it interesting?"

The men laughed. "That's one word for it," said Ben. "But they'll be all right. It's not too strong as yet."

And he was right. When Alex finally chose a club and hit his tee shot it landed safely on the green. While they waited for the next group Mollie heard about Arnold Palmer and Ken Venturi. "Arnie's first green jacket that was, nineteen-fifty-eight, and my first Masters too," said Ben.

"We hadn't met then," Bill took up the tale, "I was here when they came through, Arnie and Ken. It was the year after Ken turned pro. Arnie's ball plugged in the back bank and he played it out and shot a five. But he was certain there was a local rule about embedded balls, so he played a provisional and parred the hole. And that was the one they counted."

Ben said, "The thing is, it wasn't a provisional, was it? He just played a second ball, but he didn't announce it."

This meant nothing to Mollie. She watched the green as the two old men discussed whether Arnie should have played the other ball.

"Nineteen fifty-eight," said Ben finally. "That was the year it was named, when Herbert Warren Wind wrote a piece called "Shouting at the Amen Corner." And now they've installed a heating and drainage system under that green so you don't get embedded balls any more."

Mollie heard about the bank in front of the green, the few feet of grass falling to Rae's Creek. "They shave it so close at night, Mollie, that nothing will hold on it."

"Except for Freddy's ball." They chuckled together and told her how Fred Couples in 1992 had landed a ball on that bank and, impossibly, it had stayed dry. And Freddy had hustled over the bridge and crept gingerly toward his ball, and managed somehow to take a stance on the bank without disturbing the ball, had got the clubface on it and chipped it close and made his par, and went on to win the tournament.

She heard how Jack Nicklaus in the 1960s shanked his tee shot over the heads of the two founders of Augusta National, Bob Jones and Clifford Roberts, who were standing watching. Ben turned to Mollie: "I think that's what Bobby was referring to when he said 'Mr. Nicklaus plays a game with which I am not familiar.'"

Bill laughed at this and so did a man sitting in front of them. Mollie studied Ben. His long face was straight as a judge, but she discerned the twinkle in his eye.

"You're pulling my leg, aren't you, Ben?" she said. "Let me tell you. Lhakpa idolizes Jack Nicklaus and that doesn't sound like him."

Ben smiled. Really, she thought, they were sweet, these two old fellows.

"Oh, he did hit a shank," said Bill, on her other side. "But what Bobby Jones said about Nicklaus, he said that on another occasion." He looked at her. "Lhakpa—that's your son?" He opened his program. "This L.G. Pinasa?"

The man in front turned. "Is he the Asian who got into some trouble?" His expression was polite but Mollie wasn't fooled.

"Spit it out," she said cheerfully. "He seems to have landed himself in it yesterday, but he doesn't cheat." She looked straight at the man.

"I'm glad to hear it," he said, and nodded at her. Then he held out a hand. "I'm Doug." Mollie shook hands and introduced herself.

"Is his father here, Mollie?" Bill asked.

"Most people call him Tony," she smiled at Bill. "His father died some years ago. He was a Sherpa."

Several people heard that, along with Bill and Ben and Doug, so Mollie was quite busy for a few minutes answering questions about Sherpas in general and her son in particular. Then she glanced at her watch. Time to go. Bill was looking up at the tops of the trees, now swaying in the breeze.

"Augusta Country Club lies over there, Mollie. The first time I came here, Bob Rosberg took a four-iron in a strong wind, which died as he hit. His ball went clear over the trees to their ninth fairway." He smiled at Mollie. "Of course, that was in 1956. The trees were shorter back then."

Kat's Story

We stood one side of the first tee, Stillson and Monk the other. Gordon, Tashi and Mollie were nearby, outside the ropes. We were waiting for the group in the fairway to hit and move off. When we first arrived, Tony had pulled out his visor from the back of the big pocket in the bag, and it dawned on me that this might be a daily ritual. Yesterday he'd worn a plain white visor with RNLI stitched on it in bold green letters on both sides, above his ears. Royal National Lifeboat Institution, he told me it stood for. A charity. "They're big in Cornwall because we have such a long coastline," he'd said and I thought no more about it.

Today was different. Still white and green, but the lettering was on the front, smaller because there were more words, but easy to read. "Real men play cricket." *What the hell?* He saw my expression. "Yes, well. Tashi ruined it." He started to turn away and I stopped him.

"But what's the point? Real men don't play golf? Why would you want—"

"No, no, no." He turned back. "It was supposed to say, 'Real men play cricket, not baseball.'" He grinned.

I remembered yesterday's short-lived baseball chat, late in the round. I glanced over at Tashi and she gave me a hard-done-by look.

"Are you trying to offend people?" I spoke distinctly but softly.

"No."

"You seem to be going out of your way to get in their faces."

"It's just a conversation starter."

I tried to reason with him. But he just didn't get it or didn't want to and finally he turned away. I heaved a sigh and stared at the ground. In a tournament it's often the only safe place to look, if you don't want some God-awful expression on your face to be captured on TV for all time.

Across the tee box, Monk happened to straighten up from his bag just as I looked up, and we gave each other the ghost of a grin, allies in enemy camps.

Tony and I had been first on the tee, and the crowd had watched with interest when Stillson arrived. Tony had been first to reach the middle and first to extend his hand, but Stillson was not one to nurse a grievance so they shook hands and smiled with a fair semblance of civility. Even so, I thought, it will be a long day.

At least my player looked good today, light blue shirt with a woven pattern, dark blue trousers and shoes. Very tidy. We could hear the snap of the flags along the right-hand side as we waited. I wondered whether the wind meant rain was coming later today. Right now it was sunny and warm with bigger fluffy clouds than earlier. There was a chance the wind might drop toward evening, which would help the later groups like us.

Tony's job today was to shoot one under par. If he could do that, we might stand a chance. In the old days the cut was low forty-four plus ties plus anyone within ten of the lead. Once or twice that had led to huge fields on the weekend. So they'd changed the rules and now it was low forty-four and ties. Period.

What did that mean in terms of score? If Tony played par golf today, his two-day total would be one-fifty (seventy-eight plus seventy-two). Unfortunately, the cut had been one-fifty or higher only three times in the past thirty years. Conditions had to be bad—low temperatures, lots of rain or wind, or some combination—for scores that high. The cut would not be one-fifty this week.

If we could shoot one under, we might—*might*—play the weekend. Two under or better should give us a good chance. At close of play yesterday, thirty players had shot higher than Tony's seventy-eight. No good waiting for others to play themselves out. We had to make good things happen. We had our work cut out for us.

The starter lifted his clipboard and read from the pairing sheet. “Fore, please!” It was 12:46 pm. “Greg Stillson driving.”

We were off.

o o o

“I never actually went to prison,” said Tony.

“That’s good, because I don’t caddie for jailbirds.” We were sitting behind the fourth tee, waiting as we had waited on every hole. Gordon had said Tony had had more than one run-in with the police and I’d asked him about it.

“Oh, I was in jail once.” He saw my look. “Just for an evening. I was stuck in a cell with this drunk who kept trying to put his arms around me. I wasn’t that big at the time.”

“How old were you?”

“Eleven. Then he threw up, all over the floor. Just missed my foot. So gross.”

We were at even par, compared with yesterday’s two under at this point. Tony had bogeyed the first, a big disappointment after yesterday’s birdie, but the hole had played ten yards longer into a stiff breeze. His second had shot off behind the green and he’d narrowly missed the par putt. He’d got the stroke back on two and had parred three.

On every hole, on every shot, we waited. The two players weren’t talking, so he’d talked to me. Earlier I’d heard about his recorded putts. We’d been in the second fairway at the time. He had a thumb-drive full of putts that he’d cut and spliced from more than ten years' worth of Masters tournaments, putts from each day of each year on each hole. He'd started off with all the putts from one hole on a specific day together, "except that I noticed they weren't all from the same hole location." He laughed. "I had to think about whether to group them by day or by hole location, and decided that days were pointless."

"So, wait a minute." This was giving me a headache. "You grouped say ten putts from number two, left back hole location last year with a bunch more, same green, same hole location the year before?"

"Something like that."

"What were you hoping to accomplish?" I asked. The amount of work involved was slightly boggling. "Did you think you'd be able to read the greens better?"

"Not really." He pulled out his water bottle and took a swig. "Bik asked me the same thing. He's a friend of ours—of mum's really. He's a colonel in the Nepal Army and he was over in England helping the Gurkhas, the ones who fight in the British Army. He thought I was mad, but he was too polite to say so." He stopped and gazed at his shoes, then lifted his head and looked round at the trees, at the patrons. I sometimes had trouble reading his expression, but not then: he looked like a man in love. He saw Tashi with the others on the hill above and behind us, and smiled when she gave a small wave. I said nothing, just waited curiously. "Anyway," he said at last, "I did all that work not because I thought it would help but because it couldn't hurt." He looked at me. "Know what I mean? I reckoned anything that might make me feel more at home here was worth doing."

There's an expression about a capacity—an infinite capacity, I think it goes—for taking pains, and it applies to people like Tony. They'll go to any lengths to shorten the odds, even when there's no guarantee that what they do will make any difference.

Augusta National greens are in a league of their own. Huge and fast. Three to four feet of break over a ten-foot putt: that's the Augusta hallmark. The greens have never been officially rated on the Stimpmeter, as far as I know. I did read once that when they first changed over to bent grass in 1981 the greens were rated at just under ten. They only got faster after that; ask some of the old players. These are the fastest greens played on tour. Today, the players reckon the speed is somewhere between twelve and fifteen. (A Stimpmeter works roughly like this: a ball is rolled down an incline onto the surface of the green. The distance it travels is measured, and the procedure repeated several times, then averaged. The faster the green the farther the ball rolls.)

Tony welcomes the greens. You might say he embraces them. He views them as a challenge, not a threat. His putting is all about process, not outcome: did I put the right weight and break on it? In other words, he doesn't beat himself up if the putt doesn't drop, as long as he did everything he was supposed to do. I wouldn't know whether all that seemingly pointless work with the video actually helped his game. But one thing's for sure: he putts with confidence, and that's essential. You have to come here believing you can make every putt. Tony does.

The fourth green was finally clear and we stood up. Stillson had the honor and we waited and watched while he and Monk had a conference about the wind. Today, number four was about as devilish as this par three hole ever gets. I'm not sure why the wind is such a factor here, except that this is another corner of the course, just not as well known as Amen Corner. We'd had the breeze behind us coming up three, and I could still feel it slightly at my back. But the fifth fairway runs at right-angles to the fourth, and it often has more effect on the fourth green. In other words, you want to pay attention to the flag, not to the wind up here at the tee.

Yesterday's pin had been back left. Today's was at the front, in the neck of the green right between the two bunkers. Stillson's ball was safely on, middle of the green. We had two-thirty to the front flag. I could see the tops of the trees on five swaying right, not a lot but enough. Tony decided he'd rather miss short left, if he had to miss at all, and he planned to aim left and let the wind push the ball to the right. He executed the shot well, except that halfway there, the wind died completely and the ball dropped like a stone into the bunker.

I was nervous about his sand game. He said he was feeling a lot more comfortable about Augusta sand and one thing's for sure. You can't play the entire tournament praying you're never going to have to play to your weakness, because it doesn't happen. Best to get tested as early as possible, so you can settle down. Tony got tested all right. His ball was buried and it took him two to get out, leaving a twelve-foot uphill putt which he drained, good man. So now we were one over for the day.

I had a quick word with Gordon on the fifth tee—quick because the pace picked up somewhat, and we didn't have long to wait—but it was still too early to get any conclusive idea of the cut line. A total of twenty-two players so far had finished with scores higher than one-fifty.

We added another stroke on five. This was the hole Tashi and I had watched, and I'd thought it would play to Tony's strength. But the wind changed that, and he chose to punch a low six-iron into the green. Unfortunately, he overcooked it and the ball ran past the pin and off into the back-left bunker.

"Gimme the club," I said. "Give me the club." His hands were wrapped around it as though he was about to bend it across his knee. "Give. Me. The club."

I took the club and heard a muttered string of pungent comments that I'm not going to repeat here. "Just look down at the ground when you do that," I suggested during a break in the stream. "Or up at the sky. See if that works for you." I heard somewhere that it's harder to stay angry when you look up. He bent over, put his hands on his knees, and had a one-sided conversation with the fairway.

Again, his sand game was tested. This time he produced a fair shot that stopped in the flat middle section, about fifteen feet from the hole. That putt should have dropped, but instead it slid by, leaving a two-footer for bogey.

"I've got to tell you, I'm not worried about your putting," I said as we walked over to six. "You're looking good. Just be patient. You know."

We heard a colossal roar as we reached the tee box, I'd say from the eighteenth green. I looked across at Monk and we both mouthed "Alex." The crowd roar at Augusta differs depending on the type of player, but for favorites you can always tell the roar. This was an Alex roar, for sure.

Alex Figueres is the best player in the world and has

been for the past three years. He's thirty-eight or -nine, married with four daughters. His home base is Barcelona, and when he's not on Tour or spending time with his family he's a superb bridge player. He's personable, even charming. He has tenacity and a piercing intelligence and occasionally displays a fiery temper. His presence livens any tournament. He virtually owns the British Open and he's got two green jackets.

Play was slightly faster than for the first four holes, but as a twosome we still had plenty of waiting. I was curious to hear about Tony's daffodil incident, so after we'd driven off eight I asked him about it. "I hear you got off to a rocky start with Tom Dowling." I handed him an apple.

"It's true, I did." He bit into it then glanced around as we walked along the fairway. "What do you see?"

"Huh?" I looked round. "I dunno, what?"

"What do you smell?" He grinned and took another bite of the apple.

I wanted to hear about the daffodils.

"What do you hear?"

I refused to rise to the bait.

"What do you feel, lad? There was I, swinging away for hours on end, and all he would say was what do you see? Or hear. Or feel. Or smell." He shook his head. "It drove me wild. I started trying things I was reading in books, and he'd come along and tell me not to do that. He never spent any time with me, you understand. He was always busy in the pro shop except when he came out to the range with someone. They'd get a proper lesson, but with me it was always 'what do you see, lad?' as he went by back to the shop."

"Finally," he said through a mouthful of apple, "I asked him. 'Mr. Dowling, when can I have a proper lesson?' He stopped and turned and asked me to hit some balls. Back then I was into world domination. I gripped the club so hard my hands already had breaking blisters. My entire body would become as rigid as a board. Tom stopped me after a few hits. 'Look, lad,' he said. 'Golf is played outdoors. In wind and sun and rain, sometimes all at once.' I thought he was completely potty. I mean, hello?" I laughed and Tony grinned, then continued. "He put his hands each side of my head. 'If you want to play good golf you must be part of the environment. You must see and hear and feel and smell it. You must look outwards, lad, not inwards. When you can show me that, we'll have a lesson.'"

We turned our attention to the ball at that point. He'd bogeyed this par five hole yesterday. Today I thought we might come away with a birdie. He was well positioned in the fairway, and chose to lay up rather than going for the green. We had to wait for Stillson then, and Tony returned to his early golf days.

"Did Gordon ever tell you about the daffodils?"

"You mean, about taking the heads off? Yeah."

He smiled and looked up at the sky. "I didn't mean to do that. At least, I didn't consciously mean to. But I had to tell mum about it that evening, because I needed her help to make things right with Tom. He was seriously upset. We talked about it and she brought up some things I did when I was in the gang, and I began to realize I was trying to hurt people or things that were weaker than me. I was trying to be like the Crown Prince."

I stopped him. "Whoa. The guy who killed your dad?"

He nodded. "I hadn't realized that till then. I've always had a temper. I got it from mum. But my anger has—had—rage on top of it. That's how she put it and she was right."

We walked ahead to our ball after Stillson's second. "Anyway, she picked me up after school the next day and we bought some plants and she dropped me off at the pro shop." He glanced at me, then made up his mind and continued, speaking rapidly. "I apologized to the daffs and told them I was putting in some friends and neighbors to keep them company—shut up."

I stopped laughing.

"Well, I always say if you've got to do something, make a meal of it. Now what have we got here?"

We had eighty yards to a back left pin for the third shot, and Tony left it about six feet below the hole. He spent some time muttering about this as we went up to the green, because he'd hoped for a tap in. This time the ball didn't slide past the hole. It did a horseshoe and stopped about eighteen inches away on the right. So another par.

We parred nine as well, and Gordon joined us as we walked to the tenth.

"One-forty-eight," he said. That was where he estimated the cut would fall.

Oh boy. We'd shot thirty-eight on the front nine. Two over. We'd have to shoot four under on the back.

"We'll just have to jack it up another notch." Tony was cheerful, but added, as though between gritted teeth, "Just let a few putts drop and I'll be happy."

"Your mother's fit to be tied," said Gordon. "The suspense is killing her. I'm using her as a runner on the back nine. She'll check the main scoreboard for us and that way I can keep an accurate count."

"Good old mum."

"She met up with another mother, which seemed to help. They've gone off with Tashi for an azalea cocktail, if you're wondering."

An azalea cocktail is a mixture of lime and pineapple juice with a healthy dollop of gin, and grenadine to make it red. "Those things are lethal," I said and we started the back nine in reasonably good spirits. While Thursday is for opening nerves. Friday is for making-the-cut nerves. Although Tony had battled fiercely over every shot so far, he had precious little to show for it.

"I'm trying not to second-guess myself on the putting—" he said as we walked down the tenth fairway.

"Good."

"—but it's pretty obvious that if they don't start to drop we'll have to rethink our strategy for the par fives."

I said nothing, because he was right. It was getting down to Hail Mary time unless we could find a birdie or two soon. Stillson had been playing steady golf and lay even par at the turn. How I wished Tony had that score! Both men, by the way, had been punctilious (isn't that a great word? It means "strict or exact in observance of the formalities" and I had a time finding it) about announcing their scores as they left each green. Tony had giggled about this after the second hole, "Could I—should I—have said it any louder?" He'd immediately had a change of heart. "Poor Greg, stuck with me."

Anyway, after a punctilious exchange of scores on ten, we walked up the path to eleven with Stillson and Monk leading, then Tony, with me last. Tony's visor had drawn a few looks and one or two audible comments similar to my own initial reaction. Most people watched him with what looked like courteous caution, as though they didn't want to prejudge him but on the other hand he had this reputation. Anywhere else on Tour he'd have been razzed right round the course. En route to the eleventh tee, he got a taste of that.

People lined the path as we approached the tee box. One of them, seeing the visor with its "Real men play cricket," said audibly, "Real men don't cheat, however." Tony stopped abruptly and I nearly ran into him. I followed his glance toward a burly fellow on the right, who folded his arms and returned Tony's stare. "You wanna throw one my way?" he added, and made a "bring it on" gesture with one hand.

Oh yikes. I was going to say something, to step forward, to get between them, when I heard Tony reply.

"I'm busy right now," he said softly. He started to move forward then stopped and looked straight at the burly guy. "I don't cheat," he said, still softly. "I don't have to." He held the other man's look for a moment then started forward and I followed. I could hear behind me the collective whispers:

"Did you hear what—"

"I don't cheat—"

"That guy said—"

"What guy?"

"That guy in the boots said real men don't cheat can you believe that will they throw him out?"

I put the bag down and saw Monk across the other side say something to Stillson, who looked sharply at Tony.

"I'm not really the flavor of the month am I?" He looked rueful.

"No," I said briskly. "And you're probably not going to be for a while, so get used to it."

"What do you mean?"

Oh come on, kid! I took a moment, then answered quietly. "You're a newcomer with a bad temper and a reputation for throwing clubs and fighting. Just for icing, rumor has it that you cheated yesterday." I was tempted to add something about the visor and yesterday's clothes but decided enough was enough. "Don't worry about it. Some of the best players got off to rocky starts. We have more important stuff to worry about."

I'd picked up some pimiento cheese sandwiches earlier, and now he rummaged in the bag for one of them. Don't know what he sees in them, although they're great for the toothless. But I was glad to see some carbs going in, to soak up the adrenaline. We could not afford another bogey.

"Know one of the great things about being a Sherpa?" He stuffed the remainder of the sandwich in his mouth.

"What?" I had to wait while he processed the cheese. He pulled out the driver, took off the cover and began to swing.

"Lower heart rate." Swing. "And more efficient lung action." Swing. "Comes from living at altitude." Swing swing.

"Oh? Well, hello, you've been living at sea level—"

"And heredity."

He was trying to tell me this latest encounter had not upset him. I hoped he was right. "Wonder if it's going to rain?" I asked, to change the subject. The clouds had covered most but not all of the blue sky. It was cooler now than earlier, but on the bright side, the wind seemed to have lessened. It was still a following breeze on this hole and Stillson launched a huge drive down the right. Tony's drive was a controlled draw that ended up in the middle, a fine shot. Stillson's extra length didn't seem to bother him, which was a relief. You don't want your player to start trying to force extra yardage in the middle of a tournament. One of Tony's strengths was that he was comfortable with his game. In fact, I was beginning to see that he marched to his own drummer.

The ball was lying one-ninety-eight and the hole position was center. The difficulty with this green is that everything runs toward the pond on the left, and you have some awkward mounds front right. I studied the trees. Right-to-left wind, but not overly strong.

"What are you thinking?" I asked.

"Six'll put it in front of the green or maybe on. Six faded to the mound on the right should be safe if the wind pushes it left, and the chip's not bad either way." We had spent a couple of hours last Monday working on short shots—chips, pitches, lobs—from likely landing areas on the right.

I handed him the six-iron and watched as he shaped a shot, oblivious of the water at the left and Rae's Creek at the back. "Nice." It landed in front and hopped forward onto the green, running a couple of yards toward the flag.

"That felt good," said Tony, handing me the club.

We waited while Stillson sized up the lie and made his shot. Not so good: he got an unfortunate sidehill kick off the mound beside the green and the ball ran across and down the bank into the water. After he'd taken a drop and the dust had settled, Tony took plenty of time studying his eighteen-foot uphill putt, but in the end it slid by an inch on the left. Stillson bogeyed the hole and so, for the first time today Tony had the honor.

The twelfth was fractious, you might say, like a spoiled child that's been asked to be quiet but keeps jumping to its feet and making a ruckus. The trees would still momentarily, then suddenly rustle left, right. We came rushing through here yesterday and I had other things on my mind, but I may as well give you an idea of the challenge facing the player on this hole.

The seventeenth at Sawgrass, the "island green," is more glamorous than twelve, but no more difficult. This hole is called Golden Bell because of the yellow *Forsythia intermedia* (you learn these things when you're married to a landscaper) that blooms behind the green. Never mind that, though. It's a hundred and fifty-five yards of concentrated misery. When the wind is up it can affect the ball flight from three directions: from the east initially, then from a western crosswind, and finally from swirling winds above Rae's Creek. The setting may be soothing to players who are out of the competition, so far back that they can relax and enjoy the round. Those in contention have eyes for nothing but the green.

Unfortunately, this green doesn't fit anyone's eye. It's wide but extremely narrow front to back, and it runs away on the right. Leave the ball short and you'll roll back into the creek—unless you're lucky enough to go in the bunker. Hit long and at best you're in the steeply sloped fringe; at worst in one of the two back bunkers or in amongst the shrubs. Yesterday Tony had hooked a shot up onto the bank above the green. Today there was a wind and he was looking for birdies wherever he could find them.

Whatever you decide here, you have to commit. The flag was on the left. We stood there watching it and the trees and the flag on eleven, seeing conflicting stories of wind and calm. Sometimes all you can do is choose your club and wait until the moment seems right then hit and pray. Tony hit. I prayed. The wind died completely as he hit and he overshot the narrow green, landed in the middle-back fringe and rolled into the bunker. He had a long pitch shot, but with plenty of green to work with. Unfortunately, he left the ball short and missed a difficult fifteen-foot par putt. Another bogey.

The cut had been one-forty-eight at the turn. We were now sitting one-fifty-two. We had two par fives between us and the clubhouse, and yesterday Tony had taken a nine on the first of them, this thirteenth hole. His strategy from the start had been to play the par fives in three and go for the birdie. It's a good strategy, one that has given many players a green jacket. But it wouldn't do the job for us today.

Stillson had the honor, and Tony went into the bushes behind the tee box to commune with nature, or something. The wind was fitful, and the group in the fairway still hadn't moved off, so I sat down and ate an energy bar and gazed out at the fairway.

This is a great hole. A sharp dogleg left, with a good three hundred yards to the corner. There are azaleas—hundreds and hundreds of them—all down the left fairway and behind the four bunkers back of the green. Rae's Creek runs down the left and across the front of the green. Tony had had intimate knowledge of this yesterday. Adding a bit more zest to the hole is the sloping fairway, higher on the right running down left to the creek. A gorgeous hole where birdie is expected and eagle possible.

"This is the first golf hole I ever saw." Tony came and sat down next to me and stared out at the fairway. He spoke to himself, so softly I could hardly hear. "And if you think yesterday is going to define my experience here, you can think again." He rummaged in the bag for another pimiento cheese sandwich. "I told you about landing in jail?" He took a mouthful and I nodded. "I saw this hole on a Saturday in March after Mum picked me up from the bike shop. I had to work there every Saturday morning, part of my community service deal, what Uncle Gordon had sorted to keep me out of prison. We'd—my gang—had tried to lift a couple of their Harleys. That's when my life of crime came to a screeching halt."

"What a piece of work you were," I nudged shoulders with him and he shook his head reminiscently.

"Anyway, one of my mates had been in that morning telling me about MMA." He glanced at me and I nodded. I'm familiar with Mixed Martial Arts. Can't say I care for it much. "They were starting up a class in town, and it sounded fantastic to me. Mum wigged out when I asked her, but she did the 'ask your uncle' cop out, so I came running in the house to pop the question."

"How old were you?"

"Just turned twelve. Anyway, I came into the den and Gordon had the TV on. It was a filthy day, late March, wind and pouring rain, so he'd decided to watch one of his Masters tapes. He's got lots, but the one he had on was the 1986 Nicklaus win."

I guess millions of people thought enough of that year to buy the tape. Josh and I have it and I believe Charlie does.

"He paused it when I came bursting in, and it happened to be on this hole. I asked him about MMA and he said he'd think about it and let me know later, and I was trying to think of a polite way of saying 'get a move on' when he started the tape again. So the hole happened to catch my eye. I stood there watching for a moment, and I forgot about telling him to get a move on, and that was that."

I wondered why, exactly. He gazed out at the azaleas massed along the left fairway. "It reminded me of a place my dad took me to, a month before he died." He glanced at me. "It was a little glade near a waterfall, covered in rhododendrons all round and up the banks. I hadn't thought about it in years until that Saturday in March."

He fell silent and I thought about what he'd said. There had to be more, and almost as though he'd heard me, he went on. "It wasn't just this hole and the look. Everything I saw appealed to me. The precision. The control when you got it right. . . . The shape of the shots and the shape of the putts." He stood up and so did I. "I was enthralled with golf, right from that first day."

The fairway had cleared, and Stillson stepped up and hit a colossal fade that must have travelled three-twenty. His ball would be on the higher right-hand side of the fairway. No need to ask what club Tony wanted. It was do or die time. On the plus side, this hole played to his strength.

If you can execute it, a draw is the perfect shot here. Not only does it play into the dogleg, it gives you the extra length that helps get you round the corner. However, both shot shapes have risks. With a fade you can run through the far side of the fairway into the trees. With a draw, your ball may catch the slope and run down to the creek. (Or you can do what Tony did yesterday and just hook it in there.)

There's nothing like commitment for producing a good golf shot. Tony took a moment to close his eyes and become calm. Then he began to swing the driver, visualizing the line, then went into his routine. He produced a superb shot that curved right to left, landed and pitched forward on the slope, running ahead and staying left.

"Okay!" I said, taking the club. He'd made a clear statement here, and I hoped his family had seen it. We walked across the bridge, Tony ahead, and I found Monk waiting for me. We hadn't had a chance to chat all day, so we walked down the fairway together. He wanted to know about the guy on the eleventh tee so I told him. "Nothing to worry about, Monk," I said. "He seems to have accepted it."

He changed the subject and we talked about the Braves for a bit before he had to hoof it to catch up with his player up on the right.

We were away as usual, but this time not by much. We were looking at one-ninety to the middle of the green, with a front-left pin. The ball was sitting cleanly on the slope above Tony's feet, which of course promotes a draw. I studied the trees. The wind was against us, but fitful. The green was, from our position, slightly elevated.

"Draw a five?" I asked. He had the whole green to work with, and a five would reduce the risk of getting wet. Tony wasn't having it.

"There's no point getting on the green with a forty-foot putt for eagle. I've got to try and put it closer. Give me the six."

He began to swing the club, stepped behind the ball to trace his line, went back to swinging. "You know," he said, "I like this. I feel very calm with it."

"Let's be clear. One-ninety to the middle, so the wind should take off a couple of yards. Solid contact should do it just fine."

"I'm good with that." He continued to swing and I lifted the bag and moved away. I recalled what he'd said on the tee and as he hit I thought, *you won't be defined by yesterday.* Because the second shot was as exquisite as the drive: a perfectly shaped six-iron that landed front right, took a hop left then ran left, stopping behind the flag. We exchanged a look.

"Sweet." I cleaned the club and replaced it. We could hear applause along the fairway.

"Thanks, my little sherpa," he said with a cackle, and shoving his hands in his pockets he headed off down the fairway singing some dumb song that began, "Nice one, Cyril." Of course, he had to stop because Stillson was up there on the right. I managed to bite off a rude remark about Sherpas and instead mentioned the three guys Tashi and I had seen earlier today. I was too late, however. Tony had already had their good wishes, while he was on the practice range.

"I told them to bring their prayer wheels tomorrow."

"What's a prayer wheel?" *Why do you say these things?,* I asked myself. A prayer wheel, he said, comes from Tibet. It has Buddhist sayings written on it, and when you turn it, the sayings spin round. Turning a prayer wheel is like actually speaking the words. Some stupas have prayer wheels turning with electric power. "And I saw one in the mountains with big stainless steel bowls around the top of it, four of them. They were wind vanes, turning prayer wheels with wind power."

"No kidding?" I liked that; sort of bringing religion into the modern world. "So you wouldn't have to spend time saying your prayers. Just set your wheel up in the back yard and you're as holy as hell."

He gave me a look. "The little handheld ones make a sort of sound when you turn them. Rather like those noisemakers at New Year. The chaps promised to bring them tomorrow."

I stared at him. "You're kidding me, right?" He stared back solemnly. This had to be payback for the "holy as hell" comment. I tried to picture McWatters's face if he came across three Sherpas waving noisemakers. Gave up. "What's a stupa?" We began walking toward the green. A shrine, he said. Like Amen Corner, I guess.

The ball was ten feet back of the hole with a swale to the left, meaning it would break hard and fast down to the hole. He stroked a beautiful putt without a sign of nerves, judging the line perfectly so that it motored down and fell in smoothly, and rattled at the bottom of the cup. I think I jumped three feet in the air, but Tony didn't. He just had a huge grin on his face, and we tapped knuckles. Then Stillson was there with an equally big grin.

"Tony, that was outstanding! Congratulations," and they were shaking hands and I looked out along the fairway and there were Gordon and Tashi doing some sort of jig, with their elbows linked, dancing round, then changing elbows and dancing the other way, while patrons stepped out of their way. Mollie was nowhere in sight.

So! Suddenly we were at one-fifty-one, needing to shave another three shots off par. Assuming the cut line stayed at one-forty-eight.

Stillson was generous with his praise. Say what you like about him, he never begrudges another player's good fortune or good play. Once he'd putted out for a birdie, they walked off the green together through the crowd of patrons and he made his positive opinion of Tony very clear. That ought to go some way to offsetting all the bad press, I thought, especially when they were caught squarely on the TV camera. I'd have to ask Charlie if he saw them.

Some people think the fourteenth hole is just a way to get from thirteen to fifteen. No bunkers, no water, nearly straight fairway, yadda yadda. But the green is gigantic, with a large ridge running across it and a surface like lumpy porridge. The first priority is to get your second shot close enough to the pin to make a two-putt a reasonable prospect. That means deciding which side of the fairway you want to be on, and that depends on the pin position, which was back left. The fairway slopes left to right: if you threw a ball from the top left of the fourteenth fairway, it would roll down across fourteen, through the trees and down across thirteen into Rae's Creek. That's how the slope works here.

I was quite deliberate at the tee box, wanting to see if Tony had come down from his high, but he was all business. He took a minute to drink some water, then we discussed strategy, concluding the right-hand side of the fairway gave more green to work with.

"I'll take the three," he said. "Fade it down the left. That'll put me in the middle right and give us a good look at the pin. If I can land behind the ridge it should come back to the hole."

Both drives landed in the middle of the fairway, Stillson's well ahead and to the right of Tony's, but both in good shape for attacking the green. But that's misleading. This is a hole to treat politely, not to attack, and I was just hoping for a solid par, nothing more. Tony's ball was about one-sixty out, to a green with maybe ten feet of elevation. From the fairway the distance was deceptive because the green has a large false front. Visually, two large mounds stand one each side of the flagstick. Land the ball between the mounds and it will roll back down into the fairway. The goal is to land beyond the mounds in what passes for a flat area. Do that and the ball may feed toward the flag; even if it doesn't, you're still looking at a reasonable two-putt.

The cooler afternoon air meant the greens hadn't dried out as much as they might have, so a draw would give us the whole green to work with. However, the lie, ball below the feet, promoted a fade and that's what Tony opted for. He aligned himself to the left of the flag and hit a fine eight-iron that landed behind the mound and rolled right, ending up about fifteen feet from the hole. The break was only two feet or so, less severe than some putts on fourteen, and he managed to par the hole. We went to the fifteenth looking for another miracle.

This is the easiest hole on the course. That means it's the easiest hole to par. Today, for us, that's irrelevant. We need a three: a great tee shot, a fantastic second, from probably the two-fifty range and one putt. In short, a Hail Mary. Tony's normal strategy for this hole would be to play it in three for the birdie, so he would have to go outside his comfort zone, just as he did on thirteen, and try for a longer than normal drive. The whole plan was fraught with danger, but we could not think about that.

He did in fact get a reasonably good drive into the uphill fairway, but trying for the additional length he pulled it slightly, and when we reached the ball my heart sank. It was in the first cut, which at Augusta is not so bad, but the shot was blocked by a pine five feet in front of the ball: he would have to go back to his normal strategy, advance it a hundred and twenty yards or so, then play a knockdown wedge into the pin and get the birdie. We wouldn't be out of it if he did that, but we would have to find two more birdies going in.

"I can see a shot here, Kat."

I turned back from studying the fairway and green to see him standing well back of the ball gazing out past the tree to the fairway.

"What? No. Too risky."

He said nothing but strolled over to the bag and pulled out a wood, his five-wood. I could feel my pulse speeding up but I kept quiet. He came back and gently began swinging the club while I consulted my yardage book. I had already paced off from the mound on the right fairway up ahead. Middle of the green from here was two-forty-seven with ten yards off for elevation. No shot to the left. None. Which meant a draw. Normally that would be the safer shot anyway, from the point of view of clearing the pond. But the ball would not hold the green off a draw. It would run off the back, leaving a chip and a putt. Why bother? The percentage play is to get on in three and try for a birdie.

I was about to say this when I noticed his practice swings: long, wide, shallow path back and through. Weight on the back foot. He was going for a high draw, a difficult shot at the best of times, but one with more chance of holding the green. The problem here was the tree. The shot required him to maintain full extension after impact. He would have to force himself to make the full swing knowing he would hit the tree with an almighty bang right after making contact with the ball. Club aside, he risked real damage to his wrists. It was a crazy shot and I was about to say so when he finally spoke. He had taken several swings from a yard further back than his stance, so he could estimate where in the swing arc the tree would be hit.

"This'll be fine. I'm okay with it, Kat. I'll tell you, I had a shot similar to this a couple of years ago at Launceston, and it was just gorgeous. Same sort of tree."

Is there such a thing as a soft draw? After that shot I had to say yes. The ball came pure and clean off the clubface a nanosecond before the *crack* of the tree contact. My eyes were on the ball although peripherally I saw Tony shake his wrists for a second before he ran into the fairway to watch with me. It described an arc right to left over the pond and I thought it was going to be long, or land and hop right off the back, but it landed and held: one hop and stop.

"That's unreal. That's not possible." I'd have given a lot to see a replay.

"Oh sure it is. Nick Faldo used to hit that shot with a three-wood, never mind a five. . . ."

"On this course? To these greens?"

He shoved his hands in his pockets and turned his face up to the sky and said, with the applause in his ears, "I am so brilliant, I am, I am."

I was surveying the wreckage: one five-wood snapped just above the hosel. We'd have to get hold of Henry at TaylorMade after the round.

I had a word with Gordon as we approached the green. Tony had taken his putter and I lagged behind and met him and Tashi at the rope just before the bunker.

"My God, Kat, what a shot! Isn't he a marvel? My boy?" Next to him, Tashi looked as though she was hugging herself with glee. Then she saw the club.

"Gordon, look at that!"

"What are we at? Still one-forty-eight?"

Then Mollie was there demanding to know what she'd missed, and Tashi took her to one side after she'd given Gordon her marked up program. He compared it to his own, checking the players whose final scores were now posted, and agreed. One forty-eight. "So what does he need? A one-putt here and then a birdie?" I wasn't saying anything so he answered himself. "It seems too much to hope for."

"Take it a hole at a time." I nodded at him, then took off, hiking the bag over the other side of the fairway and using the Sarazen Bridge to reach the neck that gives access to the sixteenth tee box. It was shorter that way, and after dumping the bag I went back to the green. Stillson, who had gone off the back left, chipped up toward the center pin, then putted for birdie. Then it was Tony's turn and I took the flag from Monk and waited for the putt, watching him for signs of stress. But he seemed perfectly calm and focused, and he stroked a pure putt into the heart of the cup. Eagle.

We came off fifteen having made up four strokes in three holes and needing only a birdie on any of the last three holes. Patrick Geoghan was doing his color commentary as we walked past him to the sixteenth: "—in a serious bid to make the weekend. He'll be the only amateur if he does. . . ."

Reality bit Tony on the sixteenth tee and I realized how good his control had been up to this point. Now he had trouble breathing. I don't care what kind of lungs you've got, stress at this level shortens the breath. He wanted to reach the weekend, it was within his grasp, and he had to fight to regain his calm. I gave him a piece of banana and a Five Alive and made sure he took a good swig from it. He was still away, but the group in front had waited until he putted out before proceeding, so we were able to take a minute while they were still on the green.

It made no difference.

We'd wanted a birdie: we came away with a bogey, and Tony fought for that, having been in the right-hand bunker.

I was braced for trouble when he took a long time bending to retrieve the ball from the cup. Monk held the flag because I'd been busy raking the bunker, and when Tony straightened, red-faced, I offered myself up for the sacrifice, stepping forward, hand out for the ball and putter. But he turned his back on me, stalking off the green and throwing the club—nothing dramatic, just flinging it down—near the bag on his way to seventeen.

He disappeared into the washroom. When he came back he was all business again and the look in his eye didn't bode well for the ball. He went through his usual deliberate-with-speed routine, striped a good drive, a good second and sank his birdie putt by sheer force of will as much as skill. What a shame: with that we might have had a chance. As it was, unless he could birdie eighteen we were probably out of it. And in the end, though he tried desperately, he was unable to make the tricky twenty-footer he needed for birdie. He stood there, looking at the ground, putter in hand as I replaced the flag. Then Stillson, who had already putted out, extended a hand and when Tony turned he took hold of his shoulders.

"What a fight! I don't know if you've made it, Tony, but I've got to tell you, thirteen and fifteen, those were two of the finest second shots I've ever seen. You're a player, fella, and no mistake." He gave him a quick hug as the crowd extended its applause. I saw Mr. Anderson in among the patrons on the front left and I knew he was waiting to give his spiel for the next group, but he was clapping along with the rest with his three-by-fives in hand. I shook hands with Monk and Stillson and then Tony, and we were done.

o o o

I looked at the picture of Clifford Roberts, co-founder of Augusta National, framed and hanging on the wall next to the door. Lots of people know Bobby Jones founded the club; far fewer know that Mr. Roberts was his partner. I sometimes think the qualities it took to build this place in the middle of the Depression—nerve and determination, and perseverance and dedication—are the qualities shared by those who win here.

The sign on the door said Club Manager. I knocked. It was opened by one of the decorative guys who hang around the front office. They look to me like Ivy League ads from the last century and I'm not clear what they do. This one stepped aside and draped himself over the door handle.

"Evening, Kat," said Peter Burke, "come on in. Are we done, Alden?"

Alden said they were and with a murmur he took himself off, closing the door behind him. Peter put his head down again as he spoke, and seemed to be checking off names from one list against another. "What can I do for you?"

I sat down and pulled out an envelope. He was a tanned, neatly dressed, slender man and I got on well with him as a rule. "I wanted to thank you for sticking up for me yesterday. I know you must have, Peter, and I appreciate it."

He glanced up and smiled, shaking his head slightly. "Kat. If you'd wanted to visit Amen Corner you only had to ask. Good round today?"

"Not really. I'm not sure." I was having trouble processing his first remark. There's no way they would let people go visiting Amen Corner at night. No way. I had even considered asking him and rejected the idea because I didn't want to hear the answer. I was staring at the front of his desk and I realized he was looking at me.

"You're family, Kat. We don't throw people out on their ear if they're family. But you can surely understand Horry's position."

Horry? Short for Horrible?

"In fact, we all envy him now. You gave him a leg up when you made your little midnight visit." He leaned back and rubbed his eyes and laughed.

"What do you mean?"

"You know we have performance reviews following the tournament?"

Everyone knew about the annual performance reviews. I don't know who dreaded them more, the committee heads, the suppliers or the network. The idea was to find new ways to improve the tournament presentation, and the whole deal was started by Mr. Roberts back in the dark ages. Every year they improved things, and no aspect of the tournament, from toilets to tee times to TV presentation, was exempt. "Well, Horry's got it nailed. He's already identified three improvements to his security arrangements, thanks to you." He looked at me. "Cheer up, Kat. Oh—sorry, I—"

"No, no." I waved it off. He'd already expressed sympathy; and this was nothing to do with Josh's death—not directly, anyway. I straightened up and looked him in the eye.

"Chad Flack got fired because of me."

Peter shrugged. "What did you expect?"

I chewed my lip. "Would you give me his address?"

He regarded me. "I'm not sure I can. In any case, Horry would be the person to see—," he saw my expression, "and you can relax, there's no point. Flack broke protocol. He violated security. He won't be coming back, Kat."

I gazed out the window into the parking lot, at rows and rows of white Escalades. "Then would you see that this gets sent to him?" I pushed the envelope across the desk to him. "It's some compensation for his trouble." I'd endorsed Gordon's check over to him. It seemed the least I could do.

Burke picked up the envelope and eyed me. "You're sure?"

I nodded and turned to go. I'd included a note apologizing. It didn't seem enough. "Yeah. Thank you." Then I remembered the other reason I was here. "Could I have a day pass for tomorrow?"

O O O

The sky was odd—overcast, but with brightness all around the edges and a pink sky in the west. It was cool, not cold, and I sat down at the umbrella table between Gordon and Mollie, putting the broken five-wood by my chair. On the other side of Mollie, Ann Jameson smiled a greeting, and so did Tashi. She sat opposite me with her arms crossed, leaned back in her chair listening to Tony and Gordon rehashing the round. Tony had one arm round her and his beer in the other hand.

"I spent all day in the sand, that's really what did it. And not one of my outs—not one!—was within three feet of the flagstick. That's what did it."

"You couldn't get a putt to drop," said Gordon. "That's really what did it. Remember eight?" He looked at Tashi, who shook her head sadly.

"The horseshoe."

I suppressed a smile. She was right in there with the lingo.

Tony groaned. "That putt would have done it. Just that one putt . . . oh hell." He sighed and took a mouthful of beer. Gordon indicated the beer cup next to my elbow. "That's yours, Kat." Mollie gazed out at the western sky.

"I sent those specs to you," Tony looked across at me. I nodded. He wanted me to go ahead and get him a new five-wood, just in case he made the cut.

Mollie heaved a sigh. "It's not much like that tournament in California, is it, darling?"

Tony laughed. "Not much, mum." I knew he'd played in two Tour events, the other one in Hawaii.

"No prayer flags," said Mollie and Tashi scrutinized her.

"Just pennants they were, mum. For decoration."

If she was looking for differences between the Masters and every other tour event on earth, we could count the ways.

"No mobiles," she said, and Tashi grimaced. That was still a sore point.

"No blimp," said Tony. "No wind puppets."

"No sponsors' pavilions," said Gordon. "This thing is run the way the Open ought to be."

"No little handheld TVs," said Mollie dreamily, "so your old mother could watch things properly instead of having to run up and down hill all day." Ann laughed.

Gordon and Tony exchanged a glance.

"And no electronic scoreboards." Tony got to his feet and pulled Tashi up. "So we'll go and check out the scores on the main board."

Ann got to her feet as well. "I'm going to go home now," she said, "because I've had enough for one day. Either he'll make it or he won't." She and Mollie said their goodbyes and I bent over the program.

Tony and several other players stood at five over for the two rounds, or one-forty-nine. "The way I see it," said Gordon, "we've got four players to watch." I listened as he ran down the situation with the last few groups. It didn't look good at all. I wasn't familiar with the two international players he mentioned, but the other two were Americans, and I understood what Ann had meant because her son, Eric, was one of them.

Charlie and I once spent a rain-delayed afternoon in a trailer with Eric Jameson and his wife Erin, who caddied for him. They were a nice couple, Missouri-born, in their late twenties, with two or three small children, living and travelling in a big RV. "It's the only way we could do what we wanted," Erin had said, "have kids and be together. Otherwise Eric was going to quit golf, get his MA and teach."

Eric had won two or three times on Tour, so they were quite comfortably off financially. I knew the RV would be here this week in the lot off Berckmann Road with several others belonging to players with similar lifestyles. And the kids would be on the course, accompanied by one or both sets of grandparents. I liked the Jamesons. They were unpretentious people who had clear priorities and stuck to them. Erin had a shrewd eye for putts and a full understanding of her husband's moods and they worked well together on the course. I guessed Mollie had heard all about them from Ann.

Eric looked like coming in at well under Tony's total, but the other three had possibilities. I glanced at my watch and picked up the five-wood with its dangling head.

"Oh dear, oh dear," said Mollie sadly. "Did Lhakpa take a divot?"

"I told you, old girl." Gordon made a don't-mind-her face at me but I smiled at Mollie. I know what those azalea cocktails can do.

"Oh. The shot I missed," said Mollie sadly.

"Oh Moll, it was sublime." Gordon's face lit up and he was caught up in the moment again. "It came blazing out from behind that tree and began to climb and climb in a long shallow arc, up and up and up. Then it stopped and looked around—"

I laughed and Mollie's gaze moved to me, then back to Gordon again.

"—and began this long . . . inevitable fall, Moll. Not in the water. Not behind the green. Right, smack dab in the middle."

"Honestly, I don't know why I bothered coming," said Mollie sadly.

o o o

Luckily Henry picked up. And was in his motel room, not out somewhere for dinner. And was a stone's throw from the semi.

"Let me get out there while we talk, Kat. How's Charlie?"

We talked about Charlie's back for a minute, then he said, "Okay, I'm inside. Now, what we got?"

"I sent the specs. Did you get them?" I pictured him in the lounge area of the semi, near the entrance.

"Hang on." A pause. He was walking back into the workshop area while he found my email with the specs. "Oh sure. Hang on." Another pause, then, "Was it the five-wood you wanted?" And when I said yes, "Okay, let me put the phone down so I can read the specs while I hunt up the pieces."

I heard the rattle of shafts in a drawer as he poked through them. One drawer, another, then a third. I heard the drawers shut and reckoned he'd found the right shaft. Now he was looking through drawers of club heads. I waited patiently.

I'd picked up my phone from my locker and found Tony's club specs among my messages. Muted the ring and took the phone along to the pro shop but they didn't have Tony's five-wood. There are hundreds of clubs and his wasn't one of the newer models.

So I'd called the TaylorMade trailer. It had been here until Wednesday, alongside the trailers for Nike and Ping and Callaway and others. They're huge semis, and they always park in a corner of the shopping mall parking lot across Washington Road, courtesy of Walmart, the mall's biggest tenant. And they always leave on Thursday morning, setting out for the next PGA stop, which is Hilton Head, South Carolina.

I love visiting the trailer. You get to sit in their waiting area and have coffee and listen to Henry and his assistant, or play video games or listen to music. Whatever. Charlie always liked trying out different drivers as part of his warm-up for a tournament. It gave him a better feel for his own driver. So I'd often wander over to the semi and see what Henry had to offer in the way of new and exciting technology. They'd fit out a club in Charlie's specs—they have all their pro players' specs stored—and I'd take it back to the range for him to try out for a day or so.

Sometimes Henry would let me come on back into the workshop, and I'd look through the stacked drawers full of shafts, heads and grips ranged along the walls. The center area was a long workbench with all kinds of tools and machines.

Henry could build a new club in about a minute, almost as quickly as he could find the parts. The nice thing about Tony's club was that the hosel sleeve came attached to the shaft, so you could just insert the head and tighten the screw. He would adjust for loft (17°) and lie by resting the club head in a nifty machine with a thing like a protractor on the side; then he'd measure and cut the shaft, abrade the grip end, wrap it with two-inch tape (Tony had specified a spiral wrap rather than the vertical wrap that leaves a seam down the back), add glue and the correct grip, bond it for two minutes to dry the glue, and hey presto: one new Tony Pinasa five-wood.

"All done, Kat."

I remembered something. "You put on an E head, right, Henry?" You could get your woods matched tonally if you wanted—that is, you could have all your woods make a C sound, or D or E. Tony had specified C for driver, D for three-wood and E for his five. As I understood it, they used an epoxy layer inside each club head to vary the pitch.

"Yup. Now what?"

"Okay, now first of all, Henry, you've got to include a bill."

"A what? Are you kidding me?" Henry worked with pros all day every day. He wasn't used to amateurs so I explained that we'd have to pay for the club.

"Aw, c'mon Kat, I'm not set up for that." I let him complain for a little bit, then encouraged him to find a piece of letterhead, so he went away and did that. Then he had to find a pen. He cheered up only when it became clear that I was going to dictate what to write.

"Okay, put the date. Now put Tony Pinasa, Augusta National, Augusta GA." I let him decide what to charge and he put a hundred. Then we nearly hit a roadblock. He wanted to know what to put for sales tax and I had no idea. Luckily,

Henry had purchased a shirt earlier today so he dug out the bill for that and we used the same tax rate.

"I'm changin' it to fifty dollars, Kat. A hundred's too much. So that's half the tax. . . ."

Finally, I told him to tape the bill to the shaft and wait for a call from Al. Al, I explained, was the nineteen-year-old son of my landlord in Hilton Head, who had said he'd be thrilled to deliver a golf club to Augusta National. I thanked Henry for all his help, rang off and called Al to give him Henry's number, rang off and alerted the pro shop, who alerted the front gate, so it looked as though we were set. Lucky for Tony that Charlie Jorgensen is one of those golfers who likes to play events immediately following a major. Otherwise, Hilton Head is one tour stop I might never have made. No stop, no landlord, no landlord's son.

I found Mollie alone at the table. We listened to the crowd down around the eighteenth green where the last group was finishing up. I couldn't be bothered trying to find a gap in the crowd, though I could see Gordon was trying. Tony, on the other hand, stood on a mound overlooking the green, holding Tashi's hand. I could watch his reaction.

The situation had resolved itself to this point: forty-two players had made the cut. Two were left on the eighteenth green: Eric Jameson and his playing partner, who was comfortably under the cut line. Eric, however, had had one of the meltdowns that you get when you think you made the cut and your mind starts planning tomorrow's play, then you make a bogey and another and another. . . . Eric had been at one over. He was now lying four over (one-forty-eight), right on the line. If he parred eighteen we were finished. If he bogeyed, he joined Tony's group at five over and all of them would play tomorrow. I hoped he would not double bogey.

Mollie looked strained and tired.

"You should be very proud of your son, Mollie," I said, leaning toward her. "He played some outstanding golf today."

Her face lightened and she turned toward me to answer. Suddenly we heard the "ahhhh" of disappointment that means a missed putt. A moment's pause, then the crowd of players on the mound to the right, Tony and Tashi among them, began deliriously jumping up and down.

"He's done it! By God, he's in!" Gordon was with us, face alight as he pulled Mollie to her feet and hugged her joyously, then did the same with me. I also got kissed on both cheeks, which I wasn't expecting. Then Tony and Tashi were there, and Tony had his mother by the waist and was dancing round with her and Tashi and I exchanged victory high fives, laughing. Then Mollie asked to be put down (Tony was swinging her round by this point), so he hugged Gordon instead, while she sat down and suddenly burst into tears. Taken aback, Tashi took her hand.

"Mum! What is it?" Tony was kneeling in front of her.

"I'm sorry, darling," Mollie tried to smile. "I'm terribly happy for you but I just don't think I can take any more of this."

FRIDAY-SATURDAY

O O O O

Namche Bazaar

Namche Bazaar is an old market town in eastern Nepal where Tibetan traders used to bring their wares, and where today Sherpas still come over the high passes with their yaks laden with cheap Chinese wares for trade in Khumbu. Namche is the capital of Khumbu. At eleven thousand three hundred feet it lies on the route from Lukla to the monastery at Tengboche and beyond that, the great mountain Chomolungma, goddess mother of the world.

Thousands of tourists visit Solu-Khumbu each year, most of them choosing to head up to Khumbu and Everest rather than down to the gentler slopes and lush meadows of the Solu region. Tony's cousin Kenchi was a *sirdar* with Chhiri Sherpa Trekking. She had completed a Solu trek earlier this week and after waiting for two days for the monsoon rains to cease and the plane to arrive at Phaplu, she waved goodbye to her party of ten, as Yeti Airlines ("please pick up your heart by the gate") flew them back to Kathmandu, and hiked up to visit her mother at Namche for a ten-day break. Phaplu lies at an elevation of roughly eighty-five hundred feet. After a climb of nearly a thousand feet she came upon scores of trekkers delayed by the same rains. They were fresh off the plane at Lukla and starting on their treks up through Khumbu, sandwiched in between scores more porters, each with his or her *doko*, the wicker baskets used by Sherpas to carry the food, beer, water and kerosene required for the treks. Unencumbered except for a rucksack with a few personal items, Kenchi soon outstripped them, maintaining a steady pace up the rocky path and arriving in Namche late on Thursday.

Now, at eight o'clock on Saturday morning, she left her mother's guest house and made her way to the German bakery, already doing brisk business on market day. She bought a small loaf and set off through the narrow streets, heading west. She stopped to help three trekkers who came out of an internet café in front of her and looked around in a disoriented way. They were staying a day or two in Namche to become acclimatized and were planning a daytrip to Khumjung village, a few hours away. Kenchi walked with them to the end of the street and pointed them in the right direction.

"Will we be able to see Everest?" one of them asked.

"When you get to the top of that hill you will see Everest, and Ama Dablam and Thamserku and Lhotse," she assured them, and waved goodbye.

The trails were already busy with people and their herds coming in to market, and Kenchi wished she had been able to get away earlier. She had spent the night watching TV with family and friends. They had had some difficulty understanding the scoring and only late in the round did they realize that lower numbers were more desirable than higher ones. At some point, the Nepali sportscaster, delirious with excitement, had announced that Lhakpa would play tomorrow. But his audience, mistrustful of his enthusiasm, preferred to see it in green and white on the screen. Eventually the scores had come up and there it was, above the cut line: L.G. Pinasa. Bhuti, Kenchi's mother, had danced a little jig with her sister from Phortse, a village thirteen hundred feet higher and a day's walk away. Kenchi's cousins, one a shopkeeper and the other a Phortse potato farmer, had toasted the occasion in raksi, a grain-based beverage, potent and fresh from the still.

Bhuti owned a tea house, a whitewashed stone building with turquoise window frames. She took in trekkers during the season, and had six staying last night. Kenchi helped her mother and a girl from the village cook omelets and apple porridge for the trekkers, and while they were serving that, she cooked potato pancakes for the family. By then it was time to go, and she quickly filled her rucksack with a few necessary items, added a chunk of yak cheese and a bottle of water and set off, promising to be back for supper. One of the cousins' yaks had died and Bhuti was cooking yak sizzler tonight.

There is no motorized transport in Khumbu: the trails are its highways. The track was wide and well worn as she headed out of Namche. This particular path ran west, then northwest to Thame and north to Nangpa La, the mountain pass used by traders to reach Tibet. The Bhote Khosi (East River) ran strong on her left below, milky blue from glacial silt, and Kenchi stood off the right side of the path to make way for a boy with three laden *dzom*—yak-cattle crossbreds that were more tractable and better suited to the lower altitudes. Dzom were less likely than yaks to shove you off the path as they went by, but she wasn't taking any chances. A few minutes later a train of four yaks came past, down from Nangpa La at nineteen thousand feet and late in getting to market. Kenchi knew their owner and they exchanged greetings:

"*Tashi delek*, Phurba."

"*Tashi delek*, Kenchi."

The Khumbu scent—pine mixed with yak—filled her nostrils as she continued along the track and then she veered away onto an almost imperceptible side path, which ascended steeply along the hillside then ran through the trees. She climbed the trail through spruce and pine and juniper bushes until she came to a ridge, then descended the other side. Now she had a tributary of the Bhote Khosi on her left and the path came out into the sunlight. She passed a meadow on the right dotted with blue irises and mauve primula as the path continued its shallow, steady climb. The sun was warm and Kenchi removed her windbreaker. The monsoons would soon start in earnest and she was grateful they had held off this long. She wore a tee shirt and loose trousers, her only concession to the more traditionally minded women of the region. Her mother for instance, who wore a *yengi* (a long woolen robe made of yak hair) over her trousers. Kenchi had no time for such apparel, preferring the freedom of movement trousers provided. When the rains came she would tuck her trouser legs into long knee socks to discourage the leeches.

She came on two musk deer, a male and a heavily pregnant female. Higher in the haunch than the shoulder, they were lunching on shoots from the bushes near the trail. Musk deer are shy, reclusive creatures and these two leapt off down the trail as soon as they saw her. She gave them plenty of time before resuming her hike.

Kenchi was a popular sirdar for treks, rather than the higher-paying expeditions. You could earn more as a sirdar on a climb up Everest or Lhotse, more than twice the price for leading a trek. She had served as a porter on two Everest expeditions. But it was not what it had been when Hillary and Tenzing Norgay reached the summit. Now Everest was being climbed by people who had never climbed a mountain in their lives; they had no clue how to put on crampons or even hold an ice pick, much less use one. Indeed, it was not necessary: the summit path had fixed ropes enabling almost anyone to climb to the top.

Sherpas earned their pay on expeditions. Even when the climbers were reasonably experienced, the Sherpas still did double duty: they broke trails, fixed the ropes, set up the camp, then they went back and brought up the climbers. On treks they worked just as hard, but with slightly less risk. Even so, many westerners simply failed to realize that danger lurked on any trail, not just the vertical high-altitude ones.

Nepal offers extraordinary biodiversity within its borders. Kenchi preferred trekking mostly because her education had given her a good grounding in the different ecosystems of her country, and she enjoyed showing interested tourists some of the varied plant and animal life: there were more than 800 bird species alone.

She had learned her KaKhaGa's (ABCs) at the Hillary school in Khumjung. She spent a year there, and if her parents had had their way, that would have been the end of her formal education. In common with most Sherpas at that time, they held that everything worth knowing could be learned in the space of a year. But luckily trekking had been lucrative, and Uncle Chhiri had made no secret of the fact that he would be sending his own children to the School for Hill Children in Kathmandu. So Kenchi had been sent to SHC when she was seven, along with her older brother Kalden.

Her father had died when she was thirteen, during the civil war. Tourism had fallen to a trickle and Khumbu was hurting. Kenchi and Kalden had learned what happened to their father when they flew home for the funeral. He had taken his yaks over Nangpa La to bring back trade goods, goods he could sell in Kathmandu. He had been spotted by the Maoists on his way back and shot dead along with his yaks.

Kenchi hated the Maoists. She saw a picture of one of the leaders in the newspaper, and stored it away in her mind. Four years later, she was a porter on a trek that included Nangpa La. Making the climb over several days to allow the trekkers to acclimatize, the party eventually reached the pass. The trekkers stood near the post marking the border, looking over into Tibet but staying on the Nepal side. Tourists who strayed into Tibet had been shot here in the past by Chinese border guards. Prayer flags marked the pass itself, spreading peace and compassion on the wind. Ahead they could see the barren, bleak Tibetan plateau; to the right, or east, rose the peak of Cho Oyu. Everest was thirty miles away, its summit shrouded as always in wisping cloud.

Kenchi stayed behind after the trekking party started back down to the camp. She stared out at the plateau and summoned the picture of the Maoist leader in her mind. She prayed that he and his henchmen might each be covered in leeches wherever they were. She felt better after that, and turned to hasten after the others.

She was twenty-five now, and although she had not read any accounts of Maoists being covered in leeches, she no longer hated them. In any case, today was much too nice for hating anything. Rounding another bend in the trail she saw a pheasant pecking at a moss-covered tree. She stopped and watched him—it was a male Himalayan Blood Pheasant with the red markings on tail and throat. Then he must have sensed or seen her because he gave the warning *si-si-si* cry and she knew his mate must be around somewhere close, incubating their eggs.

At noon, she stopped to eat her lunch of bread and cheese, watched attentively by a pair of yellow-billed choughs. When she'd finished, she entertained herself by throwing pieces of bread high into the air over the gorge, where the Bhote Khosi tributary rushed by below. The two birds swooped and dived for the bread. She finished off with a chocolate bar, then packed her rucksack and continued along the path. Half an hour later, she heard the waterfall in the distance. Eventually she rounded a bend and there it was, the end of the tributary, a long slender cascade of water, dropping fifteen-hundred feet down the mountainside to the bottom of the gorge.

Along the trail, lining it and extending up the right bank were masses of dwarf rhododendrons, red, pink, white and yellow. They were most profuse in a glade near the trail. In the center of the glade, covered in moss, stood an ancient *mani* stone, one of the many prayer stones found along the Khumbu trails.

Kenchi removed a small collapsible shovel from her rucksack. Using this and her hands she stripped the moss away and cleaned it off to reveal the prayer "Om Mani Padme Hum" etched in the stone. Then she dug a shallow hole under a rhododendron, and removed a small round Simpkins Blackcurrant Drops tin from her rucksack. Inside were three photos, taken last summer. The first was in Cornwall, and showed Lhakpa with his arm round Aunt Mollie, and her brother Gordon on his other side. The second photo, which Kenchi had taken herself, was of Lhakpa and Tashi outside the office in Thamel, the tourist section of Kathmandu. Behind them the sign was plainly visible: Chhiri Sherpa Trekking. The third photo, taken in the same place, was of Kenchi herself with Ruth Cameron.

Kenchi had no memory of Lhakpa at SHC, but she had been three years older, a vast difference to young children. Her earliest memory of him was a letter she received in the autumn of 2001, after he had gone to England. It came with a letter from Aunt Mollie and both were addressed to Kalden and Kenchi. The printing was large and there were few words on each of its two pages, and Kenchi only remembered it for one thing: it was the first she'd ever heard of corduroy. "The people here have strong bottoms," Lhakpa had written, "and they wear corduroy." Kalden had divided the job of responding in two: he wrote to Aunt

Mollie, and Kenchi to Lhakpa. Since she couldn't make head or tail of his letter she simply expressed her sorrow at Uncle Chhiri's death and told him about geography class, where they were learning about Europe, including England.

They had corresponded infrequently by email after that, and last year, when Lhakpa and Aunt Mollie came to Kathmandu, they met. Lhakpa was amazingly tall, much taller than most Sherpas, but he had a funny sense of humor and Kenchi liked him. She introduced him to Pasang, her friend who was a carpenter with Pete Cameron's construction company. Kenchi and Pasang had a place of their own in Kathmandu and she was working up the courage to tell her mother about him, although she had a sneaking suspicion mum already knew. Pasang had converted to Buddhism last year and Pete was pleased with his work.

They went out to dinner one night in Thamel with Lhakpa and Tashi, and it was while they were eating their pizzas that Kenchi mentioned the corduroy letter. Lhakpa denied writing it. "It was—most strange," said Kenchi to Tashi. "We thought he must have lost his reason because of grief. He was talking about the English people having strong bottoms?" She looked to see if this meant anything to Tashi, who had lived there.

"This is a complete fabrication," said Lhakpa to Pasang, around a mouthful of pizza. "She's just making it up." Pasang replied seriously that in his experience Kenchi did not make things up.

"Strong bottoms?" Tashi was mystified.

"And wearing corduroy," Kenchi recalled.

Then Lhakpa had choked on his pizza crust and after Pasang had thumped him on the back he'd laughed his head off. Eventually he mentioned Lama Sangwa and Pangboche, and Kenchi had understood—sort of.

Lama Sangwa Dorje had great magical powers. He flew into the Khumbu region one day to survey the terrain. He went to Tengboche first, then flew to nearby Pangboche, the little village two days up the mountain from Namche. He sat down on a rock to consider his options and eventually he decided to build his first monastery there, at Pangboche. Later on, long after Lama Sangwa had left, long after the monastery had been built, the monks had taken the rock on which he sat, with its imprint of his bottom, and put it behind a screen in the monastery. You could see it there to this day, along with a mural depicting the lama himself.

"We're going there in a few days," said Lhakpa. "Tashi's never been to Khumbu and I want to show her round."

"Yes, but what about the strong bottoms?" asked Tashi.

"And the corduroy," added Kenchi.

"Powerful bottoms. That's what I meant," said Lhakpa. "It was the pews at the Anglican Church."

The Anglican Church in the village of Marstow had been renovated in the late nineteenth century—1868 according to a plaque in the nave. The renovations had extended to the pews, which had been sanded down and varnished. Someone had underestimated the time required for the varnish to dry fully, and that was why to this day, you could see the lines from the men's corduroy breeches. "That's what the farmers wore for Sunday church," finished Lhakpa. "So there was I, brought up on Lama Sangwa sitting on a rock, so I thought these Anglicans were pretty hot stuff, I can tell you."

The others considered this. "Sorry, I'm not impressed," said Tashi at last. "Stone tops wood any day," she said, and the others agreed.

"I was only seven," Lhakpa apologized.

Remembering that evening last summer, Kenchi smiled. Tashi had told her, days later, of being duly impressed by the Pangboche rock. They had also come here, Kenchi knew, although Tashi said nothing about that. Before he left, though, Lhakpa arranged for her to bring the photos. "Sometime before next April, Kench, can you?" Kenchi had promised.

She made sure the Simpkins sweets lid was secure on the tin, pushed it down into the soil under the rhododendron bush and replaced the topsoil. Then she got to her feet and repacked her rucksack. This offering to the spirit of Chhiri was Lhakpa's idea, to let his father know that his family and business were well. If the monsoons had not delayed her, it would have been done before Lhakpa had started on Thursday. Kenchi was relieved he had made it through to the weekend.

She turned and began her walk back to the main trail and home to yak sizzler for supper and seven more days' holiday before her next trek.

Kathmandu

Vineeta looked up from the transcript as Jay, another reporter from Dharmedia, came down the stairs to the basement, nodded to the policeman and sat down at the long table across from her.

"Did you find them all?" she asked.

He nodded. "One died. I talked to the others. They confirmed they were away that night."

"Let me finish this interview." She bent over the document once more.

He had a newspaper cone full of *aloo chaat*—deep-fried potatoes with a savory chutney sauce—and he poured some out on to a piece of paper and shoved it across the table to Vineeta. He ate his portion using a business card as a spoon.

They were in the basement of the Home Ministry. The table was positioned in the center of the room with a long fluorescent light suspended above it. All round the walls were boxes, large plastic boxes, translucent with blue lids and labels on their sides, stacked ceiling high in metal racks. When Vineeta had first seen them, late yesterday, her heart sank. But then the Assistant to the Undersecretary showed her the section at the far end, where all the boxes were labeled June 1, 2001 followed by a description of the contents. He had instructed her severely not to touch any other boxes but these. She had assured him she had no interest in any subject but the massacre, but he left nothing to chance, and ten minutes later a policeman took up his station at the foot of thc stairs.

She began to investigate the boxes using the table as a center of operations. An hour later, following a phone call to the group manager, she was joined by Jay.

"*Ke ho ke ho,*" he said when he saw all the boxes. What to do?

"Get a box," said Vineeta curtly. She disliked that expression: in her opinion, it was tantamount to giving up. So they put their heads down, sorted through the boxes and formulated a plan of attack. They disregarded the boxes of hospital records, likewise those from the morgue. There was another containing observations from the CIA, MI6 and the BBC, all of whom had evidently put in their two bits' worth. One gruesome box contained a diagram showing where parts of the heads of two victims, machine-gunned at close range, had been found, as well as a large scene-of-the-crime diagram showing the positions of all the victims. This they opened up on the table. They found a box of ADC-related information, including shifts, holiday schedules, and a roster of the ten *aides de-camp* who served at the palace.

They decided their first task was to look for anyone who shouldn't have been there, or who was mentioned in a deposition but not listed as having been there. So, from the boxes containing all the depositions, they made a list of the survivors, ADCs and servants known to have been at the Friday night gathering. They made a list of all the victims. They stared at the list and at the diagram, and then at each other, shocked at the devastation wrought by one troubled individual.

By then it was 9:30 pm. Four hours earlier, the Assistant had come down and told them they would have to leave, at which time Vineeta had informed him that not only were they not leaving, they expected to be able to come in over the weekend. This necessitated another call to the group manager, who pulled a string or two that culminated in the Assistant arranging with the police to provide a guard for as many days as the reporters deemed necessary. So at ten they quit for the night, arranging to return early this morning. Vineeta had wakened around five to the sound of firecrackers as people came out into the streets celebrating

Lhakpa's having made the cut. She arrived at the government offices at ten to seven and a policeman let her in. Jay, as agreed, was going to track down the four off-duty ADCs and find out their whereabouts on the night of June 1, 2001.

Vineeta had decided her first task was to read through all the depositions and make sure none of them referred to a person who was not on their list. That turned out to be relatively easy, and after two hours she stopped for a break, studying the big crime diagram with a more informed eye. Now she planned to re-read the transcripts, looking for discrepancies among them. She began with the survivors' testimony, distraught and in most cases brief. The servants' testimony had little direct bearing, since none had been at the scene. When Jay returned with his bag of *chaat* she was just finishing the last of the ADCs' depositions. She sat back in her chair and they tried to summarize.

"So, no one was there who shouldn't have been."

"Or if he was," amended Vineeta, "no one saw him."

"So are we finished? There's no story here."

But Vineeta was not ready to quit. "Now we'll make our own diagram, and mark on it what each person said and where they were." She had brought a roll of drawing paper for the purpose and they tore off a large piece and used boxes to hold each end in place.

They drew a large rectangle for the billiard hall and marked the positions of all the victims: the King, his daughter, his sisters and other relatives. They marked the locations of the survivors, at the other end of the hall. Then they drew the Crown Prince's bungalow, at right angles to the hall, and marked the bodies of the Queen and her younger son, Nirajan, on the verandah steps, Prince Raman and Chhiri Sherpa in the study at the far end of the bungalow, and finally the body of the Crown Prince himself, in the garden between the hall and the bungalow. They had discovered that Jay had the better hand for drawing, so Vineeta read from each of the depositions while he marked up the drawing. The survivors' reports produced nothing but minor differences as to the positions of victims or other survivors. The ADCs' reports, however, were different. These were trained soldiers, less shocked than the family members they served, and their testimonies had been more detailed. And eventually, once they had marked the position of each ADC according to his own deposition and confirmed by at least one other person, they did indeed uncover an interesting discrepancy. They were discussing it when the group manager called.

"Find anything?"

"We think so," said Vineeta. "Five ADCs broke in through the south entrance to the billiard hall. The sixth drove round to the east end of the bungalow because he was ADC to Prince Raman. He was the first to see the Crown Prince in the garden. He should have been seen by the others when they came out into the garden. But he isn't mentioned in anyone else's deposition until much later. I estimate after nine-thirty."

There was a silence from the other end, then the group manager spoke. "Raman was the one planning the trek with Chhiri, wasn't he?"

"Yes." Vineeta motioned to Jay to pass over the official report, on top of one of the piles of documents. She leafed through it and found the place. "They were supposed to go trekking the next day," she said into the phone.

"Chhiri was the father of Lhakpa Pinasa," said Jay helpfully.

Vineeta shot him a look: everyone knew that. Then her expression changed.

"What?" said Jay.

"Oh my," said Vineeta.

"No . . ." said Jay, shaking his head in disbelief.

"Yes," responded the group manager. "This needs careful thought. Gather up all your notes and come back to the office."

o o o

The house spoke of old money, a rambling two-story bungalow on a large property north of the city, old shade trees lining the drive. A deep verandah extended round all four sides, and at the rear, facing the distant mountains, Colonel Bikram Basnet sat with a guest. Both men wore civilian clothes. They were smoking cheroots and both had drinks, served in Stuart crystal tumblers. The crystal had been brought out from England in the trunk of a Rolls Royce Silver Ghost, carried over the mountain passes in 1920.

"I hope you will pass on our concerns to your principals, Colonel," said his guest, formerly an Army captain, now an engineer in private life. He was in his early forties, ten years younger than Colonel Basnet. "A plant of that size cannot possibly be economic."

Behind them, a small study opened onto the verandah, and plans for a three hundred kilowatt hydroelectric plant lay spread on the desk.

"Please don't concern yourself," said the Colonel. "I wanted that size as a gauge of the cost. We may choose a larger plant. You have heard the American phrase, 'build it and they will come'? That is in our minds." He drew on his cheroot, and began to question his guest. The smog was not so bad today, and the Himalayan peaks were clear and clean in the distance. Absorbed in conversation, the two men scarcely noticed.

They discussed construction costs using local labor, and maintenance costs using local technicians. The Colonel was interested in the numbers of people involved at both stages. They moved on to consider the population limit for a plant of this size. The engineer suggested that the plant could serve several hundred additional families if people from remote villages were to use batteries recharged at stations located on the grid perimeter. "Carrying a battery to a recharging station once a week would be no different than carrying cans of kerosene, and the cost would be about the same or less." A thought occurred to him. "Would families be expected to pay for their power?"

"Yes. It's our thinking that if it were free, people would waste it. Tell me what kind of lighting would be used in these peripheral homes, the ones using batteries?"

The engineer described the battery-run lighting options, then ran down the installed cost per family. The quality of light would be far better, he noted. "And there would be no kerosene fumes." His host nodded, appreciating the point.

When they had exhausted the details surrounding the power plant, and the manservant had refreshed their drinks, the Colonel went over to the desk and returned with a photograph. He sat down again and leaned forward, extending it to his guest. "What does this look like to you?" he asked.

The engineer barely glanced at the photo. "It's a surveyor. Or part of a survey team," he answered, then looked more closely. "Is he Chinese? Where was this taken?"

"Inside the border," answered the Colonel, "north of Dipayal. Tell me what he's holding."

The photo showed a Chinese male standing on a rocky outcropping holding a metal pole. The angle of his glance was downward. The pole had a small square attachment about a foot below its top end.

"What is a Chinese surveyor doing, north of Dipayal? My firm is aware of every construction project underway—." He stopped and, with a glance of apology, answered the question. "It's a laser receiving rod. Do you see that small box? That receives the beam and records elevation and slope." He glanced at his listener, who nodded. "Laser beams are difficult to see in the daylight. This is a more accurate method."

He handed the photo back and rose abruptly to his feet, pacing along the verandah. He stopped, staring at the distant mountains, then returned to his chair. It was apparent that he was still agitated. "Please excuse me, Colonel, but this," he gestured toward the photo, "this is most upsetting."

The Colonel began to reply, but the engineer went on. "China, as you know, is building dams throughout Tibet to feed its industries. India is crying out for power to feed its industries. Nepal needs power to attract industry, and we have so much potential power we could export it." He tapped the photo sharply. "We have the expertise to build these plants! But what do we do?" He got up, turned away and smacked one of the verandah's supporting pillars in frustration. "We let the Chinese build them for us! Instead of using our own people, we let the Chinese do it! And why? Because investors won't touch us!"

Colonel Basnet forbore to mention that the Chinese presence was unofficial. Instead, he waved his cheroot at the drawings in the study. "Perhaps this will be the start of something—"

"With all due respect, Colonel," the engineer interrupted, "This isn't the answer! We don't need little plants, we need bloody great big ones!" He paused, and then spoke again more calmly. "We don't like China, we don't trust India, the plants we do build are sabotaged, and the government does nothing. Nothing! The politicians twiddle their thumbs and bellyache about rights and the constitution! Is it any wonder investors won't even look at Nepal?"

An hour after the engineer had departed, Colonel Basnet was still reflecting on these words. He debated pouring another drink but changed his mind. He might need a clear head this afternoon.

His wife was away visiting their married daughter in Hyderabad. His son was a lieutenant in the army, stationed with the Western Combat Division in Dipayal. He was alone except for the servants, enjoying his solitude. He returned to his chair on the verandah, and gazed absently at the mountains. What to do about China? He looked at the photograph. He'd used his contacts and made discreet inquiries. He could find no record anywhere of a team of Chinese engineers entering the country officially. He'd asked his son to check the Dipayal hotels. Nothing.

He shook his head in frustration. He would submit a report; and the report would be quietly buried. To gain exposure he would have to go outside official channels. Could he leak the story to a newspaper abroad? Quite aside from the propriety of such an action, who would care? Yes, China was gaining more and more control in Nepal, but its diplomats could argue that China only wished to help Nepal as well as itself.

The country had suffered one setback after another since the mid-90s. First the civil war, the lives lost and the decline of tourist revenues in an already poor country. Then the death of the king, and later, the post-war period: the debate about what to do with the Maoist army; the incessant strikes; the interminable constitutional wrangles..

These days the country was governed by the Maoist party, and it would probably continue to be, thought Colonel Basnet, as long as people believed their lies. He agreed with the engineer about international investors. Nepal desperately needed infrastructure and business investment. But no bank wanted to touch a corrupt, illiterate Asian country. That was how the world saw Nepal—if the world saw it at all. The world . . . most of the diplomatic, political and social world was invited to the American Embassy's all-night Masters function on Sunday night. He himself had received an invitation, along with other members of the military. That function might serve his purpose. He began to consider ways and means of using the photo to best effect—or at the very least, giving the Chinese diplomat, Mr. Hu, a great fright.

The manservant appeared at the study door. "A newspaper reporter is here and wishes to speak with you, Colonel."

This need not take long, he thought. Earlier that day, an old colleague, a former ADC to the palace had phoned.

"They're reopening the case, Bik. I wasn't even there. Have they called you?" He had been expecting a phone call, not a visit, but it scarcely mattered. He would refer the reporter to the official transcript.

He walked through to the front entrance and introduced himself to the young woman waiting there.

"I am Vineeta Bhool of the Everest Times," she said. "Colonel, are you the Major Basnet who served as ADC to Prince Raman?"

"I am." He smiled. The reporter gazed back stolidly.

"Colonel, we have an eyewitness who saw you drive off the palace grounds on the night of June 1, 2001, no more than five minutes after the shootings."

There was silence except for the trickle of a small water fountain set into the marble of the entrance.

"Please come through to the sitting room," he indicated the direction and stood to one side. "We can talk more comfortably in here." He followed Vineeta into the sitting room. "Bhool? Your family works with leather? How interesting."

SATURDAY

o o o o

The ardent golfer would play Mount Everest
if somebody put a flagstick on top. –Pete Dye

Kat's Story

Saturday. Moving Day. Now we're into the weekend and everyone, amateurs excepted, gets a paycheck. Tony was the only amateur left in the field so fifty players would share the prize money tomorrow night.

The lead was three under par, and nine players were in red numbers. A large group, half the field, were somewhere between even and three over, and we could expect to see big moves both ways today.

There are no threesomes on the weekend, and Tony was paired with the big South African, Pieter Vanderhoef, one of the nicest guys on Tour. He had a green jacket and two other major wins and the only thing wrong with his game right now was his putting.

Our tee time was 10:45. I joined Tony on the range early to find him pleased with his new five-wood. "Hear that?" he said, then off a supposed mis-hit "And that? Hear the difference?" I couldn't hear any difference but Tony said the sound was fuller and more rounded (his words) when perfectly struck. Same with his driver and three-wood. Whatever works.

It seemed to me his tempo was on the fast side and getting faster. I waited a bit, watching him, just to be sure, and eventually I spoke. "How about easing up?"

He stopped, glancing back briefly.

"We're going to have a great time the next two days. No need to rush it."

I couldn't see his face but he went very still and I assumed he was doing one of his zone outs.

"Thanks, Kat," he said finally, and resumed hitting balls, but more slowly now.

He'd picked up the five-wood from the guard at the front entrance. Hilton Head Al had left it there and been given his day pass. "Thanks for all your help," said Tony as we surrendered our spot and walked over to the short-game practice area. I asked if they'd had a good time last night. Ann Jameson had invited them for barbecue and they'd all gone: Gordon and Mollie, after she tidied up and put on some fresh makeup, and Tony and Tashi.

"Yeah. Mum had a nice time, I think. We left early."

We quit around nine. "I want to spend some time with Tashi," he said and went off to shower and change.

I spent half an hour on the caddie shack porch with coffee, a Danish and the pin sheet. When I took the bag along to the main practice green Tony was there, talking to Pieter Vanderhoef. I was vaguely surprised to see him and couldn't figure out why; then I remembered: yesterday, shortly before tee off he and Tashi had gone to sit in the Escalade in the players' parking lot behind the range, and I'd assumed they'd do that today. It was about the only place offering any kind of privacy. I'd seen them as I made my way up to the practice green, and had stopped, thinking Tony might have some instruction. He had just locked the Escalade's door and was waiting at the rear, laughing, with his hand extended. Tashi emerged from the far side and they walked in my direction hand in hand, happy in each other's company in the warm sun. Then their eyes must have met because they turned to each other and kissed, and I remembered what it was like at that age, when passion lay just underneath the skin and the slightest touch ignited it. I realized I was staring, and turned and continued on to the green, feeling a kind of emptiness inside.

That was yesterday, however. I joined Pieter and Tony.

"Sorry for your loss, Kat," Pieter greeted me. I gave him a smile and he turned back to Tony.

"Having fun yet?"

"We-ell . . ."

Pieter laughed. "Today'll be better. We got a reprieve, right?" He had his putter in hand and he nodded and turned away.

"Nice guy," said Tony to me.

"One of the best."

He too went to hit some putts and I walked over to the bag.

"Good morning, Kat! How are you?" Mollie looked relaxed and rested. People don't realize how hard tournaments like the Masters are on the families. If your son or husband is in contention the stress can be almost crippling. I'd been a bit worried about Mollie yesterday. "We had a lovely time," she said in answer to my question. She gave me a box of energy bars and said she was off to commune with the magnolias in the lane.

I waved a hand as she left, and did my pre-game check: clubs, balls, spare markers, band-aids, water, socks, rain gear. Opened the box of bars and dumped them into the bag. Filled the water bottles with fresh. We were light on balls so I walked over to the pro shop to pick up a couple of sleeves.

It was a beautiful morning, an absolutely perfect day, not a cloud in the sky. I'd heard rain in the night, not a lot but some. That meant nothing in terms of green speed: all the greens at Augusta have built-in irrigation/drainage systems. Some, like number twelve, have heating systems as well. After a rain you can hear the suction system at work even under parts of the fairways, pulling the moisture out of the ground.

I met Tashi coming back; she'd been looking at the scoreboard. She said she was fine in answer to my question and that she'd had a good time last night. I wasn't sure I believed her.

"What did they serve for dinner?" I knew she wasn't a big meat eater but she smiled and said, "It's just that I had hoped Lhakpa and I might spend some time together, that's all."

Sounded reasonable to me. "What did you think of the RV?"

"Very nice, Kat," she said briskly. "Very . . . mobile."

"Mobile?"

"I'm a bit sick of the subject, if you really want to know. Lhakpa went completely gaga over it. As far as I'm concerned, if you want mobility, take a plane."

"Hear, hear!" Gordon came up behind us, giving Tashi a one-armed hug. "Morning, Kat."

We'd reached the practice green, and I fished out my marker from one of the bag's side pockets.

"Hey! Kat! Thanks for the pass!"

It was Hilton Head Al, clutching a pairing sheet and walking on air.

"Morning, Al. Thanks for bringing the club."

"You're welcome!" Broad grin, eyes darting everywhere, trying to take it all in at once. "Wow, this is *so* great. Omigod, is that Pieter Vanderhoef?"

He was off, darting around the patrons to get to the far side of the green. I started to put Tony's mark on the new balls: a star cradled in the tail of the capital T in Titleist. Gordon and Tashi had gone down to the first tee and were chatting with the Jamesons, teeing off ahead of us this morning.

"Hiya, Kat." Kirk Wegler, Pieter's caddie, dumped his bag next to mine.

"Morning, Kirk. Beautiful day, huh?" He looked a little frayed around the edges and I suppressed a grin. "Good time last night?"

"Oh man, I got so blitzed. We were out till three." He eyed my marker. "You finished with that?"

I passed it over and he rummaged through his bag for balls, then ran over to the pro shop and returned with a box of Nikes. Ripping open each sleeve he dumped all twelve balls into his bag and began to put Pieter's mark on them: three dots under the tick. He went on describing his evening as he worked.

Kirk's a big, good-looking guy, about twenty-five, a member in good standing of the PGA high-flyers club. They're serious partyers, those guys. At each event they hook up with the Bimbettes, or vice versa. The PGA wives shun the Bimbettes but that doesn't stop them being regular as wives at each Tour stop.

I keep expecting to hear that Kirk's been fired, but it hasn't happened yet. He's habitually late and often dozy, but Pieter's easy going. I'm not sure he'd fire him even if Kirk failed to turn up at all. He'd just make do for the day and Kirk would turn up with some winning excuse and Pieter would give in and they'd go along once more. Pieter's in his mid-thirties. His first caddie was an elderly South African, surly, wily, full of course knowledge and Tour grievances. He died two years ago and Pieter's had Kirk since then. They must have something in common but I'm not sure what.

He finished marking balls and I retrieved my pen. "I'm just going off for a bite, tell Pieter, okay?"

I counted Tony's clubs. Rule 4-4 allows you fourteen clubs in your bag. You hear stories now and then about players getting penalized for having too many clubs. People ask me sometimes how a caddie could make such a basic mistake. Let me tell you: it's incredibly easy. At most tournaments, equipment reps are all over the grounds pushing their products, and players are always trying new clubs: drivers, putters, hybrids, you name it. They'll try one on the range, meet up with their caddie, walk over to the tee, strike up a conversation about the course, and fail to mention the new driver stuck in amongst all the other clubs. So there it sits in the bag: a two-stroke penalty waiting to happen, which it does as soon as the player tees off.

You don't find equipment reps at the Masters, at least not officially, but that doesn't alter my routine. I count Charlie's clubs on the practice green, then again on the first tee. I'd just finished counting Tony's for the first time when he returned. More players were arriving at the practice green, and I took his putter, wiped and replaced it in the bag. He was gazing down at the tee box where Tashi stood with Gordon and Mollie.

"Let's have clean, flush hits all day," I said, hoisting the bag. We walked over.

"Is that Kat's positive thought for the day?"

"Could do worse."

"No, it's a good one. Let's do it. Clean and flush." We reached the tee box. "If we get pushed for time I'll just think toilets." He laughed his head off.

Crowds were milling round the practice green and here around the first tee. We're into the weekend now, into the savvy patrons. They might lend their badges for Thursday or Friday play—you could discharge some serious debt by lending your badge for a day—but not on the weekend. These people are here to watch some golf. Like the elderly lady over at eighteen, hat and vest covered in year after year of Masters series badges. She sat down heavily in a chair behind the second mound on the right of the green, just outside the rope. She's been in the same spot for at least the last ten years.

I chatted with Gordon and Mollie for a moment, while Tony and Tashi stood together nearby. Whatever was going on between them seemed to have disappeared; they kissed and I heard Tashi's cheerful, "Good luck."

"Break a leg, Kat," Gordon smiled.

I stepped inside the rope and did a club recount as we waited for the group ahead to move out of range. Pieter took out his driver and began to swing, while Tony rummaged in the bag for his visor. It was no big deal today: just SHC on both sides, stitched in bold green letters on the white visor. I must have looked puzzled, because he said, "School for Hill Children. It's where we went in Kathmandu."

"Better than yesterday." I handed him the driver.

He grinned, swinging easily. "I've got nothing else to put on there, not like all these tycoons."

Pieter had logos for three different companies on his cap, shirt collar and breast pocket. These areas are valuable real estate to a pro. I'd guess Pieter, as a top ten professional, made around ten million dollars a year from his endorsements. Alex likely makes double that. And these are recession numbers, remember. Ten years ago you could have added five million to that total, or more. Tony, I thought, would be one of these tycoons soon enough.

"Fore, please. Pieter Vanderhoef now driving." And we were off.

o o o

That was a wonderful day of golf, the best day of majors golf I ever experienced, virtually stress free. Amazing. The two players hit it off, that was part of the reason. They talked about rugby and wine-making and their respective homes (Pieter spent most of his time at his home in Hampshire). The main reason, though, was that Pieter had nothing to prove and Tony nothing to lose. Neither player was protecting a lead, and neither played cautiously. They started strongly, with birdies on the first hole, but it was what happened on two that really elevated the round into something magical. Because on two they put up matching eagles.

Let me give you an idea how unusual that was. I've caddied forty rounds of Masters golf over the past ten years and I haven't seen more than three or four eagles on this hole—from either Charlie or his playing partner—in all that time. Some of the world's best golfers have never eagled number two: it's a tough, tough hole. So to see two eagles at once was almost disorienting. Pieter, who is always a long hitter, put a gorgeous second shot thirty feet from the pin. Tony, who hit first, refused to lay up. It was as though he was giving himself a prize for the past two days' effort, for simply making the cut—I don't know. Whatever the reason, he went for the green in two and put his second shot in the bunker.

"Ah! Sand practice!" He sounded cheerful. It was that kind of day.

Luckily the ball did not bury, and he connected beautifully on the shot. It dropped on to the green and rolled sedately into the hole. That was one bunker I really enjoyed raking. So then Pieter, once he and Tony had high-fived it, gave his putt a long scrutiny from all angles, read it perfectly and sank it as well. Two eagles. Just to finish the subject of eagling number two, there were only eight eagles on this hole from the entire field over all four days and I personally witnessed three of them. But I'm getting ahead of myself.

There was a slight hiccup in the magic when Tony bogeyed the tough third hole, but he managed to sink a birdie putt on the fifth. Pieter was not so lucky. His putter betrayed him on the fourth, when he missed a five-foot par putt. He got into trouble off the tee on the narrow fairway of number seven, and chose to put his second in the front bunker. He ended up with a par putt of about ten feet, below and to the right of the hole. Tony and I reckoned it would break an inch left but Pieter played it for pace, straight at the hole, and it slid by.

We chatted in the seventh fairway while waiting for Pieter. Standing in the warm sun with a gentle, untroublesome breeze, we listened to a nearby flicker. *Kyeer, kyeer,* rat-tat-tat. Earlier, on number five, as we waited in the fairway, we'd spotted a pair of cardinals in the bushes near the fairway bunker.

"It's extraordinary that I can make a living doing this," said Tony. He smiled up at the sky. "You know, Tashi was the first person to tell me it was okay to do what I loved doing best." He laughed. "She put my cousin Kalden's nose out of joint. She said we were both lucky because we knew what we wanted to do and we were doing it. He was training to be a doctor and he always said I should do something useful for my country. He was seriously disturbed when Tashi lumped golf in with saving lives."

We came to the par-five eighth hole three under, with Pieter one under. The action out of the gate had attracted some noise. That aside, Pieter is always popular, so we had quite a crowd following us. Tony was playing number eight in three, so his tee shot was left of the bunker and fairly close to it. Pieter, however, let it rip and landed in a wonderful position well beyond the bunker on the right of the fairway.

"That's a three-oh-five carry," I heard a patron say through the applause. "Uphill. Can you believe it?"

"He's on 'roids. Has to be."

I began walking immediately since we were going to be away. Tony followed with Pieter, and Kirk, looking a little less frayed, brought up the rear. Today's flag was in the front middle and Tony put his second shot out on the left, leaving a wedge into the hole. Pieter was lying about two-sixty-five from the green in the right side of the fairway, with a perfect view of the long green and front flag. In the end, he launched a three-wood that streaked upward high above the trees then fell like a stone just back-center. Lying two with a longish, downhill putt for eagle. Polite applause. He looked over at us and made a where-do-I-go-to-surrender gesture. Masters patrons can be, let's say, restrained with their approval.

A mound between us and the green obscured the bottom of the flagstick. Once we reached the ball I walked forward and retraced my steps. "Seventy-five to the flag. You can do this. No spin."

He stared silently at thc pin for thirty seconds at least, then "Yeah. Okay." He took his sand wedge and began to swing, smooth swings through the ball position. What you want here is just enough spin to stop the ball dead, but no more. If you wanted plenty of spin you'd put the ball back in your stance and hit down on it. Tony kept his arms and wrists quiet, just swinging smoothly through the ball. Finally he stepped back, went through his routine and hit a high soft shot that landed abreast of the flag to the left, then trickled slowly down and away. More polite applause.

By the time we had come to the green Pieter had finished studying his putt from in front of the hole and was now behind his ball, gauging the line. Tony marked and tossed me his ball and I inspected and cleaned it. You can change balls, but only after the hole is played, unless there's something seriously wrong, like a cut in the cover.

Pieter cosied his ball down to within eighteen inches of the hole and putted out for birdie. Tony took very little time studying his line. About six feet, uphill, slight break to the right. He dropped the putt and we walked to the ninth four under for the day.

Both players came away with pars on nine and missed birdies on ten. The flag on eleven was cruel: far left, behind the pond and with Rae's Creek lurking no more than seven yards beyond it. Tony and Pieter did what most players do, bailing out on the right and trusting to the putter for their pars. That worked fine for Tony, but Pieter left his long first putt three feet to the right of the hole, and could not sink the second. He was back to one under for the round while Tony was still at four under, one over for the tournament.

Twelve was playing short today—and capricious. The stands were packed but Tony was oblivious, absorbed in the hole and his environment. We stared at the creek. At the green. At the trees. The branches mid-level were swaying; those at the top were still.

"It's a nine."

I was not so confident. "Eight."

The wind changed, strengthening.

"You're right, it's an eight."

I was not so confident. "Nine."

The wind dropped. "Oh my," said Tony.

"Easy eight," I said. Better long than wet.

The flag was directly over the front bunker. Tony pulled out the eight and began to swing while we watched the wind. Not a breath at the flag, nor at the tree tops. Only the middle branches stirred.

"Easy swing takes the water out of play. If the wind strengthens, you're in the bunker. Nothing wrong with that. If it dies, you're in the flower bed." He'd spent an hour or so on Monday chipping out from among the azaleas. The problem with that area aside from the obvious risk of ending up in a shrub, is the vines running through the pine straw.

"Easy swing," he said at last.

"Clean, flush contact," I added. He glanced at me and nodded and I watched as he took three more practice swings to meld the thoughts.

The shot was perfect; the wind was not. It died at the apex and the ball landed long. We couldn't see it from the tee but after Pieter had hit (into the front bunker), we hiked across the bridge. Like yesterday, I had to refrain from lifting my cap in a backwards wave, as I used to do when Josh was here. We had no trouble finding the ball. It was in the pine straw just off the green behind the flag, nestled against the edge of the grass. A nasty lie.

"Wedge it out," said Tony immediately. If you used a seven, say, and tried to chip it out, you'd probably stub the club in the verge and the ball would shoot across the green into the bunker.

"If there's a vine under it and you can't get the clubface on the ball. . . ." I don't like completing thoughts like that when we're in play. We got down to green level and had a good look at the ball and the ground around it.

"Wedge," he said at last, and I handed it to him and took the bag over to the thirteenth walkway. I watched from there as he took his practice swings. He was playing it safe, aligned with the length of the green rather than with the flagstick. His angle was sharply downward, hitting down on to the ball to promote backspin. It wasn't badly executed either, but the ball would not stop until it had run the length of the green, leaving a good forty feet back up to the hole.

Pieter, who is a master at bunker play, hit a beautiful shot to within a foot of the pin, and it was back to us again. Tony gave that putt everything he had, but he'd allowed a shade too much right break and it finished up left of the hole and six inches long. Bogey.

"Now I know why I like thirteen," I heard him say to Pieter as they walked over to the tee. "I'm through twelve, that's why." I made a mental note to have a word with Charlie about attitude on twelve. You have to believe you can do well on a hole, and that particular hole can bite you in the leg if you don't.

We had a fair bit of waiting as play slowed down. It was

peaceful, with roars coming from the other side of the course where the leaders were starting out. Tony ate a pimiento cheese job and we talked about Cornwall, which he thinks of as home. "Intense sun, heavy rain" he said, when I asked what the climate was like. His life had been pretty much controlled from the age of eleven until he hit fourteen, and he'd volunteered—"ha! as if I had a choice"—with the Lifeboat Institution and any other group that needed a hand. He'd helped clear the walking paths along the cliffs in the spring, and done litter duty at the beach all summer long. "I always had to check in with the sergeant at the jail, and he was sticky about this stuff, so I couldn't get out of it."

The year he turned sixteen, Tashi and his cousin Kalden used to come on weekends. "Those two had some heated discussions at dinner, along with mum and Uncle Gordon. They made me realize how ignorant I was."

"What kind of discussions?"

"Oh, the Maoists and the war. Reincarnation. Tibet. Education."

Pieter took his second shot and landed safely on the green. Tony was sticking to his game plan, and put his third shot about ten feet from the flag. Both players made birdies, Tony's erasing the bogey from twelve.

He didn't let up, either. On fourteen he managed to pull off another birdie. Both players hit excellent second shots to the back center flag. But Pieter's ball landed ten feet short and hopped right, then trickled. And crawled. Then trickled some more. By the time it finished, he was forty feet from the flag. Tony, staring down the flagstick from the middle of the fairway, launched a high soft fade that landed front left, hopped forward and slowly approached the hole. He ended up with a tricky six-foot putt that he stroked with authority into the center of the cup.

The applause was slightly better than polite now, but not enough to suit Pieter, I guess, because he came over for a knuckle tap then pushed Tony's fist aside and made as though to punch him. He only tapped him on the chin, but Tony was completely taken aback. The crowd laughed, however, and they walked off the green together.

"You're too good, man," I heard Pieter saying. "Y'gotta cut it out." The crowd laughed good-naturedly, and I thought, *yeah, he's earned some slack, you guys.*

"He doesn't play like an amateur," said Kirk, sounding as though he'd just woken up.

Now we were five under for the day, even par for the tournament, and I began to feel some stress.

He added yet another birdie on the par five fifteenth, along with Pieter. The hole was playing short—five hundred and fifteen from the front tees—and they did it in very different ways. Pieter pushed his tee shot into the right trees and had to come out of the pine straw with a low iron. His only opening was to go across the fairway, which makes the third shot more difficult because you're short-siding yourself. With the traditional Saturday pin placement on the far left, he was giving himself very little green to work with. He left his second shot inside the crosswalk, about eighty yards from the pin. He was able to land and hold the green with his third, which considering the downhill lie was a nice bit of shot-making.

Tony, on the other hand, played the hole uneventfully down the middle right of the fairway. For his third, he chose to fade the ball in but misjudged the action. In the end he was left with a tricky downhill sidehill putt, like Pieter's. Even so, both players made birdie to enthusiastic applause. Word had got around. No matter how well the field is playing, six under par stands out at Augusta National, and Tony was now at one under for the tournament, playing like a pro with the pros. I glanced at the leaderboard as we walked over to the sixteenth tee. Someone at six under, another at four, Alex at minus two, Gardner and Lin tied at one under. It was shaping up to be an interesting tournament.

I heard Patrick Geoghan, the color commentator, as we walked over to sixteen; he was standing on the Sarazen Bridge on our left, and talking into a mike. ". . . the best round so far today. Golf's bad boy is on a roll and the two big questions are, can he keep it going? and what's going to happen tomorrow?"

"At least he didn't ask whether I did it honestly," said Tony ruefully.

He continued his good play through the last three holes, adding yet another birdie. The greens were becoming faster and on seventeen his birdie attempt was frighteningly fast. If it had not dived into the hole, it probably would have run off the green. Tony's face lit up with relief, and there was a sizable roar as it went in.

He finished the round seven under, Pieter four under, having found his putting stroke on the back nine. I thanked him as we shook hands. "No sweat, Kat," he grinned. "Say hi to Charlie, will you?"

Tony's round was the best so far today, and Pieter had a green jacket, so I wasn't surprised when an official invited them both to the press room. I saw the suppressed excitement on the faces of Gordon, Mollie and Tashi, and promised to join them as soon as I had changed. I knew we would be practicing later today, but for now I was off duty.

o o o

"Well?"

All three of them looked at me as I raised my beer.

"Cheers." I swallowed my first mouthful. Tasted wonderful. "Well what?"

Tashi laughed. "What a hard woman!"

We were sitting under one of the umbrellas. Gordon had bought me a beer and a green-wrapped barbecue beef bun. It was even warm. I leaned forward to unwrap it.

"*Come* on, Kat. Wasn't it a gorgeous round?"

"Did you ever have a better one?" That was Gordon, and I nodded at him, appreciating the question along with the bun.

"Just look at that beautiful leaderboard," said Tashi, bobbing up to admire it again. Except for the patrons milling round, we could have viewed it from our seats. Positioned between ten and eighteen, it showed Pinasa with a red two. They all talked while I enjoyed that bun. Gordon had a scorecard.

"Two was unbelievable," he said.

"I liked that putt on five," said Tashi. "I feel I know that hole."

"I liked all of them," said Mollie, "except number twelve."

I spoke around a mouthful of barbecue. "He's not happy with that hole."

We talked about the round, reveling in the score. Gordon was sure it was a record for amateurs, and I thought he might be right.

"If I had my mobile I could tell you," said Tashi cheerfully. Mollie gave her a look and they nudged each other and laughed.

"Did you think he'd play that well today, Kat?" Gordon looked at me curiously.

I shook my head. "Charlie and I talked about it. I thought maybe four under."

We relaxed in the afternoon sun, listening to conversations around us, commenting when we felt like it. Every now and then we'd hear a roar out on the course and Tashi would bob to her feet. "Lin's at three under," she said after one such roar, and after another, "Gardner's at two under, like Lhakpa! If he stays that way they could be paired tomorrow." She sat down. "We'll have to wait and see." She sounded like a seasoned patron. "I wish Lhakpa would hurry up. I want to practice."

"This is such a happy day." Mollie smiled round at us. "After yesterday."

Tashi hugged her arm and I smiled back. After the battles of the past two days I could appreciate her feelings.

I had a second beer and so did Gordon. Mollie and Tashi went off to the washroom, and I watched them leave.

"They're very close, aren't they?"

"Mm." Gordon was studying his scorecard, savoring the round.

"Where are Tashi's folks?"

Gordon carefully put the card away in his back pocket. "Gone to the four winds." He drank some beer then glanced at me, gauging the level of interest. "She's an attractive girl, isn't she?" He reached for his wallet.

"Very."

"The brothels in Mumbai are filled with Tamang women." He leafed through the transparent plastic dividers in the back of his wallet. "So Tashi said." He stopped at a picture and held it out to me.

It was a close up of a little girl. Rosy cheeks. Bright eyes. The face alive and dirty, along with the hands. Tousled hair. "Tashi?" Maybe four years old, wearing a filthy brown blanket tied round the middle with a piece of rope.

"That's right." Gordon went on speaking while I gazed at the picture. "She comes from a village in the north Himalayas. The picture was taken by a Belgian woman, a photographer there on a trek. She'd made a study of Tashi's family and she was there the morning the pimp arrived."

I looked up from the picture.

"The pimps go up into the villages and pay families to take their daughters. They tell them the daughters will be able to send home money to help out. These are desperately poor families, Kat. Pre-industrial poor, superstitious, ignorant, many of them hungry. Turn it over."

He meant the picture. I flipped the plastic divider over and there was another photo: a family portrait. Father, face filled with hatred. Mother with a baby on her hip and empty eyes. Tashi and two boys under ten, I'd guess, a girl a bit older—maybe twelve. Behind them was what I took to be a pile of rubble against a hillside, until I realized that the hole near the ground was a doorway. Then the rubble resolved itself into a hovel with a semblance of walls and a roof.

I felt something like horror. Couldn't look any more. Pushed the wallet back toward Gordon and looked out at the course.

"I had the same reaction, Kat. I keep it to remind myself how far we've come."

"How did she get out of there? Tashi."

"The pimp bought her sister and the Belgian photographer came along and wanted to buy her back, but of course the pimp wouldn't sell. So she bought Tashi instead. Gave her father all the money she had with her, and took her back to Kathmandu. She left her at the school along with a deposition containing everything she'd learned about the village and the family, the portfolio of photos and a substantial sum to cover Tashi's education. No one ever saw her again, she evidently had some sort of illness and returned to Belgium to die."

I shook my head, trying to reconcile the picture of the little kid with this present-day girl, bright, attractive and interested in hydroelectric power.

"She speaks very good English." Better than Tony, I thought.

"She attached herself to the school's administrator, an English woman." He shook his head. "Had to be weaned off her." He added, "She thinks of the school and us as her family."

"That's how it looked to me."

"Mollie's been a mother to all of them, in fact. Kalden and Kenchi as well. Paid their school fees during the civil war, after Pemba was killed. Always sending them things, socks and vitamins and so forth, whenever I had anyone flying out there."

The others came back soon after, with cups of tea. Gordon changed the subject and we talked about what to say to Tony about his round. I was glad to be back on familiar ground. "Don't single out any part of his game," I advised them. "Don't say he made a great putt here or there, or tee shot or whatever. Keep it general." The mind can do strange things to a player, I explained, especially under stress. "If you single out his putting or chipping or driving he starts obsessing about it. Just tell him he played great and leave it at that."

The others chatted about this for several moments, I recall. I remember hearing the scuffle of running feet. My mind stuck on that fact—that they were running—and refused to move further. I heard a call—"She's here!"—and we were suddenly swarmed by a ton of press. I've never seen anything like it. They ignored me, but they were all over Mollie.

"What was Tony like after the shooting?"

"Mrs. Pinasa, why did you leave Kathmandu?"

"What did Tony see?"

"Mrs. Pinasa, who shot the King?"

Tashi looked thoroughly surprised, Gordon angry, and Mollie—Mollie simply ignored them. She was only concerned with Tashi. I sat there, stunned until my elbow was jogged by a green jacket who said in my ear, "Go in through the grill room—" and helped me to my feet. Tashi was with me and several green jackets were shepherding Gordon and Mollie after us while questions came flying after them. We went inside the grill room, which was almost empty, and through a door the other side. Like most people, I've never been inside the Augusta National clubhouse. I'd have loved to linger but we weren't getting the chance. Through an entrance hall with a couple of sofas covered in flower-patterned material; I think that may be what's called chintz; then outside to the main clubhouse entrance. There was Tony in his white Escalade with the doors open.

Media Center: The Interview Room

"Good afternoon, ladies and gentlemen, we are delighted to have Pieter Vanderhoef and Tony Pinasa with us." From his seat on the raised platform, Joe Norris surveyed the interview room, off the main media amphitheatre. About three-quarters full right now, it had seats for a hundred and fifty reporters and writers, plus camera and video recording at the back and side. Joe was a balding member of Augusta National, sitting at the table in his green jacket and flanked by the two players. Normal practice would be to interview each in turn, but they had declined to be separated, and since Tony was an amateur, Joe had no objection. He continued: "We've been looking up the record books, and it seems Tony's round, at seven under, is the lowest round ever by an amateur. And Pieter won the Tournament three years ago, and had a wonderful round at four under today. So it's quite a feast here, and I'm going to say age before beauty, and let's ask Pieter first. Would you like to make a statement or just go to questions, Pieter?"

"Questions, I guess. Not much to say." Pieter grinned at the ripple of laughter that ran through the room.

Joe nodded to a reporter in the second row, who stood up.

"Pieter, is the new putter helping?"

"Yeah, I think so. I felt a lot more comfortable over my putts as the day went on."

Another reporter stood up. "Tell us about the birdie on eighteen."

"Yeah, well I know that spot. Right at the back there, you look at it and you just cannot see the break. But it's there and I knew to allow about two feet and it worked."

"Do you think you have a chance tomorrow?"

"See how the lead holds up."

"Pieter, were you two guys feeding off each other today?"

Pieter shrugged. "I don't know about that. I enjoyed watching this fellow play. He knows his way around the golf course."

"How about you, Tony? Was it helpful to have a partner like Pieter?"

"I'm happy to play with anyone as long as I can play golf. But I'd heard Pieter was a super guy and it's true. I had a great time today."

More people trickled in and found seats.

"Were you trying to prove something out there today, Tony?"

"No." He studied his hands idly, waiting for the next question. A slight movement by Joe, next to him, made him look up and he saw several reporters exchanging muttered comments. "I never think like that, that's all I meant. I made a big mistake on Thursday and I paid for it with a rotten round of golf. But Thursday's history." He frowned.

Several pens went up, but Joe glanced at Tony and waited.

"Could I say something?"

"That's what we're here for, Tony." A ripple of suppressed laughter through the room. Joe was well liked by the media.

"Look. I have a terrible temper. I've been taught to—well, to stop and think before I react, when I get like that. So on Thursday—well, look, this is what happened. I drove it in the left rough on eleven. Kat—my caddie—warned me about not getting too close to the ball and so on. The bottom line is, she saw the ball move while I was looking along the line down the fairway. I didn't see the ball move. So I was pi—I was furious with her, and if that isn't being a child I don't know what is. But I've been taught again and again, don't lose your temper. Just count to ten and wait. So I just focused on the shot, and after I'd hit it I said we'll deal with this later. Because I did not want to deal with it at that moment. I was afraid I'd get too angry." He drank from the glass in front of him, then continued. "That was the worst thing I could do. Because even though I'm pretty good at staying on focus, that issue just ate away at me, in the back of my mind. As soon as we'd finished I went in and told the officials. I mean, I was pretty sure she was right, it was a stroke penalty."

Joe leaned forward. "Well, thank you Tony for that statement. Now, any more questions?" More than a hundred hands went up, and Joe gave the nod to the *New York Times* in the front row.

"Tony, and you too, Pieter, could we go through your clubs and yardages on one and two? That was a spectacular start."

They went through club selections for one and two, then for the other birdie holes, then for all the remaining holes for both players.

"This question's for Tony. I'm wondering why you enter your name as Lhakpa Gyeltsen Pinasa instead of just Tony.

You haven't lived in Nepal since you were little, have you? Why would you use that name? Is it like an affectation?"

The two players had been kidding each other over their club selections on various holes, so Tony took a moment before replying, soberly, "I keep my Nepali name to honor my father." It became apparent he had nothing to add, so after a moment there was another question for Pieter, then back to Tony:

"Do you use meditation on the course?"

"Yes, I do. My dad taught me to meditate when I was little, and mum made me keep it up."

"Did it help you at all on Thursday, in the later holes?"

"I'm glad you mention that. You see, I tried to focus on a golf ball just sitting in the first cut, and it helped to calm me down. Then I began to wonder how many times my golf ball might have moved in the past, without me seeing it. Which is what got me thinking about signing incorrect score cards, which got misinterpreted as an admission of cheating." He heaved a sigh. "I got off to a terrible start here, I'm very sorry about it."

Joe waved to another reporter.

"This question is for both players. Do you approve of violence as a response to racism?"

Pieter leaned forward to answer. "I don't think violence is ever a good response. I've done a lot of work with young victims of violence and it's made me realize there has to be another way." He looked across at Tony, who leaned forward in turn.

"I ought to think the same as Pieter, I saw my father killed. I know what bullets can do to bodies. But I have to say, I think there's a place for violence in the world. When you don't stand up to bullies, they cause terrible trouble. That spectator I punched last year had been verbally abusing me and my playing partner for three hours round the course. He was disgusting. I asked him to be quiet or go away. He threw the first punch. I'm not sorry I hit him."

There had been some stirring among the crowd, and several reporters exited rapidly at the rear. Danny Chu stood up, along with another reporter, who got the nod from Joe.

"Have you had any other experience of racism?"

"No. None at all."

Danny tried again, but another reporter asked, "Tony, that was an amazing round today. Most first-time Masters players would tell you that kind of round is not possible until you have a few years' experience under your belt. How do you account for it?"

"I love this course. I feel at home here, and I've played quite a few rounds here in the off season. Plus I've been lucky to have a wonderful caddie, someone who knows the course like the back of her hand. I don't know how anyone manages here without someone like Kat to help them."

"Do you think you can win tomorrow?"

"Of course." He hesitated, then added, "Unless the leaders go really deep. Look, it'll be difficult. But if I didn't think I could win I wouldn't be here."

"Last question—anyone?" said Joe, and this time Danny got his attention. He was there as a stringer for several papers. He'd had a set of instructions sitting on his laptop all day and he was relieved to be able to discharge his duty now.

"Danny Chu for the *Everest Times*." There, that was the plug. "Tony, would you please tell us what you saw the night your father was killed, the night King Birendra was assassinated?"

Kat's Story

"I was playing behind the sofa. I heard this colossal rip of sound and shot to my feet. There he was, the Crown Prince, standing in the doorway in his combat gear."

We were parked halfway down Magnolia Lane. Tony had been ready to drive right off the course but I reminded him that here there was at least some protection from the press. Gordon sat in the front seat looking out his side, as did Mollie behind him. I guessed they had heard this many times. Tony was half-turned toward Tashi and me, and he had one hand on Tashi's arm while he spoke. I sat directly behind him, Tashi in the middle.

"He had a rifle and a pistol on his hip as well as the submachine gun, and it swung round to point at me. I don't know if I was terrified at the time, but in my dreams I always am."

"Oh Lhakpa. . . ."

"But he just nodded at me and turned and left."

"Nodded." I spoke involuntarily.

"Yeah."

"He nodded?"

"Don't ask me, Kat. He was a very troubled guy."

There was a small silence, then Tashi said, "What did you do then?"

Tony laughed shortly. "Waited for someone to say something." He frowned. I'd say he was trying hard to keep his emotions under control, but I really don't know. I had enough trouble grappling with what he was telling us. “Bik’ll deal with that tomorrow.”

“Lhakpa…why didn’t you tell me before?”

“It never felt right. It was such an ugly thing, Tashi. I didn’t want it to—,” he stopped, maybe searching for the right words. “My life is pretty much out there, and that’s fine. There’s not much of it and not much that’s good. I only have two secrets and this is the big one.” He stared at me but I knew he didn’t see me; he was still talking to Tashi. “Earlier this week I realized that I was ready to tell you. It felt right and I wanted to do it. I was just waiting until after the tournament. Then I got Bik’s email. . . .”

“You might have told us,” said Mollie.

“I wanted to. I was going to tell Tashi this morning but—well, . . .”

“And whose fault is that?” Tashi spoke sharply. “Honestly, Lhakpa, you make me tired.”

He hung his head. “I know.”

Gordon opened his door. “We’ll leave you two—”

“Don’t do that.” I pointed toward the entrance, where a growing crowd of reporters peered through the wrought-iron gate, zoom lenses going berserk. “They’ll just take pictures and start some crazy speculation if we get out.”

He pulled his door shut and swiveled round. “So let me see if I understand this. Bik emailed, saying you had today to let the cat out of the bag.”

“Yeah.”

“If you didn’t, they would.”

“The thing was, they were ready to splash it all over the paper right away. Bik promised, if they would hold off, to go on their TV show tomorrow. He wanted me to be able to control the timing."

"So you calmly proceeded to play lights out while formulating an announcement, which you delivered at your press conference."

"It helped me to focus." He reached out a hand and held Tashi's arm. "I didn't want any secrets, Tashi. I'm so sorry about this."

Tashi shook her head slightly.

"Oh darling," Mollie started to put her arm round Tashi but she moved away slightly, toward me. She looked down at her clasped hands.

"I remember the night King Birendra died. It's one of those moments you never forget, I suppose. I remember being held tight by one of the bigger kids. I think all of us little ones were crying because we were so frightened. How could our king, who was practically a god, be dead? That's what we all wanted to know." She paused, and no one moved or spoke. "And now to find out you were there. You were actually there."

"I wasn't there, Tashi. Not in the hall. I never saw the king get killed."

Tashi was still immersed in the past. "We heard about your dad over the weekend. You were just a day student, so we didn't expect to see you for a little bit. Then Dipendra became king even though he was in a coma. Then he died and we couldn't believe what they were telling us. We just couldn't believe he had done it, had killed the king and all the others. . . . There are still people who think the Maoists did it, Lhakpa. Do you know that?"

A sharp rap on Tony's window startled all of us. I turned

and my heart sank. The security chief, H.D. McWatters, was standing there, God rot him.

"Sorry I startled you folks," he said as Tony's window wound down.

"Do you want me to move?" Tony asked.

"You do whatever you want, Mr. Pinasa. I just want you to know we have a cabin for you and your family for the afternoon."

I slid down in my seat as he went on: "You might find it more comfortable and more private. It's round by the Par Three course." He explained how to get there, then nodded to Tony and stepped back. He glanced at me. "Ms. Archer." He touched his cap.

Tony was already starting the engine so I sat up. The car moved down the lane.

"What a sweet man," said Mollie.

Gordon laughed at me. "You should see your expression."

I scowled.

As we approached the front gate, the crowd of media heaved from side to side as photographers struggled for clear views. Tony turned right and followed a narrow service road alongside the Par Three course. Augusta National has cottages, which they call cabins, scattered throughout the grounds. The most famous are the three along the tenth fairway, the Butler, Eisenhower and Jones cabins, but there are many others, used by members and for corporate hospitality. They're all two-storey cottages, white with green trim.

We came abreast of the practice putting green and a guard indicated a left fork in the road. I caught a glimpse of the tenth tee box, then we were moving away into the trees.

The Par Three course is built round two small lakes. We drove past the seventh and eighth holes, then the road curved to the left. Another guard was waving us into a driveway before a cabin with a profusion of spring flowers near the door.

We came to a halt in the driveway and climbed out. The guard touched his cap as he came abreast of us. "If you folks'll follow me. . . ." he said, so we trailed after him into the house and got a quick tour of the ground floor: living room, dining room, kitchen, study-den and a washroom. He left, and we gravitated toward the kitchen because it had a nook with a table in it, and looked out over one of the lakes. The ninth green was on our left and the eighth was visible across the little lake. It was tranquil and quiet, with the afternoon sun streaming in at the window.

The guard had said help ourselves from the fridge, so Gordon and I brought bottled water to the table. There were only four chairs, so he motioned me to the fourth while he stood, leaning against the kitchen counter.

"Tashi, may I tell you why—?" began Mollie, but Tashi interrupted her. Judging by Gordon's expression, I thought that was probably unusual. She had clearly been shaken by Tony's revelation and was trying hard to cope.

"We never understood why you left," she said. "I'm sorry but we didn't. We thought—I heard a couple of the teachers say—it was wrong of you to uproot Lhakpa like that and take him off to a strange country."

"Let me try to explain how it was. Will you listen?"

Tashi crossed her arms. After a moment she nodded, and Mollie began to tell her about that night in June of 2001. "I've thought many, many times that I did the wrong thing, Tashi. I was guilt-ridden about it for years but it was the right decision at the time."

"It was absolutely the right decision," Tony piped up, "otherwise I'd never have—"

"Shut up, Lhakpa," they both said at once, Gordon and Mollie together.

Are you brain dead, I wondered, *to think about golf at a time like this?*

Mollie was continuing. "Lhakpa's uncle and aunt were against it and so were my friends. I know now that the abbot at Tengboche would probably have been just as good for him as the psychologist we went to in England. But Tashi, there was rioting in the city and our parents' house was available and Gordon was the only close family I had. And Lhakpa was terribly traumatized."

Tashi regarded her, then put out a hand and patted Mollie's. "I understand," she said with a small nod.

"No, darling, you don't. I haven't finished. I was terrified they'd want to interrogate my little boy. Because you see, he tried to kill the Crown Prince." She saw the disbelief on Tashi's face. I felt the same but she wasn't looking at me. "Yes, he did. You know what a temper he has. *Ang Tak* his father used to call him. Little tiger."

Tashi and I both looked at Tony. He shrugged. "I was angry. Papa was dead, and the prince's brains were all over the table, it was disgusting."

"Lhakpa, you were awfully little back then. I towered over you."

"You did not."

"You always say you don't remember school. . . . What did you do?"

"I attacked his knees." He laughed. "Then he fell on top of me and knocked me out." He glanced at his watch and then round at me. "Kat, can we meet on the range later?"

That sounded like English for "get lost." I stood up and it seemed he was sending the same message to Gordon and Mollie because they came with me to the door. He offered us the Escalade but we decided to walk. I'd already headed for the front door when I heard Gordon's voice.

"What was your second secret?"

"What do you mean?"

I stopped and so did Mollie. She retraced her steps. I stayed where I was but I could still hear.

"You said you only had two secrets. What's the other one?" He paused. "Just so we know."

"I want to implement Dipendra's plan. Once I turn pro."

"What plan?"

"To train people for jobs. It's like the Prince of Wales's Trust. You know, training inner city people? Dipendra's plan was meant to cover the whole country. He had it almost fully developed then his parents vetoed it, or something."

"Are you mad, Lhakpa?" Mollie's voice was frigid.

"No, I'm not mad, mum."

"Who else knows about this?" Gordon looked as though he was braced for the worst.

"Just Tashi and Bik. It's just something I'd like to do if I have the money. I wanted Tashi in it because I think she'd be good at getting women to come forward and apply. Bik's going to be chairman because he's high-caste Hindu and from one of the families."

Mollie opened her mouth, but Gordon overrode her. "Well, let's keep it quiet for now, okay?"

"Yeah, okay," Tony said readily. "It'd sound a bit silly right now anyway. Coming from me, I mean."

o o o

I got back to the caddie shack and had a rest in the lounge, watched some of the action on TV, phoned Miss Grace and put my name down for pork barbecue. Tonight was poker night for me and my two housemates, and I was looking forward to it.

I snoozed a bit and just vegged out. When I headed out again, jumpsuit back on, Tony was nowhere to be seen, so I strolled over to the range entrance and met up with Mollie and Gordon. We decided to visit the main scoreboard off the first fairway, to admire Tony's score and see how the rest of the field were doing.

"Hey! Gordon! Wait up!"

Beyond the big oak, a large guy waved an arm, striding in our direction. I was about to turn away and follow Mollie when I glimpsed Tony beyond him, up by the practice green. I nudged Mollie.

"Mike! I wondered if we'd meet again," Gordon had a big smile on his face. "How are you?"

Something about the guy seemed familiar. He towered over Gordon and they shook hands enthusiastically.

"I'm great, Gordon. Gee, this is fantastic. I've been—," he glanced at me and looked away. I recognized him. He was the crying guy from Thursday. He looked a hundred percent happier now. He was going on:

"—following Alex and I thought you were too, but I've never seen you around." He stopped abruptly and looked at me and neither of us heard Gordon's reply because I had just realized he was also the "come and get it" guy from Friday. He was the "real men don't cheat" guy, and he had just realized I was the caddie behind Tony.

"How's Will?" asked Gordon, but Mike was watching me intently.

"Look," he said. "I am so sorry about that, you wouldn't believe. Where's your player? Where's Tony?"

"Why?" I wasn't taking anything for granted with this guy.

"What are you two talking about?" Gordon looked from the guy to me.

"I have to apologize—" he said to me, then looked at Gordon. "I screwed up about something."

"This is Tony's uncle," I said to him. Turned to Gordon: "This guy called Tony a cheat and a coward, that's all."

"Oh Jeez!" He took a breath. "Gordon, you've got to believe me. I made a mistake. Big time. I—well, I just hated to think of anyone cheating here. I thought that player was—" he expelled a lungful of air and looked at his boots, a huge guy with a hangdog expression. I was tempted to laugh. Mollie did laugh.

"What? What did you think he was?" she asked.

He heaved a sigh that came up from his boots and muttered, "A loser. And now I'm looking at the scoreboard and he's shot the lowest round ever by an amateur, and I'm wondering where do I go to surrender?"

I thought Gordon's attitude might have been very different if this meeting had occurred yesterday, when we were struggling to make the cut. As it was, he laughed along with Mollie and introduced us to the guy, Mike something. They began to behave like long lost buddies again so Mollie decided to find the Jamesons.

"Hey!" It was Tony, coming along from the club house, Tashi behind him. He put on speed when he saw who it was. Mike started toward him.

"Oh man! No reason why you should talk to me, but I want to tell you I made a huge mistake. Ranks right down there with the worst I ever made." He hesitated then added, "I'd like to congratulate you on your round today."

He started to hold out his hand, then stopped, waiting. He was six four or five and at least fifty pounds heavier than Tony. He didn't want to crowd him.

Tony's face relaxed. "Hey," he said at last. "I just thought you were going to mix it up with my caddie and I need her." He grinned.

Oh ha ha, I thought. *Very funny*. They shook hands while the rest of us looked on.

o o o

Early evening, a soft Georgia spring evening. Tony was hitting high fades, shot after shot. He'd started with his seven (his favorite start-up club), hitting to a green about one-eighty-five out. Now he was using the two-ten green as a target, working with a longer iron, swinging easily, looking in good form. They set the precise yardage for each day's tees on the practice range, and the greens are bent grass, meant to duplicate the real thing.

Mollie and Ann Jameson sat in the stands chatting and watching their sons and a few other players. Some were alone, others had caddies or swing coaches clustered round.

The attitude at each tee spot depended on the state of the player's swing. Some were refining or rejoicing; others cursed or puzzled over their swings. A few were trying desperately to find the form that brought them here. One or two were as content as anyone can be whose natural state is chronic dissatisfaction. As for Tony, he said the ball felt good and was coming clean off the face. He was uninterested in the gossip about him. He said it was ancient history and he hoped he wouldn't have to go on and on about it. When he noticed my expression he stopped hitting balls and stood looking at the ground for a minute before speaking.

"I think about my dad every day. I think about the way he died most days." He looked away, along the fairway. "But the fact of his death is ancient history for me. That's all I meant."

We were facing more or less west and the sun had fallen behind the pines on Berckmann. I ambled over to the ball building. The club brings in more than a ton of balls before the tournament, direct from the manufacturers. They provide the ten most popular brands, repackaged into mesh bags of forty balls apiece. I grabbed two bags and started back.

The day's rounds would not be finished for a couple of hours, but no matter what happened, Tony would be taking home crystal, probably enough to stock a sideboard: two goblets for each of his three eagles and in all likelihood a crystal vase for low round of the day. On the main scoreboard, Pieter's round was the nearest to Tony's sixty-five.

Maybe twenty players were still on the course, but many others had come over to offer their congratulations and best wishes. Greg Stillman had been genuinely thrilled. He'd had a so-so day himself and was well back in the pack but he was as excited for Tony as if it had been his own round. Pieter had come by to tell him to stop stirring up trouble and get a good night's sleep.

Two players were chatting near by, trading stories, relaxing, enjoying the evening. Tony began to work the ball, using his nine-iron to shape draws and fades, landing around the flagstick a hundred and forty-five yards away. The two players fell silent, watching. He swapped the nine for his pitching wedge and continued, dropping the shots ten yards closer in but still hard right and left, wider and wider swings. The shorter the iron, the harder it is to work the ball, yet he was making it look easy. It was pretty to watch.

"Lee Trevino used to do that with his sand wedge."

The voice was unmistakable, and we both turned round abruptly. There he was, the Grand Old Man himself, Tony's idol, Jack Nicklaus. Tony was speechless.

"Kat," Mr. Nicklaus gave me a nod and a smile. "Give my best to Charlie."

"Yes sir," I smiled, touched my cap and left the two of them to get on with it.

"Well, young man," I heard him say, "that was a stellar performance today."

I picked up a bottled water and a Five Alive from the booth and chatted with Jonas, one of my housemates. He was heading home in a few minutes. "Say, Kat, did I hear your player saw his dad get killed?"

I nodded and he went on, "So—why do we care?"

"We don't. Just ignore it."

He looked relieved. "He's not going to burst into tears or anything?"

"Of course not. This all happened like years ago."

"Poker tonight, right?"

"You better believe it. You owe me big time."

He laughed and went off to join his player.

Tony was alone again and I wandered back to find him squatting down, playing marbles with a couple of balls.

"Did you see who was here?"

"Of course. Have a nice chat?" I handed him the Five Alive.

"I can't remember." He looked distressed. "I simply can't remember what he said."

"Don't worry. It'll come back to you, probably in the middle of the night."

Loss of memory is a sign of stress, but I didn't think of that.

o o o

They say our generation of caddies is different from those of the last century. I wouldn't know, although the increase in money was bound to make some difference. We probably aren't any smarter than the old crowd, but you do get a more educated caddie today: MAs and PhDs, doctors and lawyers. People who graduate but decide not to take up their professions right away.

Tucker was an example, my other housemate. Tuck had graduated law school somewhere. Maybe not Ivy League but a good school even so, because his family had money. Instead of joining his dad's law firm he had decided to caddie for a classmate who started out a rising star and kept rising, at least for several years. He hadn't shone this week, but he managed to win at least once most years, so Tuck was comfortably off aside from any family money he may have. Their wives were friends too, and were off shopping in New York for the week.

Tucker was my age, Jonas a couple of years younger but also married. He had two young children and his wife was beginning to make noises about him getting a regular job. His player makes a good living, but these days most of it comes from appearance fees and endorsements. Jonas had caddied for him a lot in recent years, the old caddie having retired, but I had a hunch this would not be going on much longer. His golf winnings wouldn't keep a fly alive.

Today it's much harder for rank and file caddies to find steady work on the PGA Tour. Once there were thirty events per season. Knock off the majors, unless you're lucky enough to caddie for someone who qualifies into the U.S. Open, knock off four World Golf events, restricted to small fields of elite players, and another three or four tournaments restricted to the top seventy. Nowadays you're looking at twenty events at most where caddies are even eligible to get jobs.

The Tour is incredibly competitive. If your guy loses his card—and these days many players manage to keep their cards only for two or three years—then you're back paying your own expenses, camping out in your car. Even if he keeps his card, you could be fired at any moment. When a player's game goes south the caddie is often the first to feel it. Either way, you soon become one of ten or twenty caddies calling the same players with the same pitch each week. The young guys just breaking in find work on the Nationwide Tour, in the Billy Bob city sweat-hole tournaments with low pay and high expectations. The rest go back to the nine-to-five world.

An average Tour player might make around twenty million dollars in career earnings over a couple of decades. His caddie's take would be anywhere from five to ten percent—it's a private arrangement between the player and caddie. Some players pay all expenses up front plus a percentage of winnings. Others pay a bigger percentage but leave the caddie to pay his own travel and hotel expenses. Let's say the caddie has a ten percent deal, same as I have with Charlie. Over twenty years, he's grossed about two million dollars, or a hundred thou a year. Knock thirty thousand off that for expenses; pay tax on the rest and it's not a bad living if you don't mind the travel.

But as the player ages, the caddie begins hurting financially. The player's golf winnings might fall from half a million to fifty thousand, his ranking declining from say the top hundred to somewhere around twelve hundredth in the world. Semi-retired as a player, if he's well-liked he might get work as a commentator or some such. But now his caddie is scrambling round looking for a bag. He doesn't have the same tolerance for the rough life that he had twenty years ago.

Nor does his wife. And Jonas's wife, though they're both still young, doesn't want to hear about Jonas sleeping in his car, stuff like that.

You could find plenty of booze and drugs in the caddie corps if you were looking, but not at Miss Grace's. All you get there is good food and plenty of it, and that evening she served up the pork with slaw and Brunswick stew, followed by pound cake and strawberries with real whipped cream. We stayed outside for a while after dinner, finishing our beer. The talk was mostly about golf, veering slightly off topic briefly.

"They're getting some crazy countries involved," said Jonas. "I mean, Nepal? Isn't that all mountains?" I told him what little I knew: it wasn't very big, there were mountains and plains and six golf courses.

"Yeah, and what pisses me off is they leave out some of the top players just so they can invite these hackers from east of nowhere. Just weakens the field."

"Tony won the British Amateur—"

"Yeah, not him. I'm talking about some of the others, an' not just the amateurs either."

"Good leaderboard tomorrow, though," said Tuck. "Wish we were in there." He sat back in his chair smoking a cigar and studying his cellphone. I went inside and turned on the TV in the den. There were eight players at even or better, Americans, Europeans and Asians, then the pairings came up: we were in the third group with RJ Gardner, behind two European players. I went back to the garden, where Jonas and Tuck were discussing the pairings. Lin Jinhai had the lead at five under. He'd never slept on a lead at the majors.

"Forget Lin," Tuck said, "he'll slide off the board. Forget Pinasa—sorry, Kat—and that leaves, let's see, eight guys if you include one over."

"Who's at one over?" Jonas asked.

"Vanderhoef. And you know what? If Alex doesn't take it—"

"Alex is leading if you don't count Lin."

"Yeah, well, I'm betting Vanderhoef," said Tuck. "And why? Because Alex is going to get tied up in a dogfight with the Europeans. Pieter goes out half an hour earlier. He'll come out of nowhere and post a score and that'll be that."

A green jacket to a golfer is like a drink to an alcoholic: one is not enough. Pieter had one green jacket and he was thirsty for another. He'd looked good finishing up today.

Jonas was doing the math. "If he shoots sixty-six you might be right. He'll clean up."

"Get real, guys," I decided to join in. "Alex isn't going to settle for par. He'll go at least one or two under." Alex had a genius for making the win happen.

"Okay, sixty-five. Maybe they'll have a playoff." Tucker turned off his phone and butted out his cigar. "What are we waiting for, guys?"

We moved inside and settled down around the poker table. An hour and a half later, when I was getting hammered by Jonas, Tony called. "Can we talk about strategy?"

"What, now?"

"Yeah. I'd like to sleep on it." When I said nothing, he went on, "I could be there in five."

There was something in his voice, and to stop him begging I answered, "Okay. Sure."

Jonas was disgusted. "Gimme a break, he's got all day tomorrow."

"I remember the first time you slept on a lead, Nellie," Tuck laughed. "And you're just the caddie."

"He's not leading."

"He's not far off. And it's the Masters."

By this time Tony had rung the doorbell. But when I opened the door I saw him back on the street, talking under the streetlight to two reporters and a cameraman. He finished up and I heard, "Look I've got some planning to do with my caddie. Okay? And please—can't you leave my family alone?" One of the reporters made some remark and he shook his head then turned. They headed back to their vehicles and he came up to the porch. "Sorry. They won't let up, silly buggers."

I'd thought we could sit out front but in view of his celebrity status I suggested the living room. Tony however wanted to stay outside so we went through to the back garden and sat on the patio.

"So! How are you holding up?" I thought he looked drawn and he seemed just a little antsy.

"All right, thanks."

He didn't elaborate, so I told him to relax and went off to the kitchen. I came back a few minutes later with two bottles of beer and a large bowl of Doritos Nacho Cheesier tortilla chips. We made inroads for a while.

"I've been thinking about tomorrow," said Tony finally. "You know we're paired with Gardner?" I nodded and he went on, "I really want to attack the front nine, Kat."

"Yeah. I've been thinking—"

"I just want to go out in attack mode, okay? We can review the position after nine. If I'm at or near the lead we may decide to ease off a bit on the back. If I've fallen back then we may have to keep the pressure on. But that's what I'd like to do."

For a minute the only sound was both of us chomping away on the nachos. Then I swallowed some beer. "Okay, that sounds reasonable." It wasn't the moment to disagree with him. I spoke slowly and kept my voice down so he had to work to hear me. "I think RJ will want to do the same. But let's step back for a minute and analyze the course. What do you think it'll play like, tomorrow?"

"Won't they mix it up, like last year? Some holes playing shorter, some easier pins?"

"Why?"

"Why what?"

"They have no incentive to make it easier. Last year there were four players around the lead then a gap. This year, they've got no gap, there are at least ten players with a chance and five of them are marquee players. It's a dream leaderboard from their point of view. It makes for a great back nine."

He digested this. "It's not going to be easier, is it?"

I thought it would be brutal, but I didn't say that. "I think it'll be a great test. They won't water the greens, so they'll be tough to hold."

I refilled the nachos bowl and we talked course management. We had been playing away from the traps where possible, but now he had a different priority. "We've got to be below the hole where we can. Nothing else matters." It was a good thought. You don't want too many downhill putts on Sunday. They'll break you after a while. Trouble is, the officials know the players want to stay below the hole. They don't make it easy.

We talked about the pressure. Pointless not to. How everyone would be edgy. "Under stress the big muscles freeze. The little ones twitch." He liked that: it gave him something to think about. "Your body may start to do weird things, and it'll show up in your shots. Experienced players know this about themselves. Some get twitchy hands or legs; others find one side gets stronger than the other." I'd be watching for signs.

We discussed his routine and agreed that I'd tell him if I saw him speeding up or slowing down. We talked about what makes a champion. Patience. Courage. Honesty. Common sense. Game management. "You're going to find RJ outdriving you by at least twenty yards."

He nodded. "I've been visualizing that. I'm okay with it, it's happened before."

We couldn't really discuss more specific strategies without seeing the pin positions and tees. Tony said he'd be up early tomorrow. "I always smell the bacon. I think I'll have an early breakfast then take a look at the course, then put in a couple of hours on my short game."

"Try to get as much sleep as you can. It's going to be a long day."

We sat there on the back patio, the only light coming from the solar bug lamps round the deck. It was pleasant and relaxing. I was impressed with myself. I'd expected to feel some stress, but I guess experience really does count for a lot.

"Tashi and I have broken up."

I sat upright. Peered over at him. "I don't believe it."

He stood up abruptly and walked down the steps and out past the picnic table. I waited but he didn't come back so I gathered my wits and joined him. I thought he was simply staring at the privet hedge, then I heard a faint sound and turned and peered at him. Tears were pouring down his cheeks.

"Oh, now," I said softly and turned him gently toward the picnic table. "This won't do, and there's nothing we can't fix if we put our minds to it." Driveling on like this in a soothing tone I got him to sit down on one side of the bench table while I sat opposite. He had both hands spread flat in front of him and I covered them with my own.

"Tell me what happened, okay?"

I found my hands entwined with his, fingers interlaced, and lifted so that we faced each other with our elbows about two feet apart.

"We had a terrible argument." He spoke in a low voice, fighting to stop it shaking. His fingers were incredibly strong and he stared fixedly at me over our gripped hands. "Terrible argument."

I didn't want to hear. "Tell me."

"She said I'm a coldblooded egotistical pig. I said she was shallow and superficial and pathetic. She said I must be insane if I thought she was going to spend her life driving round America in an RV. I said she might as well, she had nothing better to do."

He wiped his nose with the back of a hand. I think it was mine. He went on reciting insults and I let him until he began to slow down. When he got to, "What am I going to do? What am I going to do?" I managed to disentangle our hands and reached for a dish towel at the other end of the table, used to bring out the dinner plates and left behind. I handed it to him. He mopped his eyes and blew his nose. "Oh God," he said finally, "I said some terrible things. Terrible." He shook his head despairingly.

"It sounds to me as though you had a good old knock-down drag-out fight. You both said terrible things."

He shook his head again. "Unforgiveable. Oh God, what am I going to do?" And he was off again, this time with his head on his hands. I waited. He'd had a stressful three days and I didn't think it was wholly a bad thing that this had happened. Eventually he mopped up with the dish towel again.

"My poor Tashi. She'll never forgive me. Never. Never."

"Can you forgive her?"

He stared at me. "Well, of course!"

"Even if she won't help with your Trust?"

He stared some more. "She didn't say that absolutely. She said we'd talk about it tomorrow evening. But that's the classic brush-off, isn't it?"

He was nearly off again, so I began to itemize every insult I could recall him putting in Tashi's mouth. I got him to agree that some of them weren't justified. I got him to concede that Tashi had known in advance what she was getting into, that he'd be busy, that he'd be sleeping in the Crow's Nest. "You're sure you told her that?"

"Of course! I told her in detail."

Reminded of these and a few other points he began to regain his perspective.

"Most couples have these arguments, you know. Sometimes it's the only way to clear the air so you can move forward." Aunty Katrina, counselor to the lovelorn.

We sat there quietly and after a few moments I began to talk about families and how hard the tournament is on them. "They'll want you to do what's best for you, so ask yourself whether it's better to leave things like this tonight? Or would it be better to go back and sit down with Tashi and try to sort things out?"

"I offered to stay there tonight, that's what started the argument." I was careful to make no comment. After a while, he said he was going back to the hotel so we got to our feet. I walked him out to the Escalade and came back in feeling flattened. The guys were still playing poker. Jonas looked up.

"You told me he wouldn't cry. You don't know nuttin'."

SATURDAY-SUNDAY

O O O O

Kathmandu

"Ten minutes, Colonel." Rab Manga's attractive assistant poked her head into the room, beamed, and withdrew before Bik Basnet could respond. He heard applause as the door closed and his stomach knotted slightly. He leaned back in his chair and reached for the mug of tea. This wasn't going to be quite the same as appearing before a parliamentary committee.

He sat in a makeup room at Joy TV, in the Dharmedia building. The room was dingy except for the lights round the large mirrors. Rab Manga was a glamour name, a big-time interviewer, and Bik's pulse rate picked up a notch. He wished momentarily that he hadn't agreed so readily to the interview. This wasn't news; this was entertainment TV, something quite outside his experience. Then he remembered the little seven-year-old he had tried to protect, and his mind went once more to that terrible Friday evening fifteen years ago.

He had been an *aide-de-camp* to Prince Raman back then, a distant relative of the Queen's. Raman had been a friend and confidante of the Crown Prince, and had betrayed his confidence on the afternoon of that same Friday.

Bik sighed. *No use blaming Raman for my being here,* he thought. It would be as reasonable to blame Edmund Hillary, and Bik had no wish to blame that good man for anything. But Mollie would not have come out to Kathmandu if her mother had not been determined to see Everest once in her life. And her mother would have had no interest in the mountain had it not been for Coronation Day, June 2, 1953, when the announcement came that two men, Edmund Hillary and Tenzing Norgay, had reached the summit. Seven-year-old Hillary Fairley had been thrilled at her namesake's accomplishment and she became fascinated by the mountain and the people of Nepal. As an adult she volunteered with the Himalaya Trust, responsible for the schools and clinics built by Hillary in Solu-Khumbu. Her daughter, Mollie, had been working in the Trust's London office for the summer when Prince Raman and his ADC called in, to kill an idle hour or two before an embassy cocktail reception. Bik and Mollie had been friends ever since that day.

No, thought Bik as he sipped his tea, of course the blame must be laid at Dipendra's door. It was the Crown Prince, drunk and stoned, who had massacred nine members of his family and one unfortunate Sherpa, then committed suicide.

Drunk, stoned and who knew what else—of the many rumors that swirled through the country in the weeks and months following the deaths was one to the effect that Dipendra's cigarettes had been spiked by his uncle, brother to the slain Birendra, and the man who ultimately succeeded to the throne. But whether the Crown Prince was high on cocaine or some other substance would never be known, because no autopsy was performed before his cremation.

Not a bad fellow on the whole: that's what Bik would have said about Dipendra if you'd asked his opinion before the night of June 1, 2001. A bit on the lazy side but a reasonably decent chap with good instincts about his job and his people. If King Birendra had lived another ten years, and if Dipendra had succeeded him, Bik thought, then the country might not today be riven by factions but instead would be working its way toward full democracy under its constitutional monarch.

But Dipendra's good instincts and his initiative had been put down time and again by his parents. A young man left with too little to do was forced to watch as his younger sister and brother were allowed to make the marriages they wanted, while he was denied the love of his life. And *that*, thought Bik, that was where Raman became culpable. He had no intention of saying any of this in the press conference, but that didn't stop him thinking it. Raman had been a two-faced hypocrite and had paid for it with his life. When Dipendra told his friends, Raman included, that—title, wealth and position be damned—he would be marrying the woman he loved in December and they should hold themselves ready to attend, Raman had made sure this information reached the Queen. That had been the final straw. At the Friday night family gathering, hosted that week by Dipendra, Raman got what he deserved. But Chhiri did not, and that brought Bik to reflect on this most unusual young man, Lhakpa Gyeltsen Pinasa.

It had been 2009 before he saw the boy again. He had been in England testifying on behalf of the Gurkhas who had fought in the British Army and who had residency and pension issues with the government. He had gone down to visit Mollie in Cornwall and was bringing her and Gordon up-to-date on his news when they heard him come home. Gordon had said Lhakpa spent most of his waking hours outside school at the golf course. Bik had gone on talking and then the boy had come into the room. He seemed abstracted, and Mollie was evidently a little annoyed with him as she made the introductions. They shook hands, and then Bik felt the hair rise on the back of his neck, because Lhakpa looked at him alertly and said "Ang Tak."

Mollie started and stared at her son. "What?"

Bik cleared his throat. "You heard?"

Lhakpa nodded. "I knew I recognized your voice. I was in a dark place and I heard that and felt safe."

"You did?" They gazed at each other and Bik felt immensely gratified. Eventually he explained to Mollie and Gordon that he'd been holding the boy on his knees as he drove off the palace grounds, taking him home to his mother. He'd heard Chhiri use the nickname and spoke it hoping it might help.

Mollie gave her son a quick hug, and said lightly that she hadn't heard the name in years, and Bik realized in that moment how scarred both of them had been by that night in 2001. Then Gordon had made some comment in his easy way and the atmosphere had lightened. Lhakpa had stayed to chat for a few minutes then left to do homework. Later in the evening, Bik found him at his computer splicing putts together, putts from past years at the Masters. It began to dawn on him that the boy's life revolved almost entirely around golf and he'd walked thoughtfully back to the sitting room to join Gordon and Mollie.

"He's too small for professional golf, surely?" He estimated Lhakpa was no more than five foot one or two.

"He's hardly begun to grow," said Gordon briefly, then added, so there would be no ambiguity on the subject, "Whatever it takes, Lhakpa will do it." (And he had. Bik recalled with amusement two emails from Mollie, the first sometime in 2010 with the postscript that Lhakpa had grown four inches in the past year and "Tom says he's actually taller than Ian Wooznam—have I spelled that right?—so there's hope for him"; the second, a year later, said simply "FIVE INCHES THIS YEAR. I AM GOING MAD.")

The following day Bik had been invited to a round of golf at Widemouth, a links course overlooking the bay with some trees on the inward nine. Bik, a member at Gokarna and a twelve handicap, found it challenging. He discovered it was a working round for Lhakpa and Tom, who were absorbed in discussions before and after every shot.

"Don't mind them," Gordon smiled. "Tom doesn't come out with him that often, not for full rounds, so he wants to make the most of it." Bik didn't mind. On one hole, he saw a three-wood he'd never forget, an exquisite shot of perhaps two hundred and thirty yards headed out into the bay—"What a shame" he'd said audibly—that caught the wind and turned, riding it and riding it . . . until it landed and ran smoothly to the hole cut away on the landward side of the green.

"Sorry," he'd laughed, and thought he detected the slightest swagger in the little fellow's baggy-shorted stride. A swagger that disappeared when Tom said, in his broad Yorkshire accent,

"Lucky gust there, lad." Bik looked a question at Gordon as Tom added, "Move t'ball an inch further back next time."

Gordon translated. "They live in a different world," he added in a low voice. Bik saw another example of it later in the round, when the boy's ball was directly behind a tree, perhaps eighty yards out, and he hit a draw that sailed out twenty yards wide of the green then swept round to the left onto the putting surface.

He would always remember that round of golf, early on a Saturday morning in June, with the sun, the gulls sweeping and wheeling overhead, and the wind blowing off the bay. "It was an honor to play with you, Lhakpa," he said when he left the next day. "I hope you will come out and play Gokarna some time."

The boy had been noncommittal back then, but last year Bik and two of his junior officers had the thrill of their lives when he accompanied them round the Gokarna course: none of them had ever seen golf played the way he played it. That was during Lhakpa's visit to Nepal with his mother. Seeing him for the first time in six years, full grown and taller than Bik himself, he had hugged the young man and slapped him on the back.

Lhakpa had got down to business in short order. "Do you know anything about the Crown Prince's charitable trust?"

he asked. Bik had raised an enquiring eyebrow, but Lhakpa volunteered nothing further, so he walked over to a filing cabinet and pulled out a cerlox-bound document, perhaps half an inch thick. Titled "A Foundation for Development and Growth," it had been the blueprint developed by the prince and his advisors for a charitable organization that would both raise money and allocate it in different regions of the country for the education and training of the rural population. He'd lent it to the young man, who came back a few days later with it. "Interesting," he'd said, and added that he'd built some of it into his own concept for an organization to accomplish similar ends. "This is all for the future," he had stressed. "I'm not earning anything yet and I guess if you look at what I've accomplished you might think I never will. But when the time comes, will you be chairman?" He told Bik he wanted the board to contain representatives from different ethnic groups. "Just one or two. In my opinion, Nepalis need to realize they're all the same under the skin." He also wanted a Maoist. Bik protested that it would never work. "Give it a year," Lhakpa had said. "Either he'll contribute or he'll leave severely conflicted."

Youthful confidence, thought Bik ruefully, wondering what he was letting himself in for. But he approved of Tashi's involvement. She was smart and decisive and in February of this year she had come to see him with her hydro plan. She had been exploring ways of reaching the women in remote regions, but her thinking had progressed well beyond that. If we want to keep families together and help them stay in their villages, she had argued, we want businesses to locate in those areas. Most businesses require a source of energy. "Did you know we have six thousand rivers in Nepal, Colonel?" Bik hadn't known, but he saw where she was going. Hydro ought to be relatively cheap, and would be more reliable than wind or solar. It would give families light in the evenings, and radios and computers would give them access to ideas and information and online learning. Plus, every hydroelectric plant would require a small workforce to provide maintenance and upkeep, so that investing in power plant technical training would reap dividends in the form of ready-made local employment.

He asked if she had discussed this with Lhakpa. "I wanted to talk to you first," she had said, fearing the proposal might be too expensive for the Trust to undertake. Bik promised to look into it and recommended saying nothing to Lhakpa. "Until he makes a success of his golf, any proposal is too expensive."

Yesterday's electrifying round had been a major stride in that direction, and when the assistant returned he was immersed in thoughts of three hundred kilowatt power plants.

"We're ready, Colonel. Now, do you understand the format? Rab Manga will introduce you—"

"Yes, I understand." He put down his mug, impatient to get it over with.

"Now, after the introduction, you'll describe what happened. Then Rab will have questions. Then you'll take questions from the floor and the electronic audience." She ushered him out of the makeup room and along to the sound stage.

Yesterday, after he had worked out the deal with Dharmedia and emailed Lhakpa, he had poured himself another drink and reflected on his next step. His superiors, he knew, would not look kindly on his actions on the night of June 1, 2001, and some sort of censure was inevitable. He found he was able to view the prospect with few qualms, for while his army career had been long and honorable, he had a strong feeling that his most important job was yet to come: the job of running Lhakpa Pinasa's trust.

Attitudes learned in childhood die hard, but long association with the Gurkhas and with Chhiri and other Sherpas had opened Bik's eyes to the prejudices that held his countrymen back. The reporter, Vineeta Bhool, had interviewed him then called her boss. While waiting for him and Rab Manga to join them, they had chatted. "Bhool" meant someone who worked with leather. To be born into a family like that, in a country where cows are sacred, was like being red-carded before you even reached the field. Her family were untouchables, and he marveled that she had managed to get an education. Vineeta was not exactly talkative, but he learned that putting her through school had been a family project, led by her father but supported by her mother and brother. She said nothing to Bik of her life at school but he could imagine it: being ostracized by classmates and teachers; having to wash her own utensils to avoid contaminating others; possibly even being denied water from the public tap. He'd heard of such cases and worse concerning untouchables. He was afraid to find out too much. But she was ambitious, he discovered, and after all the negotiations were done and Dharmedia had promised to let Lhakpa take the lead in making disclosure, Bik had shaken hands with Vineeta and wished her well. He resolved to do what he could to help kids from similar backgrounds get a shot at an education.

They had been waiting outside the sound stage. On a nearby monitor was a schematic showing Narayanhiti Palace and the eighteen acres of surrounding grounds. Someone—Bik thought it might be the General who had been head of palace security back then—was describing the buildings. The grounds had encompassed the Palace, usually empty; the separate residences of the King and Queen, Crown Prince and Queen Mother; the ADCs' office near the west gate; the Secretariat building, where the business of state was conducted, and lastly Tribhuvan Sadan, a complex of buildings that included the billiard hall where the shooting had occurred.

Bik checked his uniform once more in a mirror, then nodded to the assistant. She smiled and spoke into a lapel mike and opened the door.

He came out on to a raised area—not high enough or defined enough to be called a stage; more like what he'd seen on talk shows, with audience on three sides, from ground to ceiling. Three armchairs were positioned in the center of the raised area, two of them occupied. Rab Manga sat in the center chair with the General on one side of him. Bik shook hands with both of them while Rab Manga introduced him to the audience, ". . . and Colonel Basnet will describe the events of the night of June 1, 2001 in light of the recent admission made by Lhakpa Pinasa."

The three were seated now. Rab Manga went on, "But first tell us, Colonel, why you omitted this important information when you gave your original deposition?"

Bik had hoped to avoid questions until afterward. He took a moment to gather his thoughts, then spoke quietly and matter of factly. "Because I believed it served no useful purpose. It was a snap decision made in the immediate aftermath of this tragedy. I have thought about it many times since and I've never regretted it." He looked calmly at the two men, then glanced briefly at the audience before continuing, "The child was unconscious when I found him and he did not regain consciousness for several hours. I was with his mother when she questioned him, and there was nothing he could add that we did not already know."

The General looked annoyed, and Rab Manga glanced at him, then out at the audience. He could see a number of raised hands, and abruptly he changed tack: "Well, Colonel, without going further at this moment, may we ask you to describe what you saw that night."

There was a TV screen built into the flat surface of a table on a swivel arm of Bik's chair. He pulled it round in front of him and studied the schematic on the screen. He took the light pen offered by Rab Manga, glanced round quickly and saw that everyone was looking at the schematic on the monitors round the room.

The drawing had a north-south orientation. A rectangle denoted the Crown Prince's bungalow, with its front door on the southwest, and seven steps leading up to the verandah running along its length. On the eastern or right end of the bungalow was the study, with the label "jeep" beyond it and a road running south through the palace grounds, past the Palace itself and down to the south gate.

Directly south of the bungalow was a formal garden and in the center of that area the label "ornamental bridge." On its western side, at right angles to the bungalow, was the billiard hall, used as a presentation chamber in earlier times. Midway along it was a door, and the lower end of the hall showed chairs, settees, billiard table, drinks bar, and so on. A door on the southwestern end of the hall gave on to a road leading to the ADC office and the west gate.

"Very well," said Bik, into his lapel mike. He adjusted the angle of the table surface so that he could easily point with the light pen. "As you know, the Friday night gathering took place in the billiard hall here; the main entrance to the hall was through this door on the southwestern end. Sometime after 8:30 pm, Prince Dipendra left the hall through the garden door, went through the garden and up the steps into the bungalow. Now, in the study, here, Prince Raman and Chhiri Sherpa were finalizing some last-minute changes to the trek that had been meant to start on the Saturday morning. The boy Lhakpa was playing behind the settee at the back of the room.

"We know that the Crown Prince went up to his bedroom, changed into his combat uniform, took up a 9mm Glock pistol, an MP5K submachine gun, a Colt M-16 assault rifle and a SPAS 12-gauge pump-action shotgun. On his way out, his orderly asked if he wanted the emergency bag that he customarily took on treks. He said it would not be necessary. He came downstairs, walked along to the study, opened the door and using the MP5K, fired a short burst, most of which took Prince Raman in the back of the head. Seated to the Prince's right, Chhiri Sherpa was killed by a bullet to the temple. Lhakpa has stated that he heard a very loud bang and jumped to his feet. The Prince saw him, turned and left."

The TV picture changed from the schematic to the three men, as Bik paused to drink from the glass of water on the table between him and Rab Manga. Then he continued, and the drawing came up again. His pen traced the route he described.

"No one heard that burst of fire. It was too brief and too far away. The Crown Prince crossed the garden and entered the billiard room where the guests were gathered. As we know, he shot his father with three shots from the MP5K, then exited through the door and discarded the shotgun. He returned to the billiard room, dropped the MP5K on the floor and used the M-16 to shoot his father again, along with six other relatives, including his sister. These shots were heard at the ADC office. Several officers ran out and up the road toward the billiard hall, intending to enter through the main southwest door. Because I was ADC to Prince Raman and I knew where he was, I drove round in my jeep, parking here, against the east end of the bungalow. I could hear a woman's voice shrieking and cursing and I heard a burst of fire as I entered the garden and saw Prince Nirajan, the Crown Prince's younger brother, fall to the grass. The Queen, still shrieking, was advancing toward the Crown Prince, who was backing away from her up the verandah steps toward the front door. She followed him up the steps. I was forty feet away but directly behind her." He stopped again and sipped some water.

"I saw the boy Lhakpa bolt out of the study above me on the right and run along the verandah toward the Crown Prince. I think he was yelling. At the same moment, the Queen turned abruptly and started down the steps. The Prince opened fire. I dropped to the ground.

"When I looked up the Prince was jogging down the steps into the garden. The boy was running on a course to intercept him. . . " He paused, and saw once more in his mind's eye the wild dash, the small legs pumping, hair on end in matching righteous fury. "I leapt to my feet and followed. The Prince reached the ornamental bridge here, and turned. The boy caught up with him and began kicking and punching him. The Prince staggered, looked down, pulled out his pistol, cried out, and shot himself in the temple. As he fell, his knee hit the boy in the head and then he dropped on top of him.

"I reached them a moment later and pulled the boy out. He was unconscious but did not appear to be injured, although he was covered in blood from the Queen. I carried him back to the study and found the bodies of Raman and Chhiri, and that was when I made my decision. I could hear that the ADCs had reached the other victims, so I took the boy to the jeep and drove out the south gate. It took me no more than ten minutes to get him home to his mother. At no time did he open his eyes or speak. I returned to the palace in less than half an hour.

"At midnight, when all the victims had been removed to hospital, I returned to check on the boy. He was awake and in great distress. I was able to question him. He saw and heard nothing that we did not already know, so I left them and returned to the palace." He leaned back from the monitor and looked at Rab Manga, then at the General. "His mother has stated that Lhakpa spent more than a year in psychiatric counseling. I am convinced that repeated questioning, not to mention the notoriety that would have arisen from his action, would have been very bad for him. I take full responsibility for my decision to withhold this information. His family had nothing to do with it."

Bik finished speaking. A hundred hands went up and monitor lights flashed red.

SUNDAY

O O O O

It is not the mountain we conquer but ourselves.
–attributed to Sir Edmund Hillary

In the Crow's Nest

Email message taken from server
From: info@anmemberscores.com
Date: Sunday, April 10, 2016, 7:03 am
To: kenchi@chhirisherpatrekking.com.np
Subject: Lhakpa, Sunday at Augusta

Hi Kenchi
Don't reply to this address! I liberated this laptop from the pro shop and its what the members use to put in there scores but they won't be playing today (lol) and in any case I'll take it back soon but I've got time to kill and its easier writing on this than texting.

Thank you for your message. I got so many this morning I cant read them except for the important ones. Tom sent a message. Did I tell you what they did for him at home a couple of weeks ago? The whole town bought him a first-class round trip package but he turned it down. I mean he's not short of a bob or two but he already said he couldn't handle the suspense. I dont know how old he is but pretty old. But when someone warned him the town would be making this presentation he said they had more brass than brains (that means more money than sense) and told them to get a refund. He's with me in spirit, that's what counts.

Back to your message. I dont know why I did it, Kench. I was seven and angry. Tell Pasang I dont think it was brave, just brainless if you really want to know. But it's ancient history now. For me I mean. Tashi and Mum and Gordon are having a difficult time, with the press and so on. I'm going in to the hotel a bit later to see if I can help.

Anyway let me tell you about this place. Have you seen pix of the clubhouse? You may have noticed the bit on top that looks like a stupa. That's where I sleep! It's called a cupola and it's part of the Crow's Nest. The rest is a largish room below the cupola, I'd say almost as large as the top floor of your mum's place. Its got white walls and green carpet, and four cubicles around the walls with beds. The centre part is arm chairs and a TV and on one end there's a ladder up to the cupola. A couple of years ago, when they expanded the field they wanted another bed for amateurs. So they renovated the cupola and put two beds in it and that's where I've been sleeping. Its very bright and quite hot up there and you need ear plugs and one of those airline sleep masks if you want to get a good night's sleep but wow! It is so worth it. You can see everything, all the way round.

I slept really well last night. You know, one of those really deep sleeps where all you remember is total blackness. Then it went sort of grey. Then I heard this bird. And then I smelt bacon and woke up. What a morning! The tree trunks were pink from the sun, you know? The way it is early on. And I could see down Magnolia Lane, and the Founders' Circle and then I saw the bird. I know you've got just about every bird in the world in Nepal, but do you have robins? Cuz thats what this was, just a redbreast only bigger than the ones at home. I woulndt have known otherwise, but its the only bird I know other than seagulls (and eagles ha ha). It was sitting on a branch just singing its heart out. That little chap must have been created last of all when the world was made, because he was perfect. He made my day.

Then I went over to my roommate's bed (he moved out after two days) and looked out at the oak tree and the course. It just lay there, peaceful and with—have you ever seen tissue paper, Kenchi? There was a mist over the fairways, like a layer of soft tissue paper is the only thing I can think of, like a giant present waiting for me to unwrap it. As if I was the ruler of the universe or something.

So anyway, I got dressed and crept out without waking the other four chaps. There's all kinds of pictures on the walls, Bobby Jones and Byron Nelson and Slammin Sam Snead, its so cool. Then you go down this narrow staircase and you see a door that says "Masters Club Room—Private." Its the Champions locker room and I looked in there when I first came. It's got wooden lockers round the wall, and tables and chairs in the middle, and a big display case that's covered up and locked. I was told it has replicas of all the prizes, including the low amateur's medal, which I'll be getting, and some of the crystal, and a sterling silver reproduction of the Clubhouse, which is the Masters Trophy. Oh, and a green jacket.

Anyhow, I didn't hang around this morning, I went down another floor to the Grill Room. It looks out over the first fairway and even at six-thirty it was busy, with members and some rules officials and a couple of players all having breakfast. People kept giving me sideways looks so I expect they'd seen Bik's press conference. (I got a message from him saying it went well and wishing me luck.) Anyway, I ordered orange juice and hotcakes. Have you ever had pancakes, Kench? Same thing. It's really important to serve them on a hot plate with soft butter and warm syrup, but I've been here long enough now that they know exactly what I like. So I had hotcakes, and then I had scrambled eggs with sausages and hash browns (potatoes) and two rounds of toast. And while I was practising twitching (more in a min), Joe from yesterday joined me. He's one of the members here, and I like him. He's easy going and talks in a sort of drawl. I dont know what he does, but they're all supersuperachievers, the members. It's a bit like Sherpa Heaven here.

Anyway, Joe wanted to warn me about the media. I'm still thinking about it, but what he said was, "If the media ask you questions you dont like, you can always say 'no comment'." He said he didn't just mean "this Nepal business," as he called it. "If they see they've got a live one, the press'll ask you about the war, free trade, climate change, Tibet, and so on." When I said I had opinions on those things, he just said, "Uh huh. And you may just want to go ahead and learn the hard way, but the more you put out there, the more you'll be misquoted or taken out of context. You and your family. You might pass this advice on to them, too, son, even if you dont want to follow it." I sat there eating my toast (btw, have you tried peanut butter and strawberry jam on toast? Outstanding!!!) and thinking about what he said. "Believe me, son," he said finally. "I've been there." Then he told me to let my clubs do the talking, and off he went.

I have to say, I didn't want to hear this. I was going to kill an hour or so later on by standing under the oak tree and just waiting for any reporter who wanted to chat. Am I being an idiot, Kench? The thing is, until yesterday I hadn't done anything except use up air. Now people want to talk to me, and I have things I'd like to say. I really do.

Oh well. Consider yourself warned. You might want to say "no comment" if the reporters bother you.

I mentioned twitching, just to finish off, because I've got to go and hit balls in a minute. Kat (my caddie) said yesterday that under stress the big muscles freeze and the little ones twitch. So I thought I'd practice twitching to get a head start, in case it becomes necessary. But I was getting egg and sausage all over the floor. So I'll try it on the range.

Today's a big one.

Lhakpa

PS: Joe said I must have been a feisty little varmint. Tell Pasang.

PS2: He also said they like to take care of their guests but the press can be cruel in the big old world. I wish you could hear him talk. I guess I'm going to have to listen to him.

Kat's Story

I could hear them as I entered the hotel lobby: talking heads on the Golf Channel. I glanced over toward the monitor, then saw Tashi beyond it, in the coffee shop. I headed that way, half listening to the TV.

". . . an outstanding leaderboard, Larry. Six—count 'em, six!—marquee names, plus Lin Jinhai, who could surprise us all. A win on the West Coast three weeks ago, plus three European events—"

"Right! And let's not forget the wild card, Jay. Maybe the wildest wild card this stately tournament has ever seen."

"What do we make of this kid, Larry? What's he going to do?"

I reached the entrance. Tashi sat sideways to me, but a pillar had blocked my view of the opposite chair and I saw that she had company: a good-looking tanned dude wearing a Robert Talbott sports shirt. Charlie drops a bundle on those. I backtracked out of there.

". . . more likely he'll drop quickly down the board."

"No shame in that, Jay, he's already made his mark. But let's not jinx him—"

"Oh shut up," I muttered and headed for the elevator. I punched Up and it opened at once.

I was suffering from too little sleep. Tony had called too early and been far too cheerful. "I've been up for hours. There was a mist rising off number ten fairway, Kat. It looked so cool."

"Uh hunh. Was there a genuinely important reason for your call or did you just want to piss me off?" You have to stand up for yourself outside office hours.

"I'm off to the driving range for an hour. Can you meet me at the hotel after that? Gordon's room."

At least he had sounded okay. But I was bothered by seeing Tashi with some rich stranger, and I hoped they'd reached some sort of understanding last night.

I got off the elevator, and two guys were all over me.

"You're Tony Pinasa's caddie, aren't you? Kat Archer? Hiya Kat, would you mind if we ask a couple questions?"

I just stood there letting the words wash over my head and stared at the carpet. No pattern, just dark blue. Like my mood.

"Did Tony tell you what he did when his dad was killed?"

"No."

"Did you see it this morning?"

"Yes."

"What does it mean for his game today?"

I raised my eyes to look at the speaker, a stocky guy with longish hair. "What?"

"He looks to be impulsive, doesn't he? Short sighted? Not good round this course. Will you be able to rein him in?" He must have seen something in my expression because he changed tack. "You had a strategy session last night. What did you decide?"

I decided to walk straight ahead and too bad if I trod on one of them.

The other guy spoke. "How do you like his chances today, Kat?"

"I'm sure he'll win."

I realized they were writing this down and broke out in a cold sweat. "Aw look, guys, I was just kidding." I don't get interviewed much. Thank God. I waited till both of them looked up, then repeated it: Just kidding. And sighed inwardly because now I'd have to give them a sensible answer. Sorted round the brain for some words. Put them in order. "Tony has a solid game and a good head on his shoulders," I glared at the stocky guy. "That's really all I know at this stage. Obviously I'm hoping for good things."

The stocky guy said, "If he won, you wouldn't get a cent, would you?" He seemed pleased.

"Gotta go, guys."

I found the right door and knocked. Gordon let me in. He was on the phone, and covered the receiver briefly, smiling. "Morning, Kat. Tony isn't here." He indicated the phone. "Sorry." He turned away and resumed his conversation.

Directly ahead was a queen bed plus night tables, desk—the usual hotel stuff. The room was in the shape of an L, and I walked through to the living room part and sat down on a chesterfield opposite the TV.

I already knew Tony wasn't there: I'd seen him on my way in, surrounded by photographers and journalists in the parking lot. I'd put my head down and walked on by, relieved to get inside without being noticed. I had a pretty good idea why I was here, too. I leaned back and shut my eyes and wished I was back in bed.

Charlie had called this morning while I was eating breakfast. "That's an unusual kid. Aren't you glad I got you into this? I'm so excited I'd hop on a plane and join you but my back's shot." Then he'd dropped his bombshell. "No need to worry about this now, Kat, but I'm releasing you. If you want to join Tony permanently, you've got my blessing. I'm gonna hang it up and focus on the fish." My heart took a header into my shoes. And why tell me this now? Then he went on and I understood: "Tony called me. He'd like you to caddie for him, wanted my permission to ask you. Well, Kat, you know how it is. I didn't want him having doubts or anything during the round and I was going to make the announcement anyway, next week—"

"Yeah, it's always about Tony, isn't it," I'd snapped. "Nobody stops and thinks what about me, dammit." I was being unreasonable—after all, Charlie's back has been getting worse in recent years, so his news wasn't all that surprising—but I didn't care. I hated being the last to know. I felt deserted and didn't like it, especially not today. Told him I'd get back to him later. I doubted I'd be caddying for Tony if Tashi stayed in his life, but at that moment, the thought of going home to Vancouver and just vegging out was so appealing I didn't care.

Gordon's call ended and he came round and sat down opposite me in an armchair.

"How are you?"

"I'm fine," I made it sound upbeat. "Where's everyone else?" I'd thought this was supposed to be some kind of team thing, make sure we're all on the same page, resolve any differences, etc. etc.

"Mollie's next door. Not in a very good mood. Tashi's downstairs meeting with a patron." He saw my look. "From the course. He came up to us yesterday, curious about Tony's visor, and Tashi answered a lot of questions about the School for Hill Kids then agreed to meet him this morning to answer more." He leaned forward. "Now let's get back to you. Are you worried about being on your own?"

I looked at him suspiciously. Did he know? "What do you mean?"

"You're worried because you haven't got Charlie's experience to lean on. Aren't you?"

Very perceptive. I've been in one of the last groups before, and in majors, too, but Charlie always took the brunt of the load. He was older and had more experience than me. Now I'd be the senior and the more experienced, and everyone would expect me to keep my head, and it was worrying me more than I'd realized.

"Relax." He smiled. "I have every confidence in you. You've done a wonderful job all week, why should today be any different?"

I could give him a gazillion reasons but just the thought of them was sending my pulse racing. He changed the subject.

"I just had a call from the agent we've had our eye on for years."

"I'll bet. They'll be coming out of the woodwork today."

There's a school of thought that says the agencies have ruined a lot of promising young golfers, by signing them too young to lucrative endorsement deals. The kids begin to think they're special, and they embrace the good life and forget about practicing. They drop off the radar for a year or ten, and sometimes they make it back and sometimes they don't. Tony's an interesting contrast. By his own admission, he hasn't played decent golf since he was fourteen or fifteen, and his lackluster career and doubtful reputation meant no one was interested in representing him. Gordon had contacted this particular agent, an older man with a reputable agency, a couple of years ago. He hadn't been enthusiastic and they left it that Tony would contact him when he felt he needed an agent. That all changed yesterday.

"He called for two reasons, first because he thinks he's too old for Tony, but wants him to consider his younger partner, who apparently hopped on the red-eye out of Heathrow last night. We'll see him this evening."

"Do you agree about the age thing?"

"I always did, but Tony was set on having this chap. We'll see how he gets on with the partner. And the second reason he called was to express the hope that we wouldn't try to whitewash Tony's background." He glanced at me. "Did you see Bik's interview?"

"Has anyone not seen it?" We were both silent for a minute. I wondered if Gordon had heard the questions about Tony's character. Decided not to bring it up. Thought about the agent's comment. "If you mean about his gang, and the stealing and so on, I agree with him. No point trying to hide that stuff, or fake his background."

He nodded. I had another thought. "If you mean the shrink stuff, so what? Lots of people see a shrink. He's not psychotic. Is he?"

Gordon hesitated. "I don't think so." He saw my expression and grinned. "I'm pulling your leg, Kat. Please relax. I mean it. You're going to be fine today."

He changed the subject, and as we helped ourselves to coffee from the carafe on the desk, he went on telling me about the agency. "It isn't huge but Tony likes the way they've handled other athletes. He's heard about players being overtraveled and overexposed and he doesn't want any part of that."

When a player first wins on tour, his agent may try to milk the win for all it's worth. The player finds himself flying all over the world for fat appearance fees, and changing his clubs for fat endorsement fees, and generally after a year or so of this his game goes to hell in a hand basket. It used to be called being IMG'd because the biggest talent agency in the business, IMG, was also the best at generating these extraordinary earnings for its roster of players. Good agents make sure their players aren't overworked or overtraveled, even if the agency's fees are less in the short term, because such players are apt to have a longer shelf life.

Tony called while we were talking about this. He'd led the press on a fine chase round Augusta, luring them away to give his family some peace. He was back at the course, and since Gordon had calls to make and Tashi hadn't put in an appearance, I finished my coffee and left.

o o o

Mollie was in a foul mood. "At least you're not wearing that overall."

"It's a jumpsuit."

"You must be joking. It's what they wear at the garage to change the oil. An overall. I suppose they used to have little darkies all kitted out in them. Lovely contrast. Very antebellum. Or is it ante post bellum? Or what do I mean?"

"I don't know." I'd only looked in to say hi. I'd followed her into the room and was about to sit down but now I turned to leave.

"Kat, don't go. I'm sorry."

"This business is nothing to do with me, you know."

"I know."

"I'm just the caddie."

"I know. I really am sorry." She waited until I came back and sat down, then went on. "No one blames you for anything. Quite the contrary." She picked up her phone. "I've had so many calls. So many 'why didn't you tell us' messages. I don't know why I didn't tell them. I honestly don't."

"Isn't it like the colonel said? If people had known it would have been harder for him to recover?"

Mollie gazed out the window, black mood meeting bright sunlight. She sighed. "We always seemed to be going from pillar to post. One precipice to another. All his life." The first three years, she said, had been a period of adjusting and putting down roots and visits to the therapist. Just when he seemed to have recovered, his uncle was killed by the Maoists, and for two years it was gangs and nothing but trouble. "We were terrified he was going to get his hands on a gun of some sort. Terrified." Then three years of comparative peace after he discovered golf. "We might have said something then, but what was the point? It all seemed so distant, past and buried." Then another three years of adolescent hell. "We had Kalden and Tashi down on weekends. We should have told them, Kat. But Lhakpa was struggling with growth spurts, his golf was a mess and frankly he was monstrous most of the time, poor love."

"You might tell Tashi all this. I'm sure she'd understand."

"I did. We had a lovely heart to heart last night before dinner, bless her." She changed the subject. "We can't set foot outside, you know. It's absolute hell."

I told her what Tony had done and that lightened her mood, but not much. Poor Mollie. I studied her as she stared out the window. She looked tired and harassed and middle-aged.

"I wonder if we were right to put our own lives so completely on hold?" She scrolled through a message and I leaned back and dozed for a moment. She began to speak but I didn't move. "I work at Portsmouth hospital three days a week. I've got a flat there. And a lovely man I met five years ago. He's wanted us to move forward, you know, and I never would because I didn't want to rock the boat. Gordon's the same. He takes out the occasional woman but he made a commitment to me and Lhakpa the year we came back and he's been like a rock. Every weekend he would come down. You have no idea what a sacrifice that was, Kat."

I did, though. I sat listening to Mollie and thought about what people do and don't do for love. About how much I could have done for Josh, and didn't. All the times I could have flown home on Sunday night and instead just grabbed a ride with one of the guys to the next event. It had been all give and take with us: Josh gave and I took. I'd tried to make it up to him in the last few months and I know I helped, but it was much too late in the day.

"You know what you should do, Mollie?" I sat up. "You should enjoy the day. You should book an appointment at the spa downstairs. Get the works—hair, facial, nails. Take Tashi with you. Then come on out to the course, where there are no phones and the media are on their best behavior, and smell the flowers." I stood up and added heartlessly, "You might even try an azalea cocktail."

"Wretched girl!" she laughed and walked me to the door.

I went back down to the lobby. Tashi wasn't in the coffee shop so I left.

o o o

Back in uniform, I stood with Tony's bag near the entrance to the practice range, watching him autograph hands and programs, flags, visors, caps and pairing sheets. Other players were also working the line but he was clearly the main attraction, and he was enjoying himself. I could have gone on in and found a tee spot, but I liked watching.

I'd been round the course earlier, checking pins. More than half were traditional Sunday positions. The yardages were mixed: some tees were right up to the forward markers; others were way back. The speed of the greens was a puzzle, though. I saw some shots into a couple of greens—seven, for instance—that should have bounced right off. Instead they held. If players could stick the ball we'd be seeing some low scores. It was a pleasant day but not hot, and I wondered what the greens would be like in a couple of hours. I discussed it with Tony when we met, as arranged, near the umbrellas. He'd spent an hour going round the course himself, and we concluded that a couple of holes might reward a more aggressive approach.

He was working his way back down this end of the line now, and stopped in front of two kids, one white and the other that ebony color that you see in black Africans. The black kid was a bit taller and maybe a little older. Tony signed his yellow course flag and his dad gently drew him back from the line. There was an African player—a non-South African, I mean—in the field, though I don't recall which country, nor whether he made the cut. Maybe these guys were his guests. The little white kid had something in his hand and Tony was scrunched down eye-to-eye with him. He opened his hand to show a golf glove, and he talked while Tony listened. I guess Tony asked him a question because he nodded and held out his hand. Tony took the glove and carefully pulled it on his own left hand while the kid's eyes watched intently. Then asking another question and getting a nod he rested his left arm on his thigh, made a fist and signed the glove. The kid stepped in close to watch, putting his hands on Tony's writing arm, but I guess it didn't bother him. Then he carefully took the glove off, loosening each finger first, and folded it into a square. The kid took it, they talked some more, then Tony gave the kid's back a quick rub, one-two. He stood up, signed a couple more autographs and joined me, and we walked into the range.

"What was all that about?"

"The Danish kid? His dad died on a peace-keeping mission in Africa."

I glanced sideways; I reckoned he would be getting a lot of that sort of thing. He appeared to be good at it.

The range wasn't full. I could see Alex at the far end by himself. Gardner and Lin were working with their caddies. We found an open spot to practice and Tony did his stretching exercises while I picked up a couple of bags of balls. The trouble began immediately. He started off with his seven, tried a shorter iron then longer, tried a wood then another wood. Made no difference. He couldn't hit the ball. Oh he could hit it—but he said it felt like hitting a rock, and more than once he skulled it, hitting a thin low skittering shot with the edge of the blade instead of the face. They kind of stuck out in that crowd. The guy next to us glanced back briefly, not wanting to seem rude. If Tashi had been standing there it would have been less surprising. Skulls are commonplace on a public range.

He couldn't feel any muscles twitching, he said. In between checking his posture and alignment, he'd pull out his cellphone. He had it on vibrate, and he'd flip it open, then put it away and try hitting some more. I'd been careful not to ask how things went last night, but now seemed like a good time to change that policy.

"I didn't get a chance to talk to Tashi this morning. She okay?"

"Yeah." He tried to hit a five-wood draw. Failed. Stopped, looking down at the club. Exchanged it for his seven-iron and tried to dribble a ball. Dropped it. Finally opened up.

He'd had a good chat with Tashi last night, he said. They

both apologized and she sent him back to the Crow's Nest, saying it had worked for him so far. He'd come back and slept soundly and when he hadn't been able to get into the hotel this morning he had left her a message. He'd had a text back saying she'd be coming out later on.

It didn't sound exactly rapturous but he needed to stay positive. "Perfect! She's probably at the spa with Mollie, and we'll be seeing them in a couple of hours."

He perked up at the spa news, and shot off a message to his mother then resumed practicing. I left him after another visit to the ball building, and went to sit in the stands with Gordon and Danny. They were discussing Ladbroke's, the British betting company.

"He's fallen from five hundred to fifty to one, Kat," said Gordon cheerfully.

"No kidding?" I felt a twinge in my cheek and rubbed it.

"I saw a quote from you earlier, Kat," said Danny. "Perhaps that was a factor? You said you thought he would win."

I groaned. "I was just kidding."

"You mean you don't think he will win?"

I wanted to tell Danny to get lost, but I'd promised him an interview on Thursday and he was still waiting. Now I said nothing, just sat there worrying. He changed the subject. Did I think Tony would agree to an interview with the same guy who had interviewed Colonel Basnet? I said I'd ask. Gordon spoke as I stood up.

"Anything I can do?"

"I don't think so." I started to leave and, telling Danny he'd be back in a moment, he came with me. We stopped by the low hedge between the stands and the tees and watched.

Tony was looking a little better, now beginning to work the ball.

"Is he feeling the stress, Kat? Christ!"

We watched as a shank flew off to the right.

"I'd better get back."

But Tony had propped the club next to the bag and was walking over. He checked his phone and stopped in front of us. "I'm going for a walk. Put the bag away, would you?"

I stood there, flat-footed and speechless, as he turned toward the entrance. Gordon was quicker, and put a hand out to stop him.

"What is it?"

"Nothing."

"Rubbish."

He stared at the ground, the stands, the ball building.

"I don't know if I can explain."

"Try."

Danny was behind me, and I let the other two walk ahead a few paces. "We're just discussing it, Danny," I lied. "I'll give you the sign if it's a go, okay?"

"Yes, Kat. Please remind him that everyone in Nepal is awake and would be very excited. . . ."

I promised to bear it in mind and rejoined the others. Tony said, "I know I have obligations, Gordon, and I'll do my best. But if I've lost her—"

"What's happened?" I asked in alarm. "Have you heard from Tashi?"

"She isn't with mum. She didn't come out with Gordon." He looked at us both. "I'm unbelievably thick. Nothing matters without Tashi. Not golf. Nothing. And I—" he had difficulty finishing it, "—I only realized it this morning."

He walked off.

"Wait here," Gordon told me and went after him.

"Is something the matter, Kat?" Danny was back like a persistent fly and I wanted to swat him. Mustered a smile. "Just Sunday nerves, Danny."

"If we cannot speak to Tony, Rab Manga said he would like to interview you. Could we do that? It's just over the way, here." He indicated the BBC studio in the trees beyond the short-game practice area.

"Oh sure." *In another life.*

But Gordon was waving Danny up and he joined them. The studio entrance is off the main drag, and the pair of them headed out of the practice area. Gordon came back to join me.

"This is just nonsense, right?" I asked. "Just stress."

He shrugged. "I don't know, Kat. I'm sorry it happened now, but I'm not sorry it happened. He has to get his priorities straight." He fell silent so I decided to put in my two bits' worth.

"She had a long way to come, Tashi."

"She did."

"Tony—we've been doing a lot of talking out on the course. It worried me that she might not understand."

"She understands, Kat. And she wouldn't have minded at all except that they've spent almost no time alone since she got here." He folded his arms and we watched Mike the soldier chatting with Tony and Danny at the entrance. "Tony had very clear ideas on what he had to do coming in here. He just didn't factor in time with Tashi." Mike started toward us. "Don't misunderstand me, Kat. He loves her. He always has."

"I got that," I said drily.

"He's a warrior! You should have told me, Gordon! Morning, Kat." Mike beamed at each of us in turn.

"I like that colonel. Takes care of his men." He looked out over the range and up at the sky and heaved a contented sigh. "Isn't this fantastic? Too bad it's Sunday." His gaze returned to Gordon. "Got time for coffee?" They headed for the umbrellas. "I'm changing my allegiance," I heard him say, "Alex is a great guy but this is the brotherhood."

I parked the bag and made my way back to the caddie building. Way too much excitement for one day and we weren't even on the course.

I found a chair in front of the TV and closed my eyes and must have dozed off because the next thing I knew, someone was shaking my arm as I tried to pull out the flagstick and the trapped ball came up with it and dribbled onto the green and I shot upright in fright.

"Kat? Someone to see you."

"In a minute," I muttered and went off to my locker and the washroom. I washed my face then put on moisturizer and sun block. Mollie was waiting when I stepped outside, a younger-looking, more cheerful Mollie who gave me a hug.

"Dear Kat, how are you feeling?"

We sat on the porch and she held out a little gift-wrapped box.

"What?"

"I want you to have this, Kat. You've been so good for my son."

I shook my head. "Just doing my job, Mollie."

"Yes, dear. Don't argue. Open it."

It was a little gold four-leaf-clover pin. I loved it.

"Here. Let me pin it on your—ahem!—lovely jumpsuit," she said and we laughed. I asked her to pin it on the underside of the collar so that it wouldn't glint in the sun and distract someone.

"I'll know it's there, and that's what matters." I thanked her.

We were en route to the umbrellas when we met Tony walking up from the BBC studio. He seemed subdued, resigned almost.

"Darling," Mollie embraced him. "She'll be here."

"Have you heard from her?"

"No, but she's probably been delayed in traffic. Stop worrying." She smiled up into his face. He looked at me.

"Might as well see if we can hit a ball, Kat."

So I retrieved the bag and we tried again. He treated it as a mechanical exercise: could he fashion a shot, any shot, that would allow him to advance the ball toward the green. It still felt like a rock on the club face, he said, but he was able to achieve some success with the five-wood and we concentrated on that. "Interesting idea, hitting two-forty all the way round the course." He even perked up a bit at the challenge.

The interview had been okay, he said. The BBC feed evidently goes to quite a lot of countries other than the UK, and he was questioned by the English commentator and Rab Manga, the guy who interviewed Colonel Basnet. "I thought of telling them I can't hit the ball, but they'll work that out for themselves."

Thirty minutes into the session, I stood back behind him and watched critically as he tried to work the ball with the five-wood. He was looking a bit more fluid and I turned to grab another bag of forty balls from the ball building—and stopped dead. Tashi was sitting in the stands directly behind us, all by herself. She gave me a small wave and I hustled over.

"Where have you been?"

"Oh Kat, it is a saga, my morning." She laughed. "I arrived in great state, in a rubbish—in a garbage truck. You should have seen the expression on the guards' faces." She looked past me and I turned round. Tony was standing watching her. I turned back to see her give him the same small wave. We had no time for this.

"He was afraid he'd lost you," I said bluntly and I was relieved to see the alarm in her face. She came to her feet and I turned to find Tony a couple of feet behind me. He looked unsure and shoved his hands in his pockets then immediately pulled them out.

"Oh Tashi, I'm so sorry, I'm so sorry—"

"No, no, no, darling Lhakpa, it's my fault, I should have come out—"

"No, it's me, Tash—"

They reached for each other and I went to get the balls, taking the time for a short chat with one of the other caddies. Watched as RJ hit a sweet fade out to the two-ten green. Came back to find them on the bottom row of the stands, their heads close together. Hovered nearby. I hoped he'd made his feelings clear—then I glanced over just as Tashi looked up. A tinge of pink under her cheekbones, a deep upwelling happiness in her eyes. Guess he did. I looked away but I could hear them.

"You haven't lost interest?"

"Lost interest? Oh Lhakpa, I have so much to tell you, I don't know where to begin."

I glanced at my watch. Cleared my throat.

"Look, there's less than two hours till tee time."

They separated. Sort of. He took her face between his hands and kissed her. "Where were you, anyway, Tash?"

"It would take too long to tell you. Go." She kissed the palm of his hand. "Go and hit balls." She pushed him away.

The American Embassy, Kathmandu

At 11 pm the American embassy was ablaze with lights as guests streamed inside, passing through a comprehensive but efficient security check. The largest reception room had been set up for the occasion, with clusters of chairs in front of large screens all round the room and down the center. Dress was less formal than usual, since this was not a typical Embassy affair. The gathering was shot with color: saris of fuchsia, tangerine and turquoise, patterned Dhaka topis for many of the Nepali men, Sherpas with dark suits and pale yellow prayer scarves, Tibetan refugees in robes and mala beads, the women with brightly striped aprons. Waiters in white jackets circulated with drinks while around the room, Marine guards in dress blues looked on.

All day long, Rab Manga's show had been the talk of the town, and people found themselves remembering and rehashing the details of that dreadful night in 2001. Curiously, the action of Chhiri's child seemed to add a rational note to a national nightmare. It made sense that the Crown Prince would take his own life, and it explained why he'd done it so badly, under the battering of an outraged child. For the first time, many people found an element of closure, of finality to the tragedy.

Wearing a light suit with an open-neck shirt, Bik Basnet took a drink from a hovering waiter and declined a momo from another. He heard his name called, and turned.

"Hello Ross!" The two men shook hands. Ross Korbin was an American aide with whom he'd had both professional and social dealings.

"Who knew we had so many golfers in Kathmandu?" Ross grinned and punched him lightly in the shoulder. "That was good, what you did for the boy. I'd have done the same," he said, and issued an invitation to join a group of aides and attaches at one end of the reception room.

Bik promised to join him in a few minutes, and strolled round the room looking for the Chinese diplomat. He was congratulated on his television testimony by several guests and caught a nod from Rab Manga across the room, mingling with several Bollywood celebrities in town for a film shoot.

"What do you think of your protégé's chances, Bikram?"

The leader of the main Opposition party was a Brahmin, tall, thin, a clever politician and able speaker. The two men had been school mates but had little in common.

"He's not my protégé," said Bik, then added, "but I think he'll manage."

"Mm. I expect he'll fold early. The pressure's dreadful, isn't it?" Like Bik, the Brahmin was a member at Gokarna. "Still, he's done well for a little Sherpa boy." The tone was condescending. He saw Bik's expression. "What? You don't agree?"

Bik surveyed him. "You should listen to yourself sometime," he said finally, and turned abruptly away.

Kat's Story

Tony bent over his putter on the crowded practice green. He looked good: charcoal grey pants with black belt and shoes, pale yellow shirt that worked well with his skin color and reminded me of Nicklaus's shirt in 1986. RJ Gardner and his caddie, Jake Witterich, were across from us on the far side of the green.

I'd like to be able to say that, once Tashi showed up, Tony's swing had miraculously returned, but it wouldn't be true. He said it felt a little better, and ventured to try the driver, with moderate success. We worked through the woods and long irons, then stopped, meeting the others under the umbrellas for a quick lunch. Tashi told us about her morning. Don't recall the details except for the garbage guys. "Clovis Winter," she said. "A huge black man, he was. And Deke, Deke was just little." Tony said the name seemed familiar and Tashi said there were at least four calls on his phone from Clovis Winter. "But you wouldn't answer."

"All I was looking for was your name."

"They were coming back from the repair shop in Augusta. I sat in the middle, and I told them in Kathmandu the people who pick up the garbage are untouchables. And do you know what Clovis said?" Gordon and Mike were relaxed with beers, only half-listening as they tried to watch the action on the putting green while listening to the roars on the course.

Mollie had a lemonade. "No, darling," she said dutifully. "What did he say?"

"He said, 'That's what Deke is on a hot day.'" She looked round at us all, her eyes alight. "Untouchable, he meant. Isn't that wonderful? I thought that was an amazing thing to say." She looked at Tony. "This is an interesting country, Lhakpa. We can learn a lot here."

Tony had wolfed down one BBQ sandwich and was working on a second. "Maybe in an RV, Tash?" I wished I could eat something.

She patted his hand. "Yes, my sweet, if you like. Frank Junior says they have lots of drawers. It's an appealing thought." She was talking to me. Who the hell was Frank Junior? "I like drawers. Even if I haven't anything to put in them, do you know? I like the idea of them."

"Sure thing," I replied. I ran over the contents of the bag, thought I might grab a couple of pimiento cheese now, rather than out on the course.

Tony finished his sandwich. "It's like having our own home, Tash. Just while we're on tour."

He left to change and I went to the pro shop for distraction and bought a ball-mark repair tool. Already have several, but you never know when you might need another. They make change with new bills there, so I gave them a twenty and got back a couple of crisp fives.

o o o

Finished my pre-game routine, counting clubs, checking the water bottles, balls, making sure of the band aids and energy bars. From different parts of the course you could hear applause and the occasional crowd roar. The early groups were well into the back nine by now. A crowd three or four deep circulated round the putting green. "He was meditating when I went up," I heard, "you know, sitting on the floor with his legs crossed." "It's called the lotus position, dummy." I glanced round and saw three of the teenage amateurs walking in Tony's direction. I had been watching him in between other jobs. He was sinking three-, four- and five-foot putts round the hole. He looked fine, no twitching, but I could feel a muscle in my cheek doing something odd and I wondered if it showed.

Thirty minutes. "I wanted to talk to you, Kat." Tashi slipped an arm through mine and I turned to look at her, full face. Her eyes didn't go to my cheek that I could see.

"Me, too." I gathered my wits. Had to tell her about Rule 8.1, the advice rule. Once a player hits his tee shot on number one and until he putts out on eighteen the only person he can take advice from is his caddie. Often times, it's just easier and safer for a player to talk only to his caddie during the round and if it's a slow round, they're apt to talk a lot. Doesn't mean anything. I wanted to make sure she understood that.

"Isn't he dear?" she said softly, gazing at Tony on the putting green. "Look at him, so absorbed, lost to the world." Then her focus came back to me. "Kat, would you consider being his caddie? Gordon and Mollie and I would be so pleased. That's what I wanted to say." I opened my mouth to reply, but she went on: "I know you already have a player, but just consider it. That's all I ask." She smiled. "You make a good team." And she was gone.

So much for the advice rule. Some other time, I guess.

Twenty minutes. I moved round to the far side, standing near Tony. "Hey, Kat," said Jake, walking by. "No trunk slammer here. Guess you were wrong about that, huh?"

Tony straightened. "Trunk slammer?"

"I was disloyal to you after Thursday's round. Jake just wanted you to know that." He was watching Tony. "Feeling threatened, Jake?" I asked.

Tony bent over another putt. "I see." Level of interest: zip.

Fifteen minutes. I was eating a pimiento cheese sandwich. Years since I last tried one. Plenty of carbs, and I hoped it would quieten my stomach. LinJin had three balls down; he putted the first about fifteen feet, the second eighteen and the third twelve. Checking for feel and distance control. His caddie knocked the three back and he did the same thing again. This time it was more like twenty, twenty-three, seventeen. A crowd of young Asian girls watched avidly, dividing their attention between him and Tony. Latent Bimbettes. Two men were more interested in the drill itself. "I'm going to try that," said one, "I average thirty-one putts all season. If I could just knock off two strokes. . . ."

Ten minutes. The group ahead had teed off and we walked to the tee box.

"Kat." Gordon came up and gave me a hug.

"Is my cheek twitching? Can you see?"

He looked at me. "No, it's not twitching." He smiled. "Good luck, Kat. God bless."

Tony kissed Tashi and gave his mother a hug. "Are you okay, mum? You look different." He patted her shoulder absently, looking out at the fairway. "Try not to get excited."

I had the bag down inside the ropes, counted the clubs, pulled out the driver and removed the head cover. Mollie and Tashi both waved, and I nodded back. I was trying not to think about the tee shot.

Tony and his uncle embraced, then Tony turned away and stepped inside the ropes. He was met halfway across the tee box by RJ Gardner.

"I hear you don't think much of baseball. My brother's with the Orioles. I'd be happy to get you tickets any time." He was courteous but unsmiling. His words were audible to the patrons and the buzz went round the ropes from one side to the other. They shook hands and Tony came back, made a comical face, leaned down and unzipped the pocket where he'd stashed his new visor. Pulled it out. Stitched on both sides, in bold green letters on the white visor, two words: Be Good. I stared at it, and kept staring, hoping the words would work.

"I thought I just couldn't throw a club if I'm wearing this." He took the driver and began to swing.

"Fore please, Lhakpa Gyeltsen Pinasa now driving."

We were off at last.

o o o

It wasn't possible to implement Tony's strategy. He had wanted to be aggressive right out of the gate. Quite aside from anything else, he hadn't bargained on the intense pressure. The combination of the moment, Sunday at the Masters, and the crowd, was more than he had been able to imagine in advance. The sheer numbers, thick along the fairways, were outside his experience. He could not ignore the intent gaze of hundreds of pairs of eyes, most of them belonging to golfing fans older than him, more experienced, knowledgeable, connoisseurs of the game of golf. For three days he had flown under the radar. That was over. Now he was squarely in sight, his every move exposed.

Some players, confronted with this phenomenon, convince themselves that it's just a game and they're out to have fun. I've never been sure that this approach works, but in any case it would be out of character for Tony. Others seek refuge in the known, the familiar: they run home to mother, so to speak. That's what we did. We took refuge in the details around each shot. We followed the shot routine we had used for three days. That not only helped with the crowd and the pressure, it took Tony's mind off his earlier attempts on the driving range.

"Lose no ground" was our first priority on those early holes. That meant making pars, not aggressively seeking birdies. That's what we tried to do, starting with his mediocre but safe tee shot on number one.

What's the lie? Is the ball sitting up clean? Sidehill, uphill, downhill? Okay. What's our distance? Pace off from the sprinkler head, consult the yardage book and each other. Distance to the front, the middle, the back. Next, wind. Strong or weak? Helping, hindering or neutral? Should we add or subtract a club to compensate? How about elevation? Adrenaline? Shot shape—do we want a high soft fade that will drop onto the green and hold? Is that even possible today? Or should we run a low draw into the flagstick?

We didn't just follow this routine, we embraced it, we submerged ourselves in it. Whenever those eyes threatened to overturn our intentions and intrude on our discussions, one or the other of us would talk a little louder. Like when your brother tried to insult you and you stuck your fingers in your ears and went "na na na na, I'm not listening, I'm not listening. . . ." Tony might say "yeah, easy seven should be perfect" and when he repeated it word for word three seconds later, and three seconds after that, it was no different from me saying, as I bent over his back looking at the line of his putt, "it'll break hard right two feet from the hole," except that he muttered "that's the third time you've said that."

In this manner, drawn in to our own tight little world, armored by the dozens of decisions that go to make up the playing of a hole, we arrived at the third tee at even par. I considered that quite a feat, especially since Tony still wasn't comfortable with his long game. The shots still felt hard, and while they were not so far horrible, they weren't going quite where he wanted. What saved him early on was his putting.

However, while we were prepared to settle for par, RJ Gardner had come blazing out of the box and stood three under after two holes, five under for the tournament, tied for the lead. We had discovered early that he was the crowd's favorite. Not that they were rude to Tony, not at all. They were just polite. But they thought a lot of RJ. He was the bright young talent who had won six times already on tour and at the age of twenty-two had stated that he was ready to start winning majors: he had put in his time, learned his trade, and he was ready to take it to the next level. He stood on the tee at number three and launched one, looking like a man who, having gone three under for two would be happy to make it four under for three.

The third hole is, at three hundred and fifty yards, the shortest par four on the course. It's hardly been changed at all over the years, which tells you something. It's a topnotch, challenging short hole and you can card a five or six here more easily than a four or three. The green is shaped like a boomerang and the common Sunday pin placement is on its left arm, which is only eleven yards deep front to back. Both the green and the fairway slope from right to left. The best strategy here is to decide your preferred yardage into the green, then play your drive to leave that yardage. Tony played five-wood off the tee then three-quarter wedge, keeping his arms still to remove spin.

To my left, in the trees behind the fairway bunkers, stood a leaderboard and I studied it as we stopped to wait for RJ. Not counting the main scoreboard off the first fairway, there are ten leaderboards around the course. They're massive structures, some on raised platforms, others on pedestals. Some, like this one on number three, are nestled in the woods near a green or fairway; others are out in the open. They have three components: a central leaderboard listing the top ten players and their hole-by-hole scores, and two smaller flanking panels. The panel on the left is a duplicate of the thru board shown at the tee and green on each hole: it gives the last names of the players currently on the tee or green and their scores. The right-hand panel shows the leader in the clubhouse and his score. I'd be keeping an eye on this panel later in the round.

The leaderboards are updated by volunteers connected by headsets to more volunteers at greenside. Looking over now, I could see a couple of people on the ground near the pedestal, and another one climbing the ladder to reach the board itself. For the ten leading players, the large central panel shows the player's name and to the left of it his score at the start of the round. To the right of each player's name is his eighteen-hole scorecard. To find out who's leading, scan the numbers furthest to the right.

Vanderhoef, the last name on the board (a green one left of his name showed that he started the day one over par), had completed the fourth hole. To the right of his name I saw green one, green zero, green zero, red one. That told me he had birdied number two and number four. He was currently lying one under par, two under for the day. The sixth name on the board, Gardner, showed a red two in the prior column, and then two red numbers to the right: three and five. Above him, Pinasa, also showing a red two on the left, showed the same number twice on the right. As we watched, there was a change at the top. Lin (red five on the left) now showed a red four on the right. He'd bogeyed number one. RJ was leading the tournament.

I wondered if that would last. RJ was no more than about sixty yards from the green, on the left side, which must have been a mistake because it left him no green to work with. He tried to put his pitch to the right of the pin but it rolled down past the hole into the greenside bunker. He ended up settling for bogey on the hole. Tony found the right line but the wrong weight and his putt motored over the hole. It caught the rim and slowed; otherwise, it would have run right off the other side. As it was he had an eight-footer for his par, which he managed to make, but I knew that we still had some settling down to do.

Both players parred the fourth and on five, finally, Tony hit a drive that actually felt pretty good. We had to wait out in the fairway for the group in front. A rules official and one of the players were conferring beyond the far side of the green.

"Let's talk about something," said Tony abruptly, and added, "not golf."

"How about the Stanley Cup? Or the Test Match?"

"Not sports." He paced around and I studied him. Sunday pressure, not to mention the strain of figuring out Augusta National, can grind a player down, and staying sharp mentally becomes a tremendous challenge.

"Movies, then. Or—I know. You can tell me about lama—uh, lama—"

"Lama Sangwa Dorje? Seriously?"

"That's the guy. Your uncle mentioned him. He's a hero of yours?"

Tony laughed. "Lama Sangwa rules ok!" He shoved his hands in his pockets. "That was awful back there. Didn't you think?"

"For sure. I'm feeling a bit better now, myself. You?"

"Yeah, a bit. Hm. Lama Sangwa. Sherpas are very competitive, you know."

"You don't say."

"They also believe in personal power. There are lots of words for power in the Sherpa language."

"You said 'they.' When are you not a Sherpa?"

"When I'm asked to carry something." He gave me a kind look and patted my shoulder.

"You ass," I laughed.

"So. Power words. *Chuchermu* means good at growing things or making money. There are words for people who are powerful learners, or powerful bullies. The best power word is *tsachermu,* which means you have super powers."

"So this Dorje guy had super powers?"

"He did. But not at first. He began as a trader."

"Trading what?" After hearing Tashi's history, I wasn't taking anything for granted.

"Salt from the Tibetan mines. China tea. That sort of thing. Anyhow, I guess he was a good trader, *chuchermu*. Then he became a tax collector or governor or something. Probably head man in the village, that kind of thing. So then, like all good Sherpas, he decided to give money to the monastery. Only he went one better. He founded Pangboche monastery in Khumbu. But before he decided on Pangboche, he flew all over the—"

"He flew? I thought this guy was for real? So . . . he's like a legend, right?"

"If you're going to be like that I won't tell you any more."

"Aw, c'mon."

But the green was clear. "Back to work."

We climbed back into big-game mode, but in a slightly better frame of mind. We were lying one-eighty from the flag on the middle left of the fairway opposite the bunkers. We had a good discussion about the shot and Tony decided on a low punch shot to run up the false front to the back. It's a shot well inside his comfort zone: he plays it on his home course into the wind. Six-iron, ball back in his stance, low follow-through. Coming away with a par is never a bad thing on five, and he managed it well.

He got a further lift on the sixth hole, looking at the azaleas on the slope above that short par three. You never know where the Sunday pin will be, but this year they returned to the front left, probably the easiest pin position on a difficult green. We were still away, and we took some time to weigh the wind. In the end Tony put a seven-iron into the middle-front, which left a slick downhill twenty-footer for birdie. We were on the green surveying the putt when we heard a huge roar—an Alex roar, I thought: but I was wrong. It was Pieter on eight.

Behind the Seventh Green

The stand behind the seventh green, between seven and seventeen, offers a good view of several holes: the second and seventeenth fairway and green, and the third and eighth tee and fairway. Mollie, Gordon and Tashi had decided before the round that they would come here rather than trying to follow along. Gordon had been fairly sure they would never be able to see anything because of the crowds following RJ, and he was right. So they came directly to this spot after watching Lhakpa tee off, staked out their seats and waited.

"This is hopeless, Gordon!" Mollie spoke more sharply than she intended. "Sorry, G. But really, we can't see the green for that whacking great scorecard."

"Leaderboard, Moll," said Gordon patiently. "You can however get a good look at him coming down number two. And we can practically touch him on the third tee."

The stand was positioned behind a large leaderboard facing the seventh green. This was a two-sided leaderboard so they got to watch volunteers running up and down the ladder and along the platform on both sides as they adjusted the scores. They had seen the first change when Pieter got his birdie on two. He was a popular player and his play was met with loud roars. They shared that feeling because he'd been good to Lhakpa. In fact, Mollie and Tashi had privately agreed that if Lhakpa didn't win they wanted Pieter to. They didn't say anything to Gordon because they didn't want to put him on the spot. No one expected Lhakpa to win, they knew that. They knew it was ridiculous even to think it themselves. They had listened to the comments of those around them: people with no ax to grind, people who had been coming here for years and might be expected to know a thing or two.

"Fantastic that an amateur's got this far. Bob Jones would approve."

"Just a question of when he'll start the big slide."

"Remember Venturi, 1956?"

"Nobody remembers that, it was back in the dark ages."

"Saddest last round ever, including Greg Norman. Don't argue with me. Venturi was an amateur. Lost by one after shooting eighty. Eighty! Wish I'd been there for support. Just tragic."

"I heard he was a good commentator."

"Hope this kid doesn't screw up RJ. Playing with someone who's playing badly can really drag your game down."

Mollie and Tashi had turned in on themselves, the way animals do in the midst of a storm (animals who haven't had the sense to get out of the weather). "We won't tell anyone what we're thinking," said Mollie.

Tashi agreed. "We'll just think it to ourselves."

They had screwed round in their seats to watch the action on two. They had an excellent view of the green and far up the fairway, they saw Lhakpa hit and watched his ball land some yards out. All four figures moved forward until they reached RJ's ball. "Oh God, he's miles ahead, G! Miles!"

"Relax," Gordon said. "Lhakpa plays a completely different game than RJ. He's not worried, I promise you."

RJ hit a soaring shot that landed in the middle of the green and started to the right, down the slope, ending up at the bottom, not far from the flagstick.

Tashi called down over the back of the stands to two patrons who had just arrived. In that way she learned of RJ's birdie on one. There was another roar, and someone nearby said, "I'll bet that's Vanderhoef on four." They watched as Lhakpa hit his third shot, which ended up much too far from the hole. Then there was a modest roar from the direction of the first hole, and Gordon surmised that Alex had done something—maybe made a par. A huge roar went up when RJ made his eagle, and most of the patrons left the second hole to find spots on the third fairway, so from the stand they were able to watch Lhakpa take his time over his second putt, the first having run by the hole an alarming amount, Mollie thought.

"That's two pars," said Gordon with satisfaction. "Good for him." But Mollie and Tashi exchanged a worried look. Three behind after two holes? This was reality and they weren't sure they cared for it.

The drama elsewhere on the course succeeded in driving Lhakpa from their minds, at least for a time, then suddenly he and Kat were almost close enough to call to. They couldn't see where the tee shots went, but someone near them said, after RJ hit, "Don't know what he was thinking there." Gordon explained that it was a mistake to use a driver; the hole was too short. Volunteers became busy on the leaderboard, and a red one was dropped into the fourth slot in Vanderhoef's line: Pieter had birdied the fourth and was now at one under. They heard that the tournament leader, Lin, had bogeyed number one, and they watched as the Pinasa/Gardner lines changed to show RJ's birdie and eagle. Some time after that they saw Alex, up the fairway on two, hit his second shot. "He won't be pleased with that," said Gordon as they watched the ball land in the front bunker.

"It's quite fun, really, isn't it, Tash?" Mollie looked at her affectionately.

Tashi nodded. It was a beautiful afternoon on a beautiful course with excitement all round. "How are you holding up?" she asked Mollie.

"I'm fine, darling." And in a *que sera sera* sort of way, she was. The human spirit can only take so much terror, and Mollie had had her fill over the first three days. She had come to Augusta reluctantly and in the certainty that at some point during the proceedings her son would have a complete meltdown, disgracing himself, his mother and uncle, the Sherpa people and England. It had not happened on Thursday. It had not happened on Friday. Yesterday had been far too pleasant a day for it to happen. Today she felt fatalistically prepared for whatever might come.

That aside, she was damn well going to enjoy herself. She had made things right with Kat, who was clearly feeling the stress. She had enjoyed listening to Tashi's saga, although on the whole she liked the first part best, and she was relieved and comforted to find that Lhakpa and Tashi understood one another and were happy.

Tashi was experiencing a strange sensation. It was a background sensation and in between watching shots, she would check in on it. Each time she found it still there: a spreading warmth as though her heart were actually expanding. *My dearest love. My love.* "You're my world, Tashi. I want us to be together forever." After last year, after that night in Khumbu on the slopes of the mountain, when, transported by their love they had planned their lives, Tashi had not bargained for this week's sensations. The separation, even when they could see each other, he in the fairway and she on the sidelines. The isolation. The solitude. She had begun to doubt him, to doubt herself, not realizing that they were both affected by the stress of the event. She met his eyes. "I want that too," she replied and their heads were almost touching as she heard him say, "I couldn't manage if you didn't."

Fleetingly her lost family crossed her mind. She would never cease looking for them. *Are you my brother?* she always wondered whenever she saw a Nepali man slightly older than herself. Had the boys been shot by the Maoists? Made to join them and shoot others? Where were her parents and—*oh my sister, are you alive, are you well?* Even as she and Lhakpa made their own family she would always wonder about them. But today, at last, she knew in her heart that she would never be alone.

She looked round at the course, the sky, the patrons. They would return here, she knew, whether or not Lhakpa won, and she was glad. She had learned so much today and she wanted to come back.

After coffee with the patron this morning, she had returned to her room. She spent a few minutes answering texts and emails, including one from a school friend who, knowing of Tashi's interest in hydroelectric power, had mentioned the Chinese engineers last Thursday. Her cousin in Dipayal had seen them while visiting his family's village. Now she wrote to say he had sent the photograph to Colonel Basnet as Tashi had urged. Neither of them had wanted to get in trouble with the authorities, so Tashi was relieved to get this news. The Colonel would know what, if anything, to do with the photo. She finished with her messages and turned off her cellphone, found her badge on its lanyard, and left the hotel room.

She wanted some time alone, away from crowds and the press and questions, so she'd wandered along the Riverwalk, watching the Savannah River, and had fallen in with a family from Charleston moving to somewhere north and west of Augusta, who had three kids and a U-Haul with all their possessions, and who were taking a break from their journey. When she finally checked her watch she was taken aback to see how late it was. The family had offered to drop her at the course. Tashi sat in the back with nine-year-old Frank Junior, his younger sister and the baby. She was fascinated that the whole family was moving and when Frank Junior began to complain about leaving friends and toys behind she said, "In my country, your father or mother would leave, and you might not see them for years. They would get work in another country and try to send money home." That had sounded like a good arrangement to Frank Junior, who was clearly nursing a grievance. For distraction she had asked their opinion of RVs and Frank Junior's mother, who was driving, had said she wished they could have afforded one. That was when Frank Junior made his comment about drawers.

Frank Senior's phone never left his ear, except when it died, just as the car broke down. "His charger was broken, too,"

Tashi had said to the others at lunch under the umbrella. "Can you imagine my frustration?" She had done the only thing she could after it became apparent that Frank Senior might be tinkering indefinitely: she had walked along the verge trying to thumb a ride. The first car that pulled in carried two men whose manner had raised a warning in Tashi. She'd declined their offer and resumed her walk. "I was quite prepared to scream loudly, but luckily it wasn't necessary."

Mollie had given her a hug. "I wouldn't make a habit of hitchhiking in America, Tashi."

Gordon agreed. "Those buggers might easily have dragged you off and raped you."

"Oh I don't think so. If I'd given them the badge, that's all they really wanted."

"I expect they wanted the badge *and* you, dear," said Mollie firmly. "And why not?"

Five minutes later another vehicle had pulled in, an SUV with a flag on its roof, red and blue stars in the form of an X. "That's a rebel flag," said Mike, perturbed. "What happened?"

"A rebel flag?"

"Yeah, it's from the Civil War. You know about that, Tashi?"

"Oh yes, Abraham Lincoln and the slaves."

"What happened, Tashi?"

The men in the SUV had stared at her expressionless, eyes stony. Their vehicle had barely come to a halt when, tires squealing, it sped off the verge and back into the traffic, "as though they were trying to tell me something." Mike was clearly uncomfortable and she smiled at him. "We hill people experience prejudice at home, Mike. They have to work so hard to behave like that, I almost feel sorry for them."

The high spot, though, had been Clovis and Deke, and they had reached the course before she had finished asking questions. Jobs of all kinds interested Tashi, especially in basic industries like waste collection. What were they paid for garbage pickup, she wanted to know. What did their truck cost? Could you get an electric one? A smaller one? Back home, she told them, garbage collection was labor intensive. Each of Kathmandu's thirty-five wards had a garbage team with a team leader, a tractor driver and a small cadre of sewer unblockers, all men. At the bottom of the hierarchy were twenty to thirty street sweepers, all women. However, that would change one day and the garbage workers would need retraining. With Deke she discussed waste composition (at home it was mostly organic) and recycling, and she took Clovis's business card so that she could keep in touch.

She came back to the present as volunteers got busy along the board. About ten minutes elapsed before a score got recorded, she had discovered. A red four was slotted into the Gardner row, meaning RJ must have bogeyed the third. Tashi and Mollie put their heads together and concluded it might be safe to hope again.

They watched what they could see of the action on the seventh green as well as players late in their rounds hiking up the seventeenth fairway. During a break in the excitement, Gordon and Tashi crossed the open grassy area behind the second green and bought sandwiches and drinks from the concession stand near number eight. The population round the seventh green was growing, as followers from different groups decided to linger, and they had a struggle to reach their seats. Pieter came through and they watched intently as he found the green with his second shot, missed his birdie, but tapped in comfortably for his par.

They were beginning to appreciate how good their seats were, because now all they had to do was swivel round to see the eighth tee, up slightly to the right. Eventually, they saw Pieter launch a drive that soared high above the trees lining the fairway and dropped, after an age, in the fairway beyond the bunker.

Now the group ahead of Lhakpa's, the group Mollie had dubbed Filler, was on the seventh tee. She didn't care that these were two well-known players, German and Irish, each with a devoted following. Unless they threatened to take the lead she had no interest in them. "I've had to learn about Alex and RJ and Lin Jinhai, and I'm very fond of Pieter. That's all I need to know," she had told Gordon. So she watched politely as they hit their seconds and approached the green, while her mind was on the sixth and eighth holes. Then they all heard a good-sized roar from the distant eighth.

"That's a birdie for Vanderhoef," said the man two rows down. This time Gordon agreed. His companion asked him a question and they heard him say, "Not loud enough."

"For an eagle?" Tashi asked, and Gordon nodded. A little while later they heard another noise—a biggish noise, they agreed afterward—from the sixth green.

"That's RJ," said the patron below.

"No it's not," said Gordon, quite loudly for him. "It's Pinasa." He jumped up and joined in the cheer from the sixth, and Tashi and Mollie did the same.

Kat's Story

You couldn't call it an argument, but we certainly disagreed on how to play number seven. Tony remembered that I'd seen a couple of shots stuck in close to the flag on this hole during my walk around. He was gung ho to try that himself. To do it, he'd need a long drive so that he could use a shorter club—a seven or eight—into the green. If he'd been a topnotch sand player I'd have said go for it, because if you happen to miss your approach the sand's not a bad place to be. As it was, I thought he should continue with his prudent play. But the birdie on six had given him some adrenaline, and more than that, he could see the shot.

"Listen, Kat. I've worked hard. I'm feeling confident. I think I'm due."

I struggled to keep my voice down. "You've just picked up a birdie and you figure you're due? *Due?* Are you nuts, are you—never mind. Shut up, Kat." I took the water bottle he was holding out. "Listen, you've worked hard to get one under on the day; you don't want to give it back here. That's all I have to say. You make your decision and let's move on."

He walked up to the front of the tee box and stood there gazing down the fairway. Closely lined with trees, it offers no safe strategy, beyond trying to make a good tee shot. I didn't want to talk about drives that go into the trees because that's just putting a lousy image on the table. You have to stay in the fairway. If you can find the left side you may have a flat lie; but with today's pin on the right, being on the right in the fairway allows you to use the swale behind the flag as a backstop for your ball.

Tony came back. "I'm okay with this, Kat. Let's do it."

One of the things I like about Tony's game is that he plays well within himself: he doesn't try to kill the ball. What worried me now was that he was going to disregard that completely—he was going to try to hammer the drive. Or so I thought. He told me later that he hit it as hard as he could while still staying inside the outer edge of playing within himself. He had to say this several times before he'd expressed it to his satisfaction, and I have to say I'd lost interest before he got it right. Just to give us every possible aid, I took out a new ball, inspected it for the mark, and handed it over. He planned to hit a fade up the left, so that the ball would work right at the end, and credit where it's due, that's what he accomplished. I took the club and we did what Tony liked to call the "victory thumb," which is like a knuckle tap except with thumbprints. It sounds silly and it is, but it amuses him. Me too, I suppose. He dreamt this one up a couple of holes ago as something to divert us both. "Nothing too flamboyant," he'd said.

As we walked off the tee I brought up stress and brain function. I had to. "You would never normally say the course owed you anything. Would you?" It wasn't a question. We drew abreast of the pampas that gives the hole its name and walked another twenty yards in silence before he spoke.

"You're right. I think it must be because I'm having to work harder than I've ever worked in my life." He studied the ground as we continued down the fairway.

"It's okay. You got away with one, so we're fine." I walked a few paces. "But we don't want to be taking that attitude, it's not helpful." I left it at that as we approached the ball. We'd ended up with one-sixty to the front of an elevated green, off a clean lie that was slightly below his feet. He used his seven, and took a lot of practice swings. He was visualizing the weight he wanted for the elevation, and I heard him say at one point, "Like number eight at the Amateur." In the end, it was a beautiful shot that looked as though it would catch the front bunker but didn't. It landed just on and ended up ten or twelve feet from the hole. He made the birdie, and this time he got loud applause with enough "yesses" to make it sound like a small roar.

Two birdies in a row, four under. That victory thumb just didn't do it for me. "Can't we high five it, or something?" I asked as we walked up toward eight.

"No, no. We need something precise and controlled."

Oh boy. Charlie is so—and I suddenly remembered Charlie was history and missed him overwhelmingly for a moment.

"Lhakpa!"

We both looked up as we passed the stands, and there were Mollie and Tashi waving frantically. Gordon was next to them, and he raised one hand in a "thumbs up" gesture, and pointed at it with the other, looked at us in a puzzled, good-humored way. I laughed.

"He's never appreciated me," said Tony as we walked to the tee. I glanced over to see him watching me out of the corner of his eye, and we exchanged a grin. We were feeling good, far better than earlier. The magic continued on eight, because Tony birdied this par five hole. So did RJ, going for the green in two and narrowly missing an eagle. Both players earned roars here, although RJ's was bigger but we didn't care. On nine we finally pulled ahead when Tony rolled in a long birdie putt, his fourth in a row, while RJ had to be content with par.

We went to the tenth lying six under, leading the tournament. RJ Gardner was at minus five. Alex had played par golf to that point (he was on seven), and Lin Jinhai was lying one under.

The American Embassy, Kathmandu

The Chinese diplomat, Mr. Hu, sat with a group of politicians and diplomatic personnel, watching a wall screen at one end of the large reception room. He was on one side of a semicircle, so that if he turned his head away from the screen he could hardly fail to see the group of refugee Tibetans further along the room. He wondered if this seating arrangement was accidental. He wished he had not come. But the ambassador had instructed him to put in an appearance since he himself would be out of the country.

Alex Figueres drove off the eighth tee. As Lin Jinhai came into the picture it changed to the tenth green.

"Discrimination," muttered Mr. Hu. His companion, the Nepali Foreign Minister, a Maoist, grunted an agreement. On the far side of the semicircle sat the Brahmin leader of the main Opposition party. The two politicians detested one another.

"No, no," Mr. Hu heard the Brahmin say, "they do not show a player when he's not playing well. That's all."

Not playing well. That hardly described the performance of Lin Jinhai, and the Chinese diplomat was disgusted. Clearly the young man had let his position go to his head.

He was not concentrating, not focusing, and as a result he had lost four shots.

The atmosphere in the room had become electric in the past half-hour with the play of the Nepali Pinasa. Each new birdie produced an eruption of sound, a tumult of cheers accompanied by a flight of topis. Nepalis! It took all Mr. Hu's diplomatic training to preserve a pleasant exterior.

Kat's Story

In the old days, CBS used to say the tournament began on the back nine on Sunday, although Johnny Miller once observed that if they'd been given the right to televise the whole round they would have changed their slogan. Nowadays, of course, the whole round is televised. I haven't watched it for years, but I'd say that for viewers the old saying still applies. From the players' point of view, however, it's not so clear cut.

Tony and I had followed the same methodical routine for nine holes; and we would try to follow it for the next nine. But everything would be harder. It would be harder to breathe, harder to concentrate, harder to picture the shot. Already, I was having trouble with my own breathing and I was watching my player closely for signs of trouble. It was unfortunate, I thought, that he had gone on his birdie binge so early. It's like sleeping on the lead, which Lin had done. The pressure is suddenly double when you're leading, and you only have two options: you can go up or down. You cannot stay where you are. Players who try to protect a lead almost never succeed.

No one knew this like Tiger Woods. When you're one up (or two or three) you pour the coal on, as Josh's grandpa used to say. You try to bury the field. There's no other option. It's that or be buried, and anyone who doesn't get that doesn't belong at the top. It's not a matter of sportsmanship or good manners. It's the reason you're there in the first place: you want to win. So you make your par or birdie or eagle and you put your head down, go to the next hole and try to do the same or better, regardless of what the rest of the field is doing.

Tony began the back nine in great form. Before he teed off a roar came up the hill from the tenth green: Pieter had made another birdie. I doubt that made any difference to Tony. He was completely focused on his own game. While the group ahead of us hit their seconds, he took a little longer on the relaxation thing he does to combat stress, where he shuts his eyes and his whole body relaxes. Then he stepped up and hit a beautiful drive that drew slightly, caught the slope and trucked on down to stop back of the fairway bunker. Perfect. A good second, and an eight-foot putt that showed no hesitation or twitchiness and nice pace. Birdie. Seven under, two ahead of RJ.

The trouble began after we hiked up through the trees to the eleventh tee. Pieter's group was just teeing off and we had to wait. And wait. RJ came over and they had a thrilling conversation: Tony said "slow, isn't it" and RJ agreed, then RJ said "nice day, though" and Tony agreed. It was the first exchange between them since we teed off, other than announcing their scores after each hole. Jake glanced over and I nodded. He nodded back.

The pace had been slow but steady on the front nine; now it became glacial. The group ahead of us teed off and we were joined after a while by one and then both of the final groups. Eventually we were able to tee off and in between shots we had a good chat about the NHL; then cricket; then the Olympics. We'd started on the World Cup, which was still two years away, but we were running short of subjects.

We went back into play mode once the green cleared. The wind was from the right and the pin was on the back right, with Rae's Creek and a bunker behind it, on a green that had become lightning fast. Tony wanted to play it conservatively and trust to his putter, so he aimed for just left of the mound on the right of the green, and produced an effective draw. The ball should have landed in front of the green and hopped on, but the wind caught it. I watched, heart in mouth, as it landed a couple of yards on and ran up the green, past the flagstick, off the back and into the bunker. We exchanged a look of relief. It could have been worse.

It was worse. We discovered the ball had rolled a couple of inches up the far side of the bunker and stopped, so it was on a slight downslope. To get up and over the front lip would be hard enough. To stop the ball anywhere near the flag on a rock-hard green sloping away from us would be virtually impossible. Tony was absorbed in the challenge of it, however, and after we'd examined the lie and discussed the shot he took his sand wedge and climbed down into the bunker. I moved off. I remember it crossed my mind for a second that I should have argued more strongly for the lob wedge, but that's hindsight. He had a high comfort level with the sand wedge and you can't discount that.

He took his stance and addressed the ball, took the club back—and suddenly he was climbing out of the bunker and facing away from me, toward Rae's Creek. I felt dizzy, wondering how I'd missed whatever I'd missed. The ball was still there. RJ and Jake were still at the bottom front of the green. The sun was still shining. Now he was bent over, hands on knees. I walked over and waited until he felt like talking to me. He was cursing freely and then in among the curses I heard "caught the sand."

"I can't see anything." There was absolutely no depression or line in the sand behind the ball; nothing.

"Caught it with the back edge." He straightened.

"Tony, are you sure? I didn't see anything and I—"

"Of *course* I'm sure, you—," he turned and his face was bright red with anger at himself, at me, at the two-stroke penalty. He yearned to say more, I could see.

"Let it out!" I was sick of this stoicism. "Screw your rules! Spit it out and get it over with, for chrissake!"

He resisted. Instead he let out a sound of mixed anger and anguish, turned away, and directed a low-voiced stream of Sherpa at Rae's Creek.

You can't ground your club in a hazard like a sand trap. Rule 13-4. It's called testing the condition of the hazard. You have to hover the club over the ball until you take the stroke. The underside of a sand wedge has a pronounced trailing edge, designed to prevent the club head from digging into the sand. A lob wedge doesn't. Because of the downhill lie, the ground would rise under the backswing. Tony had taken the club back and the trailing edge had caught the sand and moved a few grains.

I turned to see RJ being joined by an official. Went to meet them, explained the situation. They both peered into the bunker.

"Did you see this?" The official was looking at me. But no one had seen it, not me, not RJ. Just Tony.

He had recovered by now, and was reaching for the lob wedge. "I grounded my club," he said to the official and RJ. He was ready to move on; the others weren't. They insisted on taking another look at the scene of the crime. Tony became absorbed in his practice swings.

"Are you quite sure about this, Mr. Pinasa?"

He nodded at the official. "Yes." He looked at RJ: "Two strokes. I'm playing five."

RJ nodded. "Bad luck."

There was nothing more to be done, so they moved off and we were alone. My concern now was that, fearing a repeat of the infraction, he would fail to get the club under the ball. We talked about it during his practice swings and he got his imagination fully in gear on it, so that when he finally took the shot it was excellent, popping up and dropping two feet left of the flagstick. Of course it didn't stop, but we both watched the path intently. He ended up with a 30-foot putt for a double bogey, but it was on virtually the same line as RJ's ball and just inside it. We both went to school on RJ's putt and Tony was able to drop his. Double bogey six.

We didn't talk about it as we walked over to twelve. What was there to say? You don't get a medal for being honest in golf. You just do it, with as much grace as you can muster, because that's part of the game. They had a camera on the eleventh green and I heard there were endless replays of the shot, but tight as they focused, no one saw any sand move. Just Tony.

With the backlog on twelve we had not caused any delays. Pieter and his caddie were on the tee, trying to figure out the wind. We found a place to sit. Tony seemed fine at first, but as the wait lengthened, he had trouble maintaining his composure. We both wanted to make up that two-stroke loss, but this was a poor place to start: twelve had not been kind to him in the past three days. My cheek began to twitch again, and it was joined by a strong twitch in my thigh. The group ahead moved up to the tee and we took their places. Tony leaned forward, forearms on his thighs, staring straight ahead. He took several deep breaths and closed his eyes for a moment. After a silence,

"Remember I told you about that place my dad took me to?"

"Yeah."

"I saw a red panda there."

I'd never heard of a red panda. Turns out they look like raccoons. Seen lots of those. It happened after they'd eaten, he said. His father had a short meditation, and Tony did too, "for all of ten seconds, I should think. I opened my eyes, and there he was, this little fellow, peering out at me from the rhododendrons." They stared at each other, Tony and the panda. "Then I giggled, and quick as a flash he disappeared. Only the leaves trembling to show that he'd been there—"

The gallery behind us erupted into a full-throated Sunday afternoon roar. We shot to our feet and looked over at the green. Pieter Vanderhoef straightened up, raising his hand with the ball between the fingers. Birdie. He now stood at five under, tied with us and RJ. The gallery was clapping, and so were we.

We sat down. Tony's expression was lighter and I let him alone, but only for a minute. We needed some help on twelve and I wasn't fussy where I found it.

"So anyway, which is better? Buddhist or Anglican?"

He smiled. "Come on, Kat. As if you cared."

"No, really, I'm interested," I said, "what's the difference?"

"Oh gosh. Ten Commandments, Eightfold Path. The hymns. You can't beat Anglican hymns. You know. All Things Bright and Beautiful? That kind of thing?"

"Oh yeah? Hymns are okay. I know about the Ten Commandments. What are the eight thingies?"

"The Eightfold Path." He gazed out at the eleventh. "It defines the right ways to behave. It's like the Ten Commandments, but more positive. Right speech, right work, right action. Buddhism stresses compassion. It's more of a philosophy than a religion, and there's an awful lot of good in it, Kat. But you know, it only works up to a certain point for someone like me."

"Oh yeah? How come?" He was beginning to sound better, I thought.

"It's all about moderation. I'm sorry, but some things are too important to be moderate about." He straightened and took a deep breath. "This is getting a bit intense."

The group ahead had teed off and we walked over to the tee box. I was trying to come up with a positive thought.

"Do you want to talk about the hole?"

"Yeah. You know, I can't visualize the shot. It's just a one-fifty shot, but that wind messes it up completely."

Our strategy was simply to get on the green and trust to the putter. Tony didn't care about getting close. On the green and two-putt, with a birdie as an off-chance. I searched for something helpful. "Some players—I mean decent players, not goof-offs—say they just hit it and pray." This was kind of outside my area of expertise. But I asked anyway. "Do Buddhists believe in God?"

"No, they follow the Buddha."

Duh. Wait a minute. "So, did he believe in God?"

"No. He was like Moses or Jesus or I don't know, maybe Mohammed? Leaders who wanted to show people a better way to live." He paused, then grinned tightly. "Maybe you could sing a hymn."

Shouting at the Amen Corner

Mollie sat between Bill and Ben and watched as Lhakpa walked up to the tee box with Kat. The atmosphere was electric. Not only was it Sunday afternoon at the Masters, but the leaderboard had turned out to be a classic.

Pieter Vanderhoef was popular: no one would begrudge him the win. Alex was—well, Alex. Number one in the world. Doing what champions do: making the best of his game, watching for opportunities, staying patient. Everyone was waiting for him to set the course ablaze. LinJin was struggling, but that might change on the back nine. Then you had RJ Gardner. He was far too young to be called "best player never to win a major" and yet that's what people were calling him at the ripe old age of twenty-two. He had a towering game, and if his personality was just a touch conventional, if he didn't quite have Alex's charisma, well—

maybe he would develop and ripen like fine wine. And lastly, playing with RJ was a kid who was supposed to have done a disappearing act by now. You had to hand it to him, this Asian with the tragedy in his past. He appeared to be a fighter, and Masters patrons love a fighter. He'd birdied ten to pull ahead by two. Let's see how he does through Amen Corner.

"He's left it in the sand," someone said when Tony climbed out of the bunker on eleven, and they waited for him to go back in. Then, with the others, Mollie saw an official walking over.

"Oh no. . . ." said Doug, the fellow in front of them.

"He grounded his club."

"The ball's buried."

"Maybe it came out so hot we didn't see it."

Eventually the small group near the bunker dispersed and play resumed. The official rejoined the crowd at twelve and the word went round: two-stroke penalty, along with the phrase "called it on himself." Mollie knew what that meant, and she knew you were expected to do that sort of thing but she was proud of her son just the same.

The leaderboard behind eleven finally changed, and they saw the score: Pinasa minus five.

"We've seen everything today," Ben had said when she first arrived. "Birdies on down." He didn't elaborate. The crowd had cheered Pieter's birdie, Mollie too. When she saw the others looking at her she had told them of her priorities. No longer was it ridiculous to suppose Lhakpa might win. "But if he doesn't I'd be thrilled if Pieter does. He's such a nice man, isn't he?"

Now they watched as Tony and Kat conferred, studying the trees. Late in the day though it was, the wind was not quite ready to die out. Stronger from the east, where it funneled through from number thirteen, it was swirling round in the trees.

"No reason he can't do just fine," said Bill and they watched the tee shot, which reached its apex and seemed to hit a wall. It fell to the bank near the front bunker, and rolled back into the creek.

"Oh honey," Ben put an arm round her shoulders.

Mollie watched, hands clasped beneath her chin, as her son turned away from the tee box, and then back. *He's disoriented,* she thought, as Kat stepped up and spoke to him. They both moved to the drop area. *Such a cruel game,* she thought. *Dreadful, dreadful.* She remembered what Bill and Ben had said about the bank, and the player who hadn't used a big enough club.

"He bailed," she heard someone say. "I mean, where was he intending to go? Crazy to go for that pin, so let's assume he's not crazy. Should have been somewhere on the green or worst case, in the bunker. Gutless shot."

She heard someone "shush" the speaker, and at the same moment Doug spoke up.

"Excuse me?" He sounded annoyed, looking at the culprit, three patrons along from him. "I think he's proved he's got guts."

Murmurs of agreement.

"I only meant—"

"Swallow it."

They watched in relief as Tony's third shot landed on the middle of the green.

"Stay here for a bit, honey," said Bill.

He had a long putt for a bogey, and although you could hardly see the green from the stands, Mollie wasn't about to leave. She had just seen her son lose at least three shots. He had continued to play without an outcry, without cursing or throwing a club, and she knew he was doing the best he could. He was coping, and she suddenly ceased to be afraid for him. He would always find a way to cope, she realized, and suddenly she did not want Pieter or anyone else to win. She passionately wanted Lhakpa to win.

He had missed the putt, so that meant he had fallen all the way back to three under and she waited for the leader-board to change. Doug turned round to face her. "Mollie, that kid of yours has a great future. I'd like it if you'd give him my best wishes after the round." That seemed to be a signal because several others turned with similar comments. Mollie thanked them and got to her feet. It was nice of them, but she wished they didn't sound quite so—so valedictory, as though Lhakpa were history. Saying goodbye to Bill and Ben she left the stand. She wanted to see the action on the thirteenth.

Kat's Story

I normally like the egg salad sandwich here, but this one tasted like sawdust. I forced it down anyway. We might be done but I had a bag to carry and six holes before I could put it down for good.

I sat on the bench in back of the tee at thirteen. Tony sat next to me, leaning forward, hands loosely clasped, staring at the ground. I'd shoved an energy bar between his hands and it stayed there, ignored. I put down my sandwich and found a pimiento cheese. He shook his head. I put it next to his foot. Didn't have the energy to argue. Finished the sawdust.

We heard a huge roar from out on the course. No need to wonder what that was: Pieter had eagled the thirteenth. I drank some water and walked over to the bin to ditch my sandwich wrapper. RJ and Jake had their backs to us, standing together looking out at the fairway, discussing their strategy.

I stayed by the bin looking out at the hole. Shame to just quit. What was the right play here? If you left out his Thursday score, Tony had shot three and four here. He loved the hole. Go for the eagle or play it safe? It had to be his call, but I knew which I preferred.

I came back to find him finishing the pimiento cheese; the energy bar had disappeared.

"We'll have to go for it, Kat." He stood up and walked over to the cooler, returning with a banana. I let him sit down before I answered.

"There's a headwind. We'd be going in with a five or six-iron to a lightning-fast green."

"Pieter's at seven under. If he eagles fifteen he'll be nine under."

RJ had pulled out his driver. I watched him without really seeing him.

"If you eagle thirteen and fifteen . . ."

He looked at me. "I'll be at seven under."

I waited.

"We can't win it on those two holes." He thought it through. "But we could lose it. Hunh." RJ stepped up to the tee and we waited in silence until he had hit off, a huge fade to the higher right side of the fairway. We moved up to the tee and Tony took out the driver and began to swing by the side of the tee box. Time to put something out there.

"You've shown you can be patient. You've shown you can reel off a string of birdies."

He kept swinging.

"Let's keep doing what we've been doing."

A swing and a glance at me. He rested the club head. "Okay. I hear you."

We got down to details then, and eventually he hit a good serviceable drive down the middle and laid up to sixty yards on the left fairway. The Sunday pin was at the far right, as near to the creek as is legal. Our position gave us a good length of the green to work with.

We waited for RJ to hit his second. Tony looked up at the sky, then his gaze came back to the hundreds of azaleas lining the fairway and rested on them as we walked forward.

The American Embassy, Kathmandu

Alex Figueres's second shot landed safely on the eleventh green. Sitting with a group of aides, attaches and army comrades, Bik watched as Lin Jinhai on the left-hand side of the fairway reviewed the options with his caddie.

"He's been duck-hooking all day, what's to discuss?" said Ross Korbin, the American aide, next to him.

Bik grunted in agreement. "He'll fade an iron to the right, wouldn't you think?"

But in the end, Lin hit a successful draw that landed off the green and rolled on. Murmurs of appreciation from the golfers among the crowd.

"Brave shot."

The room was still relatively subdued, although the shock of Lhakpa's two-stroke penalty had caused a furor. Reactions had ranged from admiration and respect, to incomprehension, to contempt. An argument had broken out when a wealthy Nepali matron, whose tenure as chair of an international aid fund had comfortably swelled her fortune, stated that Lhakpa had disgraced the country, inventing the infraction because he couldn't take the pressure. The argument became loud and increasingly disruptive until she stood up and stalked out, hapless husband in tow.

Then Lhakpa dropped two more strokes and the atmosphere became funereal. Now the camera moved to the thirteenth hole, where RJ was taking his second shot to the green. It landed safely on.

"Doing all right," said Ross, leaning forward. "Y'know, he could still pull it off."

The camera found Lhakpa, standing in the fairway with his caddie, preparing for his third to the green. He did not look defeated, Bik thought; he looked as he had all week long. His caddie moved away with the bag and he lined up, went through his customary routine and hit the shot. Also safely on.

In the fifteenth fairway stood Pieter Vanderhoef, lying seven under, three clear of the field. He launched his second shot, and they watched as the ball landed barely a foot beyond the pond and rolled back into it.

Murmurs of amazement round the room. "That wasn't even close!" Bik and Ross exchanged mystified stares.

In the Caddie Shack

Eyes intent on the screen, the audience watched as Tony lined up his birdie putt on thirteen. He made a smooth stroke and the ball ran a shallow arc and dropped into the hole, chased by comments and calls:

"Arrright!"

"You go, kid!"

Jonas and Tuck exchanged high fives. The group fell silent again as the screen changed to the fifteenth hole. Jonas, after recovering from the shock of Pieter's catastrophic shot, had bet Tuck that his caddie had given him the wrong yardage. Now the camera panned from Pieter, stalking his putt, to Kirk, standing off the green by the bag. "He is such a loser," muttered Jonas. They listened to the voice-over:

"After a fabulous eagle at thirteen, Pieter Vanderhoef is looking at this testy five-footer for bogey." Silence as they watched the putt rim the cup and drop. "Oh my. So that will put Pieter at six under."

"Shit! I had twenty on Pieter to win."

The screen changed to thirteen again, with RJ lining up his eagle putt.

"We had one there," said Tuck. "It'll break sharp right, you watch."

They watched, listening to the voice-over: "The bank and the creek both affect this putt—has he allowed enough? Oh—look at that!" The ball turned toward the hole and stopped, an inch short. "Little too much borrow. A huge disappointment for RJ, you can see. Good birdie, all the same. Back to fifteen."

Patrick Geoghan appeared onscreen near the fifteenth green, speaking into his mike. "It's pretty clear Pieter had the wrong yardage for his second. Apparently a miscommunication with his caddie."

A round of catcalls greeted this remark. Tuck shook his head and handed ten dollars to Jonas, who looked smug.

A globe appeared on the screen: "It's time for the next stop in our round-the-world series. We leave Melbourne and head northward, to our friends at Nepal TV. . . ."

There was a rush for food. Tuck stood in line for burgers and beers amid chat and general grousing.

"How'd you do?"

"Couldn't drop a putt. You?"

"Aw, he was smashin' grass all day."

"He can't play dead. Why d'you stick with him?"

"Least they give you somethin' for the weekend."

Jonas saved Tuck's seat. The screen showed a cluster of women in thin, faded saris on the pavement outside a shop. Through the window bars they looked at a television screen—at themselves. They stirred and the screen changed again, showing a Nepali reporter on a street corner, narrating in careful English: "It is four o'clock on Monday morning, but as you can see, only the street cleaners are out. The government has declared a public holiday today." Behind him, the picture changed to show a building with its lights blazing. "The American Embassy is having a party. We have heard a rumor that the American and British ambassadors played a round of golf to decide who would be host." A transition to a room filled with teenagers. "Here we have students at the

School for Hill Children, where Lhakpa Pinasa went to school until 2001." Two skinny arms in the front row suddenly held up a large piece of construction paper with the word "Lhakpa" reproduced all over the page. "As you can see, these students are very partisan. . . ."

"No kidding," said Jonas, as Tuck rejoined him with the food. The screen changed again to show Jim Nantz and Nick Faldo in the broadcast booth. Behind them the scores came up, Vanderhoef and Gardner at minus six, Pinasa and Figueres at minus four. The caddies ate, watching as the picture changed to thirteen again, where Lin's nightmare continued as he hooked his tee shot into the left bank of the creek.

"Anyone needs yardages from the left trees, Sammy's got 'em," someone called. Sammy was Lin's caddie.

Ten minutes later, the action was on the fourteenth green. The players had just arrived and they watched as RJ marked his ball, about ten feet from the pin. Tony's ball was poised just off the green on the right side.

"How did it ever stop there?" Tuck was amazed, a feeling shared in the broadcast booth, as they could hear:

"That's a little funnel area that normally takes the ball right off the green. The committee'll be looking at that tomorrow morning, I'm sure."

Tony took his seven-iron and began to study the hole from both sides in preparation for his chip. The voice-over continued: "There's a tiny ridge between him and the hole. I don't know if we can see it but I'm sure they can. He's got to chip up to feed over that little ridge and the ball will turn left as it comes off it to the hole. It's actually not the worst place in the world to be."

Tony made his chip and the ball ran into the hole. The crowd roared and so did the caddies.

"All right!"

"Jeez! Double, double, birdie, birdie. The kid just won't go away."

"Look at Kat dancin' around. Shit, what is it with this thumb thing?"

"Y'know," said Tuck, "it probably helps keep him in the moment."

Monk, Stillson's caddie, flopped down next to Jonas. "I'm betting fifty he takes it." He got their attention. "Yeah, you heard me. I played with him for two days and I'm telling you." He took a swig of Jonas's beer, dodged the hit and addressed the group. "Any takers?"

Both Jonas and Tuck declined. "I'm not betting against him." But several RJ fans took him on.

"Holy shit! If the kid does win, what'll they do with the prize money?"

"Spread it over the field?"

This affected everyone, and the talk became animated.

Kat's Story

"When my father applied for a passport, the official wanted money for putting the second 'h' in his name."

"Are you kidding me?"

"No. It happens all the time. They gave all the airport personnel new uniforms without pockets to stop them soliciting the tourists. It's a very poor country, Kat."

We stood in the fifteenth fairway, sixty yards out from the green, waiting for RJ. His second had landed on the green then taken a turn backward, then another, and ended up in the pond. He and Jake were discussing where to drop for his third. We had to assume he'd make his par; you don't want to wish a bogey on anyone.

Tony found an energy bar and told me about the robin he'd heard this morning.

"It's a thrush," I explained, when he mentioned the size. "At least, it isn't a thrush, of course it's a robin," I was trying to remember what Josh had said, "but it's a different species than the English robin. That's all."

He didn't care either way. "It made a beautiful sound."

Tony had done exactly what he had to. He'd stayed patient and made a couple of birdies. Pieter had fallen back, and Alex had yet to make a move, but if we could birdie this hole we would pull into a tie for the lead.

The birdie on fourteen had helped reduce the stress. We'd had a bit of a laugh doing the thumb thing, and the crowd had begun to appreciate my player in a way I thought was appropriate to his level of play. My twitches had stopped twitching, at least for the moment. And nothing could be worse than that hell at Amen Corner. Tony's tee shot on fifteen had been pushed into the trees on the right but we had intended to play the hole in three, like all the par fives, and luckily he was able to come out and advance the ball, so no harm done. He had a nice wedge from one-twenty for his third, which spun away a little more than we had hoped for. The ball lay about fifteen feet from the hole.

The flag was in the back right, up a little ridge. RJ was hitting his fourth from the left side of the fairway. His added pressure came from wanting to run it up the ridge if possible, to leave himself a makeable par putt. He'd chosen a lie that seemed difficult to me, downhill and tight, and about eighty yards from the flag. He hit a beautiful half-swing, landing the ball below the hole. It ran up the ridge and dropped in the cup.

The stands on fifteen erupted, along with the crowds in the fairway and on the bank across the pond on sixteen. We could almost feel the sound waves.

Tony had finished his energy bar, and he applauded with the wrapper between his palms, then turned and handed it to me. I was already rummaging in the bag. You don't want to spend too much time watching another player's brilliance. I handed him the water bottle, hoisted the bag and started down to the green. RJ had gone to minus seven and Tony had to make his putt just to stay one behind.

Chanting began: "RJ, RJ, RJ."

On the Bank Behind the Sixteenth Green

"Sonofa*bitch*." Mike was careful to keep it under his breath, because they were clearly in RJ country. He had joined Tashi and Gordon more than an hour ago, sitting beyond the sixteenth green, so high up the slope that they were not far below the sixth fairway. The slope was massed with patrons, below and all along to their right behind the pond. They were all on their feet cheering and waving for RJ's miraculous birdie save.

The excitement reduced somewhat and they sat back down. A short while later, they watched as Tony stalked his putt and conferred with Kat. His back was to them, but they could see the green, beyond the sixteenth, where the

Fillers, as Mollie called them, were going about their business. He bent over the putter, and Tashi whispered, "go in go in go in. . . ."

The silence was suddenly broken, and one of the Fillers stepped away from his putt to wait out the roar.

"Yes!" Mike and Tashi were on their feet. "To-ny, To-ny, To-ny!"

"Oh gosh," said Tashi. "I can't stand it. He's still a stroke behind. . . ."

They'd had enough excitement for one day, from the delirium when Tony reached seven under, leading the tournament, to the despair of the two doubles. Tashi had flopped back on the grass and covered her face, and the two men felt like doing the same. They'd hardly dared to believe the scoreboard when Pinasa went from red three to red four, and Gordon's eyes kept returning to it as though in disbelief. The change from red four to red five had put fresh heart into them, and now he'd climbed back to minus six.

The shadows were lengthening, the tops of the pines alight in the evening sun. They were a welcome sight to Gordon, a relief from the tension, a reminder that this had become his favorite time of day in the past ten years. Now, as a respite, he allowed his mind to retreat back across the pond, back to England, to Staines, to the end of each week. To Fridays. On Friday afternoons, no later than 5 pm and earlier in the summer, he would be out of his office, down to the car and onto the motorway to Cornwall. Depending on how early he got away, he was often able to join Tony's group for the back nine. Sometimes Mollie would come down afterward for a late dinner at the club. God, those were wonderful times! He'd come across a poem once called "Seaside Golf." Part of it expressed his experience perfectly: "Lark song and sea sounds in the air, And splendour, splendour everywhere." He himself shot in the high seventies and found Widemouth's greens challenging. He was fascinated to watch his nephew's progress, especially after the lessons began to take effect. He broke ninety in July and in August he was playing consistently in the eighties. They used to play for ten pence a hole and it had been in some ways more exciting than the Masters.

"I'm suffering from empty nest syndrome already," Mollie told him one evening and they had a laugh about it. He'd been in to see Jack Perran one rainy Friday evening, just to assure the sergeant that, even though Tony was no longer logging any community-service hours, he was still on the straight and narrow.

Jack had cocked an eyebrow at him. "Do you think I don't know that?" he'd said. It was still fairly early so the jail was quiet and they'd had a chat, two school chums whose relationship alone had spared one delinquent from entering the penal system. Perran still liked to recall that first meeting, when Gordon had arrived at the jail to be informed that Tony would have to be held over for juvenile court because he was a repeat offender. He had listened in consternation. "If you'd go after the ring leaders of this gang," he said when Perran had finished, "then maybe kids like Tony wouldn't get sucked in." The sergeant had given him a level look. "We have gone after the ring leader, sir. His name is Tony Pinasa." Gordon had been so taken aback that he'd had to sit down. "Are you a local resident, sir?" Gordon explained that he grew up in Exeter, and worked in London but came down on weekends. They discovered they'd gone to the same school, indeed, that they were classmates. Perran had once tackled him hard at rugby, a tackle they both remembered.

"My spies are everywhere," the sergeant had said on that rainy Friday. "I hear he's fallen in love." Gordon had laughed at that, because Tony spent every waking hour at the golf course. "I remember how you used to go on and on about being a flyer. Must run in the family, that determination." Gordon said nothing, but he'd never felt the kind of passion for flying his nephew had for golf.

The following year the boy played consistently in the seventies, and the year after that, when he was fourteen, Tom enrolled him in some regional tournaments where he either won or came second. He began to display an unpleasant temper that year, and a penchant for throwing his clubs or maiming the fairway after bad shots.

"Why shouldn't I? Tiger Woods does." Gordon said nothing, but the following weekend, when Tony threw his four-iron, Gordon retrieved it and refused to return it. That evening they had a long discussion, the gist of which was that his nephew should apply the same drive and determination to his behavior that he applied to his technique.

"Use your meditation, anger management, breathing, whatever it takes." At the end of it, he laid down the rules: throwing a club, audible swearing or taking a divot after a shot were all unacceptable. Mollie refused to get involved, so he had to be content with extracting Tony's promise that he would stop doing these things. "Otherwise, you lose the club. Just to impress that on you, this goes away for two weeks." The boy had had a fit: he was playing in Exeter the following weekend, but Gordon was adamant. Later, Mollie had wondered if he wasn't going overboard. "Look Moll, he's dreaming of joining the Tour. He'll never be able to cope unless he grows up emotionally. I don't know," he'd added with a sigh, "he's far too small to be able to compete. But that doesn't mean he can't learn to behave when he plays."

Over the next three years the boy had shot up, and the more he grew the worse he played. Gordon arrived late one Friday night and asked as always, how his game was and if he was controlling his temper. When Tony said everything was fine, he brought in three clubs: a five-wood, seven-iron and sand wedge. Tony had been outraged. "You were spying on me!"

"I arrived late, so Tom put me in with the group behind you. I was a little embarrassed, actually, because they knew I was your uncle. Playing behind you is no joke."

"Look, I've got a match in Bristol on Sunday."

"Not with these clubs."

The following day he'd taken Tony with him to see Tom, and explained the problem.

"Aye, I've been hearing rumors myself."

Gordon explained the three rules. "Would it be possible for you to put him with players who will tell you—"

"Oh *shit!* You can't do that!" Tony was furious. The two men ignored him.

"Aye, Mr. Menzies. It will restrict him somewhat, because t' better players usually play in t' morning, when he's in school. Come to think of it, though, he should play with some of t' slower men, and higher handicaps. It will help him learn to be patient."

Gordon had wondered if this might be considered piling on. "Not at all, Mr. Menzies. T' lad's young." He had smiled at Tony. "I have every confidence that he can learn this aspect of t' game."

Now Gordon laughed outright, and in answer to a look from Tashi and Mike, said "Nothing," then added, "I was just thinking of the time Tony came second at Bristol, three clubs short."

Mollie joined them. "What a crowd! I could hardly move coming down fifteen. What's happening?"

"They're on the tee," said Gordon. "How're you holding up, old girl?" He looked more closely. "Good lord. You're enjoying it, aren't you?"

Mollie laughed and agreed that she was.

The Fillers finished up and moved off to the seventeenth tee. The pin was in its customary Sunday position, on the lower left of the green. Tony was away and they watched, hearts in their mouths, as his ball seemed headed for the water. It landed in the bunker between them and the flagstick.

"Oh God," said Mollie, "not again."

RJ hit an excellent shot that landed six feet beyond the hole.

"What happened on eleven and twelve, do you know?" asked Mike.

Mollie described the action as best she could. "Why is it all right to move the sand when you hit the ball but not otherwise?"

Gordon explained that Tony must have touched the sand during his practice swing. Tashi looked thoughtful.

"That doesn't sound likely," said Mike.

"Definition of a stroke," said Tashi suddenly. She turned to Mollie. "A stroke is defined as any forward movement of the club made with the intention of hitting the ball. Something like that."

"I see, dear."

Gordon glanced at Tashi with respect. "She means, the penalty probably happened on the backswing. Good for you, Tashi. We'll ask him later."

Mike looked at Tashi in surprise. "When did you learn the rules?" Mollie began to laugh.

"I had nothing to do in the evenings," said Tashi sedately, "except read the rule book."

The players arrived at the green. "That's an awkward shot," muttered Mike. The ball was at this end of the trap, leaving a downhill sidehill shot. They watched as player and caddie studied the lie and the angle, then Tony climbed in from the end of the bunker. His shot came out, to their united relief, but carried past the hole about four feet up the slope.

They watched as RJ addressed the ball. They had already seen several birdies from that spot, so when the roar erupted they were prepared.

"Oh dear oh dear," said Mollie. "He's two ahead again."

The noise died down and it was back to Tony and Kat. Gordon glanced at the leaderboard behind. "Pieter's finished. Look at that, he lost another one on eighteen." The right-hand panel now showed "Thru eighteen Vanderhoef" and a red five.

Mike dropped his head on his knees as Tony addressed the ball. It was a ticklish downhill putt, one he'd seen many times on TV, and he couldn't bear to watch. Unusually, for a downhill putt, it circled the hole before dropping. They leapt to their feet in jubilation, clutching each other, jumping up and down, exulting.

"Dear little horseshoe," crooned Tashi over and over to herself.

The players walked to the seventeenth. Chants of "RJ, RJ, RJ" were met with "Tony, Tony, Tony."

Kat's Story

We were on the big climb back up to the finish now. The seventeenth rises about thirty-five feet, tee to green. Not much happening on this hole; you have Ike's Tree on the left, of course, and I've heard some murmurs that it's time to do something about that, because it just keeps on growing. The pin was in the front of the green between the two bunkers.

Tony said much later that he felt bruised after sixteen. I wasn't bruised, I was numb. We had been close to a tie at fifteen and then *bam!* we were two back. I sat like a lump, staring at nothing. Tony spent some moments up at the hexagonal Records Fountain, where tournament records and past winners are displayed. He came back to the tee. "Let's stay with our routine all the way in." Suited me. RJ had the honor and launched a high fade over Ike's Tree that landed well up the fairway. There was little guesswork for us on this hole but we went through the whole routine even so. Tony hit a good draw that landed safely in the middle. We hiked up the fairway. "Beautiful evening," he said at one point, and then smiled. "Smell the cigar?"

I glanced over as we approached the ball. Maybe that was what did it for him, what the old pro had taught him about using his senses: what do you see, what do you feel, what do you smell. . . . Whatever it was, you couldn't keep the kid down.

I shook my head. "You're amazing."

He looked at me in his lemon-colored shirt and his "Be Good" visor, hair stuck up on the crown of his head, maybe sensing a joke. Saw my expression. If we'd been standing on flooring I think he'd have shuffled his feet. As it was, he just shoved his hands in his pockets.

"Will you caddie for me, Kat? I mean, regularly?"

I dumped the bag. Glanced at him. "I'd be proud to." I meant it, too.

The second shot was on an uphill lie, one-fifty-eight to the hole. Again, we went through the routine: distance, lie, wind, club, shot shape. . . . He made good contact but pulled the shot slightly, landing in the bunker left of the flag.

"More sand," he said grumpily, but a few minutes later, after RJ airmailed one over the back of the green from about one-forty, he added, "sooner mine than his." We had quite a long wait in the end, because RJ's chip rolled down to the hole and kept on going. He chose to putt from off the green and nearly pulled it off but had to settle for a bogey. Tony managed to splash a bunker shot within a yard of the flagstick and took a long time to survey the line before stroking his par putt. We did a victory thumb, and went to eighteen one behind, and I thought, as I have so many times with Charlie, how hard it is not to let your mind wander to the finish and afterward, even if you're only thinking about how much you'll enjoy a beer. But you have to stay focused. I heard a long train whistle as we reached the tee. Nice to be on it.

The number in the clubhouse was minus five. We were sitting at minus six and RJ at minus seven. We'd heard two huge roars behind us earlier and knew that Alex was now at five under with the par five fifteenth still to play. Things were shaping up for maybe a playoff.

Everyone knows the eighteenth, four hundred and sixty-five yards, dogleg right uphill. As the person who does the carrying, I would like to point out that not only is the green seventy feet above the tee, you drop down forty feet once you leave the tee box. So it's a vertical hike up to the finish. The drive looks ugly and intimidating but it has never bothered Tony. You focus on the bunkers in the distance and aim straight for them. "Easy swing, clean contact," I said and he nodded slightly, going through his pre-routine practice swings. He looked tired, which is typical, but calm and he hit a nice drive out to a point just shy of the two bunkers. RJ took his three-wood, which I thought was a smart play, and put one ten or fifteen yards behind Tony's.

For the first time all day, RJ hit first, and he came out of the swing. His ball landed in the right greenside bunker. Tony and I conferred. We had one-sixty-five uphill off an uphill lie. We reckoned seven-iron. There's a false front to get past, and you cannot go long on this hole or you're putting back down the green and likely to roll off the front. A high, soft fade would do it, and when I saw the light in Tony's eyes I knew he was going to pull it off. I knew.

It landed just on the false front, took one hop and stopped. Five sweet feet from the hole. We heard the roar. How I wanted to jump up and down! I took the club, wiped it, bagged it. Tony hadn't moved. I looked at him and he held out his blankety blank thumb. I wanted to say "You da man."

I wanted to high five, jump up and down, do a jig. I wanted to say "Yes!" many times. What I actually did was, I matched my thumbprint to his. In these circumstances, you do what your player wants. I carefully didn't look into his eyes, just in the general direction of his face.

I could hear Zachary Anderson doing his shtick as we hiked upward. Tony took off his glove for the last time—and then, as we drew up to the green I heard a colossal roar out on the course, back down to the left: the fifteenth. I wondered if it would indeed be the last time, or whether Alex had made a birdie, or what. Too tired to think about it now, anyway.

The pressure on RJ was cruel. I knew he had already conceded Tony's putt in his mind; that's what you do in his position. So you just have to par the hole to stay in the game. He made good contact, but his bunker shot ran nearly ten feet by the hole and the putt back rimmed the hole but stayed out. He'd bogeyed the last two holes and stood at six under. It was Tony's turn. He didn't need the flagstick, so I stood off near the left bunker.

I can't describe what strength of character is required in this situation, to take no more than your normal routine, to be able to think, to be able to absorb what your eyes show you and know how to act on it. He made that putt and I stood there with the tears running down my cheeks, holding the flagstick, unable to move. The crowd roar was overwhelming. I felt his arms round my back and my feet actually left the ground as he swung me round, blindingly happy, "Kat! Oh Kat!"

I heard the exchange with RJ as I picked up the flagstick.

"I got ahead of myself." The pain in his voice was raw.

"Oh man!" Tony took hold of his arms. "This was amazing. We have to do it again."

They were shaking hands, looking each other in the face. Then RJ gave Tony a powerful hug. "Listen, guy. You make sure you take it all, okay?"

The American Embassy, Kathmandu

Bedlam. Tumult. Topis flying. Yelling, cheering and sustained clapping from the entire room, Nepalis and foreigners alike. Bik watched with the rest, laughing uncontrollably, shaking hands whenever another hand grasped his own. Lhakpa embraced Gordon, RJ walked through the crowd to the scorer's cabin, and Bik's mind kept replaying that last iron shot, that last putt, the hug from RJ. . . .

"The most extraordinary comeback I've ever seen."

"Can you imagine what good this'll do for the country?"

"Unbelievable guts—"

"Fantastic—"

"That was epic," Ross was full of appreciation. "Real shame about RJ, but that was one of the best ever."

The scores came up: Pinasa at minus 7, Gardner one behind, Figueres two behind, then the picture changed to the sixteenth green and they heard a monstrous roar as Alex poured his putt into the hole. The room fell silent. Figueres was now one behind with two to play.

"Doesn't matter what happens now, Bik. He's made his mark. He's arrived."

Bik smiled in agreement and gradually calmed down.

As Alex and Lin (now at plus two) walked up the seventeenth fairway, he came to a decision, patted his breast pocket to make sure the photograph was there, and stood up.

As he made his way toward the far end of the reception room, the American Ambassador called him over. He had taken his British counterpart off to a study for the night's entertainment, and they had only now emerged to join the throng. Bik reached the two dignitaries and inclined his head. He had played golf behind them at Gokarna. They shot in the low nineties and enjoyed themselves immensely.

The American Ambassador smiled. "Speaking as a father, Colonel, I'm glad you took the boy home to his mother. I hope it doesn't cost you too much."

The British Ambassador murmured his agreement, then asked, "How well do you know Lhakpa, Colonel?"

Bik hesitated, wondering how to answer, and the American Ambassador added, "He's going to have a great many demands on his time, that young man. We wondered if there was a chance he might pay us a visit?"

"Do the country enormous good, you know."

Bik made up his mind and gave them a noncommittal answer. He had no idea when Lhakpa would visit again, although he'd made it clear he wanted to move forward with his Trust as soon as possible.

He chatted with the two ambassadors for a few moments, excusing himself as soon as he decently could. As he continued along the room he saw an odd sight. He saw a Tibetan woman and beyond her the Brahmin leader of the main Opposition party and although they were in different groups facing screens in opposite directions they sat in curiously similar postures, with their hands held prayer-like in front of them, the woman with fingers touching her lips, the Brahmin with his chin propped on his fingertips, elbows resting on the arms of his chair. The woman's face, careworn, was lightened, as though for one evening she'd been taken out of herself. The Brahmin looked as though he'd been drawn in on himself.

He stirred, as though sensing Bik's gaze, glanced up and around, and saw him. He stood up and approached, and Bik could see that his customary sophistication was gone. His eyes had the open, defenseless look of one grappling with the overturn of a basic preconception.

"I've never seen anything like it," he said.

"No," agreed Bik.

"Are they all like that? All Sherpas?"

"I don't know."

"Was his father—"

"Excuse me," Bik interrupted. A semicircle away, a seat had opened up next to the Chinese diplomat. "Sorry," he nodded to the Brahmin, walked over, dropped into the seat and reached into his breast pocket.

"Ah, Colonel!" Mr. Hu managed to find a smile. "How glad I am that you did not take me up on a bet! Pinasa is a fine golfer."

"He is a superb golfer," corrected the Maoist Foreign Minister next to him. His glance took in Bik, and he nodded coldly. "Colonel."

"Minister," said Bik, loathing the man. He extended the photograph to the diplomat.

"What is this?" asked Mr. Hu.

"This is one member of the 'mythical Chinese horde' we talked about on Thursday. Do you remember?" The Foreign Minister watched, puzzled. Bik decided he had nothing to lose. He spoke directly to the Maoist and since Hu refused to take the photo he extended it to the Minister. "This is a Chinese engineer, and he's holding a laser receiving rod. That's not something the average tourist carries. It's a surveying tool, and this picture was taken inside our northern border."

Mr. Hu sat immobile, his eyes on the photo. The Brahmin joined them, pulling a chair round so that he sat facing them, listening.

"Let me see that." The Foreign Minister took the picture. "When was this taken?"

Mr. Hu found his voice. "It could be anywhere—"

"It was taken last Monday," answered Bik and explained that a group of villagers had seen a party of Chinese engineers, and data from the cellphone confirmed the location as well as the date.

"What are they doing?" asked the Foreign Minister. "Are they planning to build another dam, inside Nepal?"

"Minister, I assure you—," began Mr. Hu.

Bik interrupted him. "Sir, I don't see that it matters what they were doing, so much as the fact that they came in, as far as I can determine, undocumented and unofficially."

The Foreign Minister looked away. "*Ke ho ke ho,*" he muttered, after a pause.

The Brahmin reached for the photograph.

Bik held his temper. "I know we do more or less whatever China wants, so asking them to enter the country officially, like everyone else, is probably pointless, but—"

"You are being foolish, Colonel," snapped Mr. Hu. "China is a good friend to Nepal, and a good neighbor. Nothing more."

The Foreign Minister frowned at the parquet flooring. Guests passed, voices audible in the silence.

"To come back like that, from four down—"

"Shows extraordinary character."

"Strength of will—"

"Now the whole world will know where Nepal is, won't they, father?"

The Brahmin looked up from the photograph and gazed pensively at the diplomat.

"I have learned a great deal this evening," he said. "And one of the things I've learned is that my country has a future."

"Of course Nepal has a future!" Mr. Hu was relieved at the change in subject.

"I discovered this evening the resilience of our hill peoples," the Brahmin went on. "I learned that they do not give up in the face of adversity." His glance took in the Foreign Minister and dislike colored his voice as he added, "But you already knew that."

Bik kept his expression unchanged. The Maoist had been one of the insurgents' leaders during the civil war.

Mr. Hu plunged into the silence. "Pinasa had a great day, of course," he said. "It is a pity he is a westerner now, playing a western game," he ignored the two golfers and emboldened by the Maoist's silence added, unwisely, "and the child of a royal lackey—"

Disgusted, Bik began to rise.

"That is past," said the Foreign Minister. He lifted his head. He gestured for the photograph. The Opposition leader put it into his hand. "That is in the past." He studied it and came to a decision. "Colonel, you are submitting a report of this incident?" And as Bik nodded, he continued, "Please copy me on it."

Bik nodded. "Yes, sir."

Mr. Hu protested. "Whatever the nature of this action, I assure you it was taken without the knowledge or consent of the Chinese government."

"I will be glad to hear the Ambassador explain that, tomorrow morning, in my office."

Mr. Hu stared at him. His face had acquired a greasy sheen. "Then—then," he rose to his feet, "I must advise him at once," he said. His mind held an unpleasant vision, of a path—his path—both stony and steep. *Aieee.*

Bik was satisfied. At least the incident would not go without some sort of reprimand. He left the two politicians and returned to his seat at the other end of the room to see Alex miss his birdie on seventeen, and both players walk to the eighteenth. The camera showed Lhakpa, his family in the background, sitting in front of a screen in the Jones cabin. The BBC announcer began an historical survey of those who had previously sat in the Jones Cabin pending a playoff.

"He ought to hit balls," muttered Bik, and Ross grunted agreement.

They both yawned, then laughed. It was after five in the morning.

Another guest stopped by to comment on Bik's testimony, and he stood up and turned round. When he next glanced at the screen, Alex was lining up his putt, and it ran by the hole, and there was an explosion of sound. Lhakpa shot to his feet, dazed, elated.

Bik sat down abruptly, his mind a riot of thoughts, his breath catching in his throat. The Chhiri Sherpa Trust was going to be a reality. . . .

"The first amateur to win the Masters," rejoiced an English ADC, "and he's a Brit to boot!" He leapt in the air, fist pumping.

Outside the Embassy, fireworks burst into the morning air.

Bik became aware of shoes in front of him. Two pairs. He looked up to see the Foreign Minister and the Opposition Leader standing there.

The two politicians surveyed him. It seemed to his eye that both of them were fizzing with energy. *Now what?*

The Maoist spoke first.

"Colonel, how well do you know Lhakpa?"

MONDAY-TUESDAY

O O O O

A Win for Mr. Jones

--Augusta *Chronicle*

Triumph of the Amateur

--The *Times* of London

Sherpa Wins Masters Golf!

--Nepal *Times*

Historic Win Aided by Local Caddie

--Vancouver *Sun*

EPILOGUE

O O O O

I heard about Kirk from the guys. Pieter had signed his card then fired his caddie. I had a chat with him before the presentation ceremony—the real ceremony, the one that happens on the practice green with speeches and everything—and told him Jonas was looking for a change. I wasn't sure their personalities would work together but figured they could find that out for themselves. I gave him Jonas's number but he didn't want to waste any time; he hiked over to the caddie building and hired him right away. Jonas has always been a hard worker, but now he had a good income as well. His wife was happy, so he was happy, and Pieter too. There was so much happiness floating round the pair of them, in fact, that Pieter had one of his best years, winning three times including the PGA. Like I said, I wonder how many decisions get made for a quiet life.

Tony turned pro after the Masters, and roared through last year, winning four more tournaments after Augusta. He went head to head with RJ at the US Open, with Alex at the British and with Pieter at the PGA, and came second each time. And every day he battles his temper. Every day.

He spent the late fall and winter working on his trust. He's a genuine hero in Nepal, of course, and the first time he went back they had a national holiday and everyone turned out to see him. The downside was that everything he did became news, including the bad stuff. They had some friction on their Board of Directors, and some bribery allegations, but Tony refused to be deflected. They kept moving ahead with the scholarships and loans and so on, and a couple of months ago they finalized their first hydroelectric plant, in a village in the north Himalayas. I believe that's supposed to start up sometime this year. Investors are starting to take the country seriously and Mollie thinks the Maoists will get the boot in the next election. She's pretty happy about that.

Tony and Tashi got married in January, just before his twenty-third birthday. I could never get Tashi's background out of my head, and so just last month I signed up to sponsor two Tamang girls at the school in Kathmandu. I'd thought of sponsoring a Sherpa and Sherpette (Tony says that's not a word, but I told him it soon would be), but the Tamangs don't have nearly as much exposure. I've never been big on charity; I always figured to leave that for the Tour. But it doesn't cost much to give a kid a leg up, and it seems like a good investment.

I came home last Tuesday from visiting Josh at a little garden he created on southwest Marine. It has a section for roses in one corner, and I'd spread his ashes there a year ago because that's what he wanted. I didn't ask anyone beforehand, because you're probably violating six city ordinances when you do something like that, but his parents know and they go down now and then, like me, to stay in touch. I'd left the phone in my other coat and there was a message from Tony in Cornwall:

"Time to prep for Augusta, Kat. How soon can you get here?"

It was followed by another, from Gordon: "Have dinner with me on Friday."

I went online to book a flight and looked out at the pouring rain without seeing it, and I could feel a smile inside.

T H E E N D

ABOUT THE AUTHOR

Helen Yeomans was born in England and raised in Canada. She worked in book publishing in Toronto and London, then launched her own firm, providing editing and later writing services to corporate clients worldwide. She began writing fiction more than 20 years ago. *Owen's Day,* her first novel, was published in 2011.

For more information, visit www.helenyeomans.com.

Lightning Source UK Ltd.
Milton Keynes UK
UKHW021821211020
371977UK00009B/2310

9 780969 321934